To Be Chosen

Michael Travis Jasper

To Be Chosen

Published by Wheatmark®
610 East Delano Street, Suite 104
Tucson, Arizona 85705 U.S.A.
www.wheatmark.com

International Standard Book Number: 9781587368967
Library of Congress Control Number: 2007930381

Cover Painting — Chris Ahlers

To my mom – Cherry, my Grams (Genevieve),
and Aunt Margaret.
Your belief in me made me believe in myself.
I hope Goodness and Joy are inherited.

Acknowledgments

For Mrs. Rockey, for serving as my mentor in the form of an editor on this project. You are a great teacher and your support of my interest in writing, in high school and beyond, was a great source of encouragement.

For profound friendship, and what it taught me, my thanks to Annette, Pam, and Steven for a great childhood. Kelly and Mishka, my closest siblings. From high school; Shelbe, Jessica H., Mike G., and John Glen. From the life-changing days of beauty school - Julz, Angela M., Kristi M., and Brian G. From the era of my St. Joe hairstyling career - Lee Y., Rob M., David B., Kevin C., and Vicki. From my Kansas City hairstyling career - Jeannie, Nette F., Derek, Denise, Dawn, Dana, Gina, Anna H. , Jen C., Bev, Sal, Tammy, and Sheila – even Karen. From my neighborhood gym – Jessica and Erik. From my time in quality assurance – Amy, Brandi, Cindy, Christi, Robert, Michelle, Brian W., Roberta, Brenda, Matt, Kelley, Dan, Athena, Rodney, Boomer, Noel, and yes – Mike W. My nephews; Daulton, Collin, and Reid. In memory of Max and Bliss, whose unconditional love was a great gift. The rest of my parents; Dad, Lu, and Garry. And my inner most circle; John, Patrick, Frank, and Angie S.

Special thanks to Chris Ahlers, my amazing tattoo artist for the multitude of incredible body art, and much more for the perfect painting to serve as the cover of this book.

For extended family and friends. Though your names are not written here, they are written on my heart. Your presence in my life has inspired me in ways that you will never know.

Any mistakes or errors in grammar, spelling, punctuation, facts, and philosophy are purely my own; with my apologies to anyone they might offend. I can only tell it as I see it (even when it's only pretend).

Danke

Glossary

A glossary is provided at the end of this story for your enlightenment. Names and words that may be unfamiliar to you are defined and their origins made known.

Character List

A character list, in the order of their appearance, is also provided at story's end. This list explains basic identity but doesn't reveal every secret.

Please don't ruin your experience by reviewing these before encountering them in the story.
These help-guides exist to provide clarity when you refer to them during your progression through the novel.

Chapter 1

He stood in the warm cleansing rain for what seemed like hours as it gently washed the blood from his clothes and hands. He had stabbed the big ugly bastard in the chest with one of his good steak knives. It was self-defense of course. The thug had been sent to capture him, but that didn't matter. He had become a killer. He somehow felt stronger and less afraid than he ever had in his life.......and less human.

It had all begun a week ago, when Roman had spent the day raking up huge piles of leaves all over his yard. The peaceful autumn chore had been the perfect distraction for his frazzled mind. He had started to burn a large pile in the driveway. Hazy smoke filled the air with the smell of October. The darkly handsome real estate investor let his mind drift back to his childhood, when he had watched his wrinkled old grandfather rake the leaves of these very trees. This sleepy upscale suburb of Nashville never changed.

He jumped when she said it. "Daddy." He couldn't breathe. "Daddy, look at me." He slowly turned to see her standing on the other side of the crackling fire. His daughter, Jane, was seven years old. She wore a simple white dress and her long golden hair and ocean blue eyes were those of a living doll, but her face showed concern beyond her years.

"What are you doing here, Sweetheart?" Roman was thrilled to see her. He started towards her, but the flames jumped up to intervene.

"There's no time, Daddy!" She was visibly distressed.

"What do you mean, Janie?"

"They're coming, Daddy. You have to go!"

"What are you talking about, Darling?"

"Hurry, Daddy! You have to get out of here!"

He had worked his way around the fire and reached for her arm. She took a step backward to avoid his grasp. Roman's head was spinning. He considered diving and tackling her.

"They'll be here any second. Go, Daddy, please!"

Roman turned towards the house and the unmistakable sound of movement inside. Something was very wrong. He turned back to grab his baby. Her protection was all that mattered, but she was gone. He spun in every direction, but there wasn't a trace. She had vanished. Her name froze on his lips. He knew it was pointless. They were in the kitchen which gave him only seconds to roll under the marble bench that was mostly hidden by a row of purple iris. His heart stopped beating when four men burst through the back door. They seemed crazed. Predators looking for their prey. One sniffed the wind, which fortunately favored Roman by blowing towards him, away from the intruders. Roman began to tremble as the last of the sinister strangers was about to disappear back into the house where they would rummage further. The man had paused to brush the sweaty hair from his forehead. Roman disbelieved his eyes. The intruder had horns…just like the proverbial devil. He gasped, but the stranger didn't hear him.

Roman lay there for a long time, afraid to move. It had been over an hour since the trespassers had appeared to leave, but he had to be sure. The surreal events had left him unable to trust appearances. His thoughts turned to Jane. If only he could have held her. It had been over a year since she chased her dog into the street in an attempt to bring him to safety. Neither she nor

Toto had been a match for that Dodge Ram pick-up truck. She had been killed instantly. Toto too. Roman thought he must be going crazy. None of this could be real. He didn't know what to do next. The universe had stopped making sense. "Come back, Janie," he whispered over and over, "Come back……."

Days passed without his even realizing. He had searched the house for evidence of the intruders or of Jane's visit, but there was no sign of anyone having been there. Roman now had no doubts about what he had seen, but he had no idea what it meant. He knew Janie had saved his life but couldn't figure out who was after him or why. And those horns. Had it been some sort of mask? Somehow, Roman knew they had been real. He had let the machine pick up calls from his mother and brother. He just didn't feel like talking to anyone…..anyone but Jane.

He had begged her for hours to appear again, but she silently refused. Roman assumed she had returned to Heaven. His little guardian angel for one moment. One of his first impulses had been to call her mother, but he had decided against it. She wouldn't have believed him; and even if she had, there was no point in robbing Brenda of whatever peace she had finally found with her new boyfriend.

After a week of calling in sick, things began to seem normal again, and he knew it was time to return to work. He had been orchestrating a deal that would create a massive new housing development, and there were plenty of remaining details to be settled. The Armani suit and black Jaguar seemed pretty trivial that morning, but then things like that really hadn't mattered since Janie's accident. Traffic was a bitch as usual, but it gave Roman a chance to pop in the Tony Robbins tapes that helped keep him thinking just positively enough to get out of bed every day.

Roman was just leaving the posh Green Hills area and beginning to fall into his usual rush hour trance when he heard the screeching tires a few cars back. The wreck didn't impact his car, but he felt compelled to jump out and run back to assist if he could. When he saw that the little girl of about four years had been thrown from the convertible, he stopped in his tracks. Not again. He couldn't go through this again. He ran to the child. A little Hispanic girl that looked nothing like Janie, but somehow for him, she was Jane…..and he wouldn't fail her again. Her parents were unconscious, and no one else seemed willing to help.

He knew you weren't supposed to move injured people, but he acted without thinking. He fell to his knees, scooped her up, and held her tightly to his chest. They were both covered in her blood. Roman closed his eyes, but the smell of it was inescapable. He was sobbing as he cradled the back of her head and knew the bones were crushed. "Live," was his whispered prayer. Then louder. "Live…Live, Live, Live, LIVE!!!" As he screamed it out he felt the power growing inside of him; then he saw what the witnesses saw. A bright white aura of light surrounded him, and then expanded to surround the girl. The light grew blinding and Roman was forced to close his eyes. He opened them an instant later when the child began to stir. He was so astounded, he almost dropped her. Not only was she alive, she was perfect and healed. Not a drop of blood remained on her yellow sundress or Roman's suit. Her head was normal and there was no sign that she had ever been injured.

By this time, her mother had awakened and limped over to grab up her daughter. "Thank You" and "Gracias" alternately fell from her mouth. She had seen what happened and knew that this man had to be an angel sent by the Holy Mother to save her baby. That was why she didn't even try to stop him or get his name when he stumbled numbly back to his car. Everyone else looked away in fear, and since traffic was moving again, he got in his car and drove to his office.

His co-workers and associates were all buzzing about the miracle being discussed on the radio. No one knew the identity of the Good Samaritan, and Roman wasn't talking. He couldn't explain what he had done if he wanted to. He knew he had saved the girl's life, but how? Had he been used by God? Was it simply an answer to his prayer? He avoided several meetings that day and went home early. What was happening to him? He had always prided himself on being a logical, down-to-Earth kind of guy. His recent experiences didn't have any place in the version of reality he had always trusted to be the truth.

He went to bed as soon as he got home, barely getting undressed before he fell into the deepest sleep. Roman knew he was dreaming, because he had never seen any place like this before. It was daytime here, and he wore jeans and a T-shirt. A beautiful sunny day. He was surrounded by rolling hills of grass. There was an ancient-looking forest perhaps half a mile away. And only 100 yards away, a huge stone castle. People that looked like "peasants" walked along wagons and rode horses in and out of the massive main gate. Strangest of all were the small "spaceships" that flew overhead, some even landing within the castle walls. "Why ride horses, when you could fly spaceships?" Roman mumbled aloud.

"Because it is forbidden for humans to touch their technology without permission, Daddy."

"Jane!" Roman turned to find his daughter sitting on a boulder twenty feet away.

"My name is Joppa here, Da-Roman....You should call me by that name here, and I must remember to call you Roman."

"Janie, I can't call you by another name." He had run to her, and she allowed him a brief hug.

"You must. They don't understand here how my soul moves between dimensions. If they figure out that I was your daughter on Earth, they would think they could use me to trap you."

"What?...Who?" Roman was amazed to feel that she was flesh and blood. That she was alive. "What is this place?"

"This realm has many names. The race of beings here that enslave humans is called Legion. On Earth people call them demons, but I don't know what they really are. What I do know, is that they want to capture you and perhaps kill you....You and the other Avatarn."

"The Ava-What?"

"You, Blair, and Darby—The Avatarn."

"Who are Blair and Darby, and what are Avatarn, Honey?" By this time, Roman had helped her down from her lofty perch and both sat in the grass, leaning against the rock and watching the passers-by who tended to the burdens they carried and paid no mind to the little girl who sat by the boulder talking to herself.

"You'll meet Blair and Darby very soon, Da-Roman. The Legion call the three of you the Avatarn. Thousands of years ago, on a planet far from Earth or this place, a prophecy was given by a beautiful woman to the royal court. It was me," she leaned in to whisper, "I foretold of a time when three humans would lead a rebellion against the Legion slave-masters and destroy them."

"What makes you or they think that I could be one of these.... Avatarn?"

"They have spies that live among humans on Earth and many other worlds. When you healed that kid this morning, they knew you were one of the promised ones."

"How do they know the identities of the other two? Did they heal people also?" Roman still wasn't convinced himself that he had actually saved the girl.

"No." Joppa answered with a patient smile, "They do not yet know who the other two are. Only I know. But they will find them. As soon as Darby and Blair discover their powers....which, by the way, will be different from yours. They will not have the healing gift."

"But, Sweetheart, how do you know all of this?"

"I was created a thousand lifetimes ago, to wait for the Avatarn to be born and to guide and assist you in your mission. If I can."

"None of this can be real. I'm just dreaming, right?" He embraced her and kissed her forehead.

"You are dreaming, Roman. But nothing has ever been more real. Be watching for Darby and Blair. They will be entering your life very soon.....And you're all in great danger."

"Janie—"

"No, Roman. You mu—"

"Okay....*Joppa*" he said sarcastically, "This is all just too outrageous to believe. I'm just—"

"Roman, you have to wake up now. Right now!...They've sent someone to get you. A human this time. He'll stop at nothing, Roman. Failure in his mission will mean punishment by death."

"Darling, this is crazy. It's just my body reacting to some bad pizza I ate at the office. I'm sure when I—"

"You're running out of time, Ro—"

"Okay, okay, at least tell me how to recognize this Darby and Blair. Maybe then if I meet them I'll know this wasn't just bad pepperoni."

"You'll know this is real as soon as you wake up.....If you wake up." He had never seen her so angry. "But I'll tell you in hopes that you won't miss each other somehow....Darby is a handsome, 21-year-old gay man. He works part time as a personal trainer in a gym and studies history in college....Blair is a sexy 30-year-old woman who is married to a preacher, though she is secretly a witch....It's too late! You have to wake up now!" He was stunned by the terror on her face. "Now! Daddy!" She screamed as she slapped his face with all of her might.

He sat up in bed as he jolted awake. He was home. In his own bed. And there was someone coming up the stairs. He quickly pulled on the flannel pajama bottoms that were lying on the foot of the bed. Roman scrambled to his desk where the plate and silver from some past supper still sat. He grabbed the heavy-duty streak knife just in time to see the man's face revealed in a flash of lightning that seemed right outside the window. The gigantic brute of a man was hideously scarred. He had been horribly burned. Maybe tortured. Janie...Joppa had been right. Was she right about everything?

The goon ran at Roman. He was swinging a baseball bat. Roman barely evaded his blows and watched in terror as first the lamp, then his desk, smashed to bits, knowing that his head might be next.

"Please don't do this!" Roman pleaded, but the guy's eyes already looked dead inside. Roman didn't wait for a reply. He ran out of the bedroom and turned down the dark hall. The enraged man was close behind him, swinging the bat wildly. Roman was waiting just outside the door. There was no time to think. He plunged the knife into the giant's chest with all of his strength, and watched him fall to the floor gurgling blood. Soon all was quiet. Roman stared in disbelief. Was it really possible that he had just killed someone? Could he heal him if he tried? He started to kneel, but no. He didn't want to save this man. Besides....He had a very strong feeling that he had done this man a favor. He called the police, then stumbled down to the front porch to wait. He managed the stairs down to the sidewalk and out into the rain. It was pouring. He stood in the warm cleansing rain for what seemed like hours as it gently washed the blood from his clothes and hands.

Chapter 2

Blair was having a hard time focusing on her husband's sermon. Though his delivery was passionate and sincere, she had heard Thomas lecture about "The Judgment of Others" a dozen times. Her thoughts raced ahead to the hayride and bonfire the church would be hosting after dark to celebrate a plentiful harvest. Both of her sisters had promised, via email, to be there. It had been so long since she had been able to convince them to pass on the excitement of their usual weekends in Atlanta for a few sleepy days in Juniper, Georgia. She stopped twisting the ends of her long red hair as soon as she realized she was doing it. She didn't want Thomas to know she was bored. It was the familiarity of the material that allowed her mind to wander. She always loved being in church. Their little Baptist church was filled with the presence of God. The only time she felt Him more strongly was when she cast spells with her sisters.

She knew her friends in the congregation wouldn't appreciate the fact that they are hereditary witches, not Wiccan. They worshipped no other god than the Trinity of Christianity. They just happened to be born to a family that had been gifted for generations with a subtle magic. They used these powers only for good, knowing that one reaps what she sows. Blair had never been able to work even the smallest charm on her own, but with Sarah and Molly at her side they could enchant men, quiet troubled hearts, and sometimes see angels.

The rest of the day passed quickly. Blair was busy with preparations for the celebration, and nightfall would come early for the contented housewife.

Sarah and Molly arrived before dark with plenty of time to help prepare food and flirt with Thomas. They both had crushes on him. Blair always found their overtures amusing, but her shy husband was a little overwhelmed by them.

"I know!...Let's do a spell to charm the best lookin' guys at the festival. That way we're guaranteed a good time." Sarah smiled deviously as she piled cookies into a basket.

"I know!....Let's do a spell to charm Thomas." Molly winked at Blair as she finished putting her long black hair in a ponytail and turned her back to the window that looked out on the driveway where the reverend with chestnut hair was busy loading the pick-up with enough food for an army.

"I'll help you cast a spell," Blair gave her sister's ponytail a quick yank, "but not on my husband."

They were all still giggling when Tom came in, pulling up his shirt to wipe his sweaty face. Sarah faked a swoon.

"All right, girls. What are you up to?" Thomas attempted to look stern. "No hocus-pocus tonight. I mean it. No De Sortilege."

"Just girl talk," Molly batted her eyes, "Nothing that would interest a big hunky stud like you."

Thomas smiled and blushed and went about completing his chores. He almost felt sorry for the local boys who would be bewitched by his sisters-in-law even without the use of magic.

"We'll wait till tonight, when we're in the woods. The spell will be more powerful when we're communing with nature. Don't worry; we'll find you both paramours," Blair suggested.

"Do you think that's wise?" Sarah was the blonde sister, and the worrier. "We'll be surrounded by the congregation....What if we get caught?"

"What if we do?" Molly was the rebel. "We'll turn them all into toads." Again with the wink.

"Yea, and right after that, we'll all fly away on our broomsticks." Blair offered, rolling her eyes. "No one will see us…We'll be careful…Besides, what's the worst thing that ever came of someone doing a love spell?"

Sarah cleared her throat sarcastically, "Heeellooo!.........Salem, MA!"

The flames of the bonfire were at least fifteen feet high. The witches were torn between being drawn to the magic of the fire and repelled by the knowledge that churches had burned witches for centuries. Blair shivered as the waves of heat washed over her, and her friends belted out hymns. The scene could have been from any place, from any time. She couldn't explain the sense of dread that made the hairs on her neck stand up. Her first instinct was to look for Thomas, then her sisters. She spotted her adorably rugged husband sitting on the back stairs of the church, with a few of the deacons whittling points on long sticks to be used for the weenie roast later. She caught his eye and he flashed her one of his reassuring smiles that always put her mind at ease.

"Have some lemonade, Sis," Molly had appeared on her left and Sarah on her right, "Someone spiked it," she added.

"You?" Blair scolded, but was secretly glad.

"No…But I would have if someone hadn't beaten me to it." Molly raised her plastic cup to toast Blair's.

"I don't know what they used, but it packs a helluva punch." Sarah joined the toast.

"Magic time?" Molly suggested anxiously.

"Let's do it!" Blair and Sarah chimed in unison. They made their way over to the large lawn behind the church and past the dozen or so children that were playing with the baby goats. The church's answer to a petting zoo.

The sisters entered the woods on the all-but-hidden dirt path the teenagers used to reach a little grotto that accommodated their forbidden make-out sessions. The small clearing wasn't far from the boundaries of the church yard, but the ancient trunks and reaching branches provided complete privacy. This wouldn't be the first time the girls had made magic in the moonlit temple of bark, grass, dirt, and starry sky. All three girls flinched when their entrance to Mother Nature's private courtyard was heralded by several large crows that fluttered just over head in the surrounding canopy. The sisters knew beyond doubt that 'large black birds close at hand were an omen of life-altering changes soon upon us.' The girls were usually comfortable in the night, and uneasiness was quickly forgotten.

Joining hands, they tried to stop laughing. "Count of three," Blair squeaked out between giggles, and on three all became serious and began the incantation.

"Hecate, turn your face away,
We call real power as we may,
Lovers come and lovers go.
'Tis true love's face I long to know.
Earth bring forth the man for me.
Yahweh's will our destiny."

They had chanted it three times over, when the growing intensity of light from above caused them to open their eyes. The three angels appeared to be standing in mid-air above the tree tops. They were shining like liquid silver, but the sisters knew the radiance of their visitors would not be seen by their nearby friends who were caught up in their own worship ritual. The witches had seen angels many times and in many forms, but none quite like this.

"Prepare yourselves, Daughters of the Prophets," the words of the beautiful silver lips seemed deafening, though only the sisters heard, "A time of great sacrifice is at hand. You must pay a great price to awaken the Avatarn. Blessed Be the Avatarn. God's hammer, man's hope."

Massive translucent wings unfolded behind them with lightning speed. The trio merged into one creature as they shot heavenward and disappeared into space. The witches had been unable to speak in their presence, and continued to stare dumbfounded at each other until Sarah finally found her voice. "The lemonade…I think it was drugged…Something strong."

"I know," Blair interrupted, "I can feel it…But this was real," she was still in a state of awe.

"We know it was real," Molly stepped forward. "But what does it mean?"

"We're in danger," Sarah whispered.

"I agree—" Blair's sentence was cut short.

"WITCHCRAFT!!!" The old man's voice rang out through the woods. Old Man Jenkins had been spying on them. He had heard them chanting, but had not been allowed to witness their glorious vision.

"Wait!" Molly cried out as the sneaky old man turned and began to run as quickly as his withered legs would carry him back towards the churchyard, yelling all the way.

"Let us explain!" Blair sobbed as she joined her sisters in the chase.

"Stop him!" Sarah screamed, "They won't understand!"

The entire multitude had begun to run towards the woods to see what the fuss was about. Joseph Jenkins burst from the trees with absolute terror on his face. "Witches!" They're all witches!" He managed to call out, still running towards the crowd.

"Shut up!!!" The three sisters shouted simultaneously as they emerged from the forest, stopping when they found the entire throng facing them half-way across the yard.

The old man spun around when he heard them, falling as he turned. He was dead before he hit the ground. The former celebrants erupted into screams. The horror was contagious.

"Thomas!" Blair screamed. She knew the congregation was going to misinterpret what they had just seen in their drugged-out state. And she knew they would over-react. This was what the angels had spoken of.

"What's happening?" Susan Myerhoff, the church pianist;

cried between sobs. It was Lucien Jones that boldly stepped forward. He had arrived in town just a few weeks before. The tall classically handsome highway patrolman had been instantly liked by the people of Juniper.

"You all heard the man! God help him! They're witches! Don't let them get away!" He took several steps in the girls' direction before Thomas pushed past him to position himself protectively in front of his family.

"Stop!" Thomas put on his most authoritative persona. "This is ridiculous. My wife and her sisters are not witches. They're Christian. Ya'll know that as well as you know me!"

"Then how do you explain that?" Lucien was pointing behind the reverend. Thomas spun around and stumbled backward in disbelief. Blair, Molly, and Sarah had joined hands behind their backs and were floating two feet off the ground.

"What the hell are you doing?" Thomas was terrified of what this would mean to the crowd.

"It's never happened before," Blair struggled to control her breathing; "We've never been this scared."

"Well, this isn't helping. Get down." Thomas had to suppress a smile despite his fear. He had always dreaded this day, and always knew it would come. The girls released each other's hands and fell without grace to the ground.

"See?" Lucien had turned back to the crowd that was slowly fanning out to surround the girls. Everyone wanted to be able to see what was going on. The look on the big cop's face was more one of anger than of fear, and for some reason he was wearing his uniform. "He's a witch too!" He accused. "Don't let them escape! The Bible is crystal clear about how to deal with witches! Thou shalt not suffer a witch to live!"

"What? Are you insane?" Thomas was terrified. How had things gotten out of control so quickly?

"Why don't you just arrest them?" Harold, the church maintenance man, had moved to the front of the crowd.

"Arrest us for what?" Blair screamed.

"Murder!" Tiffany Chambers was pointing at the sisters. "You all saw what happened!"

"What are you—Oh, wait…of course," Blair cut her own sentence short. Tiffany had been in love with Thomas ever since she became his secretary.

Lucien shoved Thomas aside with one hand sending him sprawling in the fallen leaves. Everyone else hesitated, unsure of which side to believe. The muscular cop sprang forward grabbing Molly by the hair. "You're gonna burn, witch!"

"Enough!" Blair instinctively threw her arms up as if reaching toward Heaven. She was as shocked and amazed as everyone else when she saw what happened next. A giant oak tree reached down to snatch Lucien up in its limbs, lifting him forty feet in the air.

Molly and Sarah stared at Blair in dumb surprise. "How?" Sarah whispered.

"I don't know," was all Blair could muster.

"My God! They are witches!" Harold was shaking.

"Run!" Thomas screamed as the crowd started forward. He jumped to his feet, prepared to do battle with those who had been his friends less than an hour ago. Molly and Sarah took off in opposite directions, around the edges of the gathering. Both headed past the giant bonfire, towards the church.

"Get them!" Lucien called down from the tangled branches. Several men ran forward and engaged Thomas hand-to-hand.

"Help us!" Blair cried out to no one in particular. The dogs that had been playing in the churchyard froze in their tracks, turning to face Blair. In an instant they ran to stand guard behind her fleeing sisters, and seconds later, the three snarling former pets were joined by a half dozen wolves that came bounding from the woods in every direction. The growling animals fell into formation to create a barrier beyond the mob.

Blair turned her attention back to Thomas.

They had beaten him down. So much blood. They were killing him. How could she stop them? Her mind was racing. She looked to Heaven again, and the answer came to her as she watched a hawk soar past the moon.

"Birds!" She cried out, too rattled to make up an incantation. "Birds! Birds! Birds! Birds!" They descended from every compass point. Mostly crows, but a few owls, and a small hawk for good measure. The winged creatures attacked the men who were punching and kicking Thomas with no more mercy than the mob was showing him. Biting, pecking, clawing. The ravens chased the vigilantes all the way to their cars.

Blair fell to her knees at her husband's side, cradling his head in her lap. "Oh, Darling," she wept. He was conscious, but he wasn't attempting to get up.

"Go to your sisters," was all he could get out before drifting into sleep.

Laughter from above demanded her attention. Lucien had finally broken free of the gnarled tree limbs, and was falling directly towards her. It was too late for her to move out of the way, but it didn't matter. Just before impact, he disappeared in a shimmer, and reappeared, still laughing, at the entrance of the church. Blair was through asking "How?" She ran toward the church. The crowd parted, allowing her to pass. They were too afraid to interfere after all they had seen. Lucien hadn't materialized on the front steps empty-handed. He was holding a torch, presumably from the fire.

The dogs and wolves had fallen in behind her. Not chasing her, but escorting her. Blair looked wild herself with her long red hair and long black coat streaming behind her as she ran faster than she had ever ran before. She had almost reached the front steps when all the windows and doors were shattered in an explosion of flames. The First Baptist Church of Juniper wasn't just on fire, it was completely engulfed. The force of it threw Blair backwards and she sat motionless for a moment. Stunned. She would have run inside, but the children surrounded her and held her back.

"Rain, fall down like Noah's flood.
To stop this fire from tasting blood.
Come to serve my new-found powers.
Come to me, torrential showers!"

She repeated the chant and soon the children were chanting with her. It was only a few moments until the clouds opened up and poured. The rain fell in sheets, but by the time the fire had been tamed, the fire department had arrived and no one was allowed to enter the church. All that remained inside were the skeletons of two women. There was no sign of Lucien. The ambulance had arrived with the fire truck and Blair had followed it to the edge of the forest where she had left Thomas. Half of the congregation had left, and the others wondered around aimlessly. No one seemed sure of what had happened. Thomas still lay where she had left him. The EMTs reached him before she did. "Sorry, lady," the tech had just checked for a pulse. "He's gone."

"He can't be," Blair managed to squeak. "I need him."

The rain had stopped, and Blair sat on the ground, wet and cold, but not feeling anything, as she watched them load his body into the ambulance. Thomas's voice kept running through her head. It was her husband's sermon against judging others. He had not exaggerated the dangers of it. It had killed everyone she loved.

The last thing Blair remembered before waking up in an Atlanta psych ward was being led by the hand to a police car by a sweet little blonde girl. She had never seen her before. "Thank you, Darling...Do I know your Mommy or Daddy?" Blair muttered through tears.

"Not yet," the beautiful child hugged her and ran away into the darkness.

Chapter 3

The only lectures Darby attended regularly were for his history classes. They were morning classes, but interesting enough for him to drag his sleep-deprived ass out of bed every other day. Besides, there were several hot guys in his Ancient and Medieval history class. The sky blue baseball cap he had thrown on over his tousled blond hair matched his eyes. He hadn't bothered to shave. He was running late as usual. He felt like a bum, but knew he looked pretty good anyway. He worked as a personal trainer at The Gym downtown on the side. A part-time job that had rewarded him with an extraordinary body. He was covered in perfectly sculpted muscles.

"Glad you could join us, Mr. Zaid." The professor scolded when Darby sauntered into the room.

"Sorry," was all he offered as he climbed the steps past a few admiring girls to reach his usual seat. Darby wasn't worried about being in trouble. He knew the teacher, Professor Taylor, had a little crush on him.

The day's lecture was about the late great city of Alexandria, and while he found it fascinating, he was soon distracted by a cute Italian boy a few rows over. His name was Paolo. And he was beautiful. Probably around 21 like him. Not a gym-bunny, but fit.

His huge brown eyes could melt popsicles, and they were staring right at Darby.

Darby had to adjust his package. It was starting to swell against his will. He tried to look away. To focus on the famous lighthouse of Alexandria, but his gaze kept returning to the bronze boy who seemed embarrassed, but refused to let go of this moment's fragile boldness and what it might bring. Paolo was also getting an erection, and when he saw Darby's his mouth dropped. Darby flashed a smile, any embarrassment completely over-shadowed by pride in his king-size pocket-rocket.

Their mildly obscene little flirtation was broken by Prof. Taylor who stepped between them in the process of handing out their graded tests from the previous week. Their excessive bulges were soon deflated, and they managed to concentrate enough to get through the rest of class. Darby kept thinking about how Cleopatra had met her best lovers in Alexandria.

Paolo lingered at the water fountain just outside the classroom. Darby wasn't surprised. "How's it goin'?" He winked at Paolo and bent to get a drink. He was acting much braver than he felt.

"Great." Paolo sneaked a peak at his behind. "I've wanted to meet you for a long time, Darby."

Darby invited him to get some coffee at Starbucks. They talked for hours before Paolo said, "I hope I can see your apartment sometime."

"How about now?" Darby held his breath as he waited for an answer.

"Why not?" Paolo kept forgetting to breathe too.

Darby had never done it before. Have sex with someone that was nearly a stranger. But he didn't hesitate. Besides, he always practiced safe sex. Paolo was so good-looking. Short spiky black hair and a 5 o'clock shadow. He just stood there, in the living room, as Darby undressed him. Darby remained fully dressed at first, jut holding Paolo's nakedness tightly against him as they kissed. The kissing was the best. Darby had always liked it better than sex. Paolo unzipped Darby's fly.

The steaming water cascaded over Darby's beefy body, washing away all the scents and textures associated with what they had just done. It had been special. Nothing casual about it, even though they really didn't know each other. He was smiling to himself and already beginning to stiffen again, when Paolo stepped into the shower behind him. Paolo hugged him from behind, sliding his hands over Darby's hairy pecs until he found his nipples. They were both ready to go again. "My client's gonna be waiting for me at the gym," Darby moaned.

"Let me tell you a quick story before you go."

"Okay," Darby had stepped out of the shower and was drying off, "Make it fast buddy…No rest for the wicked…"

"….And the righteous don't need none….Isn't that how the saying goes?" Paolo added, "That's you."

"Not me. Nobody ever used that word to describe me before. Trust me." Darby grinned.

"But you are," Paolo argued, "I mean, I realize I don't know you, but I can tell. You're a good person. I mean, in every way that matters."

"Debatable. Tell me your story. I've got to go." Darby had a hard time taking a compliment for anything but his appearance.

"You're not going to believe any of this, but I swear it's all true…When I was eight, I was playing by myself in an isolated section of the playground. It was recess and as usual, no one wanted to play with the sissy-boy so I was left to amuse myself, sitting on faded hop-scotch squares and playing with a couple of matchbox cars…Suddenly, I was no longer alone…An angel appeared to me. She was standing on some steps a few feet away. I could have reached out and passed my hand through her foot if I had dared. She didn't appear solid. She was semi-transparent. Her golden hair was in a ponytail and was so long, it almost touched the ground. She was dressed in a warrior's outfit of metallic gold. She was tall and looked like an Amazon to me. A beautiful one. I never doubted for a moment that she was real, and when she spoke she had my undivided attention. She said, "Do not be afraid. I am a messenger sent by God. You have been chosen. Someday, when you are a man, you will encounter someone God has sent to Earth on a great mission. You shall be the companion of an Avatarn. Blessed be the chosen, for you will earn a special place."

"What's an Avatarn? I didn't have a clue." Paolo mused.

"Neither do I." Darby raised his eyebrows.

"She never explained. She just said, 'With eyes wide open, you will see your destiny in the peace of sleep. Be still and await truth.' She smiled and faded into nothingness."

"Sounds to me like a little kid with a big imagination." Darby smirked as he shaved.

"I know it sounds crazy, but it's true...I wrote it all down as soon as we went inside, and I memorized it. Until today it was the most amazing thing that had ever happened to me."

"I had a great time too, but I'm not that good." Darby blushed a little.

"Not that." Paolo was serious, "I mean that was wonderful, but you don't understand...It's you. You're the one...."

"Ah, man! You're freaking me out. This shit is starting to sound pretty psycho, dude. I think you should—"

"I realized it while you were sleeping. I woke up and you were sleeping with the most extraordinary expression of peace on your face, and then I saw it...This incredible blue aura around your head."

"Now you're telling me that I have a halo?" Darby was torn between disappointment that his new friend had turned out to be mental, and fear that he might actually be dangerous.

"For lack of a better word." Paolo replied, "I can see it now. I don't see it all the time. It seems to come and go for me.

"Well, I hate to cum and go," Darby laughed at his own joke, "but I'm late for work. I need you to get dressed and leave, please."

Damn this guy is hot, Darby thought to himself looking over his still wet and naked classmate.

"I don't know what it all means," Paolo wasn't laughing, "but you are something special. Special to God. I'm not afraid. I've been preparing myself for this my whole life. I'm not trying to proselytize you for some crazy new religion; I just know how much this matters."

"If you expect me to accept this big geas you're placing on me, tell me something to convince me you're not insane. If you can." Darby was rapidly putting on his gym clothes.

"There is only one other thing the angel told me that I haven't already mentioned. I don't know if it will mean anything to you, though." Paolo reached out with a single finger and wrote her name in the steam on the mirror that covered the shower door. One lone word: "APSARA"

"Sweet Jesus!!!" Darby fell back against the vanity.

"What? What's it mean to you?" Paolo was startled by his reaction.

"But how? Where did yo….No one but my parents know that name and they wouldn't mention it to a soul. There aren't even physical records of it anymore…"

"How? What's it mean to you?" Paolo knew he was staring at someone who had just had an epiphany.

"Apsara was my birthmother's name. She died when I was born."

Darby was only a few minutes late for his appointment at the gym. The client was a middle-aged housewife who would forgive her studly trainer anything. The only reason she had hired Darby to train her was her not-so-secret hopes of eventually luring him into her bed.

Darby had been completely convinced by the revelation at the end of Paolo's story. No one else could know that name. Paolo's angel or ghost had been Darby's long dead mother. His head was swimming with strange information, and he had hated to leave, but Paolo had said he had to get home as soon as possible. Some issue with his roommate. They had exchanged phone numbers and kissed good-bye.

The hours at the gym passed quickly. Darby was in a daze and barely noticed as his muscle-bound friends greeted him as they made their way from cardio to weights and back again. He had just undressed in the busy locker room when an angry man burst in.

"Which one of you is Darby Zaid?" The guy headed straight at Darby was a steroid freak. Huge, even by gym clone standards.

"Can I help you?" Darby couldn't imagine who this guy was or what he wanted.

"Sure, if you can explain why you just fucked my boyfriend!"

"What? Who are you?" Darby was humiliated as everyone in the locker room stopped to see what all the commotion was about…And to see who had just been outed.

"My name is Cinder, and the hot little stud you spent the afternoon pounding is mine, asshole!" The Neanderthal was flexing his fist, and Darby knew what was coming.

"Believe me, I had no idea Paolo had a boyfriend. That's not my style, man. *He* picked *me* up," Darby was cringing at all the knowing grins that surrounded them, "How did you even—"

"He told me as soon as he got home. Not that he fucked somebody. I know what he looks like after sex. He couldn't wait to tell me he had met the Avatarn." It was obvious that Cinder was about to lose control. Some of the gymbots stepped forward to let Darby know that they had his back, but he dismissed them with a jerk of his head. He wasn't about to get anyone else involved in this farce.

"He told you about that?"

"He's been telling me that story for years. I know it's a bunch of horseshit, but the only way I can convince him you're not some kind of godsend is to kick your faggot ass."

"There's no chance of me convincing you that I would not have been with him if I had known about you?" Darby really didn't want to lose this job, or get his ass kicked in front of his friends.

"It doesn't matter. He'll be building shrines to you by tomorrow unless I prove to him that you're just another butch-wannabe slut that needs taken down a few notches." Cinder stole a quick glance down at Darby's dick.

"Bring it," Darby said, raising his chin.

Cinder threw the first punch. Darby threw the last. He barely had time to grab a towel in a belated attempt at modesty as the members hoisted him to their shoulders for a victory march through the showers and the co-ed whirlpool room. The kick-boxing classes had paid off.

It wasn't Darby's idea to visit a psychic. It was his friend Rachel who had heard about the woman from a work associate. The co-worker had given "Miss Luna" a ninety percent accuracy rating, so Darby and Rachel were on a clairvoyant escapade.

He hadn't told Rachel, his best friend from high school, about Paolo or Cinder. He told her the guy who picked a fight with him at the gym was just some homophobe who thought he was staring. She had no reason to doubt him. She had seen him as the target of plenty of prejudice over the years, all because of other people's personal insecurities.

Miss Luna's little apartment was in a very ghetto neighborhood. Darby was a little nervous about being there. A very white gay boy and an especially beautiful black girl might draw unwanted attention in this neighborhood. Little did he know that nobody ever bothered Miss Luna's visitors. They didn't dare. They hopped out of Darby's black Jeep and darted up the stairs of the brownstone-like apartment building.

It took a long time for the old woman to answer the door. They had started to think no one was home. "Welcome, children." The ancient-looking black woman wore her hair in braids neatly twisted into a bun. She was extremely thin and wore a long loose apple-red dress, "Sit at the dining room table, young man. I sees only your future tonight."

"But I thought," Rachel began.

"I know, Darlin'," Luna cut her off, "This isn't your time. The spirits tell me this boy needs more guidance from Miss Luna tonight. You'll sparkle in yer turn, Sweetpea." Darby glanced at Rachel and shrugged his shoulders. Who was he to argue with a nutty old fortune-teller?

Miss Luna sat across from him at the little table covered with antique lace. There was nothing on the table, but a few candles placed randomly around the room created an intimate birthing place for secrets. Darby thought the tattered little room felt magically safe, set apart from the real world. A place where a retired cook from the corner diner revealed her true nature. An oracle, casting off her nearly worn-out disguise. A prophetess took his big hands in her bony ones.

She looked at their hands for a moment before looking him in the baby-blues. "You don't need to aks me no questions, Baby," she was smiling warmly, "I'm just gonna tell ya a few things 'bout yerself. First off, ya can stop lookin' fer Mr. Right. Ya already done met him…And yer little girlfriend here…She'll find one if she's spose to 'cordin' to the Lord." She added with a wink in Rachel's direction. "Now, ya need ta know. You're not mortal."

"What?" Darby hadn't seen that coming.

"I knowed it when I saw ya get out of yer car. Blue light all 'round yer head. A halo, I calls it."

"What are you talk—?" Darby was in shock. This couldn't be happening. His life was taking on a bizarre new pattern. What did it mean?

"Now, don't go getting' yerself all worked up. I know yer scared 'bout what's been happenin'. The unknown is scary. Ya never did much thinkin' on the Unseen. But it's real. And it's headin' yer way. Ya was born fer a higher purpose, Boy. You and the other Avatarn have a mission. Time ya got 'bout yer business."

Rachel was giggling. The old lady was crazy after all. Darby was dizzy. "There are others?" Darby knew Rachel was saying something to him, but he couldn't hear her. There was only Luna. There was only truth.

"Course, Sugar," the old woman cackled like he had just asked if the sky was blue, "Two others. A woman and a man. Your destiny."

"Hey! He doesn't get a man and a woman," Rachel offered in jest. If he did end up with a woman, it had better be her. The old shining one and her spellbound querent didn't even hear her.

"Who are they? When will I meet them? How will I—?" She cut him off again.

"Shush, Baby…Just listen. I can't tell ya much at this time. That ain't the way of it. You'll hook up with'em soon, and you'll know'em when ya see'em. Now God has chose ya to serve Him in a divine mission. There is evil in this world…Don't be afraid," His hands were sweating. She squeezed them and continued, "You will stand against Legion. The slave masters of many realms. The time has come for the Great Emancipation. The Avatarn will battle to free humankind and the others from those of God's children that have turned to darkness. It is the appointed time."

"I'm no leader. I'm okay one-on-one but this is…I don't want to be *chosen*. I just want to go on with my normal life. If my pious aunts ever hear that God selected me to save the world, they would crap their…Sorry."

"Yer not just savin' the world, Sweetie. Yer freein' the peoples of countless worlds and realms ya never imagined existed. Now I've done told ya more'an I was meant to. Now go boldly, knowin' that God Himself set ya on this path."

"So I'm safe. I mean, I don't want to die. Are we talking about an actual physical war here? Or is this all just some kind of spiritual thing?"

"If you die, you die. This ain't pretend. But you always knowed deep down that death ain't the end. He'll keep sendin' ya'll back till ya get the job done. I don't think that'll be necessary though. This is it. The big one."

"But how are we supposed to stand against anyone? I can do

hand-to-hand, but how do we fight the forces of evil? I just don't see how—"Darby felt helpless.

"You will each be given a special power. An ability that will help you do what must be done. We're talkin' 'bout the supernatural here, but don't worry; you'll get your hands dirty." She patted his hands to reassure him.

"I don't have any powers." Darby wondered for a moment if she could be crazy after all, but he knew she wasn't.

"Ya will when ya need it." She stood and walked to the door. Rachel was disappointed to have been excluded, but after hearing Darby's reading, she was convinced the old bat was a fraud. She went ahead into the hallway.

Darby stepped out the door, but turned to face the old woman. He handed her a twenty dollar bill. He wasn't about to insult her by discussing money. When Rachel had called to make the appointment, she had been told that whatever donation they thought appropriate would be acceptable. He wanted to give much more, but being a poor student had its limits. Luna handed it back to him with just the slightest bow of her head. "Not from you, Blessed One." She said, her tired eyes twinkling. "It is my honor to have served ya. To have served the great Avatarn. It is the reason I was gifted with The Seeing my whole life. To assist ya at this time."

"Well, thank you so much…I think I have more questions now than when I got here. I hope we can come see you again when all this becomes more clear…I'm pretty freaked out…By the things you know, and the things I never wanted to know. Darby was starting down the steps. Rachel was already waiting by the Jeep.

"I'll always be with ya, Child. Where-ever else I am."

"Goodbye, Mame!" Darby called out and waved as he climbed into the driver's seat after opening Rachel's door.

"Not 'Bye' Baby. Just 'Later'." Luna closed the door to the outside world and hobbled back into her apartment. She was tired. Her job was done. She had never known what the true purpose of her gift was until tonight. Until she saw that beautiful golden young man. His lovely face surrounded by blue light. She done good. Told him just enough to keep him alive (she hoped), but not enough to make him as scared as he ought to be. Keep a close eye on him, God. She looked heavenward as she changed into her nightgown. He has no idea. Her bed felt better than it ever had before. As she drifted off to sleep for the last time, a whisper escaped her lips just before her heart stopped, "God's hammer. Man's hope."

Rachel couldn't believe he had taken a word of it seriously. She had laughed at him for at least five minutes. When he couldn't take any more of her mocking, he started from the moment Paolo had cruised him in class and told her the whole story up to the point when he had picked her up from work. She listened. Rolling her eyes at first, but slowly being convinced. He stopped the car in front of her house and said, "You know the rest." She wasn't laughing anymore.

Zoology was more crowded than usual. It was Darby's favorite dance club. Wild, even by gay bar standards. It was a normal Saturday night for him, Rachel, Yoshi, and Josh. Pre-party at Josh's house. Heading out around midnight. Darby had called Paolo earlier. Luckily, Cinder had been out. Paolo was meeting them on the dance floor around 1 A.M. As always, Yoshi was grinding on Darby while his boyfriend, Josh, looked on approvingly. Darby had been taken with Yoshi's exotic good looks since the moment they met, but never allowed things to go beyond the occasional grope and kiss. He knew they were into three-ways, but he felt that on some level it wasn't really what Josh wanted. Joshua's conflicting emotions could be so extreme. Darby suspected he was distressingly close to a full blown personality disorder...At least when it came to affairs of the heart. It just wasn't worth the risk of hurting his friend.

Rachel and Josh were bustin' a move right beside them. None of them could resist Madonna's siren call to the dance floor, even when she wasn't the most en vogue diva of the day. Darby was finding it more and more difficult to keep pushing Yoshi away. He allowed him to slip in a lingering kiss. (Those full lips were the stuff of dreams.) His eyelids had barely parted when he saw the look of utter sadness flash for an instant across Josh's face. Darby broke the embrace as nonchalantly as possible and started dancing in Rachel's direction. Everyone laughed to play it off as they always did. It wasn't denial on anyone's part, just one of those things no one spoke of so that they might avoid the undoing of their little "family."

Darby was flooded with relief when he saw Paolo boogying in their direction. "Paolo!" They waved to acknowledge each other. The gang stopped dancing and stood gawking as Paolo slid into Darby's arms. It was like a scene from a romantic movie. The young couple madly in love, but tragically separated by some over-the-top conflict, finally reunited. Rachel hadn't even thought Darby was that interested in the guy.

Darby was taken off guard by his own reaction. It was like reconnecting with a part of him. He wondered if he was being influenced by what Luna had told him. Was it the power of suggestion, or was he really experiencing emotions that defied logic?

"I couldn't wait to see you." Paolo wasn't letting go. He just looked up into Darby's eyes. Smiling. Radiating admiration, devotion, and love. Honest…and clean. Darby was blown away."

"Paolo, you don't even know me." Darby gently pushed him away.

"You're wrong." Paolo wouldn't let go of his hands, "I've known since I was eight years old that there was someone waiting for me out in the world. It's you, Dar. It's you."

Would there be no end to the shocks this week had brought. No one had called him "Dar" since his grandmother had died. Just hearing it infused him with love and security like the much-missed caress of Grandma's hand on his cheek. "Paolo, what are you going to do about Cinder? He's crazy, man. He'll kill you."

"He knows I won't stay with him. That I can't. And he knows why. I told him about all of this years ago when we met. I don't want to hurt him, but we've been growing apart for a long time. I would never have gone home with you if things hadn't been more or less over with Cinder for a long time…I'm not saying it will be easy. But we have to—"

"Stop. You've got this whole big future mapped out for us, and we just met. We need to take some time to see if we even like each other before—"

"I didn't map it out, Dar. God did. And you know it." There wasn't a shred of doubt on Paolo's face.

"What I know is that fate has thrown us together for some reason beyond my understanding. As part of some unfolding story that I want no part of. I know this too. I won't be told whom to love. I choose. Me. I admit that I am drawn to you. More than to anyone ever before. But I don't know you. I hope to get to know you. I am open to the possibility that this could be the real deal, but we need time. So don't be planning the honeymoon just yet. Let's just see where time takes us, okay? Are we cool?"

Paolo's eyes were glistening with unfallen tears, "We're cool," was all he said before taking a deep breath, swallowing the rejection and transforming it into the most amazing smile Darby had ever seen. He hoped Paolo was right. He would be so easy to love.

Darby slid his arm around Paolo's shoulders and turned him towards his friends. "Everybody, this is Paolo. Paolo, these are my worthless friends."

"Hey!!!" Rachel, Yoshi, and Josh were unanimous in their mock indignation. They pounded on Darby. Transformed into tickle monsters. No one hated being tickled more than Darby, and soon they had pulled Paolo into the fray, making him their willing second victim. The mostly drugged-out dancers that surrounded them paid them little mind. They were carried away by Amber's admonitions to "Love One Another" to a techno beat. The gang had composed themselves at a tall table at the corner of the dance floor and were sipping on fresh cocktails when people started to scream.

The huge video screens in the corners of the bar were filled with visions of panic. Drag queens and leather men were scrambling like someone was handing out free Prada boots in the parking lot. "What's going on?" Rachel was the first to realize that something was very wrong.

Paolo couldn't speak when he saw the source of their terror. It was Cinder. He had a gun, and he wasn't alone.

Darby was frozen. Cinder was walking straight towards them, and there was no escape. Cinder and his two sidekicks stopped about ten feet directly in front of them. All three had hand guns aimed at Darby, Paolo, and their friends. "I warned you, Motherfucker!" Cinder was yelling at the top of his lungs. He had lost his grasp on sanity. Darby knew there would be no reasoning. Cinder turned towards Paolo, "Name one thing I didn't give you. We were good together, Pal. You had to go and throw it all away, and for what? Some dime-store holy man you just met? More likely you fell in love with his big meat…I know how you are. You little fucking whore…Trickin' might not come so easy if I blow that pretty fuckin' face of your—"Cinder raised the gun as he ranted. He was pointing it at Paolo's head. Rachel's screams were echoing through the converted warehouse. The music had stopped and almost everyone was gone. Darby watched as Cinder seemed to pull the trigger in slow-motion. His reaction was purely instinctual. He stepped in front of Paolo, throwing out his arms as if to shelter his friends behind him. All they saw was a gold shimmer as the bullet ricocheted away from them shattering a neon rainbow flag. The confused gunmen unleashed their fury. They opened fire with unbridled abandon. The rapid impact of the hail of bullets revealed through golden contact flashes that a sort of energy field had formed a protective shield between Darby's friends and their attackers. Darby had found his power. He knew without question. This was it. The bouncing bullets continued to ricochet wildly until two go-go boys and one of Cinder's goons lay dead on the floor. Josh was holding his stomach. He felt sick.

"Stay behind me," was all Darby said. Cinder and his buddy rushed them, prepared to do whatever it took to remove Darby and friends from Paolo's life, and to teach Paolo a lesson he would never forget.

They ran into an invisible wall and waves of golden shimmers appeared briefly in the air surrounding Darby and the others in his party. Cinder and the other thug sprawled backwards onto the floor. "What the hell?" Cinder would have been afraid, but his madness transmuted the fear into blinding rage, "It's true. You really are some kind of magical freak. Guess you're not too holy to screw my boyfriend though, huh, asshole?"

"Don't do this, Cinder. You can't force someone to love you. People are dead, for Christ's sake." Darby had taken several steps in his direction and was hoping to at least create enough of a distraction for his friends to slip out.

"You're done, Zaid," Cinder was standing and had pulled a switchblade from his jacket.

Suddenly Darby wasn't afraid anymore. Cinder aimed at Darby's heart and threw the knife. It sailed end over end at super speed. Darby raised his hand, palm out, in front of his heart. The six inch blade slowed and came to a stop in mid-air about two feet in front of Darby's hand. It was surrounded by shimmering gold light in which it continued to revolve slowly end over end. Suddenly, with lightning speed, it hurled back in Cinder's direction. It struck his own heart and penetrated the entire length of the blade. Darby was as shocked as Cinder. He hadn't made a conscious decision to launch the knife back at his attacker. The protective energy field he had generated had acted autonomously. Darby was simultaneously relieved and horrified by the outcome. Paolo and the others had joined him and were standing at his sides. Cinder's cohort had fled the building in fear for his life. No one bothered to check any of the casualties for pulses. It was obvious that they were dead.

No one said anything as they exited the front door to wait for the arrival of the police. The witnesses were struggling to believe what they had seen. It was easier to believe it had been the drugs or the alcohol, but Darby's friends knew. It was real. People were dead. And their lives would never by the same. "I'm sorry," Darby said to Paolo, "I'm sure you loved him once."

"That wasn't the man I used to love in there. He stopped being that person a long time ago," Paolo joined Darby sitting on the sidewalk, leaning against the concrete wall painted with a giant mural of men mutating into animals. "You had no choice, Dar. They would have killed us all. You're a hero, man."

"Then why do I just feel dirty?" Darby was so exhausted; he couldn't imagine ever standing again.

None of them paid much attention to the little homeless girl that had been sleeping on the bench at the bus stop on the corner until she got up and began to wander towards them in an unintentional, casual fashion. Roaming with no destination in mind. Her long blonde hair was matted and tangled, and she was covered in filth. Her most alarming aspect was her age. She couldn't have been over eight years old. She drifted over to the weary group sitting in front of the bar. Police sirens could be heard somewhere in the background. "Can we help you, Sweetheart?" Rachel leaned down to talk to her, "Where are your parents, Honey?"

The dirty little girl just looked at her silently for a moment before turning to Darby. She leaned in and whispered something in his ear. His only response was to turn and look directly into her smudged little face. She darted away then. Skipping around the corner of the building without speaking a word to the rest of them. Yoshi ran after her, thinking he would hold her there for the police. The streets were no place for a child alone, but she was gone. Vanished into the night. Yoshi gave up and returned to the group. "What did she say?" Paolo asked Darby as the police cars finally came into view.

They all had to move closer to hear his whispered reply. "She said, 'You are the last of the Avatarn to awaken. Beware of Legion. They must not find you before the meeting of the triad.'"

Paolo pulled Darby's head down on to his shoulder and kissed his forehead, "You'll find them in time...We'll help you."

Chapter 4

Twenty thousand years before human life set foot on Earth, a small planet on the other side of the galaxy was the seat of power for a great king. The Grand Emperor Skylar the 7th was undisputed ruler of Eden, governing planet for a federation of four galaxies. He was preparing to receive a special guest in the main throne room. His only wife, Empress Draden, sat at the throne to his side, and their seven sons and seven daughters reclined casually on the steps at their feet. The huge room which often served as a reception hall was the largest in the palace and was constructed of the finest marble, minerals, metals, and gems to be found in the known universe. The servants scrambled to lay out an extensive feast. Animal trainers, acrobats, and dancers performed everywhere to amuse jaded courtiers and courtesans.

Skylar's family had ruled the intergalactic kingdom for 17 generations. His ancestors had successfully resisted invasion by the dreaded Legion. The imperial armada of starships had met the intruding fleet outside the federation perimeter time and again. The Edenite forces were slowly being crushed by superior weapons and a seemingly endless supply of soldiers that would only millennia later become known as demons.

The progenitor of Skylar's line was a great leader named Issa. Issa had not been long on the throne when Legion began to attack the outer-most solar systems, enslaving entire planets as they went. He was running out of strategies, and preparing terms of surrender when a strange encounter turned the tide. He had gone riding alone in the forest as was his daily custom. Alone with his thoughts and his favorite mount, a large black unicorn named Kali. The ancient trees and fluttering birds mixed with the dappled sunlight always soothed his war-weary mind.

When he came upon the woman, she was sitting cross-legged in the middle of the dirt path twisting the stem of a purple flower she was holding in her lap. Her blonde hair was mostly hidden by the loose hood of her cloak, but her azure eyes, far below the leafy canopy, were a window to the sky. Issa fell in love with her instantly. He bedded her on the forest floor. When they had finished, she told him he had blessed her womb with a daughter that he would call Agape, and that she would be the mother of a great dynasty. She smiled at the handsome sovereign sitting in the leaves, leaning against a fallen tree. His long brown hair was the color of soil and was tied in a loose ponytail. It was matched by the beard that accentuated the masculinity of his jaw, but did not hide the beauty of his face. She was glad their daughter would look like him. She waited until they were both atop Kali galloping toward the alabaster castle to share the secret that was the true purpose of her visit to the royal homeworld. She told Issa of the exact location on a forgotten planet where he would find a vast pool of glittery water, lost to the kingdom for eons. She said this serene pond was created by God to quench the thirst of loyal angels. She said it could be used to power weapons that would destroy Legion soldiers.

The woman called herself Juna, and never revealed her origin to Issa or anyone else. The king found the holy pool precisely where she had said it would be. He never questioned her counsel, only followed it. His scientists quickly devised hand guns and ship-mounted devices that channeled light through a chamber holding the blessed water. The beams that emanated from the weapons blew apart the very molecules of the demons leaving only a brief scent of sulfur behind. The king's foundling concubine gave birth to a princess, true to her word. Issa named her Agape and made her the light of his life. Her mother disappeared the day after she was born.

Skylar's family had coasted on the legend of Issa, Juna, and Agape for generations. He tried hard to be a good leader to his people, but he wasn't much of a warrior. The Edenic army had long ago depleted the holy pool in the petty skirmishes that constantly arose between imperial colonies and marauding members of Legion. The demons were unrelenting in their efforts to nibble away at the federation, making slaves of any species that could serve them in some capacity. Legion forces were assembling in the next solar system and Skylar was afraid. His advisors had been little help and the emperor was growing desperate in his search for a defense, desperate enough to meet with the charismatic leader of a religious cult living in the mountains on the other side of the planet. He had sent a shuttle to transport her small delegation of priestesses to the royal castle. She was said to have rare powers and frequently made annunciations in the name of God. Skylar had never really taken her seriously as long as her influence never extended past the foot of her mountain; however when his lovely wife, Draden, had suggested he grant the woman's request for an audience, he began to pray that she was indeed a tool of God, and that she would deliver them from certain bondage.

The giant platinum doors could easily have been whisked open by advanced federation technology, but custom dictated that twelve strong men from Skylar's staff slowly push them ever wider until they locked into place with a loud metallic clang. Trumpets roared the arrival of a much-anticipated guest. The busy room came to a stand-still when an incredibly beautiful woman appeared at the entrance. White tigers flanked her on both sides, and seemed her willing escorts as she started the long walk to the throne. Men and women alike were enchanted by her beauty. Her long blonde hair was piled at least a foot high on her head. Intricate twists and turns woven with strands of pearls. She wore a long cerulean gown that displayed every curve of a perfect body. She carried herself with a regal bearing that the royal princesses would do well to emulate. The palace guards had moved forward to intercept the wild animals long before they approached his majesty, but were quickly dismissed by the king himself who felt compelled to trust this strange woman.

The silence throughout the room was unprecedented, and all eyes were on the mysterious priestess as she approached the royal family. When she stopped just short of the steps, her feline protectors sat dutifully at each side and turned to her, waiting for her to speak. She dropped to one knee and bowed low as protocol demanded.

"Arise, Sister…And come forth." Skylar addressed her in the manner that was customary in her order.

She stood and walked forward, stepping onto the bottom step and staring up into the Emperor's curious face. The crowd gasped. Only persons of the royal family had ever been allowed to touch those stairs or any point above.

"My name is Joppa," she began, "I have come to you to foretell the coming of great heroes that will free our people and those of countless worlds from the clutches of Legion. They shall be known as the Avatarn, a human triad selected by God to battle the Legion overseers in a mighty crusade. I shall watch for them, and teach them what I can, for that is the purpose of all my lives."

"What about now?" The king was clearly disappointed.

"It is too late for this place," Joppa raised her hands in a gesture of helplessness, "but know that your children and many commoners will escape to freedom. They are destined to become great warriors in the never-ending battle." This news alarmed the royal offspring and they began to fidget and look to their father to quiet this doom-sayer. He did not. Truth radiated from her like light from the suns.

"How shall we know these Avatarn?" the emperor asked. "What are they?"

Her answer was booming and echoed in every corner of the massive room. "God's hammer. Man's hope." She didn't wait to be dismissed. She turned and started the long journey towards the door. She never made it.

Skylar stood to summon her back for further explanation, but it started before he spoke. Deafening energy blasts shook the palace walls, and soon the ceiling of the magnificent throne room was eaten away by the energy weapons of Legion fighter ships. The terrified courtiers ran for cover, looking over their shoulders at the one-man spacecraft that were passing low over the devastated castle. Princes and princesses scattered in every direction. The sovereign and the queen had been killed instantly and lay in a crumpled pile on the floor. The searing orange energy blasts had torn through many other victims, blood and carnage erasing centuries old grandeur. Joppa stood motionless watching as several escaped. She would not be among them. She prayed that God would take mercy on those of them that would be captured and become the slaves of monsters. In the next instant she was gone, vaporized in an atom-scorching flash from an alien fighter that landed where she had stood.

Chapter 5

Adolphus couldn't stop pacing around the bridge of his ship, *The Caiphas*. It was the flagship of the armada and carried 10,000 warriors, as well as weapons able to lay waste to the most advanced of civilizations from orbit. The fleet was approaching the planet Gehenna, home base for Legion forces. It was a shiny blue planet, much like Earth, except half the size.

Adolphus normally didn't accompany his raiding parties, but this mission had been special. Scouting vessels had only recently discovered the lovely lavender planet Vishnu. A two-man scout ship had lost navigational control and veered off course. They drifted for weeks before passing into an unknown solar system and crashing in the middle of a pre-industrial society on the giant purple planet.

The naïve people of Vishnu quickly took in the injured Legion scouts and treated them as honored guests. The beautiful natives seemed untroubled by the small horns that extended from one demon's forehead or the mouth full of fangs possessed by the other. The scouts were enchanted by them as well and contacted the fleet as soon as they were able. The villagers of Vishnu would make fine additions to the slave stables. With shining black hair, four arms, and four breasts; each would draw a great price at auction. They knew Adolphus would reward them well, and he had. Each had been promoted to the next rank, and Adolphus had chosen to lead the invasion force himself. This rare species was too valuable to risk unnecessary slaughter; besides, he couldn't wait to select a concubine from among them.

The mission had been an unprecedented success. One hundred thousand captives had been taken alive. It had been necessary to execute 200,000 natives as an example. A small number of resisters among the usually docile people of Vishnu had managed to kill a handful of soldiers before the massacre began. The swift punishment came on a grand scale. Adolphus knew he had to show the new captives that he ruled with an iron first. He had chosen Indra as his new concubine when he found her hysterically mourning her recently butchered family. The strikingly handsome leader of Legion, whose only demonic characteristic was golden eyes, did not hesitate to lift his tunic and force himself on the bewildered girl. His warriors looked on approvingly as he easily pinned her four arms above her head and slammed into her defenseless body again and again. They had come to expect it of him, and she would make a fine addition to the harem.

Adolphus was glad to be home. He had stopped pacing and was leaning against a window with a breath-taking view of Gehenna. He was tired and daydreaming of his own bed, when Lucien, his second in command, burst onto the bridge.

Lucien had left his patrolman uniform on Earth, and in its place wore a crimson toga that showcased his muscular body. "Report, Asmodai!" Adolphus commanded. Only the king ever called Lucien by that name, even he only when his mood was foul. Lucien hated it.

"Master," Lucien began with a small bow, "I have just returned from Earth. It is begun. The Avatarn have awakened."

"Are they together?" Fear flicked across Adolphus' face for a fraction of a second. Lucien quickly looked away, pretending not to notice. He was beginning to realize the seriousness of the situation. Nothing had ever frightened Adolphus. The Avatarn were a real threat after all.

"No," was Lucien's only reply.

"What is the nature of their powers?" Adolphus had resumed his pacing.

"The rich one is a healer. The witch commands the forces of nature. And the fag can project and manipulate energy fields." Lucien's tone implied no opinion. He would take his cue from his master.

"They will be a formidable challenge. The invasion fleet will leave for Earth in one day. In the meantime, you will open a dimensional portal and return there. You will alert the under-cover agents. Manipulate the human fools we have already brainwashed into the idolatry of hatred. Use them to cripple the Chosen Ones. The Avatarn must be found and killed before they unite. Use any means necessary. We need not hide among them any longer. Without the Avatarn, the Terrans will be helpless and Earth will be ours." Adolphus seemed to be re-assured by his own orders.

"Of course, Master," Lucien had waited a long time to prove himself by dealing with the long-anticipated Avatarn, "The Chosen Ones shall never meet. I shall destroy them myself."

"Do not be so foolish as to under-estimate the holy triad," Adolphus had closed the distance between them and placed his hand on Lucien's chest. "They have been blessed by the Father Himself. If they are allowed to reach each other and realize their true nature, the prophecy could come to fruition. The end of our great Legion."

Lucien boldly placed his hand on Adolphus' shoulder. A gesture that suggested they were equals. "I will not fail you....The Avatarn will die."

Adolphus indulged in a long nap after a small shuttlecraft transported him to Gehenna's surface and the comforts of his Castle Hades. He awoke refreshed and after being bathed by two of the native children, he dressed in a transparent black tunic and placed a ruby crown on his cleanly shaven head.

It felt good to assume his place on the throne. Holding court always relaxed him. The captives from Vishnu had been processed and were being prepared for auction. The peasants of Gehenna scrambled everywhere to arrange a feast and service the demonic courtiers.

Adolphus clapped his hands indicating that chairs at each of his sides were to be filled. One belonged to his beautiful daughter, Beacon. He had adopted the human girl, now a young adult, when she was born. One of his subordinates had stolen her, thinking that children raised in slavery always made the best servants. However, Adolphus spoiled his plans by falling in love at the first sight of her. His decision to make her his daughter had shocked his underlings, but none dared openly oppose his wishes. All of Legion showed Beacon the respect demanded by her station, though she was secretly despised. Adolphus adored her.

The other chair was reserved for a child stolen from the backward planet Goshen. He had recently taken her under his wing. The peasant girl, a candle-lighter in the royal court, had won his favor when she slapped a rowdy guard who dared lay his hand on the Princess Beacon's waist in a familiar manner.

Adolphus had reminded the child that it was forbidden for a human to strike a member of Legion. An offense punishable by death. The girl had defiantly raised her chin and said that she would do it again to protect the princess. Since then, the out-spoken child had become his constant amusement and sometime counselor, though she knew when to keep her mouth shut. No human, but his daughter, ever stayed in his favor for long. Joppa was careful never to displease him.

At his signal, she left her candle-lighting duties to another girl and took her place at his side. Beacon entered through a door behind the throne and took her place. Adolphus signaled the guards to bring in the prisoners he was to sentence for rebellion.

The rebels from the planet Atlantis were dragged in by their tails. Under normal circumstances, the enslaved mer-people of Atlantis were kept in pools or tanks to simulate their natural under-water living environment. Atlantis was a water world. Aside from their pale green skin, the Atlantians appeared human from the waist up. From the waist down, their bodies were composed of giant fish tails. A combination of lungs and gills allowed them to breathe above or below the surface of the sea. Because of their confinement to water, Legion had kept them mostly as pets and sex slaves.

The guards dropped the three mermaids and three mermen unceremoniously to the foot of the throne, kicking them along the way. The handsome rebel leader struggled to raise himself to a sitting position. His long green hair had broken loose from the tight bun that was the custom of the males of their species.

"How dare you plot against your masters?" The resistance factions that popped up on the enslaved planets always enraged Adolphus. The mermen's only response was to spit at Adolphus' feet. The demon king was left with no choice.

"Death!" Adolphus roared, "To the rebels and 10,000 more of their species….We will not be defied." Two dozen guards ran forward with their swords drawn.

"Wait!" Joppa yelled turning to her master. The guards raised their swords without acknowledging the seven-year-old girl, but froze in place when Adolphus spoke.

"Halt!...I will hear her…."

"Mercy, Master? Please?" Joppa was on her knees, both of her small hands clutching one of his large ones.

"Why should I? If I don't put down these pogroms when they occur, there will be chaos," Adolphus growled, angered that she would dare to interfere. Beacon sat silently watching. Her eyes glistening with tears she dare not shed.

"Because," Joppa hesitated, searching for the words that might appease him, "if you kill them, they become martyrs. Icons for new rebels to rally around."

"I'll kill them all before I tolerate this behavior."

"For me then…Spare them out of affection for me," Joppa knew she might have gone too far.

"I've never known a child that speaks like you, little one," Adolphus was amused by her constant selflessness and concern for others. He even chuckled, "Very well…I will spare their worthless lives…But take heed, little one…Do not push me too far. There are limits to my affection…Even for you…You will accompany my daughter to her chambers," he continued; "I must decide some punishment for these criminals and I will not have her witness anymore of their insolence."

"Thank you, Master." Joppa rewarded him with an amazing smile, and stood, taking Beacon's hand and escorting her from the room. She paused at the doorway as Adolphus instructed her to return to him as soon as Beacon was settled in her chambers.

She returned to a scene of such barbarism that her heart was filled with regret for her intercession. Some fates were worse than death. Adolphus had decided that the rebels would be allowed to live, but only for the carnal satisfaction of his warriors. Joppa knew that on Earth the term for what she was witnessing was gang rape.

A few of the two dozen demonic guards were still completing the gruesome task of ripping off each quarter-sized scale with metal pliers. The sharp scales had to be removed for forced sexual contact. Left intact, they formed an effective defensive layer. The flesh beneath was minty green and smeared with a sheen of darker green blood. The sexual organs and bodily orifices of the Atlantians were the same as humans. The only real difference being that the male genitalia were hidden inside a pouch of flesh unless they were aroused. Such was the state of two of the mermen. The demons had pulled their large green organs free from their folds and pumped them to full erectness, the helpless mermen responding against their will to the barrage of stimulation. Males and females alike cried out in pain as demonic appendages were forced into every orifice of the beautiful fish people as they flopped on the marble floor with no avenue of escape. The merpeople bit down on foreign flesh being forced into their mouths hoping to avenge themselves by the only means at their disposal.

Their resistance was futile. The soldiers' organs were literally as hard as steel, and they were only excited by the Atlantians' attempts to harm them. Each warrior took his turn. Chewing first on the mermaids' voluptuous breasts, then on the swollen cocks of the shamed mermen.

Joppa took her place on Adolphus' lap. She didn't say a word. In the end, she was only a slave and she had pushed the lord of demons to the limits of his patience. There was nothing else she could do. She allowed him to place her tiny hand on his massive phallus. She didn't look at him. She kept her eyes on the relentless torture, her blank face showing no emotion of any kind. She allowed Adolphus to take whatever liberties that he would, without complaint, hoping that her compliance would keep his daughter untouched.

She didn't react in any visible way when her eyes drifted toward the distant ceiling and she saw several angels there weeping. She was angry with them for not intervening, but more so at God for not letting them.

It was then that she heard God's whisper, which was somehow in her ear. "You must harden your heart, beloved princess of Heaven, that you might endure a little longer. For I have taken up my hammer, and it will surely fall."

Chapter 6

Roman was sitting on his front porch steps when the police arrived. He offered no resistance as he was taken into custody. He was still in shock, but managed to forewarn the officers about what they would find upstairs. An energetic young female officer assured Roman after a brief communiqué with the cops that had entered the house, that the cuffs and trip downtown were just a technicality. She informed him that the intruder he had plainly killed in self-defense was Jerry Dobson, an escaped convict from the state prison. Dobson was serving a triple-life sentence for multiple murders, and Roman was lucky to be alive. He smiled just a little at the irony of the situation as she frisked him cautiously for weapons while telling him he was a hero…He thought her hands lingered a little longer in some areas.

He was treated respectfully at the precinct house and his sense of guilt began to fade as one cop after another assured him that he had had no choice. The phone call to Brenda was more difficult than calling the police had been, but there was no one he trusted more than his ex-wife.

Carter answered the phone with a grumpy tone, which meant he was sleeping on Roman's side of the bed. He forced himself to remain polite while asking to speak to Brenda. Carter had just finished saying she was sleeping when she took the phone from him. Brenda didn't hide the fact that she was pissed that his first call in months was coming in the middle of the night, but her attitude changed the instant he said he was in trouble. She jumped out of bed, pulling on Carter's cowboy boots and trench coat with her red satin negligee, and ran out the door.

The D.A. reviewed the initial crime scene investigation and decided no charges would be filed. All evidence had been removed from Roman's home, and he was free to go. Brenda was still trembling when they walked to her car. Officers in the waiting area had brought her up to speed as she waited for Roman to come out.

"I don't know what I would have done if anything had happened to you." She was crying as she got in the car.

"It's okay…I'm all right…Shhh," Roman held her and wiped the tears from her face.

"I can't take anymore loss," she sniffed.

"Don't worry," Roman turned her head so he could look her in the eyes, "Nothing's going to happen to me." He hoped he appeared surer than he felt.

"It's just ….I've been having these dreams…" She began, pushing him away, suddenly uncomfortable in his embrace.

"What kind of dreams?...You mean Janie?" Roman still held her hands.

"No…Not Janie…" Brenda actually looked scared, "You…I keep dreaming that someone's chasing you. Trying to hurt you."

"Well, there you go. You must have been dreaming about Dobson…We don't have to worry about him anymore. I'm safe." He pulled her close and kissed her forehead.

"No… It isn't over. In my dreams you're in a strange place, far away. There are friends with you and you're running for your lives. Every dream ends the same. I follow you all into a castle, but just as I am about to warn you of the danger all around, a beautiful woman appears before me. I don't know how I know her name is Joppa. She says 'You're not meant to be here,' and pushes me backward. I fall back and the whole scene falls away and I'm falling and falling through space, until finally I hit the bed and wake up…Don't tell me it's not real, Roman. I know it's crazy, but it's real. Now tell me what's going on."

Roman couldn't leave her in torment any longer. As they cruised down the highway, he told her everything. Even about Janie and her true identity. Brenda had become quiet; she was trying so hard to believe, but there were limits to her imagination. She was starting to think their daughter's death had taken a greater toll on Roman than she realized.

She had been silent for a while, so he had tuned in an easy-listening station to fill the void. Both were distracted from their lives' current chaos as Celine belted out a song with haunting lyrics about how loved ones live on in our hearts even after they're gone. Each was lost in the ever-present pain of their common loss, when a newsbreak cut in with other people's sorrows.

The radio anchorman's rich baritone filled the car with the story of tragedy in Juniper, Georgia. He told of a bonfire that had grown out of control, destroying a small church. The saddest victim was the preacher's wife, whose sisters had died in the fire. As if that weren't enough, the hysterical congregation had trampled her husband to death. The poor woman had been taken to an Atlanta psychiatric hospital for observation. Her name was Blair Atwood.

"That's her!" The name hit Roman like a slap in the face.

Brenda wasn't convinced, but by the time they reached Roman's house, she agreed to help him close up his home and drive him to the airport.

She was crying again when she kissed him good-bye at the terminal. "Maybe you should wait, Roman…You're still in shock… Think this over for a while. You're going to end up locked away in that hospital yourself." It was the first time she had smiled all night. "And I'm not coming down there to get you, if you do," she added.

"Yes, you would," he hugged her tight.

"God help me; I probably would." She traced the line of his

jaw with her fingers. "Stay here, Roman. Get some professional help. I think our grief has messed up our minds."

"I'm on a mission, Hon." He was trying to convince himself. "Blair needs me."

Brenda watched from the gate. He was waving from the window as his plane slowly taxied away. "Be with him, God," she whispered, wondering why only his seat's over-head light was bright blue.

The report on the radio had said Blair was taken to Saint Joan's Psychiatric Hospital. Roman had hopped on the internet before leaving the house and downloaded the address and map to his palm pilot. The flight was uneventful. The rental car was plain, but got him where he was going.

It was a beautiful sunny morning and after assuring the receptionist that he was Ms. Atwood's cousin, he was shown to the day room. The large solarium was filled with plants and sky lights.

The room was full of patients in various states of composure, and Roman was troubled by their pitiful conditions. He knew the instant he saw the catatonic redhead sitting in the window that it was Blair. Even lost in her sadness, her beauty was breathtaking. The simple green hospital gown actually flattered her exquisite figure, and her emerald eyes, though haunted, were magnetic.

Roman had only started across the room when he was intercepted by two large orderlies. The uniformed muscle men pulled him into a bathroom before he even had time to object, and he didn't even see the syringe before it entered his neck. The dizziness was instantaneous, and he knew the needle contained some kind of powerful tranquilizer. He had nearly blacked out before returning to hyper-awareness. Somehow his body had absorbed the drug, negating its influence and protecting itself from harm.

Stunned by Roman's impossible resistance to the drug, the orderlies hesitated, allowing Roman time to see that there were no whites to their eyes, only black. His heart filled with dread. They weren't human. He feared all was lost, when each twisted an arm behind his back. His accidental rescue came in the form of a curious patient who had seen the unfamiliar men disappear into the bathroom.

No one knew why Sampson's mental development had stopped around age five, and his child-like curiosity demanded the investigation of all things new. The forty-three-year-old innocent shoved the door open, unaware of his own strength.

The door struck one of the demonic orderlies. He lost his balance and stumbled forward hitting his head against the wall. He fell to the floor unconscious. Roman didn't waste his chance. His free hand found the paper towel dispenser, which came off the wall in his hand. He swung the metal box with all of his might, smashing the other brute in the face. The bloodied face registered surprise for only an instant before he crumpled to the floor. Sampson, fearing punishment, ran to his room. Roman peeked in the mirror, smoothed his hair and returned to the sunroom. He passed a couple of depressed looking teenagers, an old woman mumbling to herself about the king's spaceship, and a young man enthusiastically playing with himself. When he reached the stoic young widow he was seeking, a skinny old man was shouting in her face. "Strega! Strega!" He was poking her in the chest with a gnarled old finger. Roman chased him off with a few gruff words. He couldn't remember how he knew that "strega" was the Italian word for "witch."

"Thank you." Blair managed a half smile.

"Sure." Roman empathized completely with her crushing grief. He knew what it was to watch your loved ones die.

Blair saw the tears in the handsome stranger's eyes and his quivering lip and didn't even ask who he was before standing and pulling him into her arms.

"I've come to take you out of here," Roman cleared his throat and wiped his eyes.

"I know," Blair said, "Who are you?"

"I'm like you…An Avatarn," Roman was a little embarrassed to say it. Blair's breath caught in her chest. She hadn't heard that word since that night in the woods. She had started to think their angelic visitation might have been a hallucination.

"How do you know that word?" Blair was startled by the notion that this man had somehow become privy to the secret annunciation that had destroyed her life.

"I was told about it by my daugh—an ambassador of God. I wasn't easily convinced, but I've come to the realization that we can't escape our destiny." He brushed her hair back from her face. He introduced himself and shook her hand, smiling.

A nurse at the solarium workstation observed the encounter. She smiled to herself, totally unaware of the scuffle that had occurred with the false orderlies. No one had been able to reach Mrs. Atwood through her numbing pain, until this sexy stranger. She could see that Blair was truly present for the first time since her arrival. The nurse wondered why such handsome visitors never called for her.

Blair and Roman wasted no time in telling each other the stories of their "awakenings." Each marveled at the other's power, trying to believe.

"How are you going to get me out of here?" Blair was afraid to use her mostly untested powers. She didn't want to hurt anyone.

"I have an idea." Roman winked at her before casually approaching the guy that was jerking off and laying a hand on his shoulder. Roman's hand began to glow, setting his plan in motion. The white light expanded, engulfing both of them. The twenty-something patient let go of his sore penis and looked at Roman with immense gratitude.

"How can I ever repay you?" The young man had never had hope of being freed of his compulsions. There was nothing he wouldn't do for this mysterious savior in Gap clothes and a baseball cap.

"Just stick around, no pun intended…You'll get your chance in a minute." Roman approached the old Italian man, assuring him that he meant him no harm. The words were wasted because the old man was lost in his past. In a time long before he spoke or understood English. He was a paranoid schizophrenic and he flinched as Roman raised his hands. Roman grabbed his shoulders and an explosion of white light encased them.

The nurse had fainted when she witnessed "Jack," the jack-off-guy's healing. Blair looked on in rapt amazement.

Roman returned the weeping old-timer's shaky hug and moved on toward the teenagers — one boy, one girl. Under other circumstances they would have labeled him a psycho perv. And each would have been subtly reaching for the sharpened spoons they kept hidden in their socks. The weapons were a necessity. Sometimes at night, some of the orderlies tried to do things. This guy was different though. They had known it, even before the healings began. They had known as soon as they saw that the same blue light encircled his head that surrounded Blair's. Both stood as Roman came near and each took one of his hands. They watched the white light travel up their arms and felt it filling their hearts and minds. They knew intuitively that the light came straight from God, and that this man was only a tool that channeled it.

Roman was growing weak from the exertion, but he wasn't about to stop. There was still one more patient in the room. The nutty old lady who talked to herself. She was ancient and shriveled. Her long grey hair worn in a bun. He assumed the yellow streaks in it were from smoking. She sat at a card table in the corner and appeared to be playing solitaire. She didn't acknowledge Roman's prescence in any way. She just went on slamming down one card at a time and mumbling about courtesans letting anyone under their skirts. He gently, but firmly, took her elbow.

She spun to face him. Only startled for an instant, as the white light swirled around them, then enveloped them and filled the room. The next expression on her sagging face was one of recognition. "Daddy…I mean, Roman…I knew you would come."

"What?" Familiarity began to flood Roman's mind.

"I've been waiting here over fifty years…Since before you were born," she smiled, exposing the few of her teeth that remained.

"Janie?" He lifted her chin and studied her weathered face.

"It's me," Joppa smiled and nodded her head.

Roman pulled her into his arms and squeezed her gently, careful of her fragile bones. "I miss you, baby," Roman was crying again. Sometimes he felt like that was all he did anymore.

"I had forgotten who I was, Roman. Locked away here all these years with these lost souls. I was lost myself until you touched me. Healed me. Thank you, Daddy," the old woman allowed herself a single sob into the young man's chest before composing herself.

"But, Joppa...How can you have been here all these years, when not long ago you were a child with me? I was there at your birth."

"You must put aside mortal beliefs about time and space, Da... Roman. For I am not mortal. It is in His service that I live in many times and places at once and in many forms. Every life I live is to serve my mission — Protector and guide to the Avatarn. That's why I waited here all these years," Blair had joined them, and Joppa was speaking to both when she said, "To give you this." She reached into her bra and pulled out a gold antique key.

"What's this for?" Blair took it to examine it more closely.

"It's to get out of here," the old woman glanced in the direction of the sliding metal doors.

"Joppa, those doors — All the doors in the building, have electronic locks. They scan palm prints. An old fashioned key like this won't open them. I plan to use the patients I've healed as some kind of distraction until we figure out how to bust the hell out of here." Roman was afraid that his healing touch had not entirely repaired her scrambled mind. Who knew what had been done to her over the decades in the name of medicine.

"Of course they'll help," Joppa replied, "but you must trust me. This key is the only way out."

That's when the demonic orderlies came bursting from the bathroom, blood still running down their faces.

"Hit the alarm!" One of them growled at the nurse who had just awakened. She obeyed him instinctively before even taking in her surroundings. Loud metal clangs sounded all over the building as the metal doors locked into place and a booming alarm echoed throughout.

The seven-foot demons started towards them. The Avatarn stood frozen with indecision. A hand signal from Joppa brought all of the patients running to their side. "Go!" she shoved Blair in the direction of the exit. The teenagers pulled out their sharpened spoons and ran to intercept the giant orderlies before they reached Roman and Blair. Roman hesitated, but assumed Joppa knew best. He grabbed Blair's hand and bolted for the door. Each demon clutched one of their attackers by the throat and hoisted them into the air. The kids stabbed at them repeatedly with their carefully sharpened spoons, but their blows were easily deflected. The demons snapped their necks and tossed them aside. Joppa grabbed a fallen spoon/weapon and lunged at the closest orderlie, sticking it in his balls. He flew into a rage, lifting her over his head and flinging her against the wall on the other side of the room. There was no mistaking the sound of her skeleton shattering on contact with the concrete wall.

"No!" Roman screamed and turned to go back, but Blair stopped him.

"She did what she came here to do, Roman. The only way you can honor her is to do what she would want. Escape." He knew she was right, and as "Jack" and the old man engaged the demons, he turned back toward the door.

As they passed the desk, the horrified nurse ran around to intercept them, stun-gun in hand. She stopped in her tracks when she saw what she could only describe as blue halos radiating around their heads. She fell to her knees in worship and fear.

"Don't worship us," Blair said, "Just help us if you can."

The smiling nurse's face was smeared with mascara. She climbed to her feet, flipping on the stun-gun and headed towards the orderlies who were making short work of the remaining patients. The Avatarn couldn't wait to see what happened, despite much guilt over the sacrifices being made for them. On impulse, Blair held the gold key up against the door's palm scanner. With an electronic click, the scanning surface turned green and the door slid open. They ran through the building, opening one computerized door after another with the antique gold key. In the confusion no one pursued them except the demonic twosome.

As Roman and Blair raced out the front door, both leaped over the large orange tabby cat that stretched out leisurely just inside the door. It was pet therapy day and the animal shelter had brought by several docile cats and dogs to comfort the patients and vice versa. The demons stopped just short of the orange cat, which jumped up and hunched its back. Seven other cats came running to surround them. Cats always recognize demons for what they are, and a single cat bite would prove very poisonous to the alien creatures. The demons de-materialized, reappearing below the steps outside. They reinitiated their chase, and the cats pursued.

Roman and Blair fled into the busy street in front of the hospital. It was only after they reached the other side that they paused to look back. They turned just in time to see the impact. A huge bus plowed into the demonic assassins smashing them against the grill. They were dead. Roman and Blair were safe. For the moment. They couldn't see the bus driver, who instead of being terrified at what had just happened, smiled contentedly to himself. It was Lucien. He had decided that he wanted the Avatarn to unite after all. If the Avatarn destroyed Adolphus, he could assume command of Legion without his allegiance being questioned.

Roman followed Blair through the revolving door of a massive office building. They needed to blend into their environment until they could plan their next move. Her hair was tousled and her hospital gown was smeared with gold dust. The key had disintegrated the instant they left the hospital. He had to find her some clothes and get her to safety. Her beauty was intoxicating, even in her present state, and Roman felt guilty about his attraction to her. After all, she was newly widowed. He knew it didn't make sense, but somehow, he already loved her.

Chapter 7

Most of the cops were throwing attitude when they arrived at the crime scene. Some were homophobic. Some were closet-cases. None of them wanted to be at *Zoology*. Darby was manhandled a little at first, but all remaining witnesses soon confirmed that he was the hero of the night. After the entire gang was taken in for questioning, Darby was released free of charges, and they all crashed at Rachel's too exhausted to make it to their various homes.

It was an unspoken rule that Darby always got to share Rachel's bed in the occasional sleep-over situation. He didn't bother to get permission before pulling Paolo in with them. Rachel didn't mind. She would snuggle with anyone while she slept. Yoshi and Josh flopped on the couch in the small apartment's living room.

Spooning with Paolo, Darby began to relax and the terrors of the night began to fade. A sense of peace and self-forgiveness slowly crept into his weary mind. The dream started the moment he was captured by sleep. He and Rachel were teenagers again. They were sitting in the 50s-style diner that had been their high school hang-out. Darby didn't question their restored youth. They were giggling in their favorite red vinyl booth and munching on fries. Rachel didn't seem to recognize the waitress when she approached, but Darby knew her. She appeared to be entire decades younger than when they had met, but he knew beyond doubt. The tired but beautiful middle-aged server was Miss Luna, and she wasn't there to take their order.

"Darby!" She slid into the booth beside him. Her message was urgent, and she silenced Rachel's attempt to interrupt with a glance. "Ya'll need to head out towards Kansas City, Baby. That's where they'll be headed."

"Kansas City? Are you sure?" Darby couldn't imagine anyone choosing to go to Missouri if it could be avoided.

"I knows what I knows, Sweetpea," Luna tried to assure him by taking his hand. Rachel was totally oblivious to the situation. She showed no sign of recognizing Miss Luna at all, and Darby realized that no one but himself and the fortuneteller were really there, "Besides," she continued, "that's where that darlin' little witch is from. I spose most folks head home when they land in trouble, don't they? Luna didn't wait for a reply, "You just gather yer friends in the mornin' and head west. I reckin' ya'll will like KC well 'nough, but don't be fooled by the friendly settin'. Legion will know yer there quick 'nough. More dangerous than ever now that the great jihad is at hand, and they're scared."

"You can't expect us all to just drop our lives and go on some crazy quest." Darby knew his spiritual guide/waitress wasn't really going to offer him any other options.

"This mission is the purpose of your lives, Sugar. I wouldn't be sendin' ya out into the darkness if there was another way. Yer journey will be hard, and the toll on this road will be paid with the life of one of yer friends," she stopped wiping down the table and arranging menus and turned her teary eyes to his, "I'm sorry, Baby. The cost of freedom is high."

"What?! Who?!...Who's gonna— "

"I don't know which one, Honey. I only know His ways are mysterious. And the one that falls will never regret to go with you. Some things are more important than this life."

"I won't let them go then," Darby was determined to protect his gang, "They won't get hurt if they stay home."

"You'll say what you have to say to them, and they'll do what they have to do. They've seen what ya are with their own eyes, Baby. Everyday life doesn't have the same kick after a glimpse of the Truth. In one short night of madness, they learned more 'bout the true nature of the world than they had ever imagined. Once a body knows that magic, and evil, and angels are real, and God's really watching, livin' by the rules of normal life just don't hold much draw anymore. Those kids'll follow you anywhere now, and why shouldn't they? Helping yuns is the most important thing any of'em will ever do."

"I wish this was all just a nightmare," Darby's lips trembled. "A few weeks ago my biggest concern was whether or not to accept some gym boy's invitation to the sauna and which CD I had to have in my car next. Now you're telling me I have to sacrifice one of my friends and save the world."

"Just do yer part, Darby. Ya won't be alone. Roman and Blair are going to complete ya. It's yer destiny, Boy. Right now, ya think it's ruining yer life, but this is yer life. Ya came to this world for a reason. Everybody does, but most people don't ever know their reason. They live their lives without purpose. Yer very lucky to know the purpose of yer life. So many waste their time here." Luna hugged him briefly and said, "You get some rest now. Mornin'll come soon 'nough. Ya'll be needin' yer wits 'bout ya, Darlin'. I'll be watchin' out fer yuns. Make me proud. God speed." She gently kissed his chin as everything faded to blackness.

Darby slept a deep and restorative sleep, but awoke with a burden he had to share. He went to the kitchen and prepared a massive breakfast. The aroma slowly roused his slumbering comrades and drew them to the dining area where he had set the table with Rachel's finest and surrounded the table with a director's chair, two bar stools, and the pair that matched the table. A cozy setting with a dorm room vibe. He wanted to create the most pleasant atmosphere possible before hitting them with the prophecy about one of them dying if they insisted on following him. Their reality was grim, but bacon makes everything better. No one spoke as each one in turn took a place at the table and they began to serve themselves. Paolo approached him with half open eyes and offered a small kiss on the lips before turning without a word and joining the others in their morning feast. None of them knew what to say, and didn't have to as long their mouths were full.

"I have to tell you guys something," Darby circled the table as he spoke, perfectly comfortable in only his boxer briefs. Everyone in the room had seen him in less. It never crossed his mind to be concerned with modesty at a time like this. The others were also in various states of undress, and though they had all had crushes on Darby at one time or another, their priorities had changed. Sexual attraction wasn't first on anyone's list that morning. "Miss Luna came to me in a dream last night. She had some terrible news." They all looked up from their plates, but continued to eat. "I have to go to Kansas City to meet Roman and Blair."

"We'll go with you," Paolo spoke first, but the others were quick to voice their agreement. It was unanimous.

"I won't try to stop you guys from coming, even though it's dangerous, 'cause I'm scared to go alone. That's what it comes down to, but there's something you have to know before you make a decision. Luna says that one of you is going to die." No one was still chewing. "If any or all of you want to stay home, I won't think any less of you…I can't stand the thought of anything happening to any of you. It has to be your call. I'll understand."

"Well, understand this," Rachel stood up, "I'm going and nobody's stopping me."

"Or me!" Paolo was the next one to stand.

Yoshi and Josh whispered to each other for only a few seconds before standing. "We're going too," Josh voiced their decision and took Yoshi's hand.

"Our lives wouldn't mean very much without you guys," Yoshi added; "besides, how often does a man get a chance to help save humanity?" They all shared a nervous laugh, but happiness and hope wasn't what they were feeling as they moved to embrace Darby in a group hug. He took a moment to hold each one tightly before his thoughts finally turned to eggs-over-easy.

It was quickly agreed that they would take Josh's company van. He requested an emergency leave of absence from his software company so that he might spend time with his ailing grandmother in KC. No one at the office knew him well enough to know she had died in Charleston years ago. The van, which read *CYBERPLANET – Changing the world one click at a time!"* was always in Josh's care, so no one would question its use in the road trip.

Yoshi called the bank, where he worked as a teller, and told them he had broken his ankle. He would worry about how to come up with the doctor's note later. Rachel called the high school at which she taught mythology and told them she had the flu. She hoped they wouldn't be gone too long, and if they were, fuck the school; she wasn't about to let Darby go off to save the world by himself. Paolo wasn't even worried enough about his part-time job at the giant bookstore to call. He knew nothing would be the same at their journey's end anyway. It was the dawn of a new day, and there would be no going back. He didn't voice this opinion to the others though. They weren't ready to here it. Paolo had known all of his life that this day was coming. Darby called *The Gym* and informed them resolutely that they would have to cancel his appointments. He told the manager in a matter-of-fact tone that his life was taking a new path, and that he would never set foot in a gym again.

The road trip had been a blast at first. Everyone packed light, but brought their favorite CD's and snacks. Time flew by as they traveled west from Pittsburgh, their current hometown. They sang, gossiped about everyone they knew, flirted with every attractive man or woman they passed on the highway, and went on shopping spree after spree in nearly every convenience store they passed. All in a vain attempt to distract themselves from the unbelievable mission at hand.

They passed through St. Louis with only a brief stop to go to the top of the Arch. It was their one bow to tourism before continuing westward. They had not yet reached Columbia, when the van broke down. It was just after dark, and the moderately high traffic volume didn't change the fact that they were stranded in the middle of nowhere. Josh called for assistance on his cell phone, but was informed that the tow-truck wait would be approximately two hours. Rachel was hungry and Yoshi was desperate for a bathroom, so when six rebel-esque, alternative types on motorcycles stopped to offer help, the stranded "pilgrims" accepted the ride. Yoshi was a little wary of the much tattooed and pierced Samaritans, but at Rachel's insistence, he joined the others in climbing on the back of the bikes. The apparent skinheads had explained that they shared a house about a mile off the highway, and it would be no trouble to bring them back to the van after they had freshened up. Everyone realized they were taking a chance, but with Darby's newfound powers, they believed they would be safe in the end. Besides, the guys seemed genuinely nice, and Darby and Josh couldn't help noticing that more than a few of them were really hot… "Don't a lot of pornos start out this way?" Yoshi whispered to Paolo.

The short ride down the dirt road was not intolerable, though Rachel felt sure that she had bugs in her teeth. Darby saw the members of his posse visibly relax as they approached the house. It was actually a large hand-built log cabin just like that of Dr. Quinn, Medicine Woman. Darby was the first to notice that some things weren't quite right. There were several children playing with a couple of pittbulls in the yard. Aside from their party, several other motorcycles and four beat-up pickup trucks were scattered on the dying grass. A number of white-trash women were waiting on the front porch. So much for the rough trade, gay commune fantasy Darby had allowed himself to indulge in while his hands were on the waist of the cute thug who had provided his transportation to this increasingly humble abode. The ladies of the house seemed more than a little shocked to see them, but with a nod and a wink from Jacob, who introduced himself as the leader of the group and host of their little bike rally, they provided a warm welcome and assured the travelers that more were indeed merrier.

Wendy, the woman of the house, hesitated when Yoshi asked to use the bathroom, but with a nod from Jacob, she smiled and said, "Sure. I'll show you." She turned and led the way. Jacob explained how they had come by their guests and told some of the girls to bring out a cooler of beer so everyone could head out to the barn. Some of the other guys were already tending a fire in front of the entrance. Seemed Darby's gang had arrived just in time to attend an old-fashioned weenie roast.

Jacob invited them to step into the barn to see the horses. The entire group had entered with the skinheads close behind before Jacob flipped a switch illuminating the cavernous room. "Oh, shit!" Darby was the first to find his voice. The others were too stunned to speak. Each wall was covered with a massive Nazi flag. A giant black swastika in a sea of red any way you turned. At the far end, a small podium and a dozen metal folding chairs were scattered on the concrete floor.

"You're …You're ...Na Na Nazis." Rachel stammered.

"That's right, you nigger bitch!" Wendy stepped forward, twisting her greasy self-bleached hair, "You picked a piss poor place for your car to break down. Thanks to you and your faggot friends, we finally got our chance to make our statement. To set an example for decent, God-fearing Americans that don't realize there's only one way to take back this country."

Darby wasn't touched by the word *faggot*. He had heard it casually tossed around too many times. Hell, kids use it the same way they use *dork* or *nerd*. But hearing his friend called nigger was like a punch in the stomach. He felt like throwing up, but there was no time for him to dwell on words used as weapons. A glance at the door confirmed that there was no clear route of escape. They were in big trouble.

It was Paolo that spoke next, "You stupid fuckin' hicks don't know what you're dealin' with. Just step aside and let us pass and maybe you won't get hurt!"

"Is that right, Sweetheart?" The biker named Charlie (it was tattooed on the side of his neck) stepped forward, grabbing Paolo by the hair and twisting his arm behind his back.

"Get your fucking hands off him," Darby started forward, but a sharp blow connected to the side of his head before he had even taken a step. The skinheads descended on the holy pilgrims like hyenas. Kick after kick and punch after punch pounded the Avatarn's group into dazed helplessness. Darby had been taken off guard before he could engage his protective power.

The children had come to the entrance to see what was going on. They watched with some interest, but not surprise. Their parents got in fights nearly every weekend, but they were curious about the strangers. "Come on in and watch this kids," Wendy's pregnant sister waved the children inside, patting the belly that carried another of Jacob's babies. "Ya'll need to learn first-hand how fags and niggers should be handled.

A large and dirty Nazi hand had found its way up Rachel's skirt. She was sobbing, but no longer had the strength to offer resistance.

"This is all fags and niggers are good for," Charlie had pinned Paolo to the floor and was sitting on his chest. He quickly unzipped his fly and pulled out his fully erect dick and shoved it violently into Paolo's bloody mouth, "Don't bite, bitch, or you'll watch all your friends die before I cut your pecker off and feed it to you." Paolo was crying as he reluctantly obeyed his rapist.

Darby was lying nearby, where Jacob had beaten him to the ground. "Bring that baseball bat over here, Baby," Jake called to Wendy as he pulled down Darby's jeans. He wasn't wearing underwear, and Jacob pulled his nearly lifeless legs up towards his chest, "We'll give him what he wants." Wendy handed the bat to one of the other guys, not quite capable of the cruelty she loved to watch. Darby couldn't fight anymore. He didn't even make a conscious decision about what to do. The bottom of the bat had just touched his exposed flesh when a golden ray of light burst from his chest.

The golden blast struck Darby's would-be-attacker with explosive force. He was thrown upward and backward across the entire length of the barn, striking a distant wall and falling to the ground in the evil flag that became his death shroud. Jacob stumbled backwards, but had only gone a few feet before a shimmering gold bubble encapsulated Darby lifting him from the ground, restoring his clothes to their proper place and spinning him to face the horrified Nazi leader.

"What the fuck are you!!" Jacob screamed in simultaneous fear and anger at being undone by some pussy-homo.

"He's the Avatarn you bastard!!" Rachel screamed in a shrill burst of bitter rage, "You fucked with one of God's chosen this time, you piece of shit!" The leather clad Nazi had removed his hand from Rachel's battered vagina. He stood but was too surprised by the impossible turn of events to run.

Darby didn't even see the pitchfork that was hurled from behind him. It stopped about three feet from his back when it was caught up in the gold energy field. It spun in the air and was launched back at the man who had thrown it. It pierced his throat and brought his lifetime of misdirected self-hatred to an end.

All the remaining skinheads fled the building. The Avatarn and friends followed with newfound strength. Their faith restored.

Jacob and Wendy jumped into one of the pickups, unable to think of anything but survival. No less than ten of the Aryan soldiers (social outcasts – forgotten by their families and hope) climbed into the back and produced guns and knives from hidden places. Darby knocked aside bullets and blades with a casual wave of his hand and the golden shimmer it created before him. It was Josh who first saw the four small children playing with Tonka dumptrucks and bulldozers in the dirt driveway. Jacob still hadn't seen them, and his truck was headed straight for them. Wendy screamed, but it was too late for Jake to react. A thick golden rope of energy burst from Darby's hands, which were clenched together and aimed at the speeding truck. The gold light encompassed the pickup full of lost souls flinging it into the air. It landed upside down fifty yards beyond the kids. A number of the bikers were crushed, the rest crawling from the wreck, a few to embrace the children in shocked relief.

None of the Nazis attempted to interfere as Darby took Paolo's hand and led his friends to the nearest truck. It was the most run down of the lot, but the pilgrims piled in, desperate to be away from this unholy place. "Damn it! No keys!" Darby cursed the crappy old vehicle.

"It's okay," Paolo said soothingly as he gently placed Darby's hand on the ignition. The truck's engine roared to life. Yoshi and Josh, who were standing in back, held tight to the roll bar as the truck jostled over the bumpy yard and sped back towards the highway.

Miraculously, the tow truck was waiting when they reached their abandoned van. The driver said he hadn't gotten any other calls and had chosen to wait awhile in case they returned. "What happened to you guys?" He was disturbed by their battered appearances as they crammed into his thankfully large truck cab, "Shall I call for an ambulance?" He was genuinely worried.

"We'll be okay now," Rachel assured him as they started down the now deserted highway, pulling the van behind them.

"You should probably call some ambulances to this house off the next road." Darby felt guilty about the much-deserved devastation they had left behind.

The driver, who had introduced himself as Thomas Atwood, slowly reached over and turned off his radio, silencing some distant dispatcher, and offered one thought, "The sower shall keep the work of his hands." The group dozed and miles passed before the kind and handsome driver delivered them to a small hotel. Too much time lapsed with Yoshi's internal bleeding going unchecked. "Wake up, Honey, we're here," Josh kissed his nose and patted him on the ass. Yoshi didn't wake up.

Chapter 8

Adolphus knocked on the ornate silver door, but did not wait for an answer, before entering Beacon's bedroom. His daughter was delighted to see him as always. She turned her head only briefly to flash him a welcoming smile, as the peasant girl, Joppa, was styling her hair.

"I'll be leaving soon for planet Earth." He seated himself on the edge of her bed not far from the dressing table where she sat.

"Please don't go, Father," though Beacon was pleading she couldn't turn away from her mirror. Joppa was weaving delicate gems from the caves of planet Vishnu into her elaborate hair-do, "I've heard gossip throughout the palace. I know about the Avatarn of Earth. You mustn't go knowingly to your doom." She was crying.

"Do not fear, little one," Adolphus patted her back to assure her. "It is the Avatarn whom will meet their doom. I will return triumphant as always."

"What if you're wrong this time, Father? The prophecy of the Avatarn is so ancient that its origins are no longer known."

"No more ancient than I, Daughter. I will meet their insolence as I have all resistance for millennia...Regardless of wives-tales and superstition." The demon king gave Joppa a scolding glare knowing that his pet was fond of entertaining the princess with folktales.

"But, Father…Surely we have no need of more slaves." Beacon felt some guilt at seeing innocent peoples enslaved, but it was the way of the universe. Who was she to challenge the natural order of things?

"The Empire can not have too many slaves, Daughter…Besides…I have had my eye on Earth for a long time. In their arrogance, they actually believe they are alone in the universe… Fools…And as for the Avatarn…They must be put down before rebels from other planets and realms start getting ideas…The *idea of the Avatarn* looms larger than any real threat from them. I shall put an end to their message before they even know what it is." Joppa saw that Adolphus was uneasy despite his confident rhetoric.

Beacon was just opening her mouth to object again, when Lucien entered the room without knocking. He stopped short upon seeing Beacon in her mostly transparent dressing gown of lavender. Her full alabaster breasts were a pornographic dream.

"How dare you enter my daughter's chambers before she gives you permission!" Adolphus was furious. He stood and raised his hand to strike a blow to his subordinate's face, only to be stopped by his daughter.

"Wait!...It's okay, Father. No harm is done."

"Very well…See that it doesn't happen again." The king was too anxious to hear the report to pursue the matter further. Lucien bowed low before speaking.

"Your Majesty…Status report on the Avatarn. They remain separated, Sire. The witch and the healer are together in hiding. The fag and his friends continue their journey, though I suspect a recent loss will be slowing them down."

Adolphus wasn't aware of Lucien's lustful glances at the princess, but Joppa and Beacon were. Beacon hated him, but wasn't quite able to deny a sexual attraction to him. The silver toga he wore revealed most of his torso which was covered with hair and muscles. She also noticed the pronounced bulge below his belt.

He was a vile creature, but she couldn't control her response to his form.

"See that they are not united before my arrival. Return to Earth and prepare for our revelation." He dismissed him with a wave of his hand. Lucien bowed again silently and stole one more peek at the nearly naked princess before taking his leave.

Adolphus reclined in the captain's chair on the bridge of the *Caiphas*. The flagship of the armada was speeding towards Earth. The scaled-down "night" shift busied themselves at their stations, no one wanting to be thought a slacker by their sinister leader. He had been too excited to sleep. He had been waiting for this confrontation for a long time. The holy triad couldn't possibly stand against his army. His ruminations were cut short as four security guards restraining a struggling crewman burst from the lift. Adolphus jumped to his feet delighted at any distraction. "What is this?" he demanded.

"This crewman was caught trying to sabotage the star-drive, Sire." The ranking security officer explained.

"Is that true, Gibril?" Adolphus recognized the crewman. He had served on board the *Caiphas* for centuries.

"It is." Gibril had ceased his struggle. He would not be a coward before his former master.

"Why? We approach our finest hour. For what possible reason would you do this?" Adolphus was genuinely baffled.

"I have returned to the service of The Father," Gibril, who appeared human except for his gray skin, announced defiantly, "I am returned to the side of good. I realized the error of my ways, and He has forgiven me." The treasonous crewman was starting to glow. Adolphus knew what was happening, but helpless to stop it, he observed in disgust.

The white light radiating from Gibril was almost blinding, but Adolphus refused to close his eyes. The former crewman's facial features and entire body began to morph. He grew taller and more muscular; though he was still recognizable as Gibril, his face became more handsome. His black hair grew long, and his gray skin became snow-white. Great white wings unfolded from his back, and a powder blue halo illuminated his head. His uniform had faded away, leaving him clothed only in a blue sash that hung around his hips. He was beautiful beyond measure, and Adolphus' blood boiled with lust and rage at seeing him again in his natural state.

"Fool...You leave us just as we are about to take the hammer from The Father's hand. After all this time, you'll not share in our victory," Adolphus pitied his former subject.

"There is no victory without The Father," the mighty angel Gibril flexed his wings, "None of the fallen shall stand against the Avatarn...Come home, Adolphus. He will take back even you." He was hovering above the floor. The guards didn't dare touch him now.

Adolphus was quiet and still for several seconds. "Do you really think He would have me back, even now?" His eyes filled with tears, "I'm afraid He would reject me." As Gibril assured him that The Father's mercy was never-ending, Adolphus stepped forward with tears streaming his face and hesitantly took Gibril's hand. The angel floated back to the floor and began to wrap his great wings around the humbled demon king. He was completely shocked when Adolphus plunged the silver dagger into his chest. He was finished. He collapsed into his former master's arms. Adolphus chuckled as Gibril's light and life faded away. "How could you have fallen for that?" Adolphus was amazed, "You know what I am. Did you really think you could just talk me into going back?"

"I guess I just wanted to believe it...for you."

"Don't feel sorry for me. You're the one that's been undone." Adolphus was thinking of the fact that Gibril was not mortal. He had no soul to return to The Father. His existence was limited to his current form. He was ended.

"They will stop you." Gibril closed his eyes and went limp before the demon could argue the point. Adolphus furiously threw the lifeless body to the floor and watched as it faded out of existence.

He dismissed the guards with a growl, and returned to the main view port at the front of the bridge. His mind drifted back over the ages to a time when he had pretended to still be sleeping (the best way to become privy to secrets) as he listened to the whispers of the two newly fallen female angels he had bedded the night before. Each of them lay stretched across his back as they gossiped about The Father's latest project. It seemed he had just dispatched humans to settle a new planet…A little out-of-the-way place called Earth.

Chapter 9

The building Roman and Blair had escaped to was nearly a city in itself. A massive structure filled mostly with offices, but including stores and restaurants of several kinds. Roman pointed out that they had to procure some clothes for her right away and suggested she pick any store that suited her taste. Blair quickly spotted an Express, and dashed in. A few shoppers in ladies business suits cast disapproving glances upon seeing Blair's hospital gown, but turned away quickly, not wanting to get involved.

Roman assured her that cost was no matter, so, after hesitating briefly, she grabbed some knee-high black riding boots, a long black A-line skirt, and a black silk shirt. She emerged from the dressing room and did a catwalk spin that took Roman's breath away. She knew she looked good, but she didn't know that he had never seen anyone more beautiful. Except Janie.

Their next stop was at a men's store. He decided they appeared too mismatched with him still in his Gap gear, so he purchased some black boots, tight black pants, and a black silk shirt for himself. They would be a vision. The kind of couple that everyone notices but few have the nerve to look in the eyes.

A sweet older saleswoman approached Blair while Roman

changed into his new ensemble. "Can I help you find anything, Baby?"

"No, thank you," Blair smiled, "I'm just waiting on my friend." She gestured towards the fitting rooms.

"You must be looking forward to seeing yer hometown? KC isn't it, Sugar?" The kindly black woman had taken it upon herself to hand Blair a selection of men's watches for her consideration.

"It is...But how did you know that?" Blair was a little unnerved and took note of the woman's nametag. It said *Luna.*

"Oh don't be startled, Honey...We all have our gifts. I can usually tell where a body comes from, that's all. It's a nice place, Kansas City.

"I guess it's okay," Blair offered, "We aren't headed there, though."

"Oh ya really should go. So lovely this time of year. Besides, Darby's group will be there soon. You wouldn't want to miss them."

Blair froze. She knew that name. Roman had told her as much as he knew about the other Avatarn. Before she could question the strange salesclerk further, Roman sprang from the dressing room to model his new attire. Blair turned to face him for a moment. Only seconds passed before she turned back to demand an explanation from the old woman, but Luna was gone. Blair scanned the store, but knew she would find no sign of her. She quickly relayed the story to Roman as he made his purchases, and after considering the possibility that it could be a trick, they agreed that they didn't know where else to begin. "KC it is," Roman said as he slid his arm protectively around her waist and they left the building.

Roman hailed a cab and the handsome couple disappeared into the busy city. They decided it would be too risky to stay too near the airport. When they had finally gone far enough to begin to feel safe, Blair pointed out a large hotel that appeared to be fairly posh though the name was not a part of any chain that she recognized. They dared not sign in as Roman Perez and Blair Atwood, so they registered as Mr. and Mrs. John Smith. The fact that the Smith's were paying with Mr. Perez's credit card didn't even cause the desk clerk to bat an eye. Roman knew he was taking a chance in using the card, but hoped they would be safe long enough to get a few hours of sleep and get out of town before dark. He didn't convey his concerns to Blair. She was still too fragile.

Roman began to undress almost as soon as they reached the room. "What are you doing?" Blair laughed casually.

"I'm getting undressed to sleep…I sleep nude." He was just unbuttoning his pants. The look on Blair's face was all it took for him to add, "But I'll just keep my undies on tonight, if that's okay?"

"It's okay," Blair undressed down to her new black bra and panties and slid into bed beside him. "Gee…This isn't awkward or anything," she added.

"I know." He said turning to take her hand. It somehow seemed a very intimate gesture in the situation of the moment. "You have nothing to worry about from me."

"I know," she replied. "You are, after all, my hero." She quickly kissed him on the cheek, turned over to set the alarm for three hours, and tried to go to sleep. He turned his back to hers and fell quickly into a deep sleep. She could think of nothing but the heat and firmness of his back against hers. Overwhelming guilt weighed on her exhausted mind.

Her whole world had been turned upside down, and all she could think of was the way this man felt against her. She was falling in love with him, and she hated herself for it. How could she, when her beloved husband was barely cold in the grave? She wondered what kind of person she must be that she could betray the love they had shared in such a way. How could she be thinking lustful thoughts about a man she barely knew when her Thomas was dead? She decided she was just misinterpreting her need for Roman. She was alone except for him, and they shared a destiny. She would keep her emotions in check and not allow this crush based on hero-worship to get out of hand. She would hold herself together long enough to complete their mission. She had come to believe that it really was God's will, and she would do it to honor her lost family. She wouldn't fail them again. "Goodnight," she whispered into the darkness a she had for so many years. She smiled a little and slipped into unconsciousness as she heard Thomas say the same.

They awoke feeling surprisingly refreshed by their brief siesta. They dressed quickly and shared a small meal in the dining room. Blair hadn't eaten much in the hospital and was famished. Roman refrained from teasing her, and encouraged her to have as much as she wanted. The concierge had an upscale rental car waiting when they finished. Atlanta was well behind them when the sun set.

They talked endlessly as they headed towards Kansas City and soon felt like old friends. In spite of everything, they were laughing and enjoying the drive when they entered the poor and mostly forgotten neighborhood of Huntsville, Alabama. They really hadn't given their surroundings any special consideration when they stopped at a red light.

Roman's door was open, and the gun pressed against his face before they even realized they weren't alone. Blair didn't even know her door had been opened. She just felt the impact of her head being slammed against the dash. She was out cold. The carjackers ripped them from the car and tossed them into the street. There were so many of them. Roman realized they were dealing with an actual gang when he saw that more than a few of the men surrounding them were wearing "Huntsville Homeboys" jackets. He couldn't see Blair, but he knew he had to get to her. Protect her. At first, no one approached as he scrambled to his feet, but then they fell on him like an avalanche. Punches like rain crashed between racial epithets like "Whitebread" and "Fucking Cracker." He had the misfortune of slipping on his own blood and falling back to the cracked pavement. It was then that the kicking began. He was no longer offering any resistance.

He struggled to see through blurry eyes what he knew had to be Blair's motionless body. He was looking under the car. She was lying on the other side. Her new skirt had been pushed up in a wad, and one gang member after another attempted to penetrate her unmoving body, only to find his dick falling limp the moment he touched her. God or her own magic was protecting her. It wouldn't be long though before they would settle for violating her in some other way.

Roman began to sense that something had changed. The street punks were backing away from him, and they looked afraid. He had started healing. Open lesions on his face had begun to close. His swollen eye was returning to normal. Roman jumped up and ran around the car to help Blair who had awakened and started to scream. The wind had begun to swirl around her, bringing litter and trash of every kind from the gutter. Paper sacks, coffee cups, and cans flew in the faces of her attackers, confusing them enough to give her a chance to stand and fling herself into Roman's arms.

The Homeboys were ready for a second round, when a woman's voice echoed all around them. "Enough!!" yelled a ghetto-fabulous girl standing on the hood of the rental car. "Ramses wants to see them!!" No one was about to question Ramses' wishes. Two huge beefy men wearing only over-sized jean shorts stepped forward to grab both Avatarn by the arms. The other gang members fell in line behind them as they were led around the block to an alley. The entrance to the alley was dark, but as the mob pushed them forward they saw that the end was well lit. A plush leather chair sat on top of some carefully stacked crates to create a raised throne effect.

A beautiful black man with long braided hair was ascending to his place on the *throne* as they approached. "It has come to my attention that you are not the kind of pigmently-challenged trash that we get through here on occasion," Ramses bellowed as they were pushed to their knees at his feet. The leader flashed them a brief smile as his eyes changed for an instant to the slitted pupils of snake eyes. Roman and Blair exchanged a knowing glance, both recognizing the demon for what he was.

It was then that the rapid gunfire of a semi-automatic weapon rang out from behind them. All heads turned, and the entire group ran towards the street including Ramses. Blair and Roman followed. There was nowhere else for them to go.

They reached the street in time to find Roman's eternal nightmare recreated with an inner-city twist. A little girl of about five with at least as many pigtails lay bleeding on the sidewalk where she had been riding her Bigwheel. It had been a drive-by. A rival gang member had been aiming for one of the Homeboys, but several bullets had ricocheted and hit Chantel instead. One of the gangsters had picked her up and was rocking her in his arms. He was sobbing. His baby sister was dying, and he was realizing too late that he was part of the reason that no ambulance would even consider coming into that area. He was part of the reason that her short innocent life was over.

Ramses was starting to give some of the more angry men instructions on how to exact revenge on the marauders that had dared to cut down one of their own. Chantel's brother, Dre, was too lost in anguish to notice that the rich white couple was walking towards them. He didn't even sense their approach until Roman's hand closed around the girl's small foot, which had somehow been freed of its gelly shoe. Dre started to object, but before he had uttered a word, white light shot up her leg and enveloped her. He and Roman were forced to close their eyes as the intensity became too great. He opened them quickly when his sister began to stir. Her wounds had all been undone. She was perfect again, showing concern only for her brother as she wiped his tears away. Dre raised his eyes to the white man who was silently crying himself. Dre was wide-eyed with amazement. It had never occurred to him that any white man might be of any use to him, especially one they had just jacked. But clearly this was no ordinary man. He was some kind of angel or something.

"Who are you?" The grateful big brother asked.

"I guess I'm a friend." Roman smiled.

"Believe it." Dre assured him. Roman had won a new follower for life.

"Seize them!!!" Ramses roared from a nearby stoop. He had figured out who the whiteys really were and was not about to miss out on his opportunity to be the one responsible for their destruction. The men of the hood hesitated, their loyalties torn. This man had somehow saved one of their own. He wasn't the enemy anymore. Suddenly two factions became visible within the gang. The faces of several guys changed to ghoulish masks as their demonic natures rose to the surface. Their human counterparts stepped in to combat them and protect their new allies, but the demons were cutting them down with minimal effort.

Blair finally found the courage to speak:

"Scurry, scurry, creatures small
Seek evil hearts and make them fall."

She held her arms out to her sides, palms up, waist level. Rats came running from every direction. Hundreds. Then thousands. They attacked only the demons. Running up their legs and swarming over them, literally consuming the evil ones. The members of Legion were reduced to screaming masses, and then were gone. The human gang members stood by in horror, not daring to move.

Ramses escaped by dematerializing. He popped up behind Blair grabbing her by her long red locks and putting a knife to her throat before she could react. Roman ran towards them, but was too late to intervene. Blair raised one hand in a swirling motion. The wind obeyed, lifting her and Ramses one hundred feet into the sky. Ramses clung to her for his life, but foolishly kept the knife to her throat. "Take us down, Bitch!!" He was furious.

"You want down?" Blair asked in her most innocent voice.

"Yes!!!" He growled into her ear.

"Your wish..." She smiled and grabbed his balls and twisted as hard as she could. In shock, he let go and began to panic, free-falling towards the distant Earth. His skeleton was crushed on impact. Ramses was dead.

Roman anxiously awaited her on the ground, but she lingered far above. Roman called out to her, but there was no sign that she heard him.

Blair stood in the sky, supported solely by the wind that was her dutiful servant. She was laughing and crying. She was talking to her husband, Thomas, who had appeared before her.

"How ya holdin' up, Babe?" Thomas took her hands in his.

"I'm holdin'." She smiled and let out a little sob. "I need you, Tommy…I'm so sorry this happened to you…What am I going to do without you?" One tear after another slid down her face, but she couldn't help smiling when he was smiling at her.

"Nothing for you to be sorry about, B…You weren't prepared to battle demons. Even the hysterical reaction of the congregation was beyond your control." She started to interrupt, but he shushed her, placing a finger to her lips. "You will have plenty to do without me…You've got a big mission, Sweetheart. One of the Chosen Ones. It doesn't get any bigger than that…You'll be fine… Your sisters and I will help you whenever we can…And…You've got Roman…It's okay, Honey. You can love Roman. You have to live life. Don't hold yourself to a code of ethics and values that applied to your life before. To normal life. Your life isn't normal anymore. You are in a situation that is totally unique. There is no one else still in the world that can be to you what Roman can be. Because you think you need it, I give you my blessing. Be happy. Don't miss out on a chance for love because you think you owe me a period of mourning.

"No one could ever replace you, Thomas." She was struggling to breathe as he wrapped his arms around her and gently kissed her lips.

"I know he's not a replacement, Wife…He's a new chance. He's hope." She closed her eyes as he kissed her forehead. When she opened them, he was gone. She heard Roman then. He was calling out her name. So afraid for her. She began her descent, spinning slowly as she floated to the ground. She landed in Roman's arms and immediately threw her arms around his neck and pulled him down into her kiss. Her mouth slowly opened and they shared their first real kiss. Roman had never felt this kind of passion for someone. Both knew that they were in love. Neither said it.

Police sirens could be heard in the distance. They were finally responding to the calls made long ago. Dre somehow knew that it was important that his new friends not be detained. "Here...Take my car." He offered Roman his keys. The Avatarn hadn't even realized that their rental car had been destroyed when the gangsters battled their demonic former friends.

"That's really thoughtful, but we can't," Blair declined looking over his shoulder at the suped-up Mustang he was offering; "We can't take your transportation." Dre led them to his car insisting that there was no other way and that he knew they mustn't be delayed any further. It was the custom paint job that changed their minds. Across the door, in big gold letters were the words, *The Hammer* underlined by the image of a blazing mallet. Blair and Roman weren't about to argue with that kind of omen. They accepted the generous gift assuring Dre that God would reward his good deed.

"I'm already taken care of," Dre smiled down at his adored sister.

The Hammer sped away into the night as the reluctant police stormed into the neighborhood arresting everyone still on the street. Including Dre.

Chapter 10

Josh's anguished sob commanded the attention of the others who had been exiting the tow truck through the driver's side from the moment they arrived at the small hotel in the college-town of Columbia. He turned his tear streaked face to them, unable to speak.

"Yoshi!" Rachel screamed. Darby ran around the front of the truck and yanked open the passenger door. Yoshi's lifeless body tumbled into his arms. Josh was struggling to catch his breath.

"Help him," Josh muttered to Darby, almost inaudibly.

"I can't," Darby looked into Josh's panicked eyes, "It's too late…He's gone." The tears that burned Darby's face splattered on Yoshi's cold one.

"It can't be too late…Tom can call an ambulance, and we'll just…" Paolo stopped in mid-sentence as he looked around for their recent rescuer, but he was nowhere to be found.

Some staff members of the Crimson Shawl Hotel had wondered into the parking lot to see what all the commotion was about. The assistant manger was approaching with instructions that the towed van would have to be left at the Amoco Station across the street, when she stopped in her tracks. Darby's gang was standing dazedly around the limp body that he had laid gently on the asphalt ground. Josh kept turning his back to them to throw up.

Suddenly, an ambulance came screeching into the small parking lot. Two beautiful young uniformed women jumped out and ran to Yoshi's side. Within seconds, they had strapped him to a gurney and rushed back to the ambulance. Josh and the others ran at their heels, shouting confused questions, only to have doors slammed in their faces.

Near the street, the air shimmered. The space around the front of the emergency vehicle began to waver. Images distorted and an explosion of red light revealed an apparent rip in space-time. Only blackness loomed inside the portal. The ambulance tires squealed as it sped into the darkness of the dimensional doorway. The portal closed as quickly as it had opened. With a shimmer they were gone. And Yoshi's body with them. Only the smell of sulfur remained.

Josh crumpled to the ground. He sat silently on the dirty asphalt, staring where the portal had been. He was in shock. So were the others. None of them noticed the old black woman behind them who comforted each and every witness to the supernatural event with a motherly touch on the arm. As she moved through the small crowd, they forgot every memory of what they had just seen. Suddenly unsure of their surroundings, they made their way back to their duty stations inside the hotel. Darby was the first to come to his senses enough to take control of the situation. He sat down on the ground and took the devastated Josh into his arms after telling Paolo to tow the van over to the repair/gas station. He assigned Rachel the chore of securing them a room and she quickly returned, key in hand. After Paolo returned, they led the still numb Josh to the privacy of their third floor room. It was only after a night of endless crying and grief that the group reached a unanimous conclusion. Yoshi would want them to go on. Josh knew there was nothing else he could do for Yoshi. He announced that he would be continuing with them to Kansas City. They finally settled into a fitful sleep after the sun rose.

Darby was the first to awake. More tired than before he had

slept, he looked around at his sleeping crew. Poor Josh. He was out cold. Exhaustion had finally gotten the best of him. In the past few days, Darby had felt God's presence more strongly than ever in his life. *How could you let this happen?* He sent the silent prayer without expecting an answer. Yoshi had been Josh's world. How was a person supposed to pick up and carry on without the person they loved most? Darby felt completely responsible. If they hadn't all come with him. "I'm so sorry, Yoshi..." He whispered into the stillness. Darby was amazed at Josh's determination to see their mission through. He could be flaky sometimes. Questionable mental health, but always pulling it together when it counted. He thought in the same situation, he would be locked in the fetal position, thinking only of himself. The fact that Josh was still putting the needs of his friends before his broken heart was a tribute to his character. It's what Yoshi would have wanted. Josh never let Yoshi down.

It was late afternoon when Rachel, Paolo, and Josh woke to a slamming door. It was Darby returning from the gas station with breakfast burritos for all. The van repairs had been completed, and the gang of melancholy travelers was on the road within minutes.

Miles sped passed without a spoken word. Darby and friends drove into downtown Kansas City still lost in thoughts of Yoshi and their own mortality.

Josh paid for their new hotel room with cash he had the foresight to obtain from a Quick-Trip ATM in Columbia. The 10th floor room afforded them an impressive view of the metallic sculptures towering above the Bartle Hall convention center. Darby was surprised to find a pleasant city with some interesting sights where he expected a colorless Midwestern cowtown.

After devouring a small feast in the hotel restaurant, the group's mood was elevated to the highest level possible under the circumstances. They decided to take a stroll in a small park-like area called the Barney-Allis Plaza. It was an unseasonably warm, clear night, and even in the city, stars twinkled overhead. The crescent moon bathed the concrete world around them in the ghostly light reserved for lovers and secret things. They had just begun to laugh guiltily at some small joke Rachel had made, when they noticed a handsome street-preacher standing on a stone bench in a corner of the courtyard. He was surrounded by homeless people, punk-style teenage vagabonds, and a spattering of hotel guests from out-of-town. Darby's gang cautiously approached. The surprisingly muscular, raven-haired preacher, calling himself Brother Lucien, charismatically relayed his twisted version of the truth.

"It will begin this very night, on All Hallows Eve. When nature bows to the forces of magic. A great heavenly army will come to battle the three false angels," Lucien shouted boldly as he paced back and forth on the bench, gently touching the homeless faces. Faces no one had touched in years. Paolo saw their rapt faces and knew that these people would do anything for the enchanting stranger. The power of touch and the sense of connection it creates should not be underestimated when dealing with outcasts long forgotten by society. 'You can be a part of that army," the preacher continued, "Stand with us against these false prophets…You never have to be alone again."

Rachel noticed that some of the lost souls were wearing costumes. Of course, she thought to herself, All Hallows Eve means Halloween. But why would this historic meeting of God's handpicked warriors take place on Halloween, a pagan "holiday"?

"Because," Darby startled her by answering her silent question aloud, "It is the day when mankind is most aware of their supernatural surroundings. When the veil is lifted, and spirits roam the Earth…It's when people come closest to remembering that the world is full of magic. They just don't remember that it's not an abomination to God…It's part of God."

The small crowd began to applaud what Brother Lucien had just said, until his smiling face turned into a bitter frown when he noticed Darby at the back of the gathering.

"Join us, friends," Lucien motioned for the Avatarn and his

cohorts to step forward. He smiled and waited for their reaction. His knowing gaze never leaving Darby's eyes.

"That's okay; we're just listening," Darby declined shyly, though he was mesmerized by the strange man's extraordinary good looks.

"But it's you that I speak of, Sir," Lucien flashed a dazzling smile.

"I'm afraid you've mistaken me for someone else." Darby and his group grew evermore uncomfortable as each of the street preacher's enrapt listeners turned to focus their attention on the ones that had distracted their charming speaker.

"Seekers of truth…This handsome young fellow, with the surfer-boy looks is one of the very false prophets of which I have warned you." The enchanted audience pulled away from Darby, moving closer to Lucien, but keeping their eyes on the blond newcomer and his friends.

"What the hell are you talking about?" Rachel wasn't in the mood for some slacker's schizo bullshit. Even if he had a pretty face.

"Dear Lamb," Lucien responded in his most condescending tone, "your anger is misdirected. It is the Avatarn that has led you to the slaughter."

Josh and Paolo's sudden expressions of fear were followed by looks of confusion on the faces of most of the small crowd.

Four of the tourists' eyes turned red and every blood vessel in their bodies appeared to rise to the surface of their skin. As they growled and ripped off their clothes revealing their seemingly marbled bodies, most of the gathering dispersed with screams of horror as fast as they could run. The homeless teenagers stayed. They had seen worse.

"Behind me!" Darby yelled out to his friends. They all squeezed in against him in the nick of time. A burst of golden energy from Darby's head encased the group in a protective bubble only seconds before the vascular demons were upon them. They bounced like toads off the shimmering force field. Lucien stood calmly watching, one hand resting on the head of a child prostitute, the other on the head of a buff hustler. Neither the boy, nor the girl, was afraid. Both fourteen-year-olds were devoutly loyal to their new savior/lover.

The Legion soldiers grew more bloody and bruised with each attempt to penetrate the energy shield. Desperate to escape, Darby threw up his arms causing the energy shield to explode outward throwing their demon attackers fifty feet in every direction. The reluctant holy warriors took advantage of the monsters' momentary weakness.

Rachel and Paolo joined forces to topple a concrete bench onto one demon's throat. The creature melted into a puddle of black liquid that seeped into the ground. They looked up just in time to see Josh tackle a demon about to stand. Josh sat on his back and grabbed a large stone, bringing it down on the alien's head with all of his might. The instant the monster's skull was crushed, it turned to black liquid and disappeared into the hard soil.

The two remaining creatures had regained their bearing and both ran toward Darby. He responded instinctively. A wave of his hand created a golden energy ball that impacted the closer demon, propelling him backwards through the air. The vein-covered nude monster landed on a tree limb, impaling him through the chest. He liquefied and vanished. The last creature flew into Darby, knocking him into the browning grass. Each punched and kicked the other until Darby's hands clenched the alien's throat. He was in survival mode and didn't stop until the demon had taken his last breath. Darby wiped his hands in the grass to remove the black ooze and climbed to his feet. The Avatarn and his friends walked shakily back towards Lucien's perch atop the park bench. He hadn't moved since the battle began, but his smile had faded away.

"This is only the beginning, Avatarn," Lucien's voice was hushed and conspiratorial, "The Legion armada will soon reach Earth, and the holy triad is not yet united. You'll be defeated…I'm gonna make you my bitch, Darby," he finished with a wink.

"We'll see." Darby raised his chin and took a step forward.

With a chuckle, Lucien turned the heads on which each hand

still rested, snapping his disciples' necks with a turn of his wrists. In the same instant, Lucien was gone, vanished before the lifeless kids crumpled to the ground. The holy pilgrims stood frozen in shock and horror until movement in a nearby hedge demanded their attention.

"It's over," whispered a young black drag queen as she crawled from her hiding place.

"Are you all right?" Rachel ran to help her up.

"Honeydew Johnson's dealt with worse tricks than the likes of them clowns, Sugar. But let's get the fuck out of here just the same…Miss Honey needs a drink."

"I'll second that emotion," Josh put his arm around the cross-dressing male prostitute.

"I think it's unanimous," Darby chimed in.

"Where should we go?" Paolo hoped a few drinks would calm his shattered nerves.

"Ya'll just stick with Honey, Baby. Get it…Stick-with-Honey… I'll take ya someplace where the freaks just wanna love ya, not hurt ya," Honey took Rachel's hand and led the group down a long set of concrete steps back to the street. They walked to the front of their hotel and piled into a cab. After their latest encounter with evil, Darby was happy to let their new friend take charge for a while.

The Mustang had been a Godsend. Blair and Roman made great time and the conversation flowed from one subject to another. They chose mostly to speak of their lives before they had met. When they were still themselves. Before destiny called them to duty. Before they knew it, they were in KC checking into a nice downtown hotel. Blair was comforted when the view from their room featured the shiny golden dome of a little cathedral. A beautiful sign of hope on this perilous mission. As she gazed curiously at the four metallic sculptures towering above a large building, she said a silent prayer. Don't take this one from me too, Lord. I never thought I could love anyone but Thomas. I can't lose this second chance.

The ringing of the cell phone Roman had gotten her interrupted her thoughts. He was calling from his. "I filled up the tank, and I'm on my way back to the hotel. I was thinking. We're gonna have to do another shopping spree. Pick up some more clothes. I'll swing by and pick you up. See what we can find," Roman sounded cheerful.

"Great," Blair didn't want to ruin his mood, but she knew something huge was approaching and shopping just didn't have the same allure it had before; "I'll be ready."

They hung up and she smiled to herself, until she heard the giggling behind her. She spun around, landing in a battle stance. Prepared to fight for her life. Somehow, Molly and Sarah were standing before her. Her late sisters were only a few feet away. Like the silvery translucent gowns they wore, Molly's long black hair and Sarah's golden tresses floated around them, gently waving as if suspended in invisible water.

"Are you really here?" Blair darted forward to embrace her smiling sisters.

"Wait!" The girls cried out in unison, "You can't ...You mustn't touch us...We're not supposed to be here. If we allow you to touch us, we might have to come back," Molly explained.

"To be reincarnated," Sarah added.

Blair stopped only inches away. Happy tears streamed down her face. She had never dared dream that she would speak to them again as long as she lived. "But what about Thomas?" A sudden look of fear swept Blair's face. "He hugged and kissed me when he appeared to me. Will he be punished?"

"No, No...It's fine," Molly reassured her, "Tom was sent to you. He was supposed to appear to you. That's a whole different story."

"Well, happy as I am to see you, I don't want you guys to get in trouble," Blair was torn between the relief of seeing them and concern for their fate.

"Don't worry about us," Sarah appeared so peaceful and serene as her hair danced around her, "We risked coming here because we want to head you in the right direction."

"The Legion starships will be here soon," Molly had grown serious, "The time has come for the Avatarn to be united. Darby and his friends are here in town. You and Roman must rendezvous with them at 3 A.M. at the Liberty Memorial. It is a symbol of freedom for all mankind and the time, symbolic of the Trinity."

"Though we can't really interfere," Sarah offered, "We'll be watching over you, and help if we can…Go to your destiny, Sis… His Plan awaits you."

"We love you, Blair," Molly kissed her fingertips and extended them in her redheaded sister's direction. Each sister did the same in turn, adding the same sentiment. That said, Blair watched in amazement as the spirits of her sisters appeared to swim through the air, passing through the ceiling, and disappearing with a flash of splendid white light.

Blair was still smiling through tears when Roman came through the door, a rose in his teeth and a Lone Ranger mask over his eyes, his small nod to Halloween; he was alarmed at first, but realized that her tears weren't indicative of another breakdown as soon as she started to explain. His dark features were flooded with relief at the news of a boost in the right direction.

The concierge sent them to the Country Club Plaza in search of new clothes. He neglected to mention that they would be driving past the Sprint Center Arena, a massive building resembling a sparkling flying saucer (crystal punch bowl or squashed disco ball). The giant hockey puck-shaped structure was spectacular, but for more than a few missed heartbeats the Avatam thought the aliens had already landed. After realizing their mistake, they laughed the rest of the way to the shopping district. They purchased flattering new wardrobes in dark colors appropriate to the season and their nocturnal mission. At Roman's suggestion, they shared a nice dinner at the Cheesecake Factory, then strolled along Brush Creek. Both were caught up in a whirlwind of romance, despite the impending danger. Hand in hand, for a few moments, they forgot the prophesied meeting only a few hours away.

The taxi driver slammed on the brakes, screeching to a halt at the front door of *Club Chakra*. He had had his fill of Honeydew. After everyone had piled out, he waited impatiently for Josh to pay him, then sped away in a cloud of smoke.

With Honey in the lead, the door man waved them passed the waiting line, looking Darby over and giving him a wink. The line of disgruntled, and mostly costumed, would-be-partiers knew better than to voice their displeasure.

Darby was taken with the bar's leather flavor. Not too hard-core, just enough to create a sexy atmosphere. The three boys were being cruised from all sides, but none of them could muster even a polite acknowledgment. They had been through too much. With Yoshi gone, and the nightmare their last trip to a club had become, even casual flirtation was out of the question. Honey led them upstairs to an enclosed "patio" bar. Some easy-listening 70s music created a more relaxed ambiance and drew a gentler crowd.

"Who ya got tonight, Sweetheart?" The attractive lesbian bartender asked their mocha-diva guide, offering her a quick peck on the lips. Honey introduced Darby and the gang to the pretty blonde bartender she called Jo. She wore a T-shirt and jeans and a man's short haircut. A little butcher than any of Darby's lesbian friends, but he took an instant liking to her. She just seemed so comfortable in her own skin. It was an enchanting quality.

Jo poured Jäger shots all around and asked everyone's poison of choice. When each cocktail had been generously prepared, she asked Darby to speak with her privately at a deserted end of the bar. He was slightly surprised, but already trusted this stranger impulsively. He had no reason to, but he was rapidly learning to depend on his instincts.

"My name is actually Joppa, Darby. I spoke to you once outside a club somewhat like this one," Jo paused, "Do you remember?"

"I remember..." Darby looked confused, "And somehow I

know you're telling the truth, but how?...You were only a child, and that was only days ago."

"I am many things…And I am always," Joppa said, handing him a frozen strawberry margarita.

"Why are you here?" Darby was afraid to know.

"To help you keep an appointment made before the stars were set in the sky," she casually replied as she wiped down the counter. Darby was dumbstruck and could only watch and wait in silence as she refilled a girl's beer and allowed the customer to tuck her tip seductively into the collar of her T-shirt.

"So," Joppa returned to him smiling, "Find the Liberty Memorial in midtown. It's a war monument. Huge. Phallic. You can't miss it…Roman and Blair will be there at 3 A.M. …Be there."

Darby was having a hard time processing this avalanche of information. He couldn't even access his usual sarcasm. It was then that they were joined by Honey, Rachel, Paolo, and Josh. Honey had decided it was time for them to dance.

"Do it," Joppa encouraged them; "It might be a long time 'til you dance again."

Roman and Blair were the first to arrive at the recently renovated World War I memorial. He was awestruck by the unexpected grandeur reaching into the Midwestern sky. A Romanesque monolith, topped with an eternal flame. Blair was still holding the hand that she had taken in the cab-ride over. Not that Roman minded. He hadn't felt this way about anyone since he and Brenda had gone their separate ways. The monument seemed plain in her presence.

With Thomas's blessing, Blair had begun to surrender her heart. She and Roman had already been through so much together. Aside from being classically tall, dark, and handsome, he looked at her as only her husband had before. She found the skyscraping tribute to the defense of liberty quite beautiful, but couldn't keep her eyes off Roman. He was the Prince Charming she had been looking for when she met Tom. She didn't regret being side-tracked by a life with Thomas for even an instant. She loved him more than the world, but some part of her knew another truth. She was destined to be with her new hero. He was the other half of her...Or maybe a third, she thought when she saw Darby walking up the long elliptical drive.

Darby's group had somehow convinced Honey to stay behind. It was still a few minutes before 3 A.M. when they arrived at the Liberty Memorial park grounds. Paolo was the first to spot Roman and Blair on the few steps that led to the base of the monument. They stood out somehow, even though several transients and hustlers were scattered around the park. Josh had just pointed out that a lot of gay men were cruising the park in their cars, looking for anonymous sex, when Darby's eyes locked with Roman's across the park grounds.

Blair knew instantly which one was Darby. He was a hotty for sure. She bet a lot of girls' hearts had been broken when they found out he was gay. She would have known even if Roman hadn't told her, but it wouldn't be obvious to most people. As he walked towards them, a series of images flashed before her eyes. First, he was in a shiny silver space-suit; then he was a furry savage, naked and barbaric; then he wore the dirty robes and bare feet of an ancient prophet of Jerusalem. Next, she saw a Viking. Then an English queen, a black slave in chains; and in the next instant, he was a small Vietnamese girl. Then Darby again, marching resolutely toward them, his blond hair floating on the breeze. Their souls had been together a long time. She understood that in the instant that he smiled. They were about to be *reunited* with someone they had never met in this life.

Darby was struck by how good-looking they both were. And how familiar. Strangers...he felt like he'd known all his life. He started to run towards them. Suddenly, he couldn't wait another second to be with them.

Roman wanted to run to him too, but strong hands grabbed his arms from behind. He couldn't turn to identify his captor, but the mystery was solved when a second later a seven-foot man;

unquestionably a member of Legion, locked his massive arms around Blair's chest and stomach. They were surrounded by at least a dozen demons that appeared in the guise of hustlers and the homeless. Darby froze. Standing still long enough for his friends to catch up.

Roman was enraged at the sight of the brutish demon pawing the woman he loved. The alien boldly fondled her breasts and rubbed against her ass as he held her prisoner. For the first time, Roman wished he had the power to do something other than heal.

Blair panicked at first, but took only moments to focus enough to compose a spell:

"Lightning, streak across the sky
To free our hands, let evil die."

The thunder began to rumble before she even finished the incantation. Darby and his friends stood in awe as lightning reached down through the night to strike the heads of the two demons holding Roman and Blair. The monsters started to explode, but then vanished leaving no visible trace. The other members of Legion still surrounded them only a few yards away, but were motionless, temporarily afraid to move. For a moment, Roman just stared at his new best friend. He was still amazed by her power. Darby ran forward, suddenly unafraid. He and Roman reached out simultaneously. Each placing a supportive hand on one of Blair's shoulders. It was this physical connection between the threesome that set into motion a power prophesied for millennia, created by God to protect his more naïve children from those that had lost their way.

The Avatarn were suddenly seized by an unseen force. It spun them around, back-to-back, lifting them about three inches off the ground. Though each one's knees and feet were forced together, their arms were extended directly out from their shoulders. Hands straight out and touching at the fingertips, each was suspended in the position of crucifixion. The Avatarn were not scared. Even when the stigmata began. Demons and friends alike moved in closer, though they were forced to squint their eyes, as dazzling blue halos, encircling the trio's heads, intensified to an almost blinding degree, lighting up the night. All present were mesmerized and horrified at the spectacle. Blood gushed from the threesome at a rate not realistically possible. From the palms of their hands, the middle of their feet, around the crowns of their heads, and open wounds in their sides, the blood poured, more than any of the humans had ever seen before.

It was then that they became aware of the slowly expanding sound that was coming from the again starry sky. There were no definable words, but all present knew the extraordinary song that was filling the night was a chorus from Heaven.

The blood of the Avatarn was pooling below them, collecting inside the invisible triangle formed by their feet. After a few moments, the blood shot up between them in a crimson geyser fifty feet above their heads. It fell like rain, baptizing everyone present in the cleansing flow. The angels' song grew to a fortissimo. The falling blood splattered the nearby demons, burning them like acid. They ran screaming into the darkness, trying in vain to stop the pain that would only end when they eventually killed themselves. Josh, Rachel, and Paolo were only refreshed by the holy blood that had rained down on them as well. In another circumstance, the friends would have been traumatized by the blood bath that had soaked them, but they knew whose blood this really was, and it washed away every fear and every pain. It restored their spirits. Full of wonder, they remained quiet as the Avatarn opened their mouths in unison. The voice that emanated from them was last heard in the dreams of the apostles, a language older than Earth, though the quivering mortals understood every word.

"Blessed be the triad for their great commission is begun.
A shield before mankind against the ancient foes of every world.
Woe to the soldiers of Legion...For I have taken
up my hammer, and it will surely fall."

Their mouths closed, and the volume of the Heavenly choir

rose to a magnificent roar, forcing the mortal witnesses to cover their ears before crumpling to the ground.

The police car's mounted floodlights had just pinpointed Darby's friends in the grass, when the miracle came to an abrupt end. The Avatarn were unceremoniously dropped in a heap. The night was eerily silent, and every drop of blood was gone. No sign remained, but there was some soreness where the wounds of Christ had been.

Two police officers quickly approached on foot, shouting orders to "Stay down!" They had been looking for the out-of-town lunatics involved in recent homicides (they had been seen leaving the hotel) half the night. These visitors had left some lifeless bodies in their wake, and the frequently bored officers were looking to make a collar.

There was no time to make a decision. Josh and Rachel glanced at each other and were up and running. She paused just long enough to turn back to the others and yell, "Get out of here!" Josh tackled the larger cop and Rachel jumped into the arms of the smaller one. Both wrestled desperately with the law as Paolo and the Avatarn hesitated, and then disappeared into the night. None of them wanted to leave their friends behind, but all knew it was their best chance of escape without hurting anyone. They didn't dare return to their hotels, but they didn't know where to hide. Torn between survival instinct and the nearly irresistible urge to rescue Josh and Rachel, they ran on, hoping to find a safe place to regroup, to figure out their next move. The moment they had all been fighting toward had come and gone. It had been brief but glorious. None still doubted their destiny; each was reaching the same numbing conclusion. Many of the people they loved would be lost along the way. The price of freedom would be paid with their broken hearts.

Chapter 11

Two young hustlers, one white, one Latino, were fleeing the park just ahead of the Avatarn. Without breaking his stride, Roman suggested they follow them, convinced they would know the best places to hide. To take shelter. None questioned the wisdom of not returning to their hotel rooms. The boys weren't afraid of them. Not after the holy vision they had just witnessed. They made no effort to evade the Avatarn, who were not far behind them, but ran on block after block. Roman and Blair were not dressed for running, but the foursome kept up. They were running for their lives.

Josh and Rachel were lying face down in the grass. Both were cuffed behind their backs. They were under arrest for assaulting police officers. The cops were clueless as to what had really gone on at the memorial, but Rachel and Josh weren't about to try to explain. Both were bruised and bleeding, as were the police officers. Neither regretted their actions. They had to protect the Avatarn at all costs. The cops would thank them if they understood that they had interfered for the well being of mankind. That secret knowledge was little solace as they were roughly shoved into the backseat of a patrol car.

"Don't worry. We'll be okay," Josh reassured Rachel in his most soothing tone, though he didn't entirely believe it when he heard the words 'faggot" and "nigger" mumbled in the front seat.

It was only a short ride to the downtown precinct. Josh didn't have anyone to call since Yoshi was gone; however, Rachel made good use of her single phone call. She called her aunt, a prominent attorney in Atlanta. Though it was not yet morning, she assured her desperate niece that she would be on the next plane to KC.

The runaway boys led the Avatarn to a deserted downtown building. The under-age hustlers lived there among a community of squatters. A warehouse that once sheltered a few misfits from the night now housed a small tribe.

Fires burned in barrels with makeshift chimneys rigged to exit through broken windows. Palettes of blankets and rugs were neatly organized in various corners in place of bedrooms, and Paolo pointed out the surprising cleanliness. Blair, however; was nearly overcome by the stench of too many unwashed humans in a confined space.

The others were not pleased by the breach in protocol when the boys let the Avatarn directly into the living area without first asking permission from the "council" elected by the group. They didn't let just anyone into *The Palace,* as the squatters referred to their humble abode. Once a storehouse for camping and outdoor supply stores, *The Palace* was an ideal haven for the homeless and forgotten.

Tyler and Mateo were busy trying to explain why they had led the strangers into the safe house, but the council leaders, some of whom were still teenagers themselves, weren't having any of their wild story. It was only after Roman started handing out twenty-dollar bills that the tribe of lost souls began to reconsider their position. They agreed to let the rich mental cases take refuge in

The Palace as long as they brought no trouble with them. The Avatarn were asked to swear an oath to keep secret the existence of *The Palace*.

They did so, and then sought a secluded corner in which to discuss the encounter they had just had and a method of rescue for Rachel and Josh. Darby pointed out that his friends might be safer kept away from them. The others agreed and it was decided that they would make no effort to contact Josh and Rachel after all. None of them wanted to risk losing anyone else. Though exhausted from their recent ordeal, the Avatarn and Paolo were awake until sunrise, getting to know each other and comparing the experiences that had brought each of them to this place. Tyler and Mateo hovered nearby, hanging on every word. They had seen enough to know their guests were telling the truth and wanted to help in any way that they could. The Avatarn had become an instant family.

"Why do you think they stole Yoshi's body?" Paolo mumbled to no one in particular before they drifted to sleep on only lightly soiled towels and rugs the boys had insisted on loaning them.

It was Darby that replied, "I think someone snagged Yoshi because they didn't want our journey to KC being derailed. They didn't want us being detained by a funeral or burial."

Roman agreed.

"The only part that is debatable," Blair chimed in, "is whether it was the good guys or the bad guys. The motives are obvious for the forces of good, to push us towards our initial meeting, but something tells me those weren't angels that swiped your friend's body," Blair finished by squeezing Darby's hand.

"The question," Roman added, "is why someone from the dark side would want to encourage our union."

The Avatarn awoke to a morning much more crisp than the one they had left behind, having sailed into an ocean of sleep that took a full day to cross. The foursome, completed by Paolo, woke up refreshed, if somewhat chilled and felt their energy restored. They had slept peacefully with Mateo's guarantee that no one would bother them within *The Palace* walls.

With a quick food run to Micky-D's, Roman provided breakfast for the entire tribe, ensuring their place among the royalty of *The Palace*.

Blair made a quick call to *Club Chakra* from her cell phone to learn that "Jo" the bartender had a daytime gig as a tattoo artist in a trendy neighborhood called Westport, an area catering to alternative lifestyles. It was Darby's hope that Joppa could guide them to the next leg of their mission, to prepare them for what was coming. A heavily pierced girl named Heather volunteered to be their guide through Westport, and, after declining her offer to steal a car, they were soon in a cab headed south.

Heather assured them that finding Joppa would be easy-peasy. There were only three tattoo shops in Westport. The lovely homeless girl had wild, chin-length black hair and striking ice blue eyes. Her white skin and ruby lips were especially sensual. She had cut, tied, and knotted her over-sized thrift-store clothes until they conformed to her centerfold figure. Her magnetic beauty was in no way hampered by the many piercings that adorned her. Ears, eyebrow, septum, tongue, and the area below her lower lip, all enhanced with silver jewelry. Roman couldn't help wondering what other parts of her body might be so adorned. He felt a pang of guilt. After all this girl couldn't have been more than eighteen years old, and he was completely in love with Blair.

Still…He was a man and Heather was one of those charismatic people that everyone is just drawn to. It didn't matter. Roman had no desire to ever be with anyone but Blair. They hadn't consummated their relationship yet, but that was okay. He knew she would need some time, and he was prepared to give her whatever she needed.

Blair noticed the way Roman and even the gay men looked at Heather. She didn't blame them. She was attracted to her herself. She was a charming little punk. An ethereal beauty. But Blair knew Roman loved her. She was secure enough not to be threatened by the momentary distraction of a pretty face. Besides, Heather didn't seem to be interested in the men. She seemed totally unaware of her gift of beauty. Smiling and laughing like a child, she somehow retained the peacefulness of the innocent even though she had been educated in the streets. And now she was pointing out the cab window, focusing their attention on a colorful commercial neighborhood. They had arrived.

Westport was filled with clothing, music, jewelry, and knick-knack stores catering to the alternative subcultures. Restaurants and businesses specializing in merchandise for the gay, hip-hop, skater, Wiccan, artistic, and hippie subsets. Freaks and rebels of every bent wandered the streets, going about their non-conformist lives.

Heather knew there were no female artists working in the shop that was part of a vintage clothing store. Tyler had just tricked with one of the artists there as payment for a tattoo.

She guided the cab instead to the ink shop with the metallic storefront and the name spelled out in purple flags. Heather bounced from the cab and spoke only for a moment to the sexy tattoo artists loitering on a bench in front of the store, before returning with an expression of defeat. Though she had guessed the right shop, "Jo" wasn't working that day, and the tattoo-covered hotties had no idea where to find her.

The Avatarn climbed out of the cab and joined her for a stroll through the curiously popular part of the city. Heather explained as they walked that, during the day, the interesting neighborhood was largely populated by gay people that live in the surrounding area. At night, however, straight people and closet cases flooded the many nightclubs and bars.

Heather and her friends resented the fact that mainstream society seemed oblivious to their own hypocrisy as they barged in and used for their own entertainment the exciting, alternative environment created by those they disrespect and oppress. Stealing the "cool" aspects of the gay subculture as whites had from blacks for decades.

Because the tank-top clad Darby and Heather had moved to

the front of the group, Roman couldn't help noticing that Dar was sporting a tattoo of his own on the back of his shoulder.

"Hey, Blondie, what's up with the ink on your back," Ro enquired.

The gay Avatarn stopped so the others could get a closer look. "It's my three-leaf shamrock for good luck."

"Oh my God," Blair exclaimed, "It's exactly like mine!" She raised her sandaled foot to show the matching green shamrock that adorned her ankle. It was exactly the same as Darby's.

"Amazing coincidence," Heather smiled, making it perfectly clear that the matching symbols were more than a chance occurrence.

"Well, I don't have one," Roman was a little envious. He found the identical body modification fascinating and as he inspected them, he touched the one on Dar's back and the one on Blair's uplifted ankle. In that instant, a blurry green image appeared inside the older man's wrist. He jerked his hands away from the others, and everyone gathered nearer to examine his up-turned arm. The image quickly became clear, stinging during the process. A shamrock, the same in every aspect as the other Avatarn.

"Holy shit!" Roman squeaked.

"Looks like God's decided you're a three-piece set," Paolo offered before the others nodded casually and resumed their stroll. Ro couldn't help stealing glances at his new arm décor.

Paolo and Blair were both distracted for a moment by window after window full of trendy clothes. They stopped briefly in the local "homo" store, it was friendly and offered some interesting wares.

At Heather's suggestion, they grabbed a quick lunch at The Corner Restaurant where her friend Chaos, also known as Tim, waited tables. Chaos threw in free desserts and Roman rewarded him with an extremely generous tip. They window-shopped some more as a brief distraction from the gravity of their plight, but decided against a visit to the fortune-teller advertised in neon, after Heather declared her a fraud. By late afternoon, with no sign of Joppa in sight, the Avatarn, Paolo, and Heather decided to head to the non-franchised coffee shop. Darby had a hankering for a frappachino, and Heather never turned down free gourmet coffee.

None of them knew the tall, good-looking bald man sitting alone at the table just outside the coffee shop door. He wore sunglasses, a black T-shirt, and jeans. The casual way he reclined in his chair suggested a regular customer, finishing the newspaper at his usual hangout. As they passed him, each Avatarn in turn felt the hair on the back of their necks and their arms stand up. Each thought he or she was the only one to experience the odd sensation until they got inside and Heather quickly pulled them into a huddle.

"Red alert!" Heather's loud whisper turned a few heads, "That hotty-boom-body outside is a demon." She was struggling to contain herself.

"What? How would you know?" Paolo sounded a little harsher than he intended.

"When you live a life like mine," she replied without taking offense, "you come across a demon from time to time."

Blair was somewhat skeptical of her vague explanation, but couldn't deny that she had an odd feeling as they entered *Espresso Express*.

Heather grew increasingly agitated as the others insisted on getting their coffee before going back outside. The handsome stranger got to his feet when the group warily took their leave of the bustling coffee shop.

"Can I help you?" Roman stepped protectively between the as-yet-unidentified man and the friends that had become his family.

"I think you can," the bald man said, "Please join me?" he gestured to the table.

"Thanks, but we're kinda busy," Roman answered as the group turned to go.

"Please reconsider, Avatarn," the man smiled and lowered his sunglasses, revealing golden irises surrounded by thick black lashes. The group froze, ready to spring into action.

"Who are you?" Blair demanded.

"I am Adolphus…I am Legion," the handsome demon king pulled some chairs from the next table as he spoke, "Please join me. I had hoped this meeting would never come to pass, but since it became inevitable, I have become consumed by thoughts of you…Just a moment of your time, that I might clarify our situation."

"Guess it can't do any harm," Darby was anxious to see what they could learn from this very appealing monster. The other Avatarn were surprised, but when he pulled out a chair and sat down, they nervously followed his lead.

"Spill it," Heather wasn't going to feign politeness.

"Stay out of this, girl." Adolphus dismissed her and turned to Roman, "My fleet of starships shall arrive tomorrow to begin Earth's conquest…I simply couldn't wait that long to meet you, so I portaled here in advance to extend to you a most generous offer."

"We're not trying to make any deals," Darby countered, "I'm gonna ask you to leave before we have to put the hurtin' on ya."

Adolphus replied with laughter.

"Let's hear him out," Blair was curious to see what kind of ridiculous proposal he would make.

"It is simple, my lovely witch," Adolphus sat forward in his seat, "I am the king of a vast empire. In one day my armies will begin the enslavement of this planet. If you surrender to me, you may live out your lives comfortably on the planet Gehenna or you may fight by my side as you choose."

The Avatarn were all smiling, unable to believe his audacity.

"We won't be surrendering ourselves…or our planet," Roman refused the demon's ultimatum.

"The vassals you have collected from the streets can't begin to stand against my army. You are children. Your lifespans are those of insects compared to ours, and you think you can defy us. We have forgotten more about the workings of the universe than you could ever learn," Adolphus sneered.

"Perhaps such extended lifetimes are to blame for your twisted minds," Blair offered, "It would be almost impossible to avoid corruption over such a long time. Maybe your evil nature is just the unavoidable result of your biology." She wasn't excusing them, only trying to understand.

"That is no excuse," Heather was almost angry, "What about the angels that serve God? They are immortal, yet they resist defilement. Evil is a choice."

"It is the choice of the bold," Adolphus flashed Heather the smile that had seduced more righteous souls than silver or gold.

"It is the way of the weak," Roman subconsciously flexed the muscles all over his body as he grew evermore indignant arguing with the alien leader, "It's easy to give in to every temptation. Real courage means having the strength to set aside selfish desires and sacrifice for the good of others."

"Bravery is defying an all-powerful Father, and doing what you will. Consequences be damned!" Adolphus shouted, unconcerned with observers.

"You will be damned," Heather stated matter-of-factly.

"I already have been, child," Adolphus chuckled at her simplicity, "Don't you understand little one...We all have been damned to hell...What do you think this thing you call life is?... This separateness. Being trapped in a body. Alone...The life you are living is the hell He forces you to endure. Apart from Him. No longer one with Him."

"If that's how you feel," Darby interrupted, "Why do you oppose Him?"

"Don't you see, fool?" The demon king was enraged, "My kind are created without souls separate from our beings. Servants to do His bidding through eternity. Even if destroyed we are not united with Him. We are apart from Him until we are undone. And then oblivion. You humans have always been his pets."

"You could be with God right now, if you chose to be?" Heather stated it as a question.

"As a slave," Adolphus roared ignoring the on-lookers, "Never to be truly re-integrated with Him. Better to rule in Hell, than lick His feet."

"I pity you," Blair sincerely offered her empathy. "You wage war against that which you most long for."

"Do not feel sorry for me, witch. I am more than content in this physical realm. Someday you mortals and even the Avatarn may return to Him, but not without the scar of our boots on your souls," Adolphus stood then, quickly grabbing Paolo's wrist. Darby's new Italian boyfriend had the misfortune of being seated closest to the Legion king.

"Take your hands off—"Darby jumped up raising his own hands, preparing to use his powers, but stopping in mid-sentence when Adolphus pulled Paolo into a head-lock, using his body as a shield. The small crowd of *coffee house types* pulled back. All lacked the aggression to get involved in a street brawl.

"Please…" Was all Paolo said to the demon as he pulled pointlessly at the massive arm around his neck.

"Please what?...Take you home and fuck you?" Adolphus licked the side of Paolo's face, "Don't worry…I probably will…As soon as my lieutenants finish with you."

Blair had jumped up with the others and was rubbing the gem of her wedding ring. All she said was "Stone!" In that instant, Adolphus' feet slowly began to crystallize, beginning to transform him into a diamond statue.

He in turn shouted, "Babylon!" which she knew translated as "the gate." A black and gray spinning vortex opened behind him like a window. The diamonds not yet having climbed to his knees, the demon simply fell backwards into the portal, taking Paolo with him.

"I'll kill you!" Darby screamed as he and Roman simultaneously dove towards their friend. Paolo and Adolphus disappeared through the spiraling energy of the dimensional doorway the instant that it closed, leaving Roman and Darby sprawled on the sidewalk. No sign of the portal remained.

"Paolo!" Darby yelled in helpless terror. Blair pulled Heather against her and started to cry.

Heather and the Avatarn were too distraught to continue their search for Joppa. Not knowing what else to do, they returned to the sanctuary of *The Palace*.

They had just built a barrel fire in the corner of the warehouse they had claimed as their own, when Tyler and Mateo joined them. Blair suspected Heather had more than a passing crush on the redheaded, brown-eyed boy known only as Tyler. He refused to divulge his last name or his age. Blair guessed him at about seventeen. Lean, but muscular. He was a cutie. She thought he reciprocated Heather's feelings, but he was fiercely loyal to Mateo. She thought he might be in love with him too. Blair thanked God she wasn't a teenager anymore. She didn't stay lost in her thoughts for long. The boys were anxious to share some news.

"Damn lucky you made it back," Tyler began. The boys were too excited to stand still, "Cops are questioning everybody on the streets, looking for you guys." Blair could tell his voice had changed recently, though it was now deep and rich. "You had better not be leaving *The Palace* during the daytime anymore," he continued as Heather and Mateo looked on adoringly; "you'll be safer in the dark."

Roman thanked him for the advice and assured him that they would be careful. Blair asked the eighteen-year-old Mateo to continue to keep them updated. He promised they would and casually slid his arm around Tyler's shoulders after noticing Heather had taken his white-as-snow hand. Tyler began to feel awkward after Heather told him about Paolo's abduction. He never knew what to say to comfort people in pain. Darby seemed on the verge of hysteria. Tyler excused himself and Mateo followed him into one of several dark corridors. Heather stayed with the Avatarn, determined to find a way to help. Darby had resolved to be strong. To remain functional. He couldn't let the others down, and relied on them to help him maintain a sense of calm.

His burden of guilt was being compounded with each loved one that was lost on this crazy pilgrimage. He had lost everyone from home now. All he could do was pray that Josh and Rachel were okay, and that Paolo was alive. He was silently begging God for guidance in the rescue of his lover, when it happened.

Their heating fire in the tattered metal barrel expanded with a surge of warmth and yellow/orange light. They had all been standing around it, warming their hands, which they pulled away just in time to avoid being burned. Darby saw it first, but a moment later, the others shared his vision. Radiating from the flames was Yoshi's face. Darby's first thought was to wish that Josh was there to see the beautifully smiling face.

"Don't worry. I'm not in Hell," were Yoshi's first laughing words, "Don't let the fire fool you. I just chose this medium to communicate with you."

"Oh, Yoshi, I'm so sorry," Darby was sobbing before the flickering image of his dead friend could explain further.

"Hush yourself, Darby Zaid. I knew the risks when I joined you on this mission. Besides, I'm with God now. You guys can't even imagine the love in this place."

"Have you appeared to Josh like this?" Blair inquired.

"I can't," Yoshi replied, "I am only here to guide the Avatarn. But please know that Josh and Rachel are okay for now...You must remain focused on your duties. Tomorrow the rape of Earth begins."

"What about Paolo?" Darby choked out the words.

"King Adolphus has taken him to Gehenna, the Legion homeworld...He is in great peril." Yoshi looked afraid.

"I know he's in fucking peril," Darby cried, "How the fuck are we supposed to get to Gehenna? We're fresh out of spaceships," he sobbed. Each of the Avatarn had tried in turn to open a portal with the "Babylon" command right after the kidnapping, but to no avail.

"I can't tell you how to get there. That answer has not been revealed to me. Perhaps you are not meant to save him. There is little time for you to prepare for the horror that tomorrow brings," Yoshi's tears were visible even through the flames.

"Bullshit," Darby hissed through clenched teeth, "I'm going to find a way to get him back."

"I hope you do," there was nothing else Yoshi could say to comfort his friend. For a moment there was no sound, but the crackling flames. "I leave you with a ray of hope... Legion shall not find you in this place... *The Palace* is under the protection of a hidden angel, bound to Earth for the protection of the lost and those forsaken by man. Her powers shield this place from demon eyes. All here owe their safety to the angel HeaTheriel," Yoshi swore his love and said his good-byes and faded away with the quieting fire. All eyes turned to Heather who only smiled and bowed her head.

Chapter 12

The spacecraft appeared in the sky around dawn to the inhabitants of Kansas City. The armada of 1,000 saucer-shaped ships wasted no time orbiting the beautiful blue-green planet. Each took its pre-determined position, hovering above a major city. Reactions from the people of Earth ranged from hysterical panic and curious observation to religious awe. Their wonder was short lived as within an hour of the fleet's arrival, every television and computer screen around the world was filled with the handsome but alien visage of the lord of demons.

"My name is Adolphus, Lord of Legion, King of Demons," the Avatarn watched helplessly with the rest of *The Palace* tribe on the small TV the community shared, "This is our planet now. You and all future generations of your race shall serve us as slaves. Resistance is fu…Aaa, never mind." He chuckled briefly to himself. "There is no escape; your destiny has arrived. We have been among you since the birth of your species: Ramses, Caiphas, Genghis Khan, Hitler, as well as certain terrorists who have become household names. We are among you still in your highest positions. Presidents of certain countries, religious leaders, military generals, even some entertainment celebrities worshipped by your children." As he spoke, images of the people he referenced flashed across every screen, revealing a conspiracy so vast that no screenwriter had even dared to imagine it. "Do not seek to avoid capture," the golden-eyed alien continued; "punishment will be immediate and severe. Transport to our ships cargo holds will be conducted by a number of methods, the most common being herding shuttles. Leave all material possessions behind, and do not bother to pack your garments. Our slaves are rarely allowed to wear clothes. You also need not bother to attempt to stay in contact with your mates or children during transport. You will be selectively bred to serve our sexual needs and to increase our herds," Adolphus paused for a moment to let the terror of his last words sink in, "Prepare yourselves for surrender. Armageddon comes early to planet Earth. A sample of our power..."

Monitors and televisions around the world returned to their normal programming. Most people assumed the broadcast was some kind of farce, a joke perpetrated by some hacker taking advantage of the incredible circumstances. The jaded attitudes of mankind evaporated in an instant, when TV and computer screens were again possessed by the alien invaders. The images being broadcast now were of a wavering violet energy beam that radiated from one of the saucer ships to envelope the Hawaiian Islands. The islands and everything on them appeared for a moment to stretch or distort and then were simply gone. All the molecules that made up the state and the people that lived there were scattered into oblivion, leaving nothing behind but giant ocean waves colliding with each other to fill the void. Every man, woman, and child around the world held their breath. This was real. Next came panic.

The Avatarn had run out to the street to see how people were reacting. It wasn't good. The traffic jams had already begun as people tried to flee the city and enter hiding. People were beginning to riot. The world had gone mad with fear. They wondered the streets for a while with Tyler, Mateo, and Heather. So far there was no sign of the shuttles Adolphus had promised, but the holy triad felt helpless in the face of the chaos that had already begun.

Their wanderings soon brought them to the front of the

gold-roofed Cathedral of the Immaculate Conception that was a landmark of the downtown area. People of every religion were scrambling to get inside. In their hysteria, a nun was shoved to the ground at the foot of the steps. She would have been trampled had Darby not thrown up his hand, erecting a shimmering gold force field around her to protect her from the mindless masses. The group of misfit warriors ran to help her to safety. It was only after Tyler and Mateo had helped the Sister to her feet, that the others saw the young nun in the somewhat tailored modern habit for who she was. "Call me Sister Mary-Joppa," she introduced herself.

"Jesus, Are we glad to see you," Blair was greatly relieved to see their mysterious friend.

"Sorry to disappoint," Joppa countered, "but He isn't coming for a while. In the meantime, He's counting on the three of you to host this little party."

"He took Paolo, Joppa," Darby was teary-eyed, "Tell us how to get him back. We each tried opening a portal, but we couldn't."

"The portal part is easy. The three of you have only to hold hands and chant the word *Babylon*. Your combined power will open the gate," the pretty nun explained.

"I don't understand," Blair chimed in, "If the demons have access to these dimensional portals, why do they need spaceships to transport an army?"

"I'll take that one," HeaTheriel smiled at Joppa and turned back to the gang, "Portals are opened by magic. It saps a great deal of energy from the one casting the spell, and weapons and most other objects can't be brought through. The same applies when demons de-materialize and appear in another place. They can't transport much with them, and it drains them to a degree."

"Why didn't you explain all this before, angel?" Roman didn't try to conceal his anger.

"Hidden knowledge is only given to me on a need to know basis, and I pass it along accordingly," Heather stuck out her tongue at him, but apologized with a quick kiss on the cheek.

Their impromptu tutorial on the ways of magic was suddenly

interrupted by countless shuttlecraft dropping from an orifice on the underside of the massive saucer that floated above the city. One landed less than a block away and Legion soldiers began to disembark, shouting commands and firing energy weapons at the defenseless humans.

A young girl from *The Palace* was separated from her mother by the panicking crowds, and soon singled out by an armored alien. He unceremoniously grabbed her long blonde hair and began dragging her toward the shuttle's cargo door. Tyler was running towards them before anyone else had a chance to react. Leaping onto the demon's back, he began a barrage of fists that distracted the monster enough for the little girl to escape. Blair was the next to sprint into action. "Power of a Puma!" Was all she muttered aloud as she ran towards the monster and her friend. As she ran, she fell on all fours and quickly morphed into a small cougar. Her demon prey turned just in time to see her approach, the redheaded boy still hanging from his neck. Blair pounced, and though her claws and fangs were ferocious, the demon grabbed her by the scruff of the neck and shot her in the chest with his energy weapon. The mountain cat stopped moving, and Tyler froze in horror. Before the remaining members of the holy group could set their feet in motion, the monster holding their friends shimmered into nothingness, taking Blair with him. Vanished in the blink of an eye, leaving Tyler sprawling on the pavement.

"What now?" Darby said turning to the lovely blonde nun as throngs of terrified people pushed past them in every direction.

Joppa's answer could barely be heard by the strangely motionless group standing before her, "I don't know."

"We have to get on that shuttle!" Mateo was nearly hysterical.

"They aren't on the shuttle," Joppa placed her small hand on his chest to stop him from lunging into the chaos; "He wouldn't have shimmered if he were only going as far as the shuttle. They're probably onboard the mother-ship hovering above us. It's the flagship of the armada. Captained by Adolphus himself. They might have teleported to the Legion homeworld, but I don't think so...

I'm betting they're on the *Caiphas*...The worst place they could possibly be..." the seemingly young nun trailed off as she turned her gaze upward toward the gargantuan spaceship.

"We have to come up with a plan to get on that ship," Roman stepped forward, automatically assuming the leadership position that everyone somehow knew was his destiny, "Let's get back to *The Palace* and put our heads together...We've got to get to them as fast as we can. Blair is in the most danger. Adolphus knows that she is Avatarn. Ultimately, he will want to kill her, but her beauty may buy us a little time...The thought of him touching her..." Angry tears filled Roman's eyes as the words caught in his throat. The others knew what he was thinking and knew that he was probably right. Her beauty might keep her alive for a while, but she might rather be dead. The others watched helplessly as Roman repeatedly hit the programmed speed-dial button on his cell phone, hoping Blair would pick up. There was no answer.

"Joppa, how can we get up there?" Darby was the first to break Roman's awkward silence, though his question went unanswered.

"Where is she?" Heather jumped up from the curb where she had been sitting. They all searched in a vain attempt to find their magical guide. She was gone, vanished into the throng of terrified citizens desperately fleeing the gunfire and lassos of the demon invaders.

"Looks like she's deserted us once again," Darby didn't disguise his bitterness, "just when we need her most."

"We can discuss Joppa's timing later," Tyler joined their huddle, "We've got to get out of here!" he yelled as Heather and Roman ducked just in time to avoid a laser blast.

"Agreed!" Roman turned and signaled with his arm for all to follow him. Their run was frequently halted by cars and pedestrians that refused to clear a path. At Tyler's suggestion, they soon decided to detour through the sewer. Darby erected a small force field at the mouth of the manhole they entered to keep out the panicked people trying to follow. They couldn't afford to have anyone follow them, endangering everyone at *The Palace*. Darby felt guilty about preventing the strangers from escaping to the relative safety of the dark sewers, but there was no choice. The Avatarn had to survive if mankind were to have a chance. The holy ones ran along the damp metal grates that covered the river of raw sewage as quickly as they could, sometimes falling and climbing back to their feet in disgust. It wasn't until Roman, Darby, and Tyler had climbed up through the drain that was actually inside *The Palace* walls, that they realized that Heather and Mateo were no longer with them.

"Let's go back, "Roman was already kneeling to descend the way they had come, "They could be lost down there forever."

"Wait," Tyler stopped him, "Give them a few minutes. Mateo knows those tunnels better than I do, and Heather *IS* an angel. They'll be here soon."

"Okay," Roman was convinced by Tyler's confidence, "But if they don't show up soon, we'll have to send a search party."

"Leave that to me," Tyler comforted Roman further with a pat on the back; "*The Palace* posse can find anyone anywhere in KC. But trust me...Mateo will find his way."

"We've got to concentrate on getting on board the *Caiphas*, Ro," Darby returned from momentarily warming his hands by a fire, "Blair may not last long up there, and the three of us together are the only chance we have against Legion..." he paused, clearing his throat and looking away nervously, "or so I'm told." Darby still found it hard to believe that the fate of mankind had been placed in the hands of a gay student, a witch, and a middle-aged man who while still hot, was never-the-less haunted by the sudden loss of his daughter. The Lord moves in mysteri—His thoughts were cut short by a massive explosion outside.

Heather and Mateo were only a few yards behind the others when he heard the little girl crying for help. Without hesitation, he turned down a side tunnel and was out of sight before she could call to the others to wait. Not trusting him alone, the pretty raven-haired, and more than subtly pierced, angel ran after the handsome Latino boy, begging him to wait. By the time she caught up to him, both were confused by the section of tunnels they had never explored; however, Mateo refused to stop moving. The child was still crying out, and they followed her sobs down one twisting turn after another. HeaTheriel was a little freaked by the rats that scurried everywhere, but kept her eyes focused on her friend.

Visibility was only a few feet in the dimly lit sewer system, so it was no surprise that she ran smack into Mateo's back when he stopped short. They had just turned a particularly slippery corner, where moss and slime combined to make the going treacherous. Heather almost ripped Mateo's half-shirt completely off as she scrambled to regain her footing, only to see what had frozen the usually fearless boy in his tracks.

There had never been an endangered child lost in the tunnels. Before them stood a seven-foot demon that would have appeared human, if not for the long forked tongue that slithered out between child-like cries. Mateo wanted to move. To run...And most of all to protect his beloved HeaTheriel. He couldn't move a muscle. He was somehow entranced by the alien's beautiful and totally human-looking blue eyes. They were just like Heather's, and for a moment he understood that this beast was somehow the same thing she was. But she is an angel, how could this—his question not fully formed when the demon dove on him, the tackle taking him through the rusty grate and into the shallow river of shit that flowed below. Mateo was momentarily submerged and came up sputtering the fowl liquid. Heather's instincts took over. In a split-second the monster could shimmer away with her friend, the friend she was falling in love with although she knew he was still torn between her and an equal love for Tyler.

It was forbidden for her to lie with a mortal, but in the end her heart would have to decide. None of these thoughts entered her head as she pulled the small silver dagger from her boot and threw herself on the alien's back. She sliced his throat in the most savage move she had ever made. No mercy. Only Mateo's safety mattered.

"Didn't know you had it in you, little sister," the demon gurgled with a half smile as he turned in surprise to face Heather, then rolled off of Mateo and melted into the sludge. Gone forever.

"What the hell was he talking about?" Mateo questioned the little punk-pixie as he climbed quickly back onto the grating and pulled her up to join him.

"It's not what...I'm not actually *his sister,*" she had to grab his face in her filthy hands to make him look at her.

"I'm listening," Mateo was looking at the girl he loved with distrust that she could hardly bear.

"I'll explain while we walk," Heather's upset began to turn to anger. She didn't have to defend herself to him...But she knew she would, "We're going to have to go to the surface to find out where we are."

"You could be leading me into a trap for all I know," Mateo was trying to sound bolder than he really felt.

"If you really believe that," Heather just looked sad now, "then don't follow me, but I'm getting out of here. We have to get back to *The Palace* before it's too late for Blair." With that she turned on her heels and stomped off through the splattering filth that clung to the bouncing grates.

Mateo silently followed.

The sun was just rising when Simone Woods arrived at the police station, anxious to do whatever she could to help her niece and the girl's friend. Rachel had never called on her aunt's legal expertise before, and Simone had no doubt that any charges pending against the girl were complete bullshit.

The elegant black attorney looked smart in her burnt orange business suit without sacrificing the charming femininity of a Southern lady. Even the asshole desk sergeant was taken with her charismatic demeanor. She had soon arranged a visit, though it turned her stomach to have to play kiss ass with the jerks in uniform. Atlanta was pretty cosmopolitan, but she dealt with their kind on a regular basis. The kind that were as likely as not to have a badge on the dresser and a white hood hanging in the closet. So she played the game. She could definitely work the game. And was soon sitting across the table from her sister's baby girl.

"What happened?" was the first thing Simone asked after holding her sweet niece and meeting her friend, who was a real doll, despite having sugar in his britches.

"We were just strolling through this park," Josh answered for Rachel who could not stop quietly sobbing; "we were minding our business, when these two crazy cops jumped us." He had to lie if they were to have a chance at getting out of this, and this conservative lawyer from Atlanta would never believe the truth. "I think it was just racial profiling and homophobia," he threw in for good measure.

"I knew it had to be something like this," Simone was pissed and had just begun to ask for more details when the building began to vibrate, "Do ya'll have earthquakes in these parts?" The usually unflappable attorney was terrified.

"Not really so far…" Rachel was removed from her self-involved sorrows by a much bigger fear. The un-nerved threesome returned to discussing the fabricated police assault that had landed the young friends in the slammer. Not more than 15 minutes had passed when a guard opened the door to the small conference room to shout an insane warning.

"Run!!!...They're here…Run for your lives!!" then the cop was gone. The door wide open. Simone and the kids thought it was a joke or worse yet, a set-up. None of them moved for a moment, but seeing and hearing the chaos outside the door compelled Simone to check out the situation. The world had gone crazy. People were running toward any exit, some even climbing out windows (They were only on the 2nd floor). Officers were freeing prisoners. Removing cuffs.

"What the fuck?" Josh mumbled as he and Rachel joined her

aunt at the door. It was at that moment that a lovely black girl in a halter-top, low-rider jeans, and high-heels ran passed their door.

"Honey!!! Is that you?" Rachel called out to her. The pretty young drag queen spun to face them.

"Rachel? Joshua? What the fuck is you two doin' up in here?" Honeydew was obviously glad to see them, though she was quaking with fear.

"What's going on out here?" Simone had moved from the doorway where she stood as a barrier between the kids and the world gone mad.

"Well," Honey began as she pulled Josh into a rather familiar embrace, "I was just tryin' to earn a livin', givin' mens what they want and Honey's got, for a reasonable fee…Next thing I knows some hot little asshole cop is draggin' my tight little ass in here… Of course they was taken their sweet time friskin' me and I was helpless to resist— "

"Honey, please," Rachel interrupted, "Why has everybody gone crazy? What happened?"

"Oh…" Honey let go of Josh to pull Rachel in for a hug and a kiss on the forehead, "Gir, you ain't gonna believe this shit.. Well I guess *YOU* might…These giant UFOs pulled up over all the big cities, and then this evil, but still hot, you know, demonized motherfucker comes on all the TVs and computers talkin' 'bout they done took over the world, and everybody's gonna be sex slaves and all this shit, but somebody needs to tell this crazy bastard, 'cause Honey don't give it away for free…'Cept for you, Baby," she turned towards Josh with a wink.

"That's ridiculous," Simone wasn't buying any of the nonsense this little gender-bending whore was putting out. Rachel and Josh just exchanged knowing glances.

"See for yourself, Granny," Honey stuck her nose in the air and grabbed Josh's hand to lead them outside. None of the cops objected, so Rachel and her aunt followed them out the front door and down to a sidewalk where people ran passed in both directions.

Legion soldiers were grabbing people in each arm and dragging them towards a nearby transport shuttle at the corner of the block. Policemen were taking up defensive positions behind a mailbox, a tree, a statue, and more than a few cars, but their hand guns and rifles were no match for the lasers, stun-guns, and slashing swords of the monsters.

Already there were as many bodies scattered in the street as there were still standing. Josh spotted a manhole cover and signaled the others to follow. Simone kicked off her heels and left them behind. Honey followed her example, but wasn't about to leave her gold glitter sandals behind. It wasn't easy finding them in a size 13. They reached the manhole cover in moments, but Josh had to resist the impulse to gag as he pushed the lifeless body of a teenage boy off the bloody metal lid and began to climb down the metal rungs. He had gone first thinking he could catch the women if they fell.

"Rachel you go ne—"Simone's instructions were cut short as the tip of a sword appeared from her chest. She looked down at the bloody point, and back up to Rachel's horrified face. Simone's mouth shaped the words 'I love you.' Rachel couldn't move, but Honey could. She pushed Rachel into the manhole, knowing that Joshua would catch her. Simone's crumpling body pulled the demon's sword downward giving Honey the opportunity she needed. A flying drop kick toppled the armored monster, and though Honey's foot was broken, she crawled to Simone to confirm with a pulse check what she already knew. Rachel's aunt was dead. Just what the Avatarn's crew needed. Something else to feel guilty about.

Honey looked up just in time to see the giant fist coming towards her face. The alien she had knocked down had taken it personally. He would have stomped her into pulp, had his first blow not flung her backward into the open manhole. She had hit her head on the metal rim of the hole, and the demon smiled to himself as he looked down into the darkness at the unconscious body lying on a grimy metal grate. Her long brown wig had landed near her shoulder and her torn halter revealed a muscular but flat chest. Josh and Rachel remained hidden just out of the light from above, wondering if their friend was dead or alive. Josh held her tightly against his chest to stifle the sobs that racked Rachel's body. Aunt Simone was dead and it was her fault. Josh's plan had worked. The alien soldier assuming they were long gone watched Honey's motionless body only a moment longer before shoving the manhole cover back into place. The demon didn't want any other Earthlings to recognize that route of escape.

Rachel and Josh ran to the boy that had saved her life. "Is he okay?" Rachel had found the inner-calm that allowed her to do whatever had to be done in these situations that were a regular part of her dangerous new life.

"He's alive," Josh replied, whispering his name and gently slapping his face in hopes of bringing him around.

"Wait just a minute," Honey slowly sat up, picked up her wig, and started tying her halter back in place, "You ain't my momma...Ain't nobody lays a hand on Honey...You ain't my pimp, Sweets...But you know you got my heart." It wasn't until she tried to stand that they all realized walking was not going to be an option for the hero/drag queen.

"Guess you'll have to climb on my back, Hon," Josh turned and squatted, offering the injured young man a ride.

"Boy, just between us I would've pictured this with *you* behind *me*, but I'll take it anyway I can get it," Honey set aside her campy voice for a moment, and it was the quiet voice of a sincere man that said, "Thanks, Joshua," as Honey climbed on his back and was glad that Josh was a bigger man than he. Rachel would have laughed at the sight in other circumstances, but the invasion going on a few feet above their heads made that impossible.

"What about Aunt Simone?" Rachel's head was pounding and her eyes burned with a river of tears that seemed to pour without end, "We can't just leave her there."

"That is exactly what we are going to do!" Josh barked at her in response, "I am very sorry for your loss, but staying here or going back up top would be suicide...We have to get back to *The Palace* to help the Avatarn any way we can...We owe it to Yoshi, and we owe it to Simone."

Honey adder her two cents, "What he said, Sugar." And with that Josh turned and they were off. Going was slow because the grating wouldn't hold their combined weight. Josh stuck to the more solid ledge that bordered the grating on both sides, but it was narrow and slippery. He struggled to maintain his balance and nearly fell at regular intervals. "Well, Aunt Simone," Rachel whispered to herself looking up at the rusty underside of the manhole cover directly above, "you always said that 'If love can't find a way, it'll make a way.' So I'm gonna go find a way to help my friends save the world…I won't let you down, Auntie MoMo." Drop after drop splattered on her face as she swore her vow to Simone and she casually wiped them away. It wasn't until her hand passed through a sliver of light that she saw the crimson stain. It was blood raining from around the hole cover. She ran then to catch up to her hobbling friends, her screams echoing through the darkness.

HeaTheriel climbed the next rusty ladder they came to. Mateo was close behind her thinking that she would need his help to lift the heavy metal lid above her head. She lifted it easily with one hand. It might as well have been a sheet of parchment. Heather was not about vulgar displays of her angelic powers, but she was distracted by the anger she felt over Mateo's lack of trust in her. She went about her mission unconscious of her secret strength. Mateo reached a new level of discomfort, watching the girl he privately thought of as his girlfriend again prove she was not human.

She dropped the hole cover suddenly, and pushing him backwards, jumped to the ground.

"What is it?" Mateo demanded, both frightened and embarrassed as he landed on his ass.

"Legion!" Heather replied in a stage whisper, "They're everywhere. Come on." She easily pulled him to his feet and they sprinted onward into the dark, sliding with every step on the slippery grates.

The onyx-haired girl was praying for a sign as she led the way, running passed side-tunnels that split off in every direction. She knew she couldn't allow herself to be distracted by the rats she nearly stepped on or the stench that permeated her clothes or she might be overwhelmed by the horror of the instant. Bad enough that she was already cut off from the omniscient timelessness of Heaven by the isolation of life lived moment-to-moment. Angels are forced to live in the moment while on assignment, something mortals almost never do. It was a blessing and a curse, but necessary to stay truly focused. To remain aligned with the force. In her head, she called out to the Father, and the voice of his servant answered.

"This way, Baby," the singsong voice of Miss Luna floated to her ears at the same time she saw the kindly old fortune-teller at the opening to the tunnel just ahead on the right. The wise black woman and the little punk girl exchanged radiant smiles as Heather ran through her, reaching behind her back to take Mateo's hand.

"Follow her," the pierced angel almost dragged her companion as she ran down the narrower side-tunnel.

"What? Who?" Mateo didn't repeat his questions, not wanting to piss her off by insisting they only follow people that are actually visible. He didn't pretend to understand the complexities of what she was, but she had already saved his life at least once that day...Besides, no one that beautiful could do anything but good in the world.

They had gone the equivalent of several city blocks, when Heather saw it. The silhouette of a large misshapen creature stumbling their way.

Josh had to stop several times to lay Honey on the filthy ground and catch his breath. It felt like they had been walking the sewers forever, and he was completely lost. Each time he suggested they take a peek topside to figure out their location, Rachel became hysterical. Losing Simone was taking a greater toll on her than he had realized. He had to get the "girls" to safety soon, before Rachel gave them away with another bout of screaming…the screaming…It was almost more than Josh could bear. Reality had always been a little blurry for him anyway. Sometimes the things he imagined could seem more substantial than the reality everyone else seemed to agree on. Historically, he had relied on Yoshi to help him sort it out…To keep from drifting too far from mental health. He was torn between wanting to join her in the screams and slapping her back into sanity. Honey's, "Sugar, you best shut that child up before she gets us kilt," was not helping. He was just as worried about Honeydew though. Her wig was soaked with blood, and she kept fading out of consciousness. He hefted the young drag queen onto his back yet again. Polished toenails and a wonder bra might help create the illusion of daintiness, but they weren't making him any lighter; still they had to keep moving. Josh knew Honey's only chance was for them to find Roman, and soon. If he didn't find a clue ahead to point them in the right direction, he would have to risk going above. Even if he had to knock Rachel out to do it. They had only gone a few more yards, when he was startled by a commotion approaching them fast.

Heather had stopped on a dime and held her arms out protectively to signal Mateo to stay behind her. She was prepared to do anything to ensure his safety.

"Kyrie Eleison (Lord have mercy)," she whispered to herself as the bizarre creature approached in the gloom. Then just as she was reaching for her dagger, the beast stepped from the shadows.

"Heather!!!...Praise Jesus," Honey was thrilled to see the dirty young girl she knew from the streets.

"Honey!!! What happened?" Mateo stepped from behind his petite guardian, terrified by the apparent injuries of the friend he had made over many shared hours hanging out in the parks.

"Joshy's my white knight," Honey winked reassuringly at her Latino amigo. She turned to introduce Rachel as well, but her head lolled to the side as she fell into unconsciousness.

"We have to get her to Roman," HeaTheriel said to Mateo as she stepped forward to take Honey's hand.

"You know Roman?" Rachel spoke the question on Josh's lips.

"Sure, we live with him," Mateo answered, "How do you know him?" He and Tyler had heard about Darby's friends, but had never seen them during the Avatarn's spectacle in the park.

"I guess you could call us acolytes," Josh offered with a handsome smile, grateful to find allies that might be able to lead them to their blessed friends.

"We can't waste anymore time," Mateo was up a nearby ladder before Heather could stop him, "We have to find out where we are." A quick look above ground told the hustler/freedom-fighter they were only blocks from *The Palace*.

Josh and Rachel were shocked into motionlessness when Heather instructed Mateo to help move Honey onto her back. Even though, the black man was easily a foot taller than she, the angel carried the cross-dressing hooker with ease.

"Angel," was all Mateo offered in the way of explanation to the others before setting off to take the lead. Josh and Rachel fell silently in line, content to trust the unusual twosome to take them to their fate.

Tyler and Roman were just preparing to lead a search party, when Mateo surfaced through a man-hole cover in the sheltered alley that bordered *The Palace*. "Dude!" Tyler ran to his battered-looking friend to help him up. Mateo turned immediately to take hold of the large limp body that Heather was holding above her head.

"Oh, my God," Roman ran to help pull Honey to safety. With the help of the other squatters who populated *The Palace*, the injured drag queen was quickly carried inside and gently placed on the nearest palette. Roman was too distracted to fully react to Josh and Rachel's unexpected arrival, but Darby had run to embrace them, ecstatic to see his lost friends again.

Roman was kneeling over Honey's crumpled body. She wasn't breathing and her pulse was nearly gone. He still wasn't sure how to use his healing powers, but he was her only chance. Roman tossed her wig aside and sat down against a concrete pillar and pulled her whole body into his embrace. He held her against him and rocked her, humming some nameless song he use to sing to Janie as he rocked her to sleep in the peaceful hours of the night. A crowd of would-be disciples gathered round to witness what they knew to be a miracle as the place where the two men's hearts were pressed together began to glow with a brilliant white light. The light expanded slowly to envelop them both completely. In a flash that filled the room, it was over. Honey's beautiful, and still perfectly made-up eyes, were staring into Roman's.

"You really are the chosen, aren't you?" She whispered into the handsome face of the weeping Avatarn who was her friend.

"Looks like," Roman replied bowing to kiss her forehead, his dark tousled bangs falling like a veil to tickle her lashes.

"I'm so glad you can look past what I am," Honey was crying happy tears as she stared into the handsome face surrounded by blue light.

"What I see when I look at you is a person that God loves as much as He loves anyone else in the universe...That's all I need to know," Roman helped her smooth her wig back into place. All traces of blood had disappeared, leaving Honey looking fresh and restored.

Roman's heart leaped with hope as he looked up and finally realized that Josh and Rachel had somehow found their way back to their makeshift family. He was actually laughing when Rachel knocked the air from his lungs with two words, "Where's Blair?"

Chapter 13

The first sensation Blair became aware of as her mind drifted towards waking, was the tingling feeling that accompanies electric shock. She knew that every tiny hair on her body was standing on end. When she moved, soreness erupted in her chest reminding her instantly of what had happened. She had been shot in the chest with an energy weapon. Her eyes flew open in sudden panic. The chaotic crowd and her friends were gone, but she wasn't alone.

"I thought I was a goner when they threw a sleeping mountain lion in here," a pretty woman with shoulder-length brown hair was smiling down at her, "I can't tell you how relieved I was when you morphed back into human form and I recognized you from my dreams…You must be Blair," she added, seating herself Indian-style beside the confused woman lying on the metal floor.

"Where am I?" Blair demanded, rolling away and jumping to her feet. She just assumed that the woman with chocolate eyes was a demon.

"We are on board the lead ship, hovering over Kansas City… And I am a captive too…A hostage, more precisely," the lovely young woman had a calming demeanor. Not as if she had surrendered hope, but she had accepted that, for the moment, her situation was unchangeable.

"Who are you, and how do you know my name?" Blair was crouched in a defensive posture, ready for whatever this seemingly docile girl might throw at her.

"My name is Brenda Perez," she explained with a smile, "And I know who you are, because I was with Roman the first time he heard your name."

"You're his wife." Blair was aghast with the improbability of what was happening.

"Ex-wife." Brenda corrected her, extending her hand. Blair shook it hesitantly, amazed at this turn of events.

With her other hand, she pulled her small cell phone from a pocket, hit the button programmed with Roman's number, and prayed she would be hearing his reassuring voice by the time she moved the phone to her ear. Her silent prayer was not to be granted. She couldn't get a signal within the alien walls of the mothership. She flipped the phone closed, slipped it back into her pocket, and refocused her attention on the ghost from Roman's past.

"But how?...Why?...How were you captured?" Blair forced a smile for her fellow prisoner, and gestured for the woman, once married to the new man in her life, to join her on the bench-like surface that extended from a slot in the wall.

Brenda's casually friendly demeanor faded from her face and was quickly replaced by a visage of sorrow and anger. "I had just settled into my cubicle at work and turned on my computer…I'm a real estate agent," Brenda explained as her eyes began to glisten with unshed tears, "when they stormed in…The ships hadn't even appeared in the sky yet…Everything was still normal except for Roman's crazy new adventures…It was like a scene out of a horror movie…Monsters rampaging into the office, slaughtering my associates as casually as you might swat a fly…Making their way toward me…It was my nightmares come to life…I didn't run…I just stood up, and waited for them." Blair squeezed Brenda's arm in a futile attempt to comfort her, but she only sobbed once before continuing her story. "One of those bastards had hands that were literally the size of your head. He walked straight up to me, but I didn't blink or even flinch…Until he grabbed my best friend by the neck and crushed her throat like a Chinese lantern…I jumped on him then. Determined to make sure he at least died with me. I broke every nail I have punching him in the face, but he wasn't even fazed…He calmly closed both of those giant hands around my waist, and in an instant, we were somehow teleported here…I knew then that everything Roman had told me was true. And that I was brought here in hopes of black-mailing him into submission." She paused as Blair wiped tears from her new friend's eyes. "It's crazy, you know, 'cause I had just seen my best friend murdered, and all I could think about was how scared Carter was going to be when he heard about the massacre at my company… Carter Sodderby…That's my boyfriend… Now that I know about the invasion…I mean, I don't even know if Carter is still alive. Is that crazy?...I'm trapped on a spaceship full of demons, and I'm more worried for my boyfriend than I am for myself."

"Makes perfect sense to me," Blair replied, pulling Brenda into a protective hug. It was then, that video images appeared on a large section of the wall across the room. They showed graphic scenes of the carnage taking place on Earth. Humans were being captured or killed on every continent of the world.

"That is how I witnessed Adolphus' speech when they arrived," Brenda explained as Blair sat transfixed, unable to turn away from the horror, "And the beginning of the invasion. I think it's their way of keeping the cattle demoralized into submission," she added, regaining some of her composure as the images faded away, replaced with a simple seamless wall.

"We should get some sleep," Blair suggested as she tied her long red hair into a loose knot; "tomorrow we have to find a way out of here."

"That's easier said than done," Brenda countered, "At night… That's when the soldiers come," her eyes were glassy again, "I don't even know how many times I've been raped in the last few days." Blair took both of her hands into her own.

"That's over now," Blair spoke with confident certainty, "I'm here now, and those assholes aren't going to touch you again."

"Please tell me you've been given some kind of supernatural

power like Roman," Brenda's facial expression revealed her extraordinary hope and need.

"As a matter of fact," Blair flashed her dazzling smile, "I was born a witch, but before my awakening as an Avatarn, I relied on help from my sisters to perform even simple magic"; she couldn't avoid wincing slightly at the thought of her sisters' deaths, "However, God has seen fit to give me an incredible Avatarnal gift...I've been given influence over nature. My powers have been magnified a thousand fold by the Father Himself," Blair paused at the relief reflected in Brenda's face, "So don't be afraid anymore." With the promise of safety, Brenda allowed herself to recline on the hard bed/shelf, still secure in Blair's embrace. This was no time for prudish self-consciousness. Besides, she knew beyond doubt that she could trust this new friend of Roman's. It was the only thing she was sure of in that moment.

"Brenda," Blair had just thought of one more question before she could allow herself to sleep, "Have you seen a young Italian man named Paolo on board this ship? He's a close friend of ours."

"No...I'm sorry. I haven't seen any other humans since I've been here," Brenda didn't open her eyes as she spoke. She was drifting away on gentle waves of sleep, and soon she would be beyond the reach of Blair's soft whispers, "but we can ask Indra tomorrow. She's been sneaking in to check on me each day. She might know if your friend is here. She spends a great deal of time in the presence of the king, and is privilege to many secrets."

"Who's Indra?" Blair wondered aloud, but Brenda didn't hear her. In her dreams, she was in a castle on a distant planet, roaming through the corridors, unobserved by the aliens that marched here and there. Drawn to the barred window of a massive door, she peered inside. A lone prisoner sat in the corner on a pile of straw. Spiky black hair, he was naked and dirty. He was badly beaten, but alive.

"Paolo?" Brenda barely recognized her own voice, which somehow seemed far away. At the sound of his name, the prisoner's head snapped up. For an instant their eyes locked, then she was falling…Through the total blackness of space…Falling deep into unconsciousness.

The demons didn't visit her cell that night.

Blair awoke early. Though she hadn't slept long, her new status as Avatarn was a source of unexpected stamina. She felt revitalized, and ready to face the challenges ahead. She allowed Brenda the luxury of a little more sleep. She needed to recover as much strength as possible. Blair said a silent prayer, asking Jesus to somehow get them safely back to *The Palace*…Back to Roman.

Brenda began to stir, and Blair hoped that her short respite would be enough. "Good morning," Blair said as Brenda's eyes fluttered open. She sat up quickly, startled once again by her surroundings, but immediately comforted by the sight of Blair standing across the room taking down her hair and shaking it out.

"Did I sleep long?" Brenda felt some guilt at having slept away valuable planning time.

"All night, I think," Blair smiled, "You needed it, girl."

"I dreamed again," Brenda couldn't wait to share her new clue, "I was in the castle. The one in the nightmares from which I recognized you…I saw your friend. Paolo. He's alive…He's in that castle."

Blair was still at a loss for words, when a door slid open revealing an alien woman of extraordinary beauty. Her long jet-black hair was pulled back from her face in a series of ponytails, each one above the other, topping out at the back of the crown of her head. She wore what contemporary Americans would call a jeweled bikini and veils flowed around her legs. Most striking of all, was the fact that she had four arms and four breasts. She was like something out of an episode of *I Dream of Jeannie* but with a Hindu twist. Blair had never been anything but heterosexual, but for perhaps the first time, she understood the sexual attraction of women.

"Greetings," the exotic woman offered as she glided into the cell."

"Hello, Indra," Brenda was clearly happy to see this enchanting creature.

Indra responded to the brown-haired woman with a sweet smile and turned her attention towards Blair. "It is an honor, great Avatarn," she bowed as she approached, "I am pleased to meet you." Blair simply smiled and respectfully bowed her head in return. "I am Indra," the alien continued, "of the planet Vishnu. Concubine of Adolphus, King of Legion…I can not avoid my fate…I am to be his wife…Another of many…However, I must do everything in my power to see to his destruction…I know who you are because my position often allows me to be present as he consults with his dog, Lucien…That one makes even my master seem only partially evil…Beware of him…Even Adolphus would be wise to do so," she paused and Blair only nodded her head, well aware of what Lucien was capable of. It was he, after all, that had murdered her sisters. "Though I may be executed for my betrayal, I am going to help the two of you escape. We will steal two shuttles. My personal servant, a dwarf named Hashup, will pilot Brenda. His people are bred as pets by the demon pigs, but I assure you that he is a most capable soldier. He will take your shuttle to the secluded ranch of a woman who has taken many children into hiding there. I know of this secret resistance, because of my hearing, which unbeknownst to the demons, is far more developed than most humanoid species. It has allowed me knowledge of the Earthlings' whispers about a rapidly formed underground spiriting their children away to the safe-keeping of one called Oprah. Subtle questioning of the harem guards has revealed to us that she is a member of Earth's royalty."

"Something like that," Blair winked at Brenda, "And what are your plans for me?"

"You will also be given a shuttle, but you will go alone. You will use the witchcraft, which my master greatly under-estimates, to pilot the transport yourself…There is little time. We must go."

"Wait, Indra," Brenda grabbed one of the concubine's four

hands to demand her attention, "Remember my nightmares that we discussed? I had another one. I think the Avatarn's friend, Paolo is being held in that place."

"The place she speaks of is the Castle Hades," Indra held Brenda's hand, while patting her on the back reassuringly and gently grasping Blair's shoulder with yet another hand, "It is Adolphus' headquarters on the planet Gehenna. If your friend is there, he is beyond our help at this time. May the Creator protect him...We must go now." She turned back towards the door, instructing the prisoners to stay close behind her. Brenda made a vain attempt to remind Indra that they had to try to find Carter, but the lovely alien, could only silence her with a finger to her quivering lips, and the promise that she would get word to her if she learned anything about her lover.

Indra addressed the guards which immediately moved to block their path, "I am taking these prisoners to the bathing chamber. His majesty wishes them to attend him later, and they smell like animals." The guards exchanged a quick uncertain glance. "Do you wish me to make known to him that you are responsible for these women being brought to his bed smelling like you," Indra showed no fear, but Brenda turned away to hide the undeserved shame she felt at having been used by these monsters. The indignant guards moved briskly aside, allowing them to pass, hoping that the favored new concubine would not inform their leader of their transgressions with his new toys.

They moved quickly through the ship, and though many demons, both male and female, paused in their duties to admire the beautiful women, they all recognized Indra, and knew better than to bother her.

As they moved into the restricted area near the shuttle bays, Blair said a short glamour to make them appear as demon girls to anyone they passed. It worked flawlessly, and no one questioned their presence until they reached the gate to the main shuttle bay. Access to the bay was controlled by a female demon enclosed in a small tank of water. The glass booth which was just to the left of the large interlocking gate contained nothing but a small control panel, the she-demon, which possessed gills and webbed hands, and a merman swimming near her feet. The Atlantian, who was clearly her enslaved lover, momentarily seemed shocked by their appearance. Blair realized too late, that she had phrased the glamour only to mask their identity to demons. The slave was unaffected, and saw them as they really were.

"What is your business here? I don't recognize you," the demon asked Indra as she laid her hand near the alarm button on her console.

"Major Teardra, we have only recently crossed over, and wish to prove ourselves to his majesty by making a cattle run on the surface. We will return with many new slaves of exceptional quality for the king," Indra had practiced this dialogue many times, but the demon didn't seem to be buying it. Teardra was about to object to the nonsense she was listening to, when her beloved slave began to convulse at her feet.

The beautiful and muscular merman was pretending to be in seizure to distract his monstrous mistress. He swung his tail wildly, knocking her off her feet. Teardra was disoriented, but most concerned about the well being of her handsome new pet.

"Open Sesame!" Blair commanded the doors to the bay; she didn't have time for creativity and they were the first words that came to mind. With a whooshing sound, the seal was broken and the doors slid open. By this time, Teardra had too late become aware of the deception. She struggled to reach the alarm button, but the merman's arm was already around her neck. He strangled her to death with one arm, and motioned with the other for Indra and the girls to pass through allowing him to close and lock the gate behind them.

The threesome strolled casually towards the nearest shuttle, still camouflaged by the magic of Blair's glamour. Hashup had been hiding on board since the night before, and started the engines as he lowered the hatch door automatically from the navigation station. Indra kissed Brenda on the lips and gently shoved her through the hatch. There was no time for lengthy farewells, and though she had only known Hashup for a few days, she knew that he would not fail her. The hatch closed, and the shuttle rose into the air. Indra and Blair moved out of the path of the craft, and it only hovered in place for a moment before gliding forward and passing through the invisible force field that maintained air pressure in the bay.

Blair opened the hatch to the next shuttle with a simple wave of her hand. To the Legion staff, Indra appeared to be just another demon with large bat-like wings, and Blair looked like a demon with antennae extending from her forehead. No one interfered as they said their good-byes.

"It is my eternal honor to have served you, Holy One," Indra made a small gesture of bowing, "Remember, though your mission is paramount, there is no higher priority than love…A messenger from a higher realm visited me last night. He said that the Creator would save many worlds through one that will come at the zenith of the Avatarn's love"; finishing Indra kissed her and guided her forcefully towards the hatch.

"Gee, profound much?" Blair didn't know what else to say.

"It is to that end that I sacrifice myself," Indra waved in a small gesture, and took a step backwards. Blair had boarded, and turned to say good-bye to her new friend. "Success, Blessed One."

"Thank you," was all Blair could say. She knew that Indra would probably be taken before Adolphus for execution within the hour. With a small wave of her hand, Blair magically closed the hatch and moved to the navigation station at the front of the small craft. She thought that magic on the scale necessary to pilot this vehicle was deserving of a proper incantation so she focused her mind on her escape, opened her mouth and let the spell fall out:

"Spirits of the Cosmos
Heed my need
And lift this craft with all due speed
Carry this vessel where my mind flies
And hide my path from watchful eyes."

She hadn't even finished the chant when the shuttle began

to hover. It glided through the force field and into the open sky. Hashup and Brenda's shuttle was long gone. As soon as her ship was clear of the *Caiphas,* it was cloaked by the powerful magic, becoming invisible to anyone looking on. With only the power of her mind, she had soon directed the small craft toward the downtown area. She saw the roof of the building she knew as *The Palace,* and finally allowed herself to exhale. She was almost *home.*

Chapter 14

Josh and Rachel were exhausted after all the commotion, and after their reunion with two-thirds of the Avatarn, they had wanted to sleep, but it was still a long time until dark. They puttered about for a while, getting to know the residents of *The Palace*. Tyler and Heather showed them how to make pallets in an isolated corner near the sleeping area that the Avatarn shared.

Josh decided to explore some of the many uninhabited floors of the building alone. He needed to be by himself a little bit. The whole world had gone so crazy; he just needed some space...He had been alone for about an hour when he turned a corner into what had once been someone's private office. The wall opposite of the door was mirrored from floor to ceiling. He jumped in surprise, but it wasn't his reflection that had startled him. The image standing before him in the mirror was Yoshi's...His beloved Yoshi.

"How ya, doin', Joshua?" Yoshi smiled his one-in-a-million smile.

"Oh, Yoshi," Josh's voice quivered with grief, and even as tears streamed his face, he returned the mega-watt smile only his martyred lover could inspire.

"I'll take that as a *Hangin' in there,*" Yoshi pressed his palm against his side of the glass and waited for his shaken friend. Josh crossed the office floor in two long strides and placed his hand against the cold glass where Yoshi's was white with pressure on the other side.

"I miss you," Josh managed to warble, "How am I supposed to just keep going without you here, Yoyo?...Nothing even makes sense…None of it seems to matter."

"It makes more sense than ever, Joshy," Yoshi was using his *soothing tone*. The one that always made things better for Josh, "I am in Heaven now…Proof beyond doubt that it's all real…God is real…And he has given you guys a special mission. You have to do what you were born to do. Free will gives you the choice, but your heart tells you there's no choice to make, because your friends are in trouble. You belong at their side. If you did anything else, you wouldn't be the man that I love."

"It's just too hard without you," Josh was sobbing quietly now and their hands stayed aligned though Josh crumpled to the floor, crushed under the burden of sorrow carried bravely for too long. "I need to be with you now." An idea began to form in his rattled mind as his eyes searched the room and fixed on a shiny letter opener on a desk.

"NO!...Don't even consider it," Yoshi became instantly angry, "I forbid it…You will not take your own life to hurry our reunion. We will be together in time…When it is meant to be…Darby and the others need you here…You weren't made a part of this by happenstance or luck…The Father chose you to play a role in all this when the universe was still just an idea he had," Yoshi was on the floor beside him, where Josh's reflection should have been, "He will give you all the strength you need until your part is done." They would have been cheek to cheek if not for the hard glass between them.

"What now?" Josh was starting to feel stronger with Yoshi's love and faith propping him up, "Why are you here…Besides giving me the will to go on I mean?" Josh grinned a little.

"Helping you is reason enough to cross the divide," Yoshi's eyes were also glittering with unshed tears, "But you are right in thinking that these appearances are only allowed to aid the holy mission of the Avatarn…You must take a message to the boys… She who is blessed will again be among you…As is a traitor most foul…Soon a disciple of The Chosen will plot the betrayal that will paint the walls of this sanctuary in blood…Judas walks these halls to carry out his destiny yet again, as he delivered The Son millennia ago, so he will turn on those selected by The Christos to protect mankind."

"What? Who?" Josh was horrified to think that anyone at *The Palace* could betray them, that Judas himself lived again behind some familiar face.

"I can not tell you everything…The traitor himself does not yet know what he is capable of, how cheap his devotion, how easily his soul twisted yet again," Yoshi was pained by the knowledge that his darling Joshua was in grave danger. "Just prepare the others…All of you must flee this place…Your *Palace* is no longer safe."

"I'll make sure we depart immediately." Josh had climbed back to his feet, finally letting his sweaty palm slide away from the dusty glass.

"No, Joshua, not yet." It is inevitable that some will die here, but first the triad must undergo a perilous journey…Paolo still lives…Imprisoned on the demon world. He must be rescued…He and the other…"

"Who else? Who are we suppose—"Yoshi cut his questions short by reaching through the mirror to lay his corporeal hand gently on his lover's face. Josh was crying again. Would the tears never end? He couldn't speak, so Yoshi did.

"I have told you more than I am allowed already. Tell the others and prepare yourselves. The road ahead is harder still."

"I won't let you down, Yoyo," Josh squeaked, the handsome man in his prime reduced to a child.

"I know," Yoshi responded with another smile that glowed as brightly as the white aura that was starting to radiate from him, "There is no way you could," the spirit of the Asian man pulled his hand back through the mirror. Josh tried to grab it, but missed.

The barrier was re-established, and though Josh slammed the mirror with both hands it didn't even crack.

"Just remember the most important thing," Yoshi added as he took a step backward. Josh hung on every word, waiting for more instructions for his holy friends. "I love you," Yoshi finished as his image floated upwards and faded away.

Josh could have cried again, but he refused. Yoshi carried on somewhere, and he would too. He would make his Yoyo proud. He took a deep breath and backed out of the office, hitting his shoulder on the doorway as he went. He didn't want to look away from the mirror until he had too. Just in case he came back. He was gone. But he was okay. Josh would be okay now too.

Roman and Darby were shocked when Josh shared the details of his lover's ghostly message. Roman reflected with amusement on the fact that none of them were even surprised anymore by an apparition of the dead, but the thought of a living person turning traitor seemed too much. They chose to wait to share the news about the coming abandonment of *The Palace,* and focused instead on the joy of hearing that Blair would be returning to them. Each of them settled anxiously on his mat or pallet on the floor and let sleep consume them. Morning would bring new hope.

The crash on *The Palace* roof awoke everyone with a fright, except Heather. Though the Avatarn had not yet shared Yoshi's message with her, she somehow knew it was Blair. The residents of the warehouse sanctuary were further un-nerved by the now recognizable sounds of shuttle engines shutting down. For a moment all were frozen, unable to react. It was only after Heather bounded from her sleeping bag and dashed to the stairwell that the holy warriors and their companions followed quickly in her footsteps.

Roman and Darby hesitantly followed their angelic friend towards the still humming shuttle on the other side of the rooftop. The other *Palace* residents held their collective breath as their leaders bravely walked towards inevitable battle.

The hatch lock clicked, and Darby braced himself for a fight, but he wasn't about to let Heather face this danger alone. He stole a quick glance at Roman, whose illusion of courage gave him strength, and kept moving.

Roman flinched as Blair leaped through the doorway and started running in his direction. In an instant, he recognized the missing third of their triad, the woman rapidly becoming his other half.

"Yoshi told us you were coming back to us, but I was afraid to believe it," Roman managed to squeak as she literally flew into his arms. "I was afraid I had lost you as suddenly as I found you."

"You're not getting rid of me that easily, Perez," Blair playfully scolded him, though she couldn't hold a stern look on her face for long, not with Roman's face shining back at her.

The denizens of *The Palace* surrounded their "queen," anxious to learn the details of her abduction and escape. Blair finally felt safe, sheltered from her adoring friends in Roman's muscular arms. The tension melted from her body, and more than once, he had to support her as they descended the stairwell. She recounted all that had happened, shocking everyone most of all with the meeting of Roman's ex-wife. Horrified to learn of Brenda's endangerment, he was greatly relieved to learn of her escape to relative safety. He no longer had to worry about finding a way to protect her from the invasion and slaughter.

Back in the privacy of the living/sleeping area the people of *The Palace* let out an enthusiastic, if stifled, cheer. Darby joined Roman and Blair in their special corner of the vast room. For a moment the three of them clasped hands. And in that moment, the rest of the crowded room saw a split-second flash of blue light exploding outward from the holy threesome. From the perspective of the Avatarn, something different happened.

In the instant that they locked hands, the world froze all

around them. The three of them were still moving, talking, but around them everything was locked in that instant of time. Flames in the fire barrels were frozen in place. Birds that flew from beam to beam near the ceiling were captured in mid-air. The people all around them were statues. Sculptures of themselves. Even Heather was a mannequin of herself.

"Wow," Blair said pulling her hands away from the men. It was an extraordinary under-statement of the circumstance; they were all too shocked to elucidate further. In the moment their connection was broken, time returned to normal and life around them resumed.

"What was that?" Roman asked aloud, as much to himself as to the others.

"I don't know," Darby replied, "but I don't even want to think about it right now. It will be morning soon, and I am still exhausted. Let's get a little more shut-eye before we start another fun-filled day in KC."

The others agreed, and Heather and the boys quickly spread the suggestion to the other inhabitants.

Even though Blair and Roman were spooning and whispering things of love in each other's ears as they drifted into peaceful oblivion, Honey found a spot near them to curl up. She still needed to be near Roman to feel safe, and her heart was bursting with gratitude that Blair had found her way back to them. Soon an uneasy quiet settled over the forlorn sanctuary and not a human stirred. Only the little creatures of the night scurried about their business, only occasionally venturing close enough to steal the crumbs of food from the hair and clothes of the intruders in their world.

It was almost dawn when Honey felt Blair gently nudging her awake.

"Shhhhh, you were having a nightmare," Blair whispered to the pretty drag queen sleeping on the floor beside her.

"Oh, I'm sorry I woke you, Sugar"; the last thing Honey wanted to do was disturb her friend's much needed rest. "It wasn't exactly a nightmare though...You won't believe this shit, Darlin'."

"What is it?" Blair knew that coming from Honeydew it would be a doozy.

"Girrlll…You won't believe who just been to see me in a dream."

"Who?"

"Princess Diana!...And I do not mean Lynda Carter," Honey was beside herself with excitement and could barely keep it to a whisper.

"No way," Blair wasn't taking the dream seriously, but the glamorized black boy lying beside her clearly did, so she smiled her encouragement.

"Way, Sweets…She was a vision too…Dressed in a long blue gown…Sapphires around her neck and drippin' from her ears…Matchin' those gorgeous baby blues of hers…She came and sat right down here beside me on this crate right here…Just pulled up a damn dirty crate and sat down like plain folk…She said she had a message for me, Blair. A message from God," Honey waited for her friend to nod before continuing, "She told me God loves me, Blair…Me!...I just started cryin' like a baby…I always knew He did, but hearin' her say it like that…Sent here by Him…She told me," she choked on the next words. A masculine sob breaking through, "She told me I have to sacrifice myself for the good of the Avatarn…And that the Lord misses me somethin' awful and wants me to come home…"

"No," Blair interrupted putting her fingers over Honey's lips to hush the words she refused to hear. She was crying.

"There ain't no arguin' with the Lord, Miss Blair…Now I ain't sayin' I ain't scared shitless…Miss Honeydew and selflessness ain't never been friends, but you don't argue with Princess Di and you sure as fuck don't argue with Him…Besides Sista, have you ever heard anything so amazin'?...He misses me…ME…"

"I'm not the least surprised," Blair whispered back through tear-drenched lips.

"Don't cry for me, Love…I'm not exactly ready to go, but what am I really leaving behind…until I met ya'll my life was nothing but trickin' and killin' the hours in some triflin' bar…Honey was meant for more than all that…And now I know what…I was put in this world for somethin' grand…I've done glamour…Now it's time for guts and glory."

"What are you supposed to do? When?" Blair was still gently crying. She wondered how long she had been crying now…Days? Weeks?

"Di didn't say when, just that I would know what to do when the time was right…I trust her, Blair…The people's princess wouldn't steer me wrong."

"Any chance this was all in your imagination? Just a plain old-fashioned dream?" Blair was really trying to convince herself.

"Not a chance," Honey responded without doubt or hesitation, and Blair knew she was right. In their crazy new lives, encounters like this were par for the course, "Now you just promise me you'll take care of our boys…They need the influence of good women like you and me in their lives…Even Darby, more than he knows or understands, bless him…You feel me, Girl?"

"I feel you." It was all Blair could do to get the words out though a smile now filled her streaked face.

"And don't you worry, Miss Atwood…Honey's gonna be watchin' out for her homegirl…I'll always be with you."

"All right enough of this kind of talk. Tomorrow will be another day and maybe there will be another way," Blair insisted, "We'll just play it by ear, okay…And you just check with me before you do anything rash…You're already a heroine in this story."

"Okay, Sweets," Honey wasn't going to argue anymore with her holy friend, "We'll see how it plays out."

"Good…Now let's catch a few more winks. It's almost light," Blair kissed her chastely on the lips and soon they were both deeply asleep. Their foreheads pressed together. Arms intertwined.

The girls chose not to tell anyone about Honey's nocturnal visitation from royalty. They both knew everyone would just try to stop her from doing whatever she had to do, and Blair was secretly hoping that when the time came she could find some other way…She had to.

Darby slowly stirred to full wakefulness by the sounds of *The Palace* community about their morning business. A group their size required a lot of food and supplies. The "gatherers" would soon be off on specific assignments to acquire the necessary items. Much organization was required, and they had it.

Roman and Blair had sneaked off somewhere to enjoy their breakfast of fresh fruit and stale bread in private. Darby was happy for them. They deserved the love they had stumbled into. Thoughts of his fellow Avatarn were suddenly interrupted as Josh appeared out of nowhere and flung himself down unceremoniously on the pallet beside him.

"What the hell are you doing?" Darby was getting pissed. He hadn't had any coffee yet, and Josh had suddenly climbed on top of him and was straddling his waist.

"It's time to go save Paolo! Don't you get it? Blair's back now. The Holy Avatarn and all that. Get your ass up, Superman. We've got a job to do," Josh was so excited and all Darby could think about was how terrible a person he was for not immediately connecting Blair's homecoming with the fact that they could leave right away to find Paolo. Forgive me, Paolo, echoed on and on through Darby's now very alert brain.

"Get off me, Freak," Darby flashed Josh his warmest smile and pushed his friend over backwards, freeing himself.

"Bet that's the first time that sentence ever passed your lips," Josh fired back at him.

"True dat," Darby had to admit, "Let's find the others," he said climbing to his feet without even trying to hide his "morning wood" and grabbing his underwear and jeans, "We have a mission."

Roman and Blair returned as Darby finished shaving. Such vanities seemed ridiculous to some under the circumstances, but both men of the Avatarn figured that anything that made them feel more "ready" to face the coming day with a sense of preparedness and normalcy was worth doing as long as they had the option.

Blair knew as soon as she saw Josh and Darby's faces that they were anticipating the same thing that she and Roman had been discussing as they ate. They had to rescue Paolo from the demon planet. The sooner they left the better.

At that moment Rachel and Heather returned from helping dispense breakfast to the others. "Well, look what the cat dragged in," Darby teased.

"It's time," Heather announced to no one in particular. No one had to ask what she meant. They were ready to go.

"We're going too," Tyler spoke for himself and Mateo as they climbed up through a grate in the floor.

"I know you don't think ya'll are leavin' without me," Honey chimed in from behind a screen where she was putting the finishing touches on the mirage that was Honeydew. She liked to think of it as putting some things away and putting some on display.

"Sorry guys, but you're not all going"; Roman took command. "I appreciate the gesture, but too large a group will just slow us down…Tyler and Mateo will stay here."

"No fuckin' way!" Mateo was immediately enraged, "I'm not staying behind like some little pussy while the chicas and the maricón get to go. Sorry, Darby."

"It's okay," Darby replied.

"I need you two here to protect our sanctuary. Nobody knows more about *The Palace* and the people here than you guys…," Roman paused for effect, "Please, guys. I'm relying on you to be the soldiers I know that you are." He knew that youth is easily seduced by the notion of bravery and they were quickly convinced.

"Okay, how do we do this?" Darby couldn't wait any longer.

"We chant *Babylon*," Roman offered, "Remember? It means *gate*."

"Everyone that's going, get inside the circle created by the three of us linking hands," Blair instructed, somehow knowing she was right. Honey, Heather, Josh, and Rachel stepped into the magic circle formed by the arms of the Avatarn.

The holy threesome clasped hands as they had the night before, and again the world around them froze. Inside the circle, the quartet of would-be-travelers spun around in awe at the sights just beyond their magic friends. Tyler and Mateo were statues as motionless as metal, the entire world a mural frozen in time. Inside the circle, they were chattering and muttering obscenities, until they were drowned out by the rising voices of the Avatarn. Roman, Darby, and Blair were chanting "Babylon…Babylon… Babylon" over and over again. As their mantra grew in crescendo, the floor beneath them seemed to give way. At first they were suspended in air, as a black void opened below their feet. Though no one had issued instructions regarding their destination, all thoughts turned to the planet Gehenna and Castle Hades. They were falling…through nothingness… blackest night…deepest space…Somehow they could still see each other and the terror on every face…falling…

They didn't see the ground until after they felt the impact. They landed hard on the grassy hillside. Every bone in their bodies should have been crushed, but there wasn't a scratch on them. Roman was sure they would be sore for a while, but no one seemed to be hurt. "Thank you, God."

The peasants shuffling along the dirt road leading to the castle draw-bridge seemed to take no immediate notice of the seven strangers lying in the field, and the holy pilgrims turned rescue squad took advantage of the chance to scramble behind a large boulder only 40 feet from the castle moat. They should all have been overwhelmed by the experience of portal travel, but after all they had seen and done in the last several days, it was just another horrifying miracle that defied everything they had ever believed.

Blair quickly realized that they really had no shelter from the small shuttlecraft that were flying overhead. She hoped their faces would be unrecognizable from the distance, but their clothes were another story. She turned to Heather to point out their blunder in teleporting to the demon homeworld without proper dress.

"But we are dressed appropriately," Heather begged to differ, indicating for Blair to turn back towards the others. They were all in peasant gear. Old style. Any one of them might have just walked out of Earth's Europe in the Middle Ages.

"How did you—," Blair's long heavy skirt twirled as she spun back towards the angel, but her question was cut short by Heather's mischievous smile. She would never tell. An angel had to keep a few secrets under her studded collar.

With Roman in the lead, the little group fell in with the steady stream of true peasants making their way onto the draw-bridge. Everyone attempted to be nonchalant, but the sight of the demon guards posted on both sides of the giant entry gate made it hard. Rachel was the first to over-hear some of the slaves talking and realized that they could see the Avatarn's blue halos. She began to push the others along, anticipating some kind of riot, but nothing happened. Just the slow but steady wandering forward of a people enslaved for too long on this alien world to trouble themselves or get worked up by a few more beings with magical powers. The holy pilgrims went mostly unnoticed as they made their way inside the thick dank walls. The giant hall they entered could have enclosed a village, so they made their way to a far wall and, secluded behind a massive pillar, planned their next move. They had made it. They were in their enemy's house.

Chapter 15

Looking around at the immense stone walls, it abruptly occurred to Blair that she had forgotten to tell the others about Brenda's dream of Paolo. Oh, well, the point was moot. They were there to find him. She would just recount the story to Roman later.

The Avatarn and friends looked on with consuming interest as the castle staff moved busily about the chores of preparing a victory feast for the army conquering Earth. The Legion officers would be returning to Gehenna in a few days to celebrate another successful invasion. There was much to do. Many human slaves would be added to the herd, and the castle had to be made ready for their initial training. Even the harem must be made ready for the anticipated concubines. The necessary alien medics would be standing by to provide the immediate treatment required after the initiation "ceremonies." There were no Legion doctors. Demons wounded beyond their own ability to heal were simply left to die. Only the strong survived in a world where monsters wear no masks and no heart knows mercy.

From their vantage point behind the pillar, they could see that behind the huge central stairs, no doubt leading up to living quarters, were another set of stairs that led down into the belly of the mammoth structure. Probably a dungeon level. Probably where Paolo was being held.

"Where to? Someone's gotta lead," Rachel whispered.

"Guess that should be me," Darby spoke up, "He's my boyfriend…Let's go." Everyone filed in behind him and they made their way toward the relatively narrow stone stairway that led into a torch-lit abyss of mostly darkness. The others weren't even aware that Heather was silently using her powers to render them invisible to the slaves and courtesans as they started down the stairway that was probably forbidden to unattended humanoids. She couldn't keep up the camouflage for long, but it was enough to get them safely out of sight. The next floor wasn't immediately below ground level as one would assume. The stairwell spiraled down further and further until Darby began to fear they would never reach the end. In that moment, they turned onto a cavernous landing. Giant hallways led away in every direction.

"What now?" Josh was the first to wonder aloud.

"Should we split up?" Rachel said turning to Roman for instructions.

"Not yet," Roman didn't hesitate, "We don't know what we are up against here. We'll stick together for now…Follow me," he took Blair's hand, but walked directly in front of her as he took the point position and turned down the left most corridor. He reasoned that they needed some kind of search pattern and if they back-tracked to this landing and moved clock-wise from the bottom of the stairs, one hallway at a time; they wouldn't miss anything. They had a vast area to search, and Paolo could be running out of time.

Many of the rooms they entered were empty. They came upon everything from storage rooms to armories, barracks, and the occasional torture facility. They found humanoids and aliens strapped to or contained in all kinds of pain-inflicting devices, but never any guards. It appeared that nearly all Legion soldiers were on Earth, part of the invasion force. Several people and creatures begged the holy pilgrims to free them or kill them, ending their misery either way. Roman sternly informed them that they could not. If they were discovered before finding Paolo, they might never make it back to Earth, and that wasn't an option. The protection of Earth was their sacred duty. They could not fail. Roman realized there was a certain hypocrisy in what they were doing. As surely as he knew the survival of mankind on Earth was more important than the lives of these tortured souls, he knew that the survival of one man was crucial to their mission. Darby needed Paolo. God couldn't expect the Avatarn to survive another broken heart.

The brave little band hardened their hearts and continued the search that finally brought them to the end of the corridor and a more formidable door than any they had tried so far. Darby sensed that this room was special and finding it unlocked, rushed inside. The others were right behind him, and entered to see him stammering to find his voice. Before them a beautiful blonde girl sat horrified at a small desk which faced what could only be her teacher. A grotesque alien that appeared to the Earthlings to be an ostrich with long bony arms instead of wings. The creature held a book and blackboard pointer, and appeared equally shocked by the intrusion. They had stumbled into Beacon's classroom.

Surprise had stopped Roman and Blair in their footsteps just inside the doorway; and Josh, Honey, Rachel, and Heather shoved their way in to see what had caught the others off guard.

"She's no slave," Honey gasped taking in the princess' long red gown and the countless rubies and diamonds that adorned her body and tiara.

"Of course not!...She is the Princess!" squawked the ostrich/tutor angered at their insolence; "Bow in her presence, slaves."

Roman indicated with a slight nod that they should comply. They didn't want this oversized bird sounding an alarm.

"Forgive us, your Highness," Blair began, "we have somehow lost our way. We were sent to prepare the Terran prisoner, Paolo, for the triumphant return of Lord Adolphus. He is to be groomed and trained to serve his majesty at the triumph festivities."

"My father doesn't speak to me of such things," Beacon responded with an air of complete disinterest. "The dungeon isn't even in this wing...Are you new? Report back to your trainer and inform him that I was disturbed by your careless interruption."

"But Mistress," Roman chimed in, "We'll be beaten…If you could just point us in the proper direction—"

"How dare you!" Beacon stood up and stomped her foot. It would have been a hilarious comic cliché if they weren't in so much danger. "You are only to speak when—"

"Hold up," Darby interrupted her, "Sorry to cut you off short there, Highn-ass, but we are wasting too much time here. You are going to take us to find Paolo yourself. We are not slaves, and there will be no more bowing and scraping, you bitch."

"The audacity!" Clucked the teacher in horror. He moved towards a communications console on his desk, clearly intending to summon security.

For a moment his eyes locked with Blair's, and she said, "You're molting." In an instant, every black feather that covered the trunk of his body fell to the floor, leaving him naked, his saggy human-like genitalia exposed. The ostrich-man was petrified to have his beloved pupil see him like this, but only for a moment. He lunged suddenly for the controls on his desk.

"Sorry, Big Bird, can't let you do that." Darby stepped forward, extending his arm and flipping his palm towards the creature. A burst of golden energy flew from his hand, impacting the bird and flinging him against the far wall. He would never get up again.

"Monster!" Beacon screamed, "You've killed him!" She started to scream for guards, but Blair ran forward and slapped her hard across the face. "I know who you are," Beacon stated with a sneer as Roman stepped forward and took her by the arms, "You're that trash that call themselves the Avatarn of Earth. The prophesies do not forewarn that you are barbaric killers."

"They're not," Rachel stepped forward, "Demons just keep forcing their hands."

"How you gonna be Adolphus' kid and call somebody else a monster, Sista?" Honey took a protective stance beside Blair.

"What else am I to believe when my tutor lies dead in a corner?" Beacon asked of Roman, the obvious leader.

"We are sorry about that," he replied; "we don't want to hurt anyone. We just have to find our friend."

"You spend your time searching for one friend, while my father takes your planet?" Beacon was incredulous, "This extraordinary selfishness prevents you from fulfilling the prophesies. You messed up…Missed the opportunity to be the heroes of your inferior race…If I weren't grieving for my teacher, this would be pathetic."

"Ooookaaay," Josh was at the end of his patience, "And we're moving." He gestured widely toward the door and waited for the others to move through it.

Blair pulled three strands of her long red hair and used them to bind Beacon's hands as Roman held them behind her back. Their royal prisoner soon realized that her farcical bonds were indestructible. Not any stretch or give. Blair shoved her toward the door, and the search resumed.

Beacon dared not scream again. Her kidnappers were proven killers, and her father and Lucien were a long way away. She would play along until the opportunity to escape presented itself. Besides, she kind of wanted to see what they would do once they had their friend back. And the blond one, the one that killed her teacher, was quite attractive in a brutish way. She wondered what he might do to her if they were alone.

Almost the entire castle staff was occupied with preparations for the triumph feast. The few remaining house guards were spoiled and lazy. They didn't take notice the few times that the princess and her captors passed. She could have called out for help, but she would not be the cause of death for another of the loyal servants she had grown up with. She was quiet except for the occasional directions she muttered to guide them through the labyrinth of corridors towards the dungeon wing.

Turning into a small, torch-lit alcove, they discovered someone waiting for them on a small bench. It was Joppa. She appeared as the high priestess of the ancient mountain cult she had ruled on a planet a galaxy away. Her long blonde hair was piled high on her head, glittering with diamonds throughout. Her long blue gown fit her womanly curves like a second skin and left nothing to the imagination. She was exquisite, and only after drinking in her beauty, did the group realize that she wasn't sitting on a bench at all. It was a white tiger, effortlessly bearing the weight of his mistress.

"Joppa!" The Avatarn all said in unison.

"Boy, are we glad to see you," Roman continued.

"That isn't Joppa, you fool," Beacon glared at the darkly handsome lunatic, "Joppa is a child."

"But it is me," Joppa stood, flashing the child image of herself for a split-second so that Beacon would know her.

"What madness is this?" Beacon felt dizzy. Nothing was making sense. Who was this stranger that could somehow look like—

"I am here, Highness…And I am always," Joppa touched her face for a brief gesture of comfort, then turned her back on the princess to face the Avatarn. Beacon felt faint.

"There is much to tell you, and so little time," the priestess began, "First, the princess shall be free…She's not going anywhere." Joppa had but to say it and the copper strands of Blair's hair fell away, freeing Beacon's hands. She rubbed her tender wrists, but made no move to escape the alcove. The holy pilgrims were a little surprised by Joppa's choice, but would not interfere.

"I want the eight of you to sit on the floor in a semi-circle. I am about to reveal a great secret to you. You will want to take this one sitting down," the priestess offered a small smile.

"I don't sit on the—" Beacon wasn't able to finish, because Rachel abruptly pushed her to the ground. She stayed down, and each took their place in the requested formation. All faced Joppa, and Roman's stomach turned anticipating what terrible universal truth she was about to make known.

"This knowledge had just been revealed to me. I'm afraid it will be difficult," Joppa paused.

"With everything that's happening," Josh broke in, "what could shock us now?"

"This concerns you, Darby," the priestess began, "and Princess Beacon…your sister… your twin."

"Blasphemy!" Beacon screamed, "How dare you suggest this creature shares my royal blood—"

"There is nothing royal about your blood, dear," Joppa cut her off, "You are human. Terran. Your mother's name was Apsara. She is dead. Your brother is sitting beside you."

"Joppa, that can't be," Darby was shaking, "My parents would have told me about a sister when they told me I was adopted."

"They never knew," she countered; "the girl child was stolen even before Apsara ever saw her. Everyone involved in your adoption thought it best not to burden your new parents with the scandal. No one wanted to scare them away."

"Lies!...I don't know who or what you are, but you are not the little slave girl I thought was my friend," Beacon could feel the panic rising in her chest, "Why are you saying these things? What do you hope to gain? You think I will convince my father to spare these abominations if I believe this one is my brother?...I will kill him myself at my first chance."

"Be silent, girl, for you know not what you say," Joppa was almost angry.

Beacon's mouth continued to move as she tried to speak, but no sound escaped her lips.

"Surely there has been some kind of mistake," Blair offered; "how would Darby's sister end up being raised by Adolphus here on Gehenna?"

"Lucien," Beacon's voice had returned, "He brought me here when I was born. A gift to my father…My people can not reproduce biologically. Longing for whatever is forbade him, Father wanted a child more than anything…Of course he would have preferred a son as heir, which is why his ever defiant lieutenant brought him a daughter. He took me into his hands with the intention of bashing me against a wall, but looked into my face and fell immediately in love…At least that's what he tells me."

"Isn't that just the sweetest," Honey whispered sarcasm.

"But why her?" Heather was next to speak, "How could the demon have known her brother's destiny. Why did he choose her?"

"This is perhaps the biggest surprise of all," Joppa joined them on the ground and leaned casually back against the tiger that had been lying at her feet. For an instant, Beacon saw the child-Joppa again. "It really was just coincidence...At least on Lucien's part. Of course, from God's perspective there is no coincidence. Lucien did not choose Beacon because of who she was. He had already taken a thousand babies of many species for his king's consideration. Adolphus had killed them all...None were worthy...Until he saw Beacon...He did love her...Does still."

Darby's usual quick wit and sarcasm had deserted him. He could only sit and stare at the Princess of Legion sitting next to him. His sister. Full of piss and vinegar. She returned his gaze. The walls of her mind were crumbling...She somehow knew that this was Joppa, and she knew that this was true. This man was her brother. Her brother was Avatarn. Her father would not stop until he was dead.

"Oh, and that's not all," Joppa spoke again.

"You're fuckin' kiddin' me," Honey's mouth fell open. How much more could they take?

"The bond of twin siblings is very special," Joppa explained, "The fact that Darby is of the holy triad makes this relationship even more profound."

"What relationship?" Darby cut in, "We don't even know each other...She's a demon princess for Christ's sake."

"You have the same genes, the same blood," the priestess insisted, "You have more in common with this stranger than anyone else you have ever known."

"My head hurts." The spoiled princess wasn't accustomed to dealing with this much drama.

"Suck it up," Rachel poked her in the ribs, suddenly very jealous of this girl that was truly Darby's family.

"You need to know this," Joppa pushed on. "When the two of you combine your efforts, you possess another power...When holding hands, you are invisible to all but the Avatarn."

"Ridiculous," Beacon stated with disgust.

"Let's see," Darby grabbed her hand before she could pull away. Nothing happened.

"I told you, fool," the princess was pissed. No one had ever touched her without permission except Lucien. And one dead soldier.

"I said combined effort, Beacon Elisondre Dragor," Joppa was out of patience.

Beacon turned back to the absurdly attractive new brother who was still holding her hand. She was feeling a little overwhelmed by his proximity, but with the slightest concentration on her part, the two of them began to fade from sight.

"It's working!" Josh barked in amazement. Score one more for the Avatarn. That is if this little bitch would be willing to help them.

Only Blair and Roman could see them, until Beacon reluctantly pulled her hand away and they both shimmered back into view.

Darby was feeling somewhat overwhelmed himself. A few minutes ago he had been an only child. Jesus protect my sister from her father, he silently prayed. And if she turns out to be daddy's little girl, protect us from her.

Beacon was crying. Darby wanted to comfort her, but had no idea how to. Honey tried to put an arm around her shoulders which racked with sobs, but the princess only glared at her briefly before crab-walking backwards on her hands and feet to the relative isolation of the other side of the corridor. Joppa was as surprised as everyone else, because she knew those royal hands had never touched a floor.

Roman turned back towards the magical guide that was sometimes his daughter, but Joppa was gone. No trace of her or the tiger remained. The group talked quietly among themselves while waiting for Beacon to get hold of herself. The shock of this new revelation wasn't going to excuse her from leading them to Paolo.

Josh was the first one to begin watching as the princess sat crying into her knees, her face mostly hidden by her falling blonde tresses. "What is she doing?" he asked to everyone listening.

"What?" Rachel wanted him to clarify as they all turned to face the girl on the floor.

"Oooohhh, Her Royal Bitchiness has done gone crazy," Honey drawled before realizing Darby might be offended, "Oops. Sorry, Baby…I shouldn't've called your crazy demon sister a bitch. I just meant she's talkin' to herself."

Darby doesn't have a comeback, Roman thought to himself. This is an occasion.

None of them could see that within the shroud of her hair Beacon was staring into a giant onyx bracelet. She was looking at her father, and talking to him live through the two-way communication stone he had given her as a child. He wore the match of the pair, and was speaking to her from Earth. She quickly informed him of the situation, and though he was horrified he informed her that he could not leave the invasion forces at that moment. He had dreamed of possessing Earth for too long.

Lucien was dispatched immediately. His mission was to protect the princess at all costs, and to take her to the safety of her father's side. Lucien's handsome face joined her father's deep below the surface of the shiny onyx, and he assured her he would be at her side in an instant. She stopped him with a warning. In a direct confrontation the Avatarn might destroy him. She instructed him not to come directly to her, but to follow them and plot his move. She said nothing of Joppa or her new brother.

"Are you all right?" Beacon jumped when Blair laid a hand on her shoulder, "Who are you talking to?"

"I was just praying that *The One Who Sits Apart* might turn His back on you. Abandon you all as the one called Apsara once abandoned myself and your friend. I prayed that He abide by His famous neutrality and leave your fates to my father," Beacon paused only for an instant to catch her breath.

"Sorry I asked," Blair shrugged and returned to her friends.

No one suspected the hidden communication, and only Beacon knew that Lucien had joined them and was nearby.

Chapter 16

"Let's go," Roman moved quickly to Beacon and pulled her up from the floor. "You'll have to mull over your new identity on your own time. Take us to the dungeon. No more stalling."

"My father will burn you alive for this!" She spat at him.

"Let him try," Roman replied calmly, "I have a feeling it wouldn't be the first time that happened to me." He was developing an awareness of the eternal nature of the human soul. How could I have been so dim about all this before, he thought to himself.

"Which way, Sis?" Darby demanded with a sneer. How could he ever have shared a womb with this spoiled bitch? A flick of her eyes indicated the corridor they were seeking, and everyone fell into line behind Darby. Roman was quick to take the princess forward to guide her new brother.

The ancient stone halls had the ambiance of catacombs, and, though torches lined the walls, they were dark by modern standards. Blair was becoming convinced that the princess was leading them astray when she turned them down another long and twisting corridor. She didn't have to wonder for long.

Darby was staring at his sister as they walked (with Roman still holding her arm). He was wondering if he would ever love her, when a group of Legion soldiers rounded the corner in front of them. It was no accident. They had obviously been made aware of the intruders. "You Bitch!" Josh wanted to strangle Beacon with her own hair. As he was about to reach for the golden curls in front of him, the unmistakable racket of more demon guards filed in behind them. The group spun to see the danger from the rear, and Blair wished she hadn't been tagging behind. Lucien stood only an arms-length away from her.

As always, he was a vision to behold. His shiny black toga matched perfectly his black hair and eyes, and his body was the male ideal. Beacon was overjoyed to see him and started forward, only to be held back by Roman's firm grasp. Lucien's face showed no trace of concern. He smiled at Blair, the lovely witch that hated him most of all for killing her sisters. Pity he couldn't taste this one before killing her too, he thought to himself. Oh, well, the princess would soon be his bride, and he would inherit the Unseen Kingdom.

"Unhand her," Lucien's command was spoken softly but with force.

"Not this time, Caligula," Roman tightened his grip.

"The king himself will kill you for laying hands on his daughter," Lucien took a step forward; Blair, a step back, but his eyes never left Roman.

"Maybe you should be more concerned about what he's gonna do to you when he finds out the infant you stole to become his daughter is the sister of an Avatarn," Darby was none too gentle as he grabbed Beacon's face, pressing her cheek to his own, "Twins… How 'bout that, you bastard?"

Lucien was speechless. It couldn't be. How could he not have known? He didn't even want to imagine Adolphus' outrage.

"Perhaps a trade then," the handsome demon began as he reached for Blair. She was too scared to react in time, but Heather was not. The streetwise angel had been standing at her side, and shoved her beyond his grasp, only to be captured herself. "Well, well, I had forgotten about you HeaTheriel. Still wasting time with humans. After all these millennia, why do you still degrade yourself?"

"You're the one that has lowered yourself, Lucien," Heather spat back at him, struggling in vain to free herself from his massive arms, "How can you have so completely forgotten yourself?"

"Spare the song and dance, little sister. I am not a prodigal son. I was never content to serve. It is my destiny to rule. My king was not the only one to adopt the great idiom 'Better to rule in Hell than serve in Heaven,'" Lucien held the petite angel's back to his chest.

"But you don't rule anywhere, Lucy," Darby interrupted his little speech.

"For now," the demon countered, and in the same instant a silver dagger appeared in his hand. It would have been over in an instant, but the reflection in Blair's horror-filled eyes showed Heather what was about to happen. Without hesitation, she reached behind her and under Lucien's toga. She grabbed his balls and squeezed with all of her might. The silver knife froze mid-swing towards her heart and fell to the floor. Lucien gasped for air and unthinkingly released the raven haired girl. She grabbed the knife and did a tuck-and-roll to avoid his flailing arms. She bounced back to her feet and lunged with the dagger. He avoided the blade by a hair's width, and dematerialized, only to reappear with the soldiers at the other end of the corridor. One swift motion freed the princess from enemy clutches, and she clung to her father's second-in-command.

"Kill them all," Lucien ordered as he and the rescued princess shimmered and were gone.

Darby started to raise a force field that would have protected them all, but it had only expanded enough to engulf himself when the first immense sword bounced off the energy shield.

A large green-skinned demon grabbed Josh's shoulder with one hand and flung him through the air to bounce off an unforgiving wall. Heather used that moment to jump on the monster's back and slide the knife across his throat. His fall to the ground sent Heather rolling across the floor, dagger still in hand.

The alien that attacked Roman wasn't expecting any real resistance, so the Avatarn's well placed kicks and punches took him by surprise. Roman took his sword and with a powerful swoosh, removed his head from his shoulders. To the amazement of the humans, the creature didn't die. The body got to its knees, feeling blindly for the necessary appendage, while the head lay where it had rolled, shouting curses at its clumsy missing parts. Roman dashed to Josh's side. He was motionless where he had landed. Roman couldn't take his attention off the swords clashing with his own long enough to heal Joshua, though one hand passed over the broken body somehow told him it was Josh's back that was shattered.

It was then that Honey stepped to his side. She took the sword and battled to provide cover allowing Roman to finally turn his powers towards Josh. Roman was gaining more control over his gift, and managed to subdue the blinding white light, confining it to his friend's injured flesh. In a flash, Josh began to stir, and Roman helped him to his feet. He offered a quick hug as thanks, and Roman accepted it humbly.

Rachel had set more than a few dozen demons ablaze with the torch she had grabbed from the wall, but she was encircled when Darby saw that his friend was in immediate peril. Balls of golden energy erupted from his chest, flying directly into the heart of each alien and exploding. The gore rained down on all of them, but faded out of existence only seconds later. Darby ran to Rachel and extended his personal force field around her.

With a few words mumbled under her breath, Blair's body began to change. When the mutation was complete, she had become a massive gorilla. Employing little effort, she began to swat the soldiers aside to clear a path for their escape. It was then that Lucien appeared, grabbing Heather from behind and snatching the dagger from her small hand.

Expecting the gorilla to attempt to rescue the angel, the demon was taken off guard, when instead, Blair reached out her long simian arm and wrangled the dagger from his grasp. She grunted a message as she turned hurling the knife towards Darby. He heard,

"Heads up, Dar. Keep this safe." As the knife approached him, it slowed in mid-air and came to a stop. Suspended a foot in front of him. Darby grabbed it and shoved it into his belt.

A kick to the face from Lucien sent Gorilla Blair scurrying away.

The fighting had stopped, as holy pilgrims and demon soldiers alike waited for Lucien's next move.

"I'm not afraid of you," Heather said, calmly looking into the eyes of the man-like being that had violently jerked her head back by a fist full of hair.

"You should be, little one," Lucien bowed his head to kiss her passionately, invasively, before moving his lips down to her neck. In an instant he was biting. Tearing out her throat. He chewed and swallowed as he raised his head to look into the Avatarn's eyes. His face and body were covered with the blood that continued to spray from HeaTheriel's body.

The humans couldn't move. Struck dumb by the absolute horror of what they had just witnessed, they couldn't even speak. As Lucien began to laugh uproariously, the lifeless angel and the gruesome spectacle of her blood faded into nothingness. Gone forever. Roman was thankful that Tyler and Mateo weren't there, knowing they would already have sacrificed their lives in a futile attempt at revenge.

"Where is Beacon?" Darby finally managed to mutter in Lucien's direction. She was starting to matter to him, despite his better judgment.

"The princess is safely in my care, my sweet young fagola," the demon responded with a flirtatious wink. "Pitiful," he continued, his gaze turning to Blair, again in human form, "You barely knew HeaTheriel and yet tears burn your face as they did for your whore sisters."

"Not as much as they are going to burn yours," Blair growled as she wiped her fingers across her face gathering a river of tears to fling towards the devil before her. Somehow the teardrops multiplied as they left her hand to splash over Lucien like the contents of a bucket. The witch's tears burned him like acid and he cried out in crippling pain. He convulsed and vanished.

Without their leader to punish them for retreat, the soldiers scattered in the directions from which they came, none willing to meet the same fate as their master. Blair smiled, but only for a moment. Heather. Their angel was dead.

Beacon was waiting comfortably in her own bedroom, far away from the danger of the Avatarn in the dungeon wing. She would see that Lucien was well rewarded for her rescue. She might even let him…Her thoughts were interrupted by bold knocking at her door. Lucien had dismissed the servants that normally attended her in her quarters so she need not suffer the indignity of being seen in such disarray. She would have to get the door herself. She had nearly reached it, when someone barged in locking the door behind him. It was the Avatarn called Darby. Her brother.

She was only frightened for a moment. He was too handsome to fear, and he was after all her brother. Besides, Lucien would be along to kill him shortly. "How dare you?" She shouted and used all of her strength to slap him across the face.

"I saw the way you were looking at me, Sis. I know you're hot for me. This is our chance to become better acquainted," he added, grabbing her small waist and smashing her against himself. She could feel that he was hard, and suddenly she *was* afraid. Anger had deserted her, and she was alone with a madman.

One hand seized the back of her head and he began kissing her. She scratched and fought, but the muscles that covered him made her efforts pointless.

"But I'm your sister!" She sobbed, as large hands tore away her ruby gown.

"Incest is best…Isn't that what they say, Sis? I know you're attracted to me…No point in playing hard to get. I know you've probably been with half your father's army by now," he added with a shove that sent her sprawling onto her bed.

"For your information, Brother, my purity remains intact. It is by my father's decree and my choice that it will remain so until I am married," she was trembling but fought to maintain an air of prideful aloofness as her arrogant new sibling stared lustily at her nakedness and slowly undressed.

"You're gonna like this, Sissy," Darby was almost drooling as he climbed on top of her, rubbing his cock against any part of her that he could.

"How could you, who are *The Chosen* of *He Who Sits Apart*, violate your own sister like this?" Beacon had become calm, no longer even crying as she resigned herself to the inevitable. Besides, she knew Lucien would cut out his heart before he even finished the deed.

She didn't resist when he forced himself inside of her, though he was big and it hurt more than she had anticipated. He fucked like an animal, and to her shame, the virgin princess found that she was beginning to like it. His brute strength filled her again and again and soon the weight and the rhythm had driven everything else from her mind. She had given herself over to him until a final savage thrust awoke her from the trance. He was cumming inside of her, and somehow it burned her and felt cold at the same time. How could he? Her body had betrayed her in this battle, but her spirit's shout for justice echoed through her mind. She couldn't take back what she had allowed him to finish. Freeing a wrist that had been pinned above her head, she lashed at him with everything her stolen innocence demanded. Her long beautifully sculpted fingernails raked across his pretty face. A double slash split the skin of his chiseled jaw, and he turned his back on her before the blood even reached the surface.

"I knew you would like it, princess," Darby picked up his clothes and headed to the door without even bothering to turn around, "Don't worry, I'll be back for more." He was still naked when he left her room.

Lucien missed his chance, she thought. I'm killing my brother myself.

Beacon had just finished bathing and dressing when her silver door flew open again. Honey strolled in with no apologies and popping her knuckles, "I know you didn't just come up here for a costume change, girl." The rest of the gang was close behind her. Beacon was afraid, but the small laser pistol she had strapped to her wrist underneath the flowing sleeves of a new gown was giving her the courage to face them.

The princess didn't question how they had found her, assuming that whatever evil powers had led her brother to her chambers had brought the rest of them as well. Blair was just thanking God that her idea to follow the slave girl carrying a tray of women's jewelry had paid off. They had first spied her after returning to the main floor. Maintaining a respectable distance, they went mostly unnoticed, lingering in the shadows until Beacon had turned the young servant away with some yelling and jewels scattered on the floor. The slave scrambled to return the treasures to her tray and take her leave before she was punished.

When Darby casually walked in with the other Avatarn, Beacon was prepared to shoot him. She wouldn't wait for Lucien or her father to exact revenge on her psychotic brother. Roman had just begun to demand that she accompany them back to the dungeon to find Paolo when she drew the weapon.

"Whoa there, Highness," Roman slowly raised his hands in a show of submission, "Nobody's going to hurt you, Miss…We can talk about this."

"Talk to my brother," Beacon hissed, "Let him explain my need to result to violence."

"What are you talking about, Twisted Sister?" Darby was baffled as he and Blair took positions at Roman's sides. Beacon turned the gun towards her brother's abdomen.

"You have the nerve to deny it?...Of course…You don't want your friends to know how vile you really are…Well, I'll tell them," she was furious.

"Be my guest," Darby had no idea what she was ranting about.

"He raped me," Beacon stated through clenched teeth, turning her head and repeating it twice more to any who may not have heard.

"Impossible," Rachel replied with a snicker until she realized she was serious.

"Darby has been with us since the moment you disappeared with Lucien," Josh assured her.

"Besides, Sugar…He be gay," Honey chimed in.

"I don't know that word," Beacon looked a little confused, but mostly angry, "I can prove it. I scratched his fa—," her words faded as she simultaneously realized Darby's lovely face was as flawless and undamaged as the moment she had first laid eyes on him, "But how?...There were two gashes on his cheek…You healed him," she accused Roman, her confidence restored.

"I promise I did not," Roman thought the day had been too much for the frazzled princess and she was probably projecting some guilt-ridden fantasy of her new brother onto his innocent friend.

"Liar!" She raised the gun slightly preparing to fire her revenge into Darby's gut.

Blair acted on instinct. It was becoming her style. She kissed her finger tips and blew the kiss at Beacon. An incredible burst of wind hit the princess, tossing her across the room. The laser was lost under the bed.

Lucien materialized at her side. "Get behind me, Princess," he commanded. She only stared from her place on the floor. The Avatarn and friends were equally stunned. Two long gashes lacerated the demon's face.

"It was you," Beacon was trembling with shock.

The demon hesitated, uncertain of his next move. Darby didn't hesitate. He stepped to his sister's side, and taking her hand, they vanished.

Lucien was stunned by their disappearance. The legends had not foretold any of the Avatarn having such powers.

Roman dove under the bed to find the missing laser pistol.

Lucien grabbed him by the ankle, hoisting him into the air without straining his arm. "Do me a favor while you're down there," the demon smirked, pushing Roman's head toward his crotch.

Unable to think of a spell, Blair leapt forward, pounding her fists against the alien attempting to humiliate the man she was growing to love.

Lucien only laughed in her face, unfazed by her physical assault. Both were too distracted by the altercation to see the laser float from under the bed and stop at waist level. It was pointed at the battling warriors. The sudden look of shock on Lucien's face stopped Blair's barrage of punches. Roman dropped to the floor and looked up to see the scorched hole, where the laser beam had burned through the demon's toga impacting at his rib cage. The alien flesh showed no sign of burns, though it was slightly red. Lucien was stunned and confused. He stumbled backwards, hitting the wall, and escaped by disappearing in a shimmer of air. Roman finished climbing to his feet and took Blair into his arms. "My hero," he said with a quick peck on her full lips.

When Darby and Beacon parted hands, they slowly became visible again. To the pilgrims' surprise, it was Beacon who held the gun. She had shot Lucien herself. This bit of revenge had gone a long way towards healing the trauma of her rape, and she was calm when she lowered the weapon and turned to face her brother. "I'm sorry that I blamed you for this sick crime. In my heart, I couldn't believe it was true, buy my mind played my father's advocate…I will help you find your friend," she finished with a quick hug, then pushed herself away. Not all of her feelings for her brother were appropriate.

"Why can't I be one of the *Wonder Twins*?" Rachel whined to Josh.

"Not easy being a muggle, aye, Sweetheart?" Darby was only half teasing.

"What *IS* that like?" Honey turned towards Rachel, "Cause Honey makes her own magic."

"So why's everybody just looking at me," Rachel was actually a bit offended and locked eyes with Josh.

"Fairy Magic," Josh stated casually with a flip of the wrist and a wink.

"You guys all suck," Rachel hated it when the gang rubbed her face in her *normalness*. She didn't quite have their flair for drama and eccentricity, but she was the one that kept them all grounded. She was the *super-hag* that kept these fairies from floating away.

With the princess as escort, the pilgrims navigated the stairs and endless corridors much more efficiently than before and were soon in the dungeon wing. They encountered some monster guards a few times, but a nod of the royal head dismissed them without fuss and they moved quickly towards a remote cell.

"This room is reserved for special prisoners." Beacon's voice revealed that she was learning to feel ashamed of her heritage and the evils perpetrated by her father. "I believe your friend will be in here."

Darby peered through the small barred window into the relative darkness for nearly a minute before his eyes adjusted enough to make out the individual curled in a ball on a nest of straw. "It's him." He was without doubt.

"Unlock it." Josh wasn't timid about giving the royal bitch an order.

"I don't have keys, you fool," she snapped back. Though Darby was feeling the beginning of a connection, it was apparent that his sister and his friends might never call a truce.

"Paolo, we're here, Baby," Darby called into the cell as loudly as he dared. Paolo raised his head for a second, but quickly dismissed the shadowy silhouette at the door as more harassment from the guards.

"We can't get in," Roman was trying to shake the immovable door.

"I can," Blair stepped forward with a grin and wiggled her nose.

Chapter 17

Blair's incantation poured out in a rushed whisper:

"Nighttime's owl with eyes so bright,
Lend me wing so that I might
Pass this door to dark's domain,
To free my friend from prison's chain."

By the time the last words escaped her lips she had begun to change. She morphed into a small barn owl, and with a brief pause at the window, flew into the cell. Darby's head blocked the others' view, as he watched his friend fly to a small ledge above his lover. Paolo refused to look, assuming another bat was rustling about.

When a human voice began to emanate from the tiny sharp beak, he spun to face the small bird and scattered straw in every direction as he scrambled for the imagined safety of the corner:

"Serpent slither, creature small,
That I might carry beyond this wall."

Blair fanned her wings and Paolo stopped trembling as he began to shrink and his form blurred and he changed into a small snake. The owl swooped down and snatched into her claws the writhing animal attempting to hide in the dirty straw. She flew to the ledge of the barred window, and dropped the snake into Darby's waiting hand. He would have been terrified of any snake but this one.

"Saints of Hades, preserve us," Beacon uttered in shock at the magical display happening before her. This kind of power was greater than even she was accustomed to.

Blair didn't have to make up another incantation. Without a word, she and Paolo slowly morphed back into human form. Paolo was still in Darby's arms, and, clearly confused, his damaged mind found refuge in his lover's embrace. Though he seemed afraid of the others, he was smiling a little, and Darby was sure he heard his name being whispered against his chest.

Rachel was quietly praying aloud for Paolo's troubled mind, and Honey took her hand, bowing her head to add her plea for God's intercession. Paolo had been scarred by horrors they didn't even want to imagine, and the boy they had come to take home was a broken replica of his former self.

"You're okay now, Baby," Darby tried to force Paolo to meet his gaze, but too many beatings had taught him not to make eye contact. The Avatarn's eyes became wet as the realization set in that *his Paolo* was gone, and the one in his arms was a frightened animal, abused beyond comprehension by hordes of demons. Darby swore an oath to himself; Adolphus would pay with his life.

"Obviously, our naked friend here is in no condition to travel, but we gotta get moving," Josh coaxed.

"Hold on," Roman let go of Blair's hand and stepped towards the reunited couple, "I wanna try something."

Paolo flinched as the raven-haired older Avatarn gently placed his palm on the trauma victim's forehead. Re-assured by Darby's tightening hug, he forced himself to resist the urge to pull away. Roman threw all of his energy into healing the battered mind, but the healing white light he was growing accustomed to failed to appear.

"Why it ain't workin'?" Honey wondered aloud.

"I…Don't…Know," Roman was as baffled as the rest.

Darby's eyes began to glisten. What was he going to do to burn away this fog that not even Ro's healing light could penetrate?

"Of course," Roman's face suddenly turned from grim to renewed hope, "I should have known." Without moving his right hand from Paolo's dirty forehead, he placed his left on Darby's muscle-hard chest. White light began to pulse from Roman's hand in time with the beating of Dar's heart. As it spread up the healer's arm and across his body and other arm, it continued to pulse. This was different from anything Roman had done before. His power was acting as a conduit for Darby's love to repair Paolo's tortured psyche. The intense white light lingered around his head before spreading to illuminate his entire bruised body. In a flash it was gone, and the familiar gleam returned to Paolo's gaze.

"I'm back," he grinned, not the least embarrassed by his nudity. Grabbing the back of Roman's head, he pulled him in for a quick peck on the lips. "Thank you," he mouthed to his healer.

"Thank God," Darby interjected, the tears finally sliding passed his cheeks into his open smile.

"Your rude friend is correct," Beacon hated to interrupt her brother's joyous moment by referring to Josh's last comment, but their very lives were in peril, "Lucien has alerted the guards by now. Escape may already be impossible, but time is still of the essence." She spun on her heels and was moving down a corridor without waiting to see if they followed. Her Highness was not in the habit of considering others. It was their duty to attend her.

As they moved through the castle, Josh, Honey, and Rachel couldn't help being distracted by what Darby already knew. Paolo had a beautiful body, and he somehow seemed especially naked with everyone else fully clothed. The display of moving muscle and bouncing maleness diverted more attention than they could spare. An amused Darby, having noticed their reaction, decided to play the gentleman by removing his shirt and tying it apron-style around Paolo's waist. It hadn't occurred to him that his own body was equally impressive eye-candy.

Their sizable group moved quickly and quietly behind Beacon's lead. Sporadically, they encountered small guard units blocking their path, but after hesitating, all stepped aside in obedience to the princess. It was dangerous for them to defy Lucien, but if disrespecting the royal daughter angered Adolphus, his wrath would be fatal.

More than a few of the holy pilgrims took note as they fled down yet another dark hallway of a cavernous room, open to much of the length of the corridor save for giant stone pillars every three yards. It was filled with cribs and children's beds. A grand nursery. An ancient chamber, filled with new life. Nannies in the forms of every monster ever imagined moved among the children, rocking infants and playing with toddlers. Many were human. Many were alien. All seemed well cared for. Honey and Blair had to force themselves to keep running, reminding themselves that their first duty was to Earth and the greater good. Roman hesitated as the habit-clad woman who appeared to be head governess locked eyes with him. He was struck by her extraordinary resemblance to Mother Teresa. A knowing nod from the old woman released him from his contemplation, and he raced to catch up to the others, convinced that the familiar visage was a remarkable coincidence.

The demonic courtiers that worked and loitered in the great hall stopped to stare at the princess' entourage, some with glowing blue halos.

No one interfered until they approached the main gate, where Lucien's most loyal lieutenants were prepared for battle.

Beacon didn't think they would stand down, even for her. She was torn by the thought of her kidnapping being stopped inside the castle confines. She had to escape Lucien, and the best way to do that was to let these humans take her to Earth. To her father. One hundred yards still separated the opposing parties, when a large black slave, wearing only a loincloth, rapidly approached the princess with the premise of offering a tray of fruit. She was prepared to dismiss him with a wave of her hand, when he spoke.

"Your Highness, I am Zanzibar. I can show you a secret way out of the castle. You have only but to take me with you."

Beacon hesitated, but Roman stepped forward responding to the bold slave with, "Let's go."

The tall and handsome Zan turned, tossing his tray to the floor and sprinting towards a small side room. The pilgrims were right behind him, and the demon guards were rushing across the modest distance that still separated them.

Josh brought up the tail of the Earth group, and ran into the room just in time to hear the slave shout, "This way!" before dashing into a giant, dark fireplace. The others didn't hesitate to follow him in and start climbing. Metal rungs lined the interior of the vast chimney. All climbed as fast as they could until halfway up, Zan stepped onto the ledge that backed another fireplace. Fortunately, Josh was well above the original floor, because the rebel slave flipped a switch on the wall causing a large fire to roar to life in the main floor hearth. The flames licked at Josh's shoes as he scrambled up the ancient ladder as fast as his usually keyboard-punching hands would carry him.

All of the Avatarn had reached the ledge when they heard the alien soldiers storm the room below. The demons lingered only a moment before moving on to search other chambers. Zanzibar's plan had worked perfectly. Thank God for disgruntled help Josh thought to himself.

The upper level room they entered via the second cold fireplace was also deserted. Their new guide hurried to a massive wooden wardrobe, jerking open the heavy doors to grab an armful of the hooded cloaks inside. He quickly distributed them to the group. Beacon sneered at the shoddy peasant garment, but a chastising glare from her brother convinced her to pull on the rough cape and raise the hood as the others donned their disguises.

"Now what, Brown Sugar?" Honey purred and batted her eyes at the well-built slave.

"Follow," Zan replied, moving to a large window. They were only about three floors up, but it was too far to jump. Zan ripped down a long velveteen drape. They tore and tied it until it was long enough to reach the ground. All held onto the end as each climbed down in turn. Honey insisted she would go last. She would tie the heavy curtain to something, and then join them on the ground. When nothing presented itself as an obvious anchor, the young drag queen prepared herself to stay behind. "Diana was right," she whispered to herself, forgetting to affect a feminine sounding voice as she recalled the prophecy the people's princess had revealed to her in a dream. She would sacrifice herself to save the others.

"Jump, damn it!" Josh was yelling up to her in a stage whisper. The others immediately chimed in. They refused to leave without her, so she finally gave in, stepping onto the window ledge and falling backwards. She expected to hit the ground with a splat, but was only a little bruised by the impact with many determined arms. Safely on the ground, Honey wondered if Di had been wrong after all.

"We must still cross the moat," Zan wasn't going to allow them a breather. All adjusted their cloaks and followed his lead as they mingled in with the parade of peasants that flowed both ways over the huge drawbridge. Honey brought up the rear, and the others had all crossed without harassment when a guard noticed the tall girl in the brown cloak reaching only to her shins. On her feet were size 13 silver stilettos. Heather's powers only lasted so long beyond her death, and their clothes had started reverting to normal.

The demon's fur-covered hand latched onto her arm, causing the lovely black Earthling to lose her balance as she swung her purse to bust the monster in his face.

"Honey!" Joppa screamed from a tower window, but it was too late. The other members of the Avatarn's party turned back just in time to see their friend topple from the rail-less bridge. She hadn't even reached the water, when a great white shark broke the surface to catch the fallen damsel in its toothy jaws.

Blood surrounded her torso as the beast chomped and Honey's eyes locked with the holy ones for a final instant. "Meet you in the clouds," she mouthed before forcing a smile. With a splash she was gone below the surface.

"She actually smiled," Rachel whispered in admiration and

horror. The gruesome incident had caused a small riot on and around the bridge. The crowd stampeded, pushing others and causing them to fall into the murky depths. Only a few resurfaced at all before disappearing forever. Blair couldn't force herself to move, and Roman was finally left with no choice but to carry her back to the boulder where they had first materialized on Gehenna. Though still in shock, Blair gathered her thoughts enough to stand and join hands with the other Avatarn around their tightly clustered friends. Since their arrival, they had lost two and gained three. Blair felt they had lost too much in the trade.

Some of the demon soldiers had nearly reached them, swords drawn, when the holy triad linked hands and began their chant. Beacon, Paolo, and Zan were especially shocked when the monsters froze in place. Giant vultures and space shuttles were motionless in the sky. Time stopped outside the magic circle as a black void opened below their feet. Suddenly the rescuers and the rescued were falling through space. They crashed hard on the concrete floor of the warehouse they called their *Palace*.

For an instant, Tyler and Mateo thought it hadn't worked. Nothing had happened except they all fell down. Then it hit them. Heather and Honey had disappeared…And in their places were Paolo, a nearly naked black man, and what looked like a movie-harem-girl. It had worked. And something was horribly wrong.

"Where the fuck are they?" Tyler shouted.

Blair started sobbing.

"Tyler, just calm down," Roman commanded. He knew the boys' reaction to the loss of their friends – especially Heather – was going to be violent and extreme. He hoped he could rein it in.

"What fucking happened?" Mateo was getting hysterical too. Many of the homeless residents of *The Palace* gathered near, afraid to hear what had befallen their friends. It was Darby that spoke next.

"They're dead…." He mumbled first, then shouted it again to the ceiling beams.

Tyler fell backwards, sitting down hard on the cracked cement. He shook his head like a horse trying to dispatch a buzzing fly. He was trying to make his brain work. It wasn't effective, because he couldn't have heard what Darby just said. Heather was an angel. She couldn't die. Worse still, all he could think about was how she had explained to him that angels don't have souls that exist separate from their bodies. Angels were created to live eternally in their semi-divine bodies. If they were somehow destroyed, there was nothing to separate and carry on. That wasn't the plan. Only humans existed as sparks of God inserted temporarily into delicate shells. If Darby was right, there would be no after life for sweet HeaTheriel. She would be gone forever.

The new arrivals from planet Gehenna had climbed to their feet, but didn't stray from the spots where they had landed. The Avatarn and friends moved to comfort Tyler, Mateo, and each other, though still in shock themselves. Beacon and Zan stood rooted to their spots, taking in the scenery of what appeared to be a poor and dreary new world.

"This is the planet Father had to possess?" The princess thought to herself.

"What happened to them?" Mateo managed to stutter. Rachel was heartbroken over Honey, but had always been a little jealous of the attention Heather got from the boys. Though traumatized by the event of her slaying, she secretly admitted to herself that she really wouldn't miss the punk angel. Slowly she slipped an arm around the trembling Mateo and proceeded to fill in the boys and the gathering on all of the tragic details. When she had finished most of the eyes were dry again. Hearts had been quickly hardened by their recently terror-filled lives.

After a silent moment, Paolo — having slipped on a pair of jeans offered by the crowd — stepped forward to take Beacon and Zan by their hands and introduce them to the *courtiers* of their new, more humble *Palace*.

As if the assembled freedom fighters hadn't been shocked enough by the losses, they were blind-sided by Beacon's astounding double identity. She was the princess of Legion *AND* twin sister to an Avatarn. More than one person fainted upon finding himself face to face with the demon king's daughter. However, none dared disrespect the born sibling of a holy one.

It was Josh who rapidly explained how such a connection was possible. For Beacon's part, she raised her chin and silently looked on with disdain. There was much grieving around the barrel fires before the exhausted portal travelers and the members of their sanctuary settled down and surrendered to the restorative oblivion of sleep's embrace.

Darby had been forced to wrestle his sister to the ground and wrap himself around her to hold her there. It was beneath her royal personage to sleep on a floor, lying in filth, so Dar had lifted from her the burden of choice. She fought him only briefly, before letting the comfort of his strong arms and the warmth of his breath on her neck soothe her fears and her resentment. She didn't want to trust him, but she did. She slept the sleep of a child whose resistance to stillness is overcome by the patient determination of family's insistent security.

No one noticed the slight violet glow of the onyx bracelet on her wrist.

The bridge of the starship *Caiphas* was abuzz with activity. Ranking officers moved from station to station coordinating the multi-pronged attacks on Earth. Though the flagship still hovered over Kansas City, the staff issued directives to every other ship in the armada, arranging transportation of the newly collected slaves, fighting on the planet's surface; and in many cases, causing city-wide destruction from the air. Violet lasers and sonic weapons rippled through the air crumbling or erasing buildings or entire blocks. It was Adolphus' intention that any surviving humans left behind by the herding shuttles would find themselves living in a stone age. Civilization would never again show its face on Earth. The demon king watched from a towering window in the saucer's hull and found himself smiling at his final confrontation with this world. He had all but forgotten the perilous predicament of his daughter when Lucien appeared in a flicker beside him.

"Your Worship," the rogue soldier bowed, "I bring news of the Princess Beacon. Her captors have escaped with her to Earth and even now lurk somewhere below this very ship."

"I shall lead a rescue team myself," Adolphus' gold eyes flashed, "Though I would have pin-pointed my daughter's location in time using our communicator bracelets, that technology has become unnecessary. There is a traitor in the Avatarn's midst. He wrote me a note and pinned it to a child's garment, then sent the child, unattended, into the streets. Of course our soldiers seized the child and transported him to the slave holds with the rest of the new herd. Some wretch of a woman read the message and thought to procure my favor by presenting it to a guard. The hand-scribbled note reveals the exact location of their sanctuary and other relevant details. Of course, I had the woman killed. Anyone who would turn on her own people that easily won't even make a decent field slave. I did have the boy taken aside though. Beacon's nanny on Gehenna has mentioned that she would enjoy an exotic pet. She's beaten to death the last several pets my daughter has given her, but this child seems of sturdy stock."

Though Lucien was bored by the digression, he feigned interest as was expected.

"Forgive my interruption Lord, but who is this that betrays the triad?" The alien second in command hoped that his insolence would not anger his master.

"What? Oh…In this life he calls himself Mateo, but I knew him long ago," Adolphus smirked, "His name then was Judas."

"I guess some people have to learn their lessons more than once," Lucien smiled back.

"This time, however, the deal will not be sealed with a kiss, but with fire. Before, he committed his vile act in service of his Lord. This time he acts in service of me." Adolphus began to pace with anticipation, his long clingy robes swaying around him, "And what of my daughter," her barked; "is she unharmed?" The demon leader held his breath for the answer.

"I'm sorry to report that she has been damaged, Majesty," Lucien was scared to even say it, "She was violated by one of His *Chosen Ones*."

Lucien flinched at the roar that Adolphus unleashed. The king's face turned purple with rage, blood vessels standing out on his shaven head.

"I'll destroy the entire species," he bellowed. All activity among the bridge crew had ceased. "I'll reduce this worthless shithole of a fringe planet to a dust cloud"; acid tears burned his cheeks as they etched their paths down his face. The king of Legion hadn't cried in over two thousand years. Lucien had seen him mad on many occasions, but nothing on this scale. He hoped his lie had not driven his master to such distraction that his plan would fail. Swallowing his fear, he stepped forward, sliding his hands over Adolphus' smooth chest, exposed by his open robes.

"Master, this talk of the carnage you will rain down on the holy ones is arousing me as nothing ever has before. Allow me to pleasure you before you take your revenge. Then I will make it my personal responsibility to learn which of the humans dared force himself on your child," Lucien closed his verbal come-on with an aggressive kiss, pushing his tongue into the other's mouth at great risk.

Adolphus was slightly surprised by his second's lusty advance. Of course they had fucked many times over the centuries, but this was not the time. The thought of violent and fatal revenge on his long prophesied opponents was giving him an amazing hard-on. He decided a full-throttle sexcapade with the only creature that could take him at full blast might be just the thing to focus his mind before he killed the Avatarn.

He broke the kiss as he rubbed his hands over Lucien's thick carpet of chest hair. His crimson toga, worn over one shoulder, allowed perfect access. It was only then that he spied the *decoration* his general had applied as an additional lure. Lu had rouged his nipples. Adolphus didn't know what manner of crimson stain had been used, but he suspected it would taste good. With a knowing chuckle, he lifted the warrior's well-developed pectoral and sucked the dark red nipple into his mouth. He feasted hungrily for a moment as Lucien moaned, until stopping abruptly, he raised his head to look questioningly into his subordinate's waiting face.

"How did you get it?" Adolphus squeaked as his throat began to swell, "He would never give this to you."

"Don't you remember, fool? I was there," Lucien sneered, "It was fun playing one of Pilate's thugs for a while. I just got in on a little of the scourging and collected His blood from the lash."

"Christ's blood," the demonic helm officer mumbled, surprised that even Lucien had the audacity to keep the divine sample through the millennia. It was the only substance in the universe sure to act as deadly poison in the body of evil incarnate, the only way to kill one so ancient and powerful.

Adolphus was still alive, though on his knees and gurgling, when Lucien ripped the onyx bracelet from his wrist and secured it on his own. The mighty demon lord was helpless to resist. Some of the bridge officers wondered how Lucien remained unharmed by the Holiest Blood, but the king knew that upper-level demons must actually ingest it for a reaction to occur.

The mutinous general was a little pissed to have to use the tracking technology of the bracelet to locate the Avatarn hideout instead of the information provided by the traitor, Mateo. However, he wasn't about to let anything ruin this illustrious moment. For a thousand years he had waited for the perfect chance to assassinate the devil lying before him. And just for an additional thrill, he fell to his knees and cradled the king's head in his lap, "Before you go," Lucien paused to allow a rapturous smile to spread across his face, "It was I that raped your daughter," and with a laugh, "Rape is the wrong word really…because she wanted it. She loved it." Adolphus' face was a mask of despair, until Lucien dropped his head and it cracked loudly on the floor. The general climbed to his feet as his master began to liquefy. The black goo puddled around his sandaled feet until it faded out of existence.

A lieutenant covered in reptilian scales was the first to bow shouting, "The king is dead. Long live the king. Long live King Lucien!"

The handsome devil proudly accepted the accolades of the soldiers that had witnessed his self-granted promotion, but he knew there was only one way to guarantee his unquestioned right to the dark throne. The Princess Beacon must become his wife.

Chapter 18

Mateo couldn't understand how everyone else seemed to be moving so quickly past their grief for Heather and Honey. Sure they were upset, but their intrigue over Zan, who though humanoid was not from Earth, and especially the demon princess, who had become their unwilling guest, seemed to outweigh their sorrow. They would all pay for their callousness. Mateo was glad he had sent the note to the evil king. In it he had demanded that he and Heather be spared, but his beloved Tyler and the rest were all fair game. He had come to the painful decision after following Ty and HeaTheriel to a clandestine meeting in a third floor closet. At first he had felt like a creep when he knelt in cliché at the keyhole. Watching as they passionately kissed, he was consumed with jealous thoughts of times when he had done the same with each of them. He could have dealt with the physical encounter, but when their whispers turned to debate over how to break the news of their deepening relationship to their Matelito, he was devastated. A switch was thrown in his heart, and his foot slid across the line between love and hate. His revenge would be as big as the world. It had taken a while for him to formulate a plan, but it had finally come to him.

He would let the devil do his dirty work. The previously good-natured boy hustler was dead inside. If Heather had lived, they'd have been together, and no one else would have mattered. Now nothing mattered, and he was glad they would all pay for their pathetically brief mourning.

Beacon had agreed to try the Pop-tarts Tyler had brought for them, but after one bite, she had wrinkled her nose and handed hers to Zan. Though she was hungry, the factory-made pastry couldn't compare to the poached dinosaur eggs that were her favorite. She hoped her father would find them before lunch.

Blair had been filling in the other Avatarn about Honey's dream of Diana, how their friend's death had been foretold. Roman's weary mind was divided between numbed pain from their most recent losses and a partially formed realization that the veil of protection that Heather's powers had afforded them would probably no longer shelter *The Palace* from demon eyes. Darby was trying to convince his sister to try some *campfire oatmeal* when Lucien materialized, standing atop a forklift. No one but Beacon understood that the silver laurel wreath that rested in his ebony hair was a crown. The implications were horrifying.

"Where is my father?" The princess demanded. The others scrambled to their feet. For several eternal seconds the demon intruder only smiled. As casually as possible, Darby changed position to place himself between his trembling sister and the beautiful monster.

"Adolphus Shaitan Dragor is dead!" Lucien finally shouted, "I am now the Legion King. Bow before your new master, lowly cattle."

"Liar!" Beacon screamed, "I'll have you skinned alive for your insolence."

"I assure you, Highness. I dispatched him myself," he replied with a sneer and mock respect.

"Impossible! When my father arrives—"

He silenced her by casually raising his arm to display the onyx bracelet on his wrist. She knew then that it was true. Standing silently, she refused to shed the tears that stung her eyes or let the sobs that would later rack her body reveal even a momentary weakness.

Lucien secretly admired her strength, "You have one option if you wish to retain your royal status. Marry me and be our queen, or stay here among these primitives and your name shall be anathema. You will die at the hands of your former subjects." He levitated and descended to the floor, and Darby responded with a burst of gold energy forming a bubble around him and his sister.

"I will die with these animals, if it is my destiny, but not before avenging my father," she had to take three strides closer to Lucien to reach her brother's side, but she did it. They clasped hands and disappeared.

The new king seemed only to be amused. Although he fully intended to screw her again —many times and many ways — he was glad she had chosen the Avatarn. It simply meant he would have to kill her to remove all threats to his reign. And he had been hoping for an excuse to kill her. It would be long and slow and painful. Perhaps more so than their next fuck. With that blissful thought, he turned his attention to the other Avatarn before they got any clever ideas.

The healer was no real threat to him; the witch was his only concern. She needed a good fucking as well, but that would have to wait.

Blair saw the demon's attention turn towards her. She bravely stepped forward and began to cast a spell, but he was ready for her.

Lucien inaudibly mumbled a Latin phrase and instantly morphed into the guise of Thomas, her late husband. Though she knew the man before her was not her adored spouse, she couldn't bring herself to move against him. Just seeing his lovely face again was over-whelming. His glamour having stunned the witch exactly as he had hoped, Lucien took full advantage of her hesitation. He could easily have brought a laser weapon, but had opted instead for an ancient slingshot. With one expert swing of the device above his head, he hurled a stone that found its mark between Blair's beautiful green eyes. She collapsed in Roman's arms, and he would have healed her in an instant if not for the hordes of demon soldiers that suddenly materialized and stormed the warehouse from every direction. His hands had just begun to glow, when the hilt of a sword struck his skull and all was darkness.

Josh and Rachel just looked at each other.

"I'm gonna get Yoshi outta here!" Joshua stammered

"What?" Rachel responded incredulously.

He blinked away his confusion, then said "Never mind."

With the Avatarn out of commission, it seemed pointless to Josh to even attempt escape.

Tyler grabbed Paolo's arm and started running towards Mateo. His best friend had gone loco and seated himself in a folding lawn chair like he had just arrived at Barney-Allis Plaza to watch a fireworks display.

They had almost reached him, when with a shimmer of air, Lucien appeared at his side. His true face restored, the Olympian-esque alien placed a large hand on Mateo's shoulder. The teenager was unafraid and only acknowledged the contact with a relaxed nod.

"What are you doing, Matty?" Tyler was terrified. Mateo flinched slightly at the sound of the nickname, which only Ty had ever called him.

"Allow me to introduce my new advisor, boys," Lucien's friendly tone sounded ludicrously out of context, punctuated by the screams of the slaughter that surrounded them. The people of *The Palace* were being butchered without a hint of mercy, a blood bath worthy of Adolphus himself.

"I had to tell!" Mateo stood as he began to scream, "So H and me could be together. I needed you gone and you needed to pay, bro…You were tryin' to steal her, puto!"

"No man! It wasn't like that, dude. I know you loved her too," Tyler had his hands on each side of Mateo's face, forcing eye contact, "but we had moved to another level...We weren't going to turn our backs on you, man—"

"Enough," Lucien interjected, "I thought exposing your betrayal would provide some amusement, but already I grow weary of the carrot-topped cocksucker's whining and excuses. He stole your woman, and now you realize your revenge." In that moment, the demon produced the silver knife he had taken from Adolphus' belt and placed it in Mateo's hand. Wrapping his own long fingers around the boy's to ensure follow-through, he forced the dagger towards Tyler's chest. With flexibility only years as a prostitute could provide, Mateo contorted to place his own body in the knife's path. At first only gurgles escaped his lips when the blade pierced his heart. Tyler's anguish bounced off the walls, echoing above the fray.

"Too late, Judas," Lucien chided. "I'll see you next on Gehenna." In that moment, Mateo knew it was true. In his vision, Tyler's face twisted with despair, flickered back and forth with the face of a Nazarene carpenter Mateo had known so long ago. With a smirk, Lucien continued, "He gave you another chance and you blew it."

"Guess I'll be back for another try," the Hispanic boy smiled at his murderer.

Tyler didn't know what the hell they were talking about, so simply held his friend's head firmly against his stomach as the dying boy looked into his eyes, "Forgive me, Rabbi," Mateo whispered. He was gone then. Tyler didn't move except to meet Lucien's gaze.

"He was thinking of someone else," the killer offered with a shrug. Darby and Beacon burst into their field of vision, as a simultaneous golden ray impacted the monster king knocking him halfway across the room.

"Too late," Ty muttered to the only conscious Avatarn.

"I'm sorry," was all Darby knew to say.

Lucien had levitated to his feet and was preparing to stomp

angrily back across the lofty room, when Josh and Rachel decided to leave the marginal safety of the crates they hid behind. They would use a ploy they had pulled off once before. Rachel dropped to her hands and knees behind the monster, and before he was even aware of their proximity, Josh flew through the air with a flying drop-kick that connected with the demon's abdomen and sent him to the floor. He would have destroyed them in seconds had he not landed on a metal spike. Once used to anchor a tent display, the rusty metal now anchored Lucien's stomach to the spot. This healing would require his full concentration.

"This is only the beginning of your fall, children of Earth," he boldly proclaimed, though unable to lift himself from the floor. Turning towards Beacon, he added, "I shall return for you, my bride." With a flirtatious grin, he vanished. Only a slight whiff of incense lingered. The princess lobbed her bracelet against the place where he had lain, smashing it to pieces. He wouldn't use it to track them again. In smoky flashes the other soldiers disappeared as well, many taking human trophies back to the ships.

Blair and Roman began to stir, and he easily repaired her head wound with a gentle brush of his fingers. It was only then that they began to take in the carnage. Darby, Paolo, Josh, Rachel, Beacon, and Tyler all seemed to be okay, though shaken. Everyone else was dead.

Even Zanzibar lay at the feet of his former mistress. His body had been hacked into several distinct pieces.

"God, no," Blair begged, but it was over. *The Palace* was no more. All but a few of those under their protection were dead. Roman thought he had seen as much gore and horror as possible, until this battle. Lucien's army, under their new liege, had set a new standard for depravity. Roman ordered the survivors to follow him up to the shuttlecraft, silently praying that it had not been vandalized. The de facto leader of the Avatarn had made an autocratic decision. They had to find a secluded new home-base to regroup and figure out their next move. No one questioned him. They simply fell into line and ran like the devil was at their heels instead of soaking in a tub in the captain's quarters of the *Caiphas*.

Blair's magic performed double duty piloting the craft and cloaking it from monster eyes and alien technology. Roman pointed out directions as he guided them out of the ruins of metropolitan Kansas City. The sculptures above Bartle Hall had toppled to the street and lay in metallic heaps. The gold had somehow been stripped from the domed roof of the downtown cathedral, and former skyscrapers were mangled skeletons testifying to Earth's defilement. Massive flocks of black birds danced from tree to tree among the concrete building shells. When only a rare farmhouse dotted the countryside below, Roman chose their next home. Blair landed the shuttle near the front porch of the large dwelling and they all knew no one would object to them moving in. The whole family — seven children — lay dead in the dirt driveway.

They filed down the shuttle ramp, too de-sensitized to react to the rotting nightmare in their new front yard. Entering one-by-one through the tattered screen-door, if any of them had bothered to look up, they would have seen the old woman in the attic window, shotgun at the ready.

The holy refugees wasted no time finding the claw-foot bathtub on the second floor. Those whose turns came last, had to make do with lukewarm water, but they didn't mind. They were just thrilled to be clean again.

Roman was last, and like the rest, wore only a towel when he entered the kitchen. Darby and Rachel were scavenging the closets for clothes. Paolo was washing the clothes off their backs, and Blair was cooking. The fridge and pantry were well stocked, and after tying her long red hair in a knot, she set about creating a feast of pasta, baked chicken, and garden salad—with rolls. The food prep was a pleasant flashback to normal life. Aside from the fact that everyone was wet and nearly naked, they were the embodiment of a Norman Rockwell painting.

Joshua and Ty were looking around out back. They were scouting for a good spot to bury their host family. It would be an ugly chore, the sooner completed the better. Fortunately, there were no neighbors as far as the eye could see, as they were also wearing only towels around their waists. It seemed the Indian Summer that arrived with the demons was sticking around. Josh could have explained to Tyler that all the fires, and probably the spaceships themselves, were warming the autumnal air. Who knew what kind of climatic effects the fleet's low orbit would eventually cause? The yard dogs and barn cats didn't seem to mind the partial nudity, and came running to make friends. Without mentioning it, both guys were glad for the presence of the cats. They would be an automatic warning system if any demons should drop in.

After thoroughly enjoying their meal—only grudgingly picked at by Beacon—each pitched in to complete the burial and show their respects in a *service* led by Roman. Not actually knowing the deceased family, he offered no threnody, only a simple prayer and some respectful silence.

They still wore only towels, not wanting to dirty their fresh clothing supply. Very little from the closets had fit the group, and though they felt a little disrespectful, the struggle to survive had wiped away all concern with modesty and societal mores.

All were battle-weary, and each grieving deeply for a loved one or another, so no one turned on the TV or radio. A few conveniently placed hills obstructed the view of the giant saucer that floated above Kansas City. For a few hours they pretended the invasion hadn't happened. After taking a few minutes to figure out room assignments, they gathered in the large parlor to alternately talk and nap peacefully.

The Chosen and their entourage felt only remote guilt over walking out on mankind in its hour of need. They all knew without a vote that they had to take this break to regroup. A plan of attack was in order. They had to step away from the madness to remove themselves from the constant defense mode and organize an offensive strategy.

Blair was talking about how it would be easier to focus on

fighting demons without worrying about protecting cowans (the unmagical), when a clatter on the attic stairs caused everyone to spring into battle stances.

Each was relieved when the old lady jumped into the room, shotgun first. Though no longer safe, after facing off against monsters, an elderly woman wielding a man-made weapon seemed like a small bump in the road.

"Obviously, you aren't any of those devils from space, so I can only assume you are looters. I guess now you know you didn't get as lucky as you thought." She paused to smooth the gray hair she wore in a bun.

"You don't understand," Roman started to explain.

"You don't understand, trespasser," she was too angry to be scared, "I appreciate you all laying my poor family to rest, but I'm not going to sit back while you take over my home. Now don't make me break a commandment by shooting one of you."

Blair introduced all of them, assuming that it would be harder for the surviving family matriarch to kill them in cold blood if she felt like she knew them.

"I'm Fernie Leaves. Let's just skip the name jokes. I want you out of this house." It was in that moment that a loving cat caused her to lose her balance. The gun went off and she screamed in agony. The mechanism had jammed on the rusty old weapon, resulting in a backfire. Her hands were bloody and mutilated. Each of the Avatarn sprung into action.

The old one had instinctively thrown the gun up into the air. With a wave of Darby's hand, it was caught in golden light, and suspended in mid air. Fernie's eyes grew wide, and she recoiled when Roman approached and grabbed her wrists. His grip was strong, and unable to resist, she watched as the flesh of her hands regenerated in a white glow.

"This isn't possible," she muttered around false teeth. With hands free of arthritis for the first time in decades, Fern felt behind her for a chair. On a day of firsts, she thought she might faint for the first time too.

"She needs some air," Joshua offered, "I think Ro's charms are making her swoon or giving her the vapors or some shit."

Blair scolded him with a look; then with a wave of her hand, every window in the room was raised. "Zephyr come. I need you," was all she said. The wind responded instantly to her summons, lifting the curtains a strong breeze swirled around the old lady, reviving her and returning the color to her cheeks.

"What are you?" Fern Leaves wasn't afraid anymore.

"God's Hammer," Rachel replied first. She would have continued the explanation, but the prune of a woman fixed her with a stare and said, "You're a little dark to be the speaker of the group, aren't you, Sweetie?" Elder or no, Rachel was about to leap across the room to teach the old bitch some manners, when Tyler's reassuring arm slid around her waist. Calmer heads would prevail. Disappointed to learn their hostess was a bigot, Roman launched into a spiel announcing that they were the Avatarn, and to the best of his own understanding, what that meant. Instead of being overwhelmed by the revelation, which made her wonder if the blue halos around some of them really were from the cataracts as she originally assumed, she seemed most concerned by the fact that Darby and Paolo were holding hands.

"You aren't going to tell me that God chose a faggot to save mankind, are you?" The old woman laughed bitterly, "More likely your powers come from your master, Satan. You're no different than those monsters that landed here and murdered my family… after raping the whole lot. I only survived because I'm too old for even them to want to rape when they have other options, and no good as a slave. They found it more amusing to make me watch. I begged the Lord to let them kill me too, but it wasn't in His plan. Maybe He kept me here to stop the likes of you." Turning towards Blair, she added, "You look angelic enough to be a servant of the Lord. How did a nice girl like you get mixed up with a bunch of queers like this?"

"You may feel differently when you know my true nature, Ms. Leaves," Blair had run out of sympathy for the woman.

"And what might that be? You mean you're one of those lesbians, I suppose," Fern made sure her face projected the disgust she felt for all of the home-invaders. The self-proclaimed "good Christian witness" had already forgotten that these people had buried her family—when she was helpless to—and healed her torn hands.

"No, I'm not," Blair replied, "but I am a witch."

Fern let it soak in a moment before responding, "Well, for cryin' in the bucket. I won't abide Satan's whores in my house...Get out of here while the gettin's good."

"Just kill the old hag and be done with it. This grows tiresome," Beacon suggested casually.

"I'll do it," Josh offered, shocking the others because he didn't seem to be kidding.

"Ignore them," Roman stepped forward and Fernie allowed him to take her arm, "You've been through a terrible ordeal, and it's too much to take in." She was still charmed by Roman's masculine good looks and gentlemanly demeanor, and though she would never have admitted it, the fact that he wore only a towel thrilled her too.

When Darby moved to take her other arm, despite her hurtful insults, she swung a walking stick she'd seemingly produced from nowhere. He caught it easily. Without a word, he released it, unafraid, pitying her instead. Roman reacted too slowly as she raised the make-shift club again, but Blair simply said, "I bind you from doing harm, Fern Leaves." In the same instant, the old woman's arm seemed to wilt, and she found she could not raise it again without releasing the wooden cane.

"Look, lady," Josh had tried to be patient. "I've had about as much of your hateful bitter old ass as I can take. We are all sorry for your horrible loss. We've lost a lot of people too. I lost my soul mate," He didn't dare linger on thoughts of Yoshi for too long. He couldn't allow that luxury, "So this is how it's going to be. We are staying. It wasn't easy to find a place that was private, but not too far from the city and the mothership." He paused and turned to Rachel, "Did I just say *mothership*?" After she nodded, he continued, "We may be safe here for a while since they've already made a killing-field of your farm."

"Over my dead body," Fern interrupted.

"I agree," Beacon chimed in, "Kill her, Brother."

"I don't think so," Darby replied, "but we are going to have to secure her somehow while we sleep."

"We can put her on the shuttle," Blair offered, "It's soundproof, and I can secure the hatch and all the controls by magic."

"It's settled then," Roman resumed command, "We need some extra rest, so we'll turn in early." He gently picked up the feather-weight old woman and carried her as a bride down the front steps and over to the shuttlecraft positioned in the shade of a giant oak. Blair followed several feet behind. The others were content to watch from the spacious porch.

Only Roman could hear the tender words Fern offered as they moved across the yard, "How did you get mixed up with these perverts and devil-worshippers, young man? Send them away and you would be more than welcome to stay here."

"They are not what you imagine, Fernie," Roman spoke tenderly as well, "Not only are they not the freaks you believe them to be, but everything we have told you is true. God chose us for this mission. We didn't ask for it, but we have come to accept our destiny, and one way or another, we will complete our task." He set her on a cushy seat near a sensor console, "You can side with us or with the demons, but if you're not with us," he was especially gentle, "stay out of our way."

Blair leaned in through the hatch, sticking her head in:

"Controls now lock for safety's sake,
For your own good this spell I make,
All exits blocked to shelter thee,
This place secure, so mote it be."

Roman handed Fern his cell phone and told her to call them if she needed anything. He knew that Blair's witchcraft would prevent the phone from dialing out to anyone else—magical call forwarding. He followed his girlfriend out of the shuttle, and turned back to watch as she symbolically squeezed her thumb and finger together like a pincer and the hatch door closed with a sealing click.

Everyone in the house was bunked down and sleeping before sunset. Everyone except Josh. Unable to sleep, he pulled on a pair of tighty-whitey underwear and wondered down to the backyard, just as the last glow of purple and orange settled on the horizon. He had just settled on the steps, when a large calico cat joined him. "Hi, Kitty," he scratched behind her ears. She responded with a purr, then said, "That's Auntie Simone to you."

Chapter 19

In a small Pittsburg cemetery, Lucien stood over an open grave. As soon as his underlings had finished digging out the coffin, he had dismissed them. When midnight rang softly from a distant church tower, he pried open the lid of the box and stared at the little-changed corpse of Cinder Gorchowski. Steroids had made a hulk of the man a report card had once referred to as the most sensitive boy in his elementary school. The muscle-building drugs and a childhood of teasing by his father had turned the boy with so much potential into a murderous lunatic. That and losing the only man he had ever loved to one of the Avatarn. His final thoughts had been wonderment at how his beloved Paolo could leave him for a poser like Darby Zaid. He had finally found peace in the great *in between,* waiting to return. A few more lessons to learn. Lucien had decided Cinder would make the return trip sooner than expected.

The self-crowned demon king began to chant in a language older than Latin. Older than Earth. Thunder and lightning accompanied the windstorm that raised Lucien's black toga revealing that he was more than a little excited by the dark miracle he was performing. Finally, he concluded in English, "Arise, Cinder…Come forth and greet your new master…Henceforth, your days as a mere human are set aside…In this new life, you shall be known as Azazel. Arise my pet, my champion."

As Cinder opened his eyes and sat up, his mortal body was healed and restored. Alive again. The shock moved in waves through his recently rotting brain. Somehow this man, this angel that stood before him, had brought him back to life. Feeling stronger than he ever had, Cinder climbed out of the box and out of the grave. Lucien was petting his face as you might a prize bull, and the newly revived muscle-stud knew he would do anything this savior asked of him.

"My Azazel," Lucien proudly christened his creation, and Cinder felt the goat horns emerge from his forehead.

Josh thought he must still be in bed asleep.

"You're not sleeping, Boy," Simone scratched his hand with an extended claw, drawing blood, "See? You'll see that tomorrow and know that we really spoke."

"So what? You were reincarnated as a cat?" Josh was very troubled by the idea.

"No. No. I haven't reincarnated, Boy. I'm just possessing this cat so I can give you a message. When you see this cat tomorrow, I won't be in it." Rachel's Aunt Simone finished explaining what she thought was obvious, rubbing her tail along Josh's hairy ankles.

"How do I know you're not some kind of demon posing as Aunt MoMo?" He still wasn't sure.

"Boy, you know demons are afraid of cats. You best stop playin' with me." The beautiful cat of black, white, and orange was losing her patience.

"So why aren't you appearing to Rachel instead of me? She'll be heart-broken."

"I'll tell you why," she placed her front paws on Joshua's knees to raise her face to his; "Darlin' it isn't Southern to be rude, but somebody's gotta tell you. Your cheese is startin' to slide off your cracker."

"What?" Josh had no idea what the talking cat was telling him.

"You heard…You're starting to lose it, Joshua. Going crazy. Oh, you got a while yet, but it's sneakin' up on ya." Concern wasn't an expression a cat's face could show, but she said it with a paw gently against his cheek.

"What the hell do you mean, Simone?" He was getting really upset and probably louder than he intended to be.

"I don't mean to suggest you are a full-on loon…I'm just trying to help you because you're my niece's friend."

"Well, if I'm in such trouble—mental health wise—why didn't Yoshi come to help me?" Josh was indignant over this whole topic.

"Yoshi sends his love, but he's on assignment and couldn't come to you right now," Simone had settled back on her haunches, but leaned forward to rub her head against his shin, trying to reassure him as best she could.

"It's like this, Boy. You got schizophrenia creepin' up on you. There haven't been any real symptoms yet besides a few mood swings, temper flares, and a little confusion, but it's coming. And it's going to come on fast."

"What does that mean, oh, wise feline?" Josh couldn't resist a little sarcasm.

"Well that comment means you're a smartass, and the diagnosis means you're gonna go bonkers." Simone hadn't become a successful attorney by taking any crap from snot-nosed white kids.

"I don't feel any different. I think you're wrong about this," Josh countered.

"I'm not wrong, damn it. What's it gonna take? Joppa gotta come here herself in a doctor's coat before you'll listen?"

"Well, I'll just have Ro heal me then. No worries."

"I don't think he can, Joshua. I don't think he'll be allowed to…If it were that simple, I wouldn't have been sent here to warn you."

"But what reason could He have for wanting me to go crazy?"

"I don't know, Boy. You know how He moves..."

"Yeah yeah...In mysterious ways," he was starting to cry some. He thought he had surely run out of tears, "I have to help the Avatarn. I don't want to be a burden."

"You won't be a burden, and I'm going to tell you the first way that you can help them."

"What's that?" He stopped sniffling, feeling some hope.

"Prepare them. One of the greatest trials they'll face is headed this way. Neither man nor demon, but both. A long feared myth that never actually lived 'til this day. He is born of your common past, and brings death to the future. Don't worry, the Avatarn will survive as they must, but the one who comes is Legion's axe and it will surely fall." Simone licked his hand once, and then fell into a seizure. A moment later, the cat was scampering away.

"Good night, Aunt Simone," Josh whispered to himself and went up to bed. His last thought as sleep stole his mind was the epiphany that Simone had said the Avatarn would survive what was coming. She didn't say anyone else would.

Everyone woke with the roosters. Although they had been exhausted, their twilight bedtime had provided ample time for rest, even for Josh, who thought his visitation from Aunt Simone must have been a dream until he checked for the scratch she had given him. Somewhere in the recesses of his mind, a separate self giggled and assured him that he had been awake. He chose to ignore it, and helped Rachel start breakfast.

"I guess we have to go get the old crone," Blair said to Roman. Fern had refused to call them during the night, even though she had been scared locked in the alien shuttle. Roman had planned to call his phone to check up on her, but sleep had its way with him, and he never woke until morning. Truth was, she was more afraid of them; though she would rather die than let them know it. No one else offered to help Blair and Ro. They knew he was the only one with a chance in hell of eliciting any kind of cooperation from the old bag.

By this time, all gathered had found a change of clothes in the drawers and closets of the Tobits (evidence of the family name was scattered throughout the house), or resigned themselves to slip back into the freshly laundered clothes in which they had arrived.

Roman and Blair held hands as they crossed the yard and entered the shaded shuttle.

Fern had finally found sleep in the wee hours, but sprang to her feet and alertness the instant the hatch opened.

"It's about time. I can only control this old bladder up to a point," she scolded.

"Sorry," Blair offered. Fern didn't even glance in her direction, just continued speaking to Roman.

"Just get me out of here, please. I won't give you people any more trouble." Mrs. Leaves took Roman's arm with a small smile.

"We are sorry to have locked you out here," Ro said.

"Whether or not you people know it, you're all on the road to Hell, but compared to those bastardly devils that butchered my family, you are definitely the lesser of two evils. I will abide your presence here. I won't be giving you any more trouble."

"Glad to hear it," Roman replied, "You are going to find that we are not what you think we are. We ARE going to stop the demons, and making us welcome in your home will be a big help."

"*Welcome* is reaching a bit, young man," Fern allowed him to help her up the porch steps, but refused Blair's assistance. "Let's just say that I will tolerate you because I have to."

They joined the others for a large country-style breakfast. After a quick bathroom break, and without a word, Fern stationed herself at the stove and began to serve. For the moment, she would have to adjust to having *guests*. At least they all had sense to thank her for her food. No one used the word *hospitality*.

When the last of the sausage gravy was gone, they all adjourned to the main parlor. This time Darby decided to try the TV.

No one really expected there to be a broadcast, but to their amazement, someone was reporting world news.

A dedicated anchorwoman and her crew were still reporting for CNN. Even Fern sat down to watch, though she had mostly given up on TV when she decided that even *Touched By An Angel* had become too liberal to watch. All the seats were full, so Beacon stood. She wasn't about to join Tyler sitting cross-legged on the floor. "Turn it up," Rachel said to Blair, who had the remote. She did and everyone was enrapt by what they saw on the screen.

The pretty blonde soccer-mom-looking journalist was reporting that every president and head of state in the world had been assassinated. A few such heads of nation had been revealed to be demon spies, but most had been proven all too human. Names and faces of the murdered leaders flashed in the corner of the screen. More than a few video clips showed politicians and royalty being lined up and executed. With no more censors, the violence was extraordinarily graphic.

For a moment, Josh was surprised that Lucien allowed the broadcasts to continue, but quickly realized that the continuous news coverage would provide visual proof that the governments of Earth had collapsed and it was pointless to resist the Legion forces.

Handed a memo from off screen, the reporter began speaking of an important announcement from the Pope. The screen filled with the image of the pontiff standing on a balcony high above a crowd filling St. Peter's square below him. The very elderly leader of the Catholic Church was surrounded by an entourage of cardinals and demons.

Paolo made the sign of the cross on his chest and said, "Holy Mother. Don't tell me he made a deal with the devil."

Over the noisy background, the anchorwoman's voice was explaining that the Pope would be beseeching Christians around the world to stop fighting and surrender to the undeniable domination by a great race of beings from outer space.

A large warrior with the head of a bear helped the shaky priest to a bank of microphones, only a staff to otherwise aid his walking. A hush filled the Vatican. Softly he began to speak in Latin, his fragile voice amplified to every corner. He spoke of the surprising attack by a species with power and means far superior to our own. Being a student of history, Darby understood a few words, but the news channel was working frantically to provide subtitles.

In a move more sudden than the Pope had made in decades, he swung his staff toward his demon overseer, plunging the makeshift weapon into his animal heart. Spinning back to the podium with more grace than his condition should have allowed, the ancient pontiff started yelling, "Jesus will be victorious!" And had done so in a dozen languages when a Legion soldier reached his side and casually snapped his neck. The head of the Church crumpled lifeless to the floor. The horrified newswoman managed to mutter something about having lost the Vatican feed, and composed herself enough to describe the new images of carnage being shown from around the globe.

"Jesus!" Tyler was struck by the terrible truth. "They really have completely taken over the world."

"I'm afraid so," Roman said indicating with his eyes alone that he wanted Blair and Darby to follow him outside. The others were too caught up in the dreadful images on TV to even notice they had stepped away.

The Avatarn settled into the large white wooden rockers on the front porch. Blair was the first to speak, "This is too big. How are the three of us going to stand against an invading army?"

"We've already discussed our fear of failure too many times," Roman countered, "Like it or not, we are the chosen Avatarn of God."

"His *Hammer* even." Darby threw in his two cents.

"We'll find a way." Ro assured them once more then wandered away, following a mongrel dog to further explore the farmyard, surrounded on all sides by fields of tall corn.

Blair and Darby exchanged a glance before following behind to take in the sights for themselves. Birds and deer seemed drawn to the new lair of the holy pilgrims, and Roman hoped they wouldn't draw undesired attention from the air. Nearly a dozen barn cats stopped chasing chickens and each other to position themselves as escorts to the shiny visitors.

Roman meandered down a small hill, finally stopping just out of sight of the house, but still inside the peony border of the property. He was ending his tour at the foot of a giant oak tree, whose thick branches supported a classic tire swing. A large black uncut tire, strung from a single rope. He bowed low, with a grand gesture, presenting the seat to his girl. Blair was glad she had put on a pair of jeans, because she didn't hesitate to climb on. Using the inside of the tire as a step, she climbed up to sit on top, the rope between her thighs. Roman took advantage of her choice of perches, by stepping through, and seating himself on the interior of the rubber swing. Darby joined their laughter; unable to help noticing their positions on the swing were decidedly pornographic. Ro was all reclined, his weight balanced on his ass. His face between Blair's knees. Dar's mind flooded with dirty thoughts, and the mutual blush on the others' faces revealed that they felt the same. When the tousled blond man grabbed the sides of the tire and casually leaned against it, it wasn't just to stabilize the swing. He didn't want his partners to see the swelling evidence of his horny daydreams.

"So what's the plan, *Fearless Leader*?" Blair was the first to speak.

"Well, we've all agreed that we need to go on the offensive. That means we need to take the party to Lucy…Put the surprise on his skirt-wearin' ass," Ro pushed off with his feet to set the swing in motion. Darby's cover was ripped away, but by then the issue had subsided.

"Whoa!...Easy on the boys in skirts," Dar reprimanded.

"Sorry," Roman laughed.

Looking down at Ro's face between her knees was making Blair a bit too warm. She joined his laughter a little too eagerly. They had been too exhausted (and stressed) to do anything after going to bed last night, but she had a feeling tonight would be the big night. Roman's thoughts paralleled hers, and his hopes were the same.

"Don't worry; I won't let you fall, Ma chère," Roman assured, grabbing her ankles, simultaneously losing his balance and almost toppling out backward.

"Merci," she replied, "But I think you better just worry about yourself."

"Point taken," he was embarrassed.

Darby placed a stabilizing hand on Ro's back in the nick of time, and gave the swing a gentle push.

"So, guys," Blair rocked back and forth to keep the swing in motion after Darby removed himself to a safe distance, "What do you think we have become, the three of us? I know *Hammer of God* and all that, but what do you think it means for us?" The wind tossed her magnificent red mane around her making her seem all the more magical and somehow like a little girl.

"Well," Darby spoke up, "the Nestorian Christians of India believed that Jesus was not God. That He was a human made divine by God."

"Whichever theory you believe about that," Roman pushed off the ground again with his feet, "you can't compare us with Jesus."

"Oh, I don't mean to," Dar clarified, "I would never suggest…I just mean, I don't think we're human anymore."

"I know what you're sayin'," Blair chimed in, "He's changing us. Giving us greater access to his power. Like Yeshua did, Jesus did, when He called His apostles and sent them on their missions."

"Our mission is to stop Lucy and Legion. We need an active plan…We can't just keep reacting to his moves." Roman dragged his feet to stop the swing so that Darby could come closer.

"I think I can be of service," a face made up of knotholes in the trunk of the giant oak tree was moving and speaking. Blair knew she was the intended audience and the only one that heard it.

"I'm listening," the lovely witch climbed up to stand on the tire top. Clinging to the rope and staring at the ancient tree.

Roman and Darby knew she was receiving a communication,

but were clueless as to the focus of her attention. They waited silently for her to go on.

"I am Cerne. Spirit of the forest," the bark of the tree had continued to morph until a perfectly realized face stared back at her. "I have waited a long time to give you a gift and an idea."

"I know you," Blair responded, "You're *the green man*. The pagan god of nature." Blair knew that he had many old names: John Barleycorn or Robin Goodfellow, even Viridios to Roman Britain, Wirdjos to the proto-Celtic, or Gwrddni to the Welsh.

Darby looked at Roman and twirled a finger around his ear, suggesting that Blair was losing her mind. Both knew he was only kidding to lighten the tension of the bizarre moment. Blair didn't joke about stuff like this. Roman responded with the shoulder shrug that was the universal sign for *I don't know*." All he knew was that his girlfriend was talking to a tree…And from their perspective it was a one-sided conversation.

"There is no god except The Father. I was created by man, through whom His power flows. I was born of imagination, and can not be undone."

"We are honored, great Cernunnos," Blair bowed her head.

"It is I who am honored to serve His Holy Hammer, the Avatarn," without wind, the tree's towering branches began to wave and bend, "Accept this gift, that the dark duke, once named for his light, may be forever extinguished."

The great tree's skyward limbs bent low to bring its highest leaves for presentation to the awestruck witch standing beside the swing she had quickly dismounted. Supported by the green foliage was a mass of mistletoe, plush with countless berries.

"How did this get here?" Blair marveled.

"I instructed the birds to bring it here, that it might take root in these branches. I have cared for and nourished it all these years. The berries are in their perfect ripeness for the potential potion."

Though he had not heard the spirit's words, upon seeing the mistletoe, Darby had deduced his plan.

"It's simple," he explained to Roman, "The ancient Druids harvested mistletoe from the trees to use in magic and ritual protection. The berries can be fatally poisonous. It is being offered as a weapon against Legion."

"Exactly," Blair smiled at them. "I need something to carry it in."

Darby stripped off his shirt and handed it to the witch as a makeshift satchel.

Envy flashed through Roman's mind. Though he knew Dar's stunningly muscular torso was no threat to his recent romance, he couldn't help comparing it to his own slightly less muscular, but also impressive, body. He silently thanked God that Dar was a big mo.

Blair spread the sky-blue T-shirt on the ground and began carefully gathering the white berries from the yellow-green leaves. When the makeshift parcel was nearly overflowing, she stepped back and looked again into the face of Cerne.

"Thank you for this gift."

"It is my privilege to assist you, Mistress. Blessed be," the giant tree raised its limbs back toward the Heavens, waving massive branches in a storm of homage. Cernunnos was gone then. As much as he is ever gone. The tree again only a magnificent tree.

"Blessed be," Blair replied in farewell. "Well, boys, whaddaya think?" She scooped the stuffed shirt from the ground and slung it across her back.

"If we wanna go the poison route, aren't there drugs and other products that would be even more effective?" Roman queried.

"There are certainly stronger toxins," Darby responded, "but I suspect that the fact that this one occurs naturally, and has been used magically for generations, will make it especially deadly for the demons."

"I'm certain that is the case," Blair patted Dar's cheek. "Guess that history major's not completely going to waste."

Roman spoke next, "Okay, so how do we get him to drink it?"

"We don't," Blair was smiling. "We brew the potion, including a drop of blood from each of us. Then we fill Fern's insulin syringes." The old lady had only grudgingly revealed her weakness—diabetes—to her unwelcome guests during breakfast, "As many as we can. We'll all try to inject him at the same time."

"I guess the next question is how we get Lucy here," Darby said.

"We don't," Roman was certain. "We can't reveal the location of this place to him. We'll ambush him on his own turf. We have to find a way onto the mothership."

The threesome made their way back to the farmhouse to get input from the others in devising a way to sneak on to the saucer. Beacon's inside knowledge would be key.

Back in the comfortable main parlor, Blair pulled her flame-like hair into a ponytail and quickly brought the others up to speed on the surprise visit by the pagan Cerne and their plans for his gift.

Rachel joined Blair in the kitchen and helped her unpack the dangerous and precious bundle. Fern followed them as they moved through her cupboards gathering the cookware and utensils they would need, spouting a continuous lecture about how she would have no hocus pocus in her kitchen. Blair hadn't even mentioned needing her hypodermic needles yet. In the back of her mind, the tenderhearted witch knew that if they failed in their mission, the old woman might not be able to replace her medical supplies. Of course, if they failed, Fern would be better off with her family in the homemade cemetery out back.

Lounging around with family, while the women worked the kitchen took Roman back to those precious years when Sundays were spent at Brenda's parents house. Ridiculously huge meals filling the entire day. Janie playing in the kitchen, tugging at her grandma's dress and "helping" her prepare all the expected dishes.

Blair held first Darby's hand, then Roman's over the simmering pot to slice a finger and squeeze, allowing their blood and lastly her own to blend red with the seminal white of the bursting berries. A touch from Ro sealed the cuts.

Fern had to be restrained by Roman, when Rachel went to the medicine drawer without asking permission, and withdrew a dozen syringes for their potion. They would have extras, just in case.

When the brew had cooled, the girls began filling the needles carefully, making sure to get none on their hands. Blair mumbled charms and incantations under her breath as they filled the vials with hope.

Roman was about to ask the princess how they should go about getting onto the *Caiphas*, when the hissing, screeching, and growls of the many cats outdoors demanded their attention. Tyler hurried to the screen door and yelled out a warning.

A single-man scout shuttle had landed beside the Avatarn's stolen shuttlecraft and the pilot, who had started towards the house, was surrounded by the scruffy felines. Others joined Tyler at the door, but all just watched in amazement. The demon soldier was really scared. Their curiosity turned to empathetic horror as a dozen cats of every color pounced on the lone demon, mauling and biting him. The alien managed to throw a few of them unharmed across the yard, but he was soon overwhelmed. Bite after bite boiled with the saliva that was relatively harmless to every other species. The warrior collapsed only inches from the front steps, and was soon only a dark puddle sinking into the grass.

The Avatarn didn't have to lift a finger.

"Why didn't they do that when your family was attacked?" Josh asked Fern.

"Those jackals that came before were prepared for the cats," for a moment Fern was lost in her memories. "They had some kind of stun gun. One blast of green light and every one of those barn cats just fell over in the dirt like they were dead as doornails. Many hours later they started waking up one-by-one. Now I know why they stunned the kitties. That was amazing. Those no-good dogs just stood back and barked like they did just now. The monsters didn't bother with them. Guess their bites don't hurt'em like the cats do."

"Of course dog bites do not hurt them," Beacon seemed appalled by their ignorance, "Dogs are from the original realm—as are Legion—cats are native to this planet. Their biology is foreign to the master race. Did none of you attend school as children?"

Josh took the bait, and soon he and the princess were off to their usual name-calling and debate. Everyone had already grown use to the casual threats and raised voices that accompanied their heated disagreements.

The rest of the group disbanded and scattered. The show was over. Having finished the potion, some ventured into the garden and gathered an abundance of produce for their next meals. They lounged throughout the afternoon and discussed strategies for boarding the ship above Kansas City. They still hadn't reached a decision when Fern announced it was time for chores. The horses and other animals had to have their food and tending for the evening.

Chapter 20

After chores and supper, Roman and Blair declared they were turning in early. They had taken over the master bedroom, much to Fern's objection. It seemed a little intrusive to them as well, but they had to sleep somewhere, and their blossoming love demanded privacy.

With the door locked behind them, they stood just inside holding each other for a long time.

"I'm ready," Blair finally said raising her eyes to meet his, somehow embracing each other with a look.

"Are you sure?" Roman couldn't help seeming eager. This beautiful woman made him hornier than he had been as a teenager. He had been patient, respecting her grief, but he longed to be with her. He needed it. Sex between them seemed as much a part of their inescapable destiny as battling evil.

Blair responded without words, by peeling off her jeans. He knew she had a fair complexion, but as she pulled her shirt off over her head, the alabaster white skin took his breath away. No freckles, just snow-white flesh. So different from his Latino coloring. Having been given the green light, Roman didn't waste any time removing his own clothes. He wasn't wearing underwear, so by the time she had removed hers, both were naked.

She was embarrassed to find herself staring frankly at his swollen dick. It was even bigger than she had expected. Her blush continued when she realized he was as mesmerized by her perky breasts as she by his manhood.

"Wow," Roman finally sputtered.

"Back at ya," she replied.

He stepped to her then, placing a large hand on each side just above her hips. As his dripping dick brushed against her private hair, a glance down confirmed that she was indeed a natural red-head. She ran her small hands up his furry stomach and through the thick mat covering his hard chest. His hands moved to cup her breasts, lifting them, his thumbs rubbing and tweaking her very erect nipples. A small moan escaped her lips. He leaned in to take her mouth and invaded it with his tongue. Only in the instant of that perfect kiss, did Thomas flash briefly through her mind. She felt no guilt. He had given his blessing and this was right. She saw his nodding head then her husband was gone. Only she and her soul-mate remained.

Still standing at the foot of the bed, Roman bowed to take the peak of an uplifted breast into his mouth. Blair actually thought she would swoon as he licked and sucked hungrily. The head of his bouncing member separated and teased the outer lips of her sex. Just as she was reaching to guide it home, he backed away.

"What is it?" She was panting.

"Sure you're ready? It's a big step," Ro had to be certain.

"It is big," she said mischievously, "but if I were any more ready, I wouldn't even need your help." She took one of his hands in both of hers and led him around to the bed. Their pillaged world was forgotten. Even their love was a separate thing, watching from behind their hearts as their heated bodies merged in a primal animal dance, performed throughout time on countless worlds. No matter the positions or genders involved, at base level it was a pounding pulsing reunion, flesh recognizing and exalting in its purpose.

Roman's hair, wet with sweat, swept down her belly as he trailed kisses from her belly-button to her furry mound. He was pleased that she kept her womanhood well groomed, and didn't hesitate to thrust his tongue in to probe the generous folds. Blair was no stranger to good sex, but this was more. In every place that his body touched hers, a faint white glow made her cells sing. She was moving quickly towards climax, when he climbed on top of her. The jamming of his wide penis inside her slippery tightness was a battering ram smashing the gates of the fortress she had erected around her soul in the churchyard when her husband died. He was coming for her. And she was coming for him. They met inside, in a place Blair had thought she would never go again. Bedtime with Thomas had been magical, but not like this. Her entire life had been leading her to Roman, and they celebrated savagely, letting their love magnify the carnal act until it engulfed them. They didn't rest before starting over. He took her from behind, with her riding on top, and finished with a sleepy sixty-nine. Both were still smiling when they were captured by unconsciousness.

Fern had promised Roman that she wouldn't try any funny business, and loathe to lock her in the shuttle again; he had taken her at her word. Darby wasn't so sure about her. He had joined her on the front porch in the rocker paired with hers. They sat in silence, rocking slowly and gazing at the star-filled sky. He hadn't spent much time in the country and was awestruck by the number of stars visible to the naked eye away from the ambient light of the city. The night sky held new meaning. Even the dismissal of Pluto from the solar system's planetary count seemed a moot point, knowing for certain that their were a million inhabited worlds circling those stars, knowing so many people and creatures and beings were depending on them for their freedom and their lives. It was overwhelming.

In short order the old woman grew tired of the tension created by the close proximity of a homosexual and went inside, not so much as a peep to Darby. He considered offering her a polite "good night" anyway, but the words died on his lips. He was tired of trying to be nice to people who hated him on principle. A quick call to

Tyler's cell phone confirmed that she had retired to her room. They had searched it for items that could endanger the group. Beyond that Ty had chosen to make a pallet on the floor outside her door.

Darby was thrilled to have a rare moment alone. The subtle sound of the animals in the night weren't really an obstruction of the natural quiet. They were a part of it. He felt attuned with nature in a way he never had before, with a strange sense of peace contrary to the bitter reality that the Earth was under siege.

He found himself pondering the current state of his life. Having always considered himself spiritual, he wasn't a church-goer and had never really been a student of theology beyond basic historical movements. He didn't remember much of the dogma taught at the neighborhood church where he had attended Sunday-school, but he was fairly certain they'd never mentioned prophesies of the Avatarn. There was no getting around it though. Clearly God had chosen them for this great mission. Darby was scared, but most of all he was honored.

If anyone had told the *moral majority* and the *religious right* that the Creator, The Omniverse, would choose a gay man, a witch, and a materialistic-business-obsessive, as the *Hammer of God* to protect the Earth, they probably would have expressed some doubts… punctuated by lynchings. Finally, proof that God's love is unconditional. Jesus was right. If only all those people that call themselves Christians actually did attempt to be Christ-like. Oh, well, the point was kinda moot now. Most people had put their judgment of others on hold (except Fern of course) in order to focus on survival. People didn't care who saved them, as long as somebody did. Idealism is the first thing forgotten when someone is coming to hurt you.

Darby had no regrets about the way he'd lived his life. He had had some wild times, sowed some oats, but he was in his prime. There was a reason the saying "*young, dumb, and full of cum*" existed. And the version that better suited him, "*young, hung, and full—*"more accurate. He had always practiced safer sex, and though he had done some experimenting, he never endangered anyone else. It was good that he had been around the block. It allowed him to appreciate what had developed between him and Paolo. If someone had said Darby Zaid would be in a serious monogamous relationship by year's end, neither he nor his friends would have believed it. He was a bit of a player, and he liked it.

That was over now. After all they had been through, all Paolo had been through because he had been destined to love an Avatarn, Darby had been won. He couldn't imagine ever feeling that same way about anyone else.

It was during this moment of realizing he was truly in love, in a way he hadn't known he was capable of, that he noticed he was being watched. A pair of eyes watched him from the lowest branch of the tree that sheltered the shuttlecraft. He wasn't frightened. Recognition occurred at the gut level. It was Paolo. His partner. His lover staring back from the foliage. He jumped down, landing in the scorched grass where Josh had used the shuttle's violet beam to vaporize the scout ship; J's innate understanding of computer technology finally having come in handy. Paolo crossed the yard in long confident strides and Darby thought he had never seen a more handsome fellow. The loving goodness that radiated from the spiky-haired twink was so brilliant Dar thought it out-shown the moon.

"Spying on me?" The Avatarn's smile was so genuine it also illuminated the darkness.

"I guess some might say so," Paolo replied, "I was out here playing with the dogs when I saw you. I didn't want to bother you."

"You couldn't if you tried. Join me."

"Hoping you would say that," Paolo bounded up the steps and settled Indian-style on the small table between the rocking chairs.

"Big mission coming up," the Italian boy took the hand of the Nordic-looking boy. "We haven't had much time alone together."

"I know, mea culpa, Honey. That's my bad. I should be more considerate of your feelings. Especially after all yo— "

"Stop," Paolo interrupted, "I wasn't blaming you. You have a duty. Gotta plan. I guess I was just trying to say I've been looking forward to moments like this."

"Me too," Darby grabbed the front of Paolo's T-shirt in his fist and pulled him down for a passionate kiss. It lingered, but finally broke when Paolo could no longer keep from smiling enough to hold his lips to Darby's.

Still holding hands, Dar led his boyfriend through the parlor and up the stairs. Rachel and Josh were still up watching a DVD of some old movie on the player. Jealousy flashed temporarily through her brain, but mostly she was glad her *Darbo* had found love. She hoped there were enough human men left alive for her to find her own some day. They just reminded Josh of Yoshi. The wound in his heart was still raw, but he covered well and just flashed a grin.

Paolo and Darby shared a little girl's room. Shelves were lined with Barbies and the Bratz. The posters were of N'Sync and the Olsen Twins.

Once naked, they hit the bed so hard the mattress only half remained on the box springs. No place on Paolo's body was left unblessed by Darby's kisses. Being fucked by someone you're in love with is a holy event, and Paolo could not have felt more euphoric kneeling at any other alter. Over and over he thrust his tongue into the deep slit in the head of Darby's cock. His blond lover moaned softly when he opened his mouth to slide his lips over the swollen knob and licked the ridges of the large plumb. One hand pumped the thick shaft and the other tugged at over-sized balls.

Darby was in bliss, but composed himself enough to reach around to Paolo's round muscular ass and begin working his wet fingers through the very furry door to the temple. He became increasingly rough as one hand shoved Paolo's head down faster and further and the other hand shoved fingers further and faster. Dar's former classmate not only took it like a sport, but the leaking of his own fat dick proved that he liked it. The Avatarn couldn't wait any longer for the communion that brought him more joy than a hundred one-night tricks. He pushed the smaller man onto his back and pushed up his legs. Paolo thought he was ready, but Darby's size still surprised him. The Chosen one entered as gently as he could, but after his *Pal* had adjusted, he assaulted the sweet ass as he might Lucien's after humiliating him in combat. His eyes never left Paolo's face as he watched for any sign that his lover didn't want it this way. What he saw there instead was ecstasy. Paolo needed to feel Dar's strength pounding into him. He was absorbing it. Storing it. Later, he would share it when they switched positions and Darby was on his hands and knees with Paolo behind him. Giving and receiving energy. Domination and surrender. Perfect balance. Panting and growling. Deep and husky oaths of love and grunting. Mostly grunting. Each had shot more than one load of cum when they finally collapsed in a sticky tangle and were lost to restorative slumber.

Blair was in the middle. She could turn her head just far enough to see Roman and Darby at her sides. No rope. No nails. No blood. She didn't know how they were suspended, but they were definitely on crosses. They were being crucified.

On a rocky hill, surrounded by desert and an eternal blue sky, populated by rolling clouds too sparse to offer shade. She guessed that their feet were two yards above the ground, their fingertips separated only be inches. Though they wore modern clothes, the terrain appeared ancient. She could hear the sounds of a town or city nearby, but she couldn't see it. Strangest of all, was the small crowd gathered below them. They wore the garments and robes of old Jerusalem, but their faces were achingly familiar.

Among them were Janie, holding the hand of an adult Joppa, Thomas, Sarah and Molly, Yoshi, Miss Luna, Mateo, Simone, and Honeydew. Though they seemed concerned, none among them were crying. Blair knew then that she must still be asleep. She turned to her right where Roman hung.

"Dreaming?" He asked.

"We must be," Darby answered from her left. He had noticed they were surrounded by a wide circle of centurions dressed in imperial armor. Though agitated, they seemed not to dare come too close.

"What does this mean?" Roman asked his other two thirds.

"I don't kn—," Blair cut short her response. Someone was approaching from beyond the soldiers. As the circle parted to allow his entrance, the warriors nearest him fell to the ground. Lifeless in the presence of this magnificent male. All of their dead friends knew him and each embraced him in turn.

"No Sovereign, the future is not theirs to know," Joppa placed herself between the crosses of the Avatarn and the handsome stranger whose violet halo glowed brightly even in the glare of the noonday sun.

"Don't worry, Wife," He touched her cheek, "I only want to bring them news of what already is."

"Time would reveal it, Sovereign," Joppa was very upset; "you know it is forbidden for you to be here in this way."

"And you know He cuts me a lot of slack, Wife."

"Careful you don't hang yourself with it," she stepped aside without further argument. Unafraid to challenge him, but knowing when to give up.

"Guys," he said looking up at each of the Avatarn in turn, "I am here to reveal a wonderful surprise. This is the kinda crap that'll knock you on your asses, or it would if you had more time to think about it, but you're just gonna have to deal."

"Blah, blah, blah…Spit it out already," Darby lost his patience.

"Since when do you have a husband, Joppa?" Roman was confused.

"Hi, Daddy!" Janie shouted.

"Hi, Baby," he beamed his love at her through a smile.

"Roman, it's not time—," Joppa was interrupted by the charismatic stranger.

"Wait, Dar's right," the stranger reached up to rub Blair's foot and she felt she should know him, "Let me get this out…Two children are coming. One born of good. The other of evil. You are pregnant Blair…And so is Beacon."

The female Avatarn couldn't speak, but Roman could, "I know who fathered Blair's baby, but what about—"

"My sister's?" Darby finished the question.

"Though demons don't normally reproduce, Lucien sired her child." There was a gasp from someone in the crowd, "My wife will explain to her how this is possible…In the meantime, know that it is true."

Roman was shedding tears of pride and joy. Shock still prevented Blair from closing her mouth or speaking. Darby was enraged by the on-going defilement of his sister and turned red with anger.

"How are we going to protect babies in the midst of this madness," Blair finally found her voice, simultaneously thrilled and terrified.

"Let's just say they'll mature quickly," the one Joppa called Sovereign seemed confident that he was delivering good news.

"Does this story seem a little familiar to anyone else but me?" Darby wondered aloud.

"I see your point," the stranger laughed, "but trust me, it's never gone down quite like this before….Don't be afraid," he continued. "This is a good thing…Really."

The sky suddenly grew dark then and lightning and thunder split the day. Rain poured down in torrential sheets. In a moment everyone was soaked.

"Remember," the stranger added, "the children shall inherit the Kingdom. Assuming you all make sure there is a Kingdom. Blessed are." With that he turned and started down the hill. Jagged lightning pierced the dark, striking the top of the stranger's head. The blinding flash forced all present to close and scrunch their eyes. Blair and Roman opened their eyes at the same time, relieved to be in the safety of the farmhouse bed.

"Guess it wasn't real," Roman was less than certain.

"Then why are we soaking wet?" She replied.

They knew Darby had shared their experience when they heard his shout through the wall, "What the fuck?"

Chapter 21

Blair and Roman were each wrapped in sheets when they burst into Darby and Paolo's bedroom. "You guys okay?" She asked the Avatarn sitting in the middle of the bed with a pillow over his genitals.

"I'm not so sure about him," Paolo answered for his soaking wet friend from safely under the covers.

"It was real, wasn't it?" Darby was still shouting.

Roman was nodding confirmation when the others burst into the room to see what was the matter. Tyler brought up the rear, "I can't find Beacon. She's gone!"

The group scattered to throw on clothes, and a thorough search of the farmyard commenced. It was to no avail. She really was gone, and Darby was finding it hard to breathe.

Lucien and Beacon materialized in her old bedroom in Castle Hades on Gehenna. He had stolen her from her bed in the farmhouse before she could even manage a scream. Her shrieking now would not penetrate her ornate doors, let alone traverse the many light-years to Earth. Lucien was thankful that the missing scout had managed to send a message before his apparent destruction. He had investigated personally, hoping to find the lair of his enemies. His hunch had proven his suspicion valid.

"My brother will kill you! I'll kill you myself, you murdering bastard!" Her rage spewed out like lava.

"What you will do, you sniveling little bitch, is prepare yourself for my coronation…At which, you will crown me the rightful king of Legion," he released the arm he had been holding and started towards the door.

"Are you mad?" The princess gave a small laugh, "I would never betray my father's memory that way."

"You will do it," he said calmly, "or I will go to your brother's demesne and kill off your newfound human family, one by one. And when I am done, I may just take your handsome brother as my concubine."

She just sniffed and angrily wiped tears from her face. He smiled and said, "Get dressed…And do something with your hair. I want your appearance to reflect your royal station. No one will question my rightful place on the throne." He was gone then. Beacon felt helpless to resist. She went to her massive wardrobe and began searching for an appropriate gown.

The peasant child Joppa was performing her duties as candlelighter throughout the many rooms of the castle when Lucien approached her and two maids tending a small parlor to re-assign them to make preparations at once in the grand throne room for the stately ceremony.

Joppa knew that the only reason to go through the technical façade of an actual coronation was if the princess herself were here to install the new king.

"May I speak with you privately, Master?" She curtsied before the demon.

"I don't see why not. You always had the ear of the previous king. Perhaps you will amuse me as well."

He dismissed the maids with a wave of his hand and seated himself in a large armchair. He indicated with a sandaled foot that Joppa should sit on the ottoman before him. Though the girl appeared to be only a child, Lucien made no attempt at modesty in the arrangement of his olive-green toga. Joppa was accustomed to his flagrant exhibitionism, and was not flustered when she sat and asked him for confirmation of Beacon's return.

"Of course, she's here," he casually replied, "Aside from the fact that this is her home, even a barbarous child like you knows that the princess must place the crown on my head, figuratively and literally. It is her duty and her responsibility."

"But you just mur—ended her father's reign. Why would she help you?"

"She recognizes that it is my destiny. Besides, she is doing what is best for Legion. She still has a duty to her people here."

"I don't believe you. You must return her to Earth. She belongs with her own kind." Joppa spoke quietly, but she wasn't afraid.

"You go too far, little girl. Adolphus may have tolerated your insolence; however, I will not. I would have you flogged, if the princess didn't require your services immediately in her chambers. Be sure her beauty is at its most resplendent and most regal. The ceremony will be broadcast live to all of Gehenna, Earth, and every other planet. I will erase all doubt regarding my reign with her demonstrated approval. Now go to her before I decide you're more trouble than you are worth." He stomped his foot for emphasis, and the child gathered her long skirts and ran from the room.

Beacon recognized the light knock at her door, and called out permission for entrance. Joppa went directly to where the princess sat crying at her vanity table.

"No more tears, Mistress," the child took a brush to Beacon's golden tresses, "Once you have demonstrated your public support by partaking in the ceremony, I'll find a way to get you out of here. Back to Earth." The princess met her gaze in the mirror, but didn't bother to speak. "Have you selected a gown?"

"Yes," she was still sniffling, "The purple, with the fur collar and cuffs."

"Very well," Joppa dabbed at her royal eyes with a small kerchief, "Let's get to your hair. We'll do the make-up last." The peasant girl didn't trouble to ask where her tiara and jewels were. She looked around. Spotted them on the marble pedestal where they always were and brought them to the table where she began to whip the long blonde strands into a towering sculpture, encrusted with pearls and purple gemstones. Beacon seemed to phase in and out of catatonia until brought to instant alertness by a small slap across her cheek. "Now that you are ready to play your part, there is more that you must know."

Joppa was about to explain when a distant gong sounded, announcing that the ceremony would soon begin.

"What is it?" Beacon could tell her friend and sometimes protector had traumatic news to share.

"Mistress, you are with child."

Beacon's brain was still reeling from the slap to her face, when the child's annunciation hit her in the chest. She stammered before finding her voice, "You mean to suggest that my body would accept the seed of that pretender to the throne?" Anger stained her cheeks.

"I know that there have been no others."

"Of course not," Beacon flitted around the room, tippy-toeing towards hysteria. "I have guarded my purity without fail. I would not disgrace my father's house."

"I know you wouldn't," Joppa's voice was an oasis of calm, "but Lucien would."

"You of all people should know that Legion are unable to procreate. It's impossible."

"Ordinarily that would be true," the peasant was worried about the trembling princess, "but you share the same blood as an Avatarn. That association lends magic to your genes. That combined with Lucien's powers allowed this unprecedented creation."

"I would know if I carried his spawn."

"Apparently not. But I would, and you do...Remember, Mistress. I am not what I appear to be. I am not wrong."

"Beloved Joppa, I can not birth the baby of the creature that murdered my father...I won't," she moved too quickly for the girl to realize her intent. Beacon had thrown a priceless vase to the floor and retrieved a jagged shard before she could reach her. The princess had already turned it on herself and attempted to plunge it into her womb. The supple flesh of her belly stretched and contoured at the point of the shard, but her skin was not broken. Beacon's jabs became desperate, but she couldn't make a scratch. The cell cluster that would become a fetus was unharmed.

"Your child is protected by unseen powers," Joppa gently removed the glass from her mistress' lacerated hand and led her to a basin of water to clean her wounds, "His or her destiny will, it seems, be realized, regardless of your actions."

"Who protects it?" Beacon screeched, "Its father's evil magic, or that of your side?"

"I don't know," the child admitted as she bandaged the princess's deepest cuts.

The holy refugees were all gathered on the late Tobits' front porch and the steps leading to it. Roman had called the meeting to reveal the news of the pregnancies and to formulate a plan for finding Beacon. Darby was surprised to find himself nearly overcome with fear for a sister he had just met. Tyler expressed concern for Beacon's ability to deal with this new burden, but all were shocked when Josh and Fern allied themselves with the declaration that the princess' baby was an abomination. Only Fern, however, extended the same notion to Blair's unborn child.

"She may have run away," Rachel tried to show some concern.

"Not now," Darby countered. "She wouldn't still do that."

"Does she know she's pregnant?" Tyler asked.

"We don't know," Blair answered. "Not from us."

"But she could know," Ty offered, "which means she might do something desperate. Hurt herself."

"He's right," Darby was pacing, "We've gotta find her fast… Can't you do something, Blair? Write a spell or something?"

"I don't know, but I'll try."

"Try real hard," he snapped, "What if it was one of your sisters?"

"It was my sisters!" Blair's pain brought the crispy leaves that had accumulated on the porch swirling around. Fire-red hair and orange and yellow leaves whipping around her grief-stricken face.

"I'm sorry," Darby took her into his arms, ashamed of himself for lashing out at such a tender spot.

"I know," she already felt like a mother. "I'll figure out a way to find your sister."

"You've got to," Darby brightened. "I'm gonna be an uncle."

"*Uncle Faggot* to the son of the devil," Fern chimed in. "Isn't that a pretty picture," she added, pouring everyone another round of iced tea.

"Swear it in the name of He Who Sits Apart," Beacon demanded Joppa's promise.

"I won't tell Lucien you're pregnant, Mistress. I may look like a child, but I'm not a fool."

"I hope not, because if he knew the truth, he would never let me go."

Beacon shuddered at the thought, and Joppa still clung to her waist when a guard walked in without asking, "It's time," he announced.

"Let's just get through this," Joppa advised, taking the princess' hand and leading her into the corridor. Neither they nor the soldier noticed Beacon's other hand now stayed protectively over her stomach. Something had shifted in her mind. Once she realized the child was destined to live, she knew that she must protect it from its demon father. Her baby would not become the anti-Christ Lucien dreamed he would be. She would see to that. And Hades help whoever gets in her way.

The grand throne room was over-flowing with witnesses and spectators. Beacon and Joppa took their places on the seats to either side of the throne, which remained empty. Black rose petals carpeted the main aisle which was lined by giant and ancient candelabras. All of the courtesans and courtiers wore black from head to toe and simple glamours had given them all black eyes and hair. As it happened, Joppa wore purple like the princess. Beacon wondered how the mysterious child had known. The girl had already been wearing the matching, though simple, frock when she came to the royal boudoir. Also being blonde, she could have been the princess' sister or daughter. Everyone whispered excitedly until the moment of the traitor's arrival. He entered through the main doors. His toga was also of royal purple. The absence of the silver laurels he had recently taken to wearing left his wavy black hair unadorned. No man had ever looked more handsome.

Lucien's happiness radiated from him. He had dreamt of this moment for millennia. He thought the name The Father had given him had never been more appropriate. He *WAS* the light of the world. At least this world.

For a moment Joppa thought the floor was bubbling and moving before him, until she realized that several black snakes preceded him, undulating through the petals as they led him to the foot of the throne.

After the slightest gesture of a bow to Beacon he took his place on the chair of empire. The crowd became silent. The ceremony's officiate, Angra Mainyu, shimmered into existence at his feet. After kissing his master's sandaled toes, he rose and with a gesture of his hands, signaled that three groups of slaves be brought forward. Each group of six human slaves from Earth was made to kneel, naked at the feet of the Legion lord. Mainyu produced a wand from the air and wasted no time in approaching the slave to the far left of the throne. He proceeded to plunge the magical tool through the slave's throat. The next one was through the heart, then a lung, a stomach. On and on, until lastly through the back of a girl's skull. Then with a proud smile, he brought the bloody instrument to the giant steps that lined the throne. Lucien remained seated, but leaned forward to receive his blessing. The old priest gently laid the wand across the top of his head and in a slashing motion, drew it down across Lu's angelic face. A shiny stripe of sacrificial blood lined his visage from inside one eye to the corner of his mouth. Lucien couldn't resist a flick of his tongue to taste the power.

The thrill of the murders and the mind-blowing importance of the day were making him hard, and as usual his garment revealed his feelings to anyone looking on. Joppa appeared at the princess' side and presented a pillow holding the ceremonial crown. A fabulous construction of silver, obsidian, and real dragon's teeth, allegedly pulled from a beast's fiery mouth by Adolphus himself.

Beacon stood and lifted the crown, signaling Lucien to fall to one knee and again incline his head. This position exposed his throbbing erection to the entire assemblage, and he was pleased. As were they. He couldn't resist giving it a few squeezes and pulls as the princess simultaneously spoke the formal words of coronation and set the ultimate symbol of Legion authority on his head.

"In the name of my father, the made prince of darkness and the air, I name you the true heir to the secret realm," after placing the crown she turned to the demons comprising the royal court, "I give you Lucien, King of Legion. Long live the king," she finished with a low curtsy and took her seat. He remained on bended knee as Joppa draped a black cape over his shoulders. When he rose, it was the girl's turn to bow as she presented him with the royal scepter. The silver-and-onyx staff was rarely used except in ceremonies or ritual. Lucien was still amused by the trident Adolphus had recently had affixed to the top in mockery of Terran mythology. After he gently tapped her shoulder with the wand to bestow his dark blessing, Joppa forced a brief smile and returned to her chair. The new king took his place on the throne to ruckus cheers from the crowd.

The royal scribe, Dashwood, came forward to present an ancient scroll to his new leader. Lucien and Beacon were both required to sign in blood to document the passing of power. One of the seven fingers on each of Dashwood's hands was extended by an especially long claw which easily punctured the human finger and the demonic one releasing the flow. The scribe returned to his corner nook and returned the scroll to the magically sealed chest upon which he perched.

Musicians set up in a balcony began playing their alien instruments. As pulsing dance music filled the chamber, the celebratory demons whipped themselves into a frenzy of dance.

Slaves served the king wine and delicate food, which the girls at his sides politely declined.

"I'm not feeling well," Beacon offered, "I'm going to my room."

"That time of the month," Lucien asked. She said it was and he sniffed the air, "No it's not." He called her on the lie.

"I am sick all the same." He started to excuse her, but as she had already disappeared through the door behind the throne platform, he stopped mid-sentence and shrugged his wide shoulders to Joppa instead.

He ordered her to dance for him, and she readily agreed, but asked that she first be allowed to go to the bathroom. He nodded permission and she too entered the passageway behind the throne.

Joppa caught up with the princess on a small balcony halfway down the hall. Though it was morning on Earth, the sky was still dark with night on Gehenna. Beacon was lost in her sorrows staring out at the beautiful landscape that had once been her kingdom. The little girl leaned her head against her mistress' hip, and Beacon rested her hand on the child's shoulder.

"I'm sorry there's no time for you to grieve for your father and the crumbling of your old life, but we have to get you home, Joppa tried to comfort her beloved friend. "This isn't your home anymore."

"How do you propose we do that, my darling?"

"Luckily, I don't have to figure this one out. Blair is composing a spell as we speak. The powers of the Avatarn are growing and because her wish is concurrent with the will of God, her incantation will work."

"What do I have to do?" Beacon allowed herself a sliver of hope.

"You have only to listen," Joppa climbed up to stand on the stone guardrail and placed a small hand on her mistress' forehead. When she opened her mouth, it was Blair's voice that poured out:

"Space must fold and time must bend,
The princess home to Earth again,
The Beacon from a world of hate,
Return to us to meet your fate."

Beacon's vision blurred for a moment, and when her sight cleared again she was surrounded by corn. The barking of dogs led her the few feet to the edge of the Tobit farmyard.

Tyler saw her first, and his whooping and hollering brought everyone else running.

After Roman healed her hand and scanned her for further injuries with a mere wave of his own, her brother embraced her and everyone retired to the backyard picnic table to catch each other up on the life-altering events that had all taken place before noon.

Chapter 22

At first Lucien barely noticed Joppa had returned to his side. Though he was drunk, he remained completely lucid when he turned to the child and said, "Where is your, mistress?"

"I believe she's in her chambers."

"I know that you somehow helped her escape, you defiant little pest. Fortunately for you, I am feeling merciful on this great historic day....I also know that she is pregnant. Human females exude an odor not unlike other breeding livestock during gestation."

"Then why did you let her leave?"

"There will be time enough to retrieve my child later."

"Your child?" Joppa feigned shock. "With all due respect, Sire. A demon can not procreate."

"I don't know how it is possible, but I smell no other man on her. Unless the faggot brother, of which she is excessively fond, has suddenly developed a taste for pussy, the child is mine." His huge smile was genuine and made Joppa shutter. "After centuries of trying," he continued, "we had given up hope. Finally, to the dark side comes a long sought prince."

Darby and Paolo strattled a fading wood bench. Blair perched cross-legged on the picnic table. Fern rested on the back steps. Tyler, Rachel, and Josh had all procured lawn-chairs, but Roman and Beacon chose to stand. Yet another urgent meeting of the Tobit House residents was called to order.

"Now that our refuge has been discovered, there's nothing to keep Lucy or his goons from returning at any time," Roman led the conversation, "We have to find a reliable way of keeping them out."

"Why doesn't your witch just use her magic?" Fern asked.

"It would weaken me too much to sustain such a barrier long-term," Blair answered.

"We need a method that won't be a constant distraction to the Avatarn," Paolo offered.

All were silent for a moment as they searched their minds for a plan of defense. They all noticed the menagerie of wild animals that surrounded the yard, watching from a cautious distance, but drawn to the collective aura of God's chosen emissaries. Deer, rabbits, a fox, skunk, and a mountain lion. Small flocks of birds from several native species populated the trees and the sky. The domestic animals lay at human feet, proud to attend the people they somehow sensed were divinely sent.

"We could all take guard duty," Tyler suggested. "The cats and the other animals would help us."

"It wouldn't be enough," Rachel chimed in. "We're no match for their strength or their weapons. They are too many."

"I have an idea," Josh looked up from the brittle oak leaf he was spinning between thumb and finger. "We could use the shields from the shuttle."

"Why didn't you suggest that when you arrived, queer?" Fern was indignant, "Are you collaborating with the devils?"

"It wasn't an option before, you shriveled old bitch," Josh didn't bother to raise his voice, "If we had used the shields before, the sustained energy output would have attracted too much attention from Legion. Since our location is now known, there is no need for stealth."

"Do you understand their systems that well?" Roman interrupted their bickering.

"I think I can get it," Josh replied with more confidence than he felt.

"Very well," Roman responded with a wink and a mock salute. "Make it so."

"Acknowledged," Joshua stood and mirrored the gesture.

Blair instructed the barn cats to patrol the perimeter of the farmyard, and they eagerly obeyed. This allowed the others to prepare lunch and continue to plan while Tyler helped Josh in whatever way he could as the former computer programmer worked diligently to decipher the shuttle controls and establish the shield projection that would protect their home. Hours later, when his analysis finally paid off, he encountered another road block. He sent Ty to fetch the Avatarn.

"How's it coming?" Blair was hopeful, despite Ty's demeanor when he requested they accompany him to the shuttle.

"I know how to activate and extend the shields," Josh wasn't smiling.

"*But?*" Ro interjected.

"But, the shuttle's energy stores are low. The shields wouldn't remain stable for more than a few minutes. We have no compatible power source."

"Maybe I can help there," Darby sat and spun in the pilot's chair, "I think I can supply a jump start. I just don't know how long the power boost will last."

"It's our best shot," Josh said, pointing out the metallic cylinders that housed the power cells, "I'm ready to initialize when you are." He keyed a few more sequences into the control panel. Darby moved to Josh's side by the power unit. As Joshua touched the final pads, Dar laid a hand against the shiny cylinders. Golden light encased the power unit which emitted a low hum. The view through the shuttle's front windows wavered for a moment as defensive shields radiated outward from the small ship and expanded to encompass the entire farmyard. The protective bubble was completely transparent once in place. Invisible to the naked eye, but virtually impenetrable. A whooping cheer from the shuttle was echoed from the house. Their home-base was secure for the time being.

Later, Josh told Rachel that decrypting the alien computer systems had been more stressful than deciding whether or not to attend the Pittsburg Gay Pride Festival. She knew exactly what he meant. Her duties as *fag hag* had required her to attend the fest annually and she knew all the pros and cons. (Great dancing, drinking, and mingling, but equal parts of shallow posers, hangovers, and Lesbos with endless kids and pets.) Josh's nerves must have been at their limit.

Unusually warm autumn nights meant wood for the fireplace was not necessary, but Darby needed to burn off some steam. He was accustomed to years of intense daily workouts, and, magical powers aside, his body had too much energy to remain idle. He had decided to lose his shirt and work up a sweat chopping wood behind the house. Taxing his muscles produced the general sense of calm that he needed.

Beacon watched him from an upstairs window. She could so easily fall in love with him. Even if he weren't gay, the fact remained that he was her brother. She didn't realize she had absentmindedly begun to touch herself in her private place. On Gehenna there had been no concept of homosexuality. Though untouched herself, Beacon knew that same-gender sex was something people and demons sometimes did, not who they were. As to the barrier of incest, not even the peasants of Castle Hades permitted it (not openly). Genetic mutations meant unproductive slaves. It couldn't be risked. It was as taboo on her homeworld as on this one.

Though carnal matters seemed somewhat trivial now that she was with child, she longed for a mate. She wanted this baby to have two parents, unlike herself. And she was determined that he not become a pawn in the battle for Earth.

The boy, Tyler, had caught her eye lately. And she his. He might be suitable. He was handsome and brave. He would be loyal and devoted. Already a devoted disciple of her brother and the other Avatarn.

She exhaled with a sigh for what could not be and felt herself one last time before turning her back on the window that allowed her to spy as her brother worked his body. She was going to look for Tyler.

Blair was enjoying her stroll as she looked for Rachel. A quick search had proven she wasn't in the house, so a search of the yard and out-buildings was in order. She wasn't to be found on either porch or in the garden. Blair waved to some of the others as she passed and wandered towards the tire swing. She allowed her mind to roam like her aimless feet.

Blair was thinking about her sisters and how they would have hated the rustic setting she found herself in. They had been city girls through-and-through. She missed them so much her chest hurt. They hadn't been dead so very long, but it seemed a lifetime had passed since they had appeared to her. She longed to confide in them all the juicy details of her new love. When she had first given her heart and her body to Thomas, they had demanded that she share every story and intimate secret. She readily had, as sisters usually do. The young preacher had possessed a naughty side and Molly and Sarah were delighted to hear of it. The gentle and conservative Roman had also revealed an animal within. Her sisters would have approved. Blair had started her adult life with a man who chose to devote himself to the service of God and wound up with a man chosen by God to serve in His plan. She didn't know which path was preferable, but her new destiny paralleled Ro's in a way that her position of support with Thomas never could have.

The universe had taught her one thing she would never have believed when she was making her vows to Thomas. It really was possible to have more than one soul-mate.

Blair's searching eyes finally landed on the lovely caramel-colored Rachel. She was sitting in the grass behind a small shed playing with kittens, momentarily distracted from the horrors of the world.

There was a purpose to Blair's quest. She had made a small gift for each of the non-magical members of their tribe, and she sought to deliver the first to the only girl in the group who was fully and only human.

"Rachel!" The witch called out to her recent "sister." At least Blair hoped that is what they would become to each other.

"Oh, hey," Rae responded with warmth and invitation. As the Avatarn approached, Rachel held up an orange tabby, offering the bundle of fur like a charm with the power to transport its possessor to the normal world.

Blair accepted the purring baby into her palms and began to coo as the nuzzling creature returned her to childhood when nothing else mattered but playing with animals and climbing trees.

"You know, Darby told me when he was a little kid, he use to dress his aunt's cats up in doll clothes. Don't tell him I told you...Did you need something?" Rachel broke her reverie. "Is everything okay?"

Blair's smile when she looked up was again the semi-jaded smile of an adult, "As okay as things ever are now. I just wanted to give you something." She set the orange kitten down with the others tumbling over Rae's legs, and reached into the pocket of her halter-top. She opened her hand to reveal a red string bracelet.

"Oh, a friendship bracelet," Rachel was surprised, "That's so sweet."

"Well, it is that," Blair responded with a small laugh, "but it's more. It's called a *roite bindele*. It's a talisman worn by kabbalists. It is worn on the left wrist to protect you from the *evil eye*—from evil in general."

"Cool. Thanks, Blair." Rachel was genuinely touched.

"I've made them for everyone in our group not already supernaturally protected. I enhanced them with a spell for an additional power boost. It's not exactly a bullet-proof vest, but can't hurt."

Rachel held out her wrist and Blair tied it on for her. At first she tried to shield her new accessory from attack by her meowing friends, but after realizing the tiny teeth and claws were unable to damage it, surrendered her arm to the pouncing balls of fluff. They purred their gratitude and Blair hopped to her feet, silently taking her leave while the kittens remained distracted.

Fern was already watching TV when Paolo and Roman joined her for a look at the news. Somehow CNN was still managing to broadcast from somewhere. Paolo commented on the anchorman's commitment. Brave professionalism 'til the end.

The young anchorman, his famous silver hair and blue eyes shining, still managed to look starched and pressed despite the fact that unbeknownst to viewers he had been sleeping under his desk and living off whatever he could pilfer from vending machines since the alien invasion. His authoritative baritone was relaying updates from around the world as reporters and laypeople called or emailed stories of disastrous encounters from all over the globe.

Roman was beginning to feel a little suffocated by the avalanche of horrors when the image flickered and changed. Where the popular newsman had sat was an anchorwoman instead. Helmut-hairdo and navy blazer aside, there was no mistaking the face of Joppa. A quick peek at Fern and Paolo convinced Roman that this *special report* was for him alone. The others were still seeing CNN's handsome reporter.

"Don't be afraid, Roman," Joppa began in a clipped pro-speaker tone, "It's time you and I have another heart-to-heart."

"I'm listening, Priestess," Roman responded mentally, not wanting to freak out the others by responding aloud. His guide clearly heard him and continued.

"I want to be sure you are not harboring any guilt regarding the love already growing in your heart as your new child grows in Blair's womb. The joy that is born of your new life is a gift, and in no way a betrayal of Brenda or Janie…Your love for your daughter—for me—remains uncompromised—incorruptible for eternity. New love—though it be equal—does not diminish it…I am happy for you (flash of Janie's face), Daddy."

Tears streamed Roman's cheeks, though he smiled at his sometime daughter, "Thank you, Baby," he mouthed.

"Are you all right, young man?" Fern was baffled by the crying leader.

"I am now," Ro replied. He wiped his eyes and the screen was again filled with the stalwart anchorman. He quietly left the room to find Blair, unable to wait to share the message from his little girl.

It seemed that Blair's usually flat abdomen grew before Roman's eyes as throughout the following night and day the gestation of their unborn child progressed at a terrifying rate.

Darby and some of the others had worried that the witch might explode until less than twenty-four hours later she felt the first twinges of cramping. She thought something must be horribly wrong, Avatarn or no. Using all of her powers, Blair tried to summon Joppa, but the spiritual chameleon failed to appear.

The household was in a near state of panic when the witch's water broke, and an angel appeared.

"I am Avalon. Sent to serve as your mid-wife," she announced before soothing Blair's brow with a gentle caress that erased the fears Roman's best assurances had failed to calm. The angel's flesh was black as obsidian; her eyes and long hair were metallic gold. She appeared naked, though her breasts and sex lacked the detail of being fully formed. She was a living statue of gold and volcanic glass. And none of them could have been happier that she was there.

Though Ro and Blair's bedroom was filled to capacity with anxious well-wishers, the "Aunties and Uncles" were content to cut a wide berth for the angel and Fern, who insisted her decades of experience required her to take an active part.

Fern was not accustomed to visitations from celestial beings, and, though dazzled by Avalon (and her unexpectedly exotic skin color) by God, she was the head nurse in the Tobit House.

Blair couldn't decide if her head were spinning from the pain or the fact that she had just experienced an entire pregnancy in a day and was in labor. Even after everything they had encountered on their miraculous journey, nothing had prepared her for this. Not every episode of *ER*. Not years of *General Hospital.* Not even *Grey's Anatomy.*

Fern was wiping her down with cool rags when Roman knelt by the bed and attempted to heal her "pain." When nothing happened, Avalon assured him that the pain was natural and because nothing was *wrong*, he couldn't ease her burden.

Blair was sobbing quietly between the racking contractions that were coming harder and faster. Each member of the team had to remind him or herself to breathe. They had been alarmed by the one-day pregnancy, and afraid of what might spring from her womb. Every mind present had been crossed by the possibility that maybe the Avatarn weren't supposed to have sex anymore. Maybe this was a punishment for letting the lure of flesh distract them from their holy mission.

Avalon positioned herself to catch the new arrival. It would be very soon. Fern began to wonder if Blair were woman enough to remain conscious and do what must be done. Fern was also on guard. She had prepared a work station where she would clean up the new babe...Unless. For Roman's sake she hoped all would be fine, but if the witch gave birth to something with hooves or a tail. Fernie would put an end to it on the spot. She still didn't trust the red-haired slut. Another few minutes would tell the tale.

That's when Blair saw *Her*. No one else could see what had suddenly commanded her attention, but clearly something invisible was at her bedside. Blair, her pain forgotten, was listening intently and nodding her head. Eventually she found her voice to say, "As you wish, Mother. So mote it be." The witch smiled at her unseen visitor, then turned to where Ro lingered at the head of the bed. She wanted to confirm that he had seen it, but knew he hadn't when he said, "What did your mom say, Honey?"

"It wasn't Mom," Blair said in a state of extraordinary peace, and offered no further explanation. Roman didn't need one. Though his Catholicism had lapsed a long time ago, he knew who her visitor had been. He didn't ask again what had been said. He knew it was for Blair alone to know. His theory was proven, as her last and worst contractions failed to even crease her brow.

Avalon's melodic voice instructed her to push one last time and a cherubic pink-red boy slid into her ebony arms.

"Beautiful," Beacon was the first to speak.

"What's his name?" Paolo asked as Fern tried to touch the baby's radiant purple halo. Beacon wondered about the color since his parents' nimbi were blue.

Though they had never discussed it, Blair and Roman responded in unison, "Atom."

No one spoke or stopped smiling as the angel helped Blair finish the birthing process, and Fern cleaned the baby. Self-appointed Nurse Leaves was glad she didn't have to kill this wee one for Heaven's sake. Though she didn't care for the mother, this one was a prince for sure. Nobody would hurt this one on her watch. If that meant she had to step between him and the parents, she was ready. She had been helpless to stop the devils that killed her grandchildren, but she was keeping this one for the Lord. The old woman hesitated when Blair held out her arms for her son, but quickly recovered and handed over the precious bundle.

Roman had climbed into the bed to hold both his woman and their child. His teeth had dried out from smiling but he still couldn't stop. Only Blair and he could see when each of Atom's cheeks was gently pressed by the translucent faces of Janie and Thomas which floated on each side of him, their ghostly lips momentarily blushing his delicate skin. The infant seemed comforted by their blessing, and his parents looked into each other's eyes to share the truth each had just recognized. God had given them a reason, and they would save the world to shield him from sorrow.

Looking at his child, Roman finally understood something about God and His Son. He somehow knew without doubt, that Yahweh or Jehovah had not sent Yeshua to Earth to die for our sins. God was not blood-thirsty. That was a primitive tribal idea. And his forgiveness knew no limits…Roman knew he could forgive Atom anything, any mistake or even misguided intention. How could God do less for his children, which we all are? He knew as he felt again the level of love that he had only felt once before. When Janie was born. Jesus came to Earth to die and be resurrected because it was the only way for Him to make us KNOW how much He loves us. It's the love only a parent feels. God became a man to get our attention and show us that He would be tortured and killed just to make us look at Him and know that HE suffers when WE do, that we are never alone, and that WITH HIM we can have eternal life. To be reunited with Him forever. Each made complete. And all you have to do is want it, and it shall be. Roman bowed his head, overcome by the simplicity of this profound truth. By the obviousness of it. How could any parent not understand and relate to Jesus' purpose? For this baby, Roman could do anything.

Chapter 23

Roman was reluctant to part from his Atom and his Blair for even a moment, but when the crowd finally disbanded and spread throughout the house, he followed Darby down to the welcoming front porch.

"Good job, Stud-muffin," Dar offered a high-five, "You musta done somethin' right. Your son is perfect."

"Thanks, Man. I think all the credit must go to his magical mother. I'm just blessed to be any part of it."

"Don't sell yourself short, Boss. As far as I know, even in our upside-down world it still takes two for that brand of miracle."

A quick scan of the yard confirmed that there was no one else around to interrupt or influence what Roman needed to discuss with his young friend, so he seated himself on the worn-smooth boards of the porch and propped his back against a white support column and faced the blond in the rocking chair.

"I need to ask a favor, Dar…And it's a big one," Roman suddenly seemed nervous.

"Anything," Darby responded without hesitation.

"We would like you to be Atom's god-father."

Darby was stunned for a moment, but quickly recovered before squaring his shoulders and raising his chin. "It would be my great honor."

"I'm so glad…Later we plan to ask Brenda to be his god-mother."

"That's a wonderful idea, Ro."

"If loving that little guy up there, gives her heart even a fraction of the healing it's already given mine, I can't wait for her to meet him."

The darkly handsome man rose up on his knees and he and the other Avatarn met in a fierce hug. Celebrating the expansion of their new family.

Rachel ping-ponged between jealousy and envy. She couldn't help being envious of Blair and Roman. The complete devotion of a wonderfully charismatic straight man and a new born baby. On the other hand, Paolo had captured the heart of the only man she had really ever fallen in love with. The ever-unattainable Darby. She was having a hard time being happy for her friends. Wanting a piece of the pie for herself; she had never felt more alone.

The lovely brown girl had slipped away to patrol the perimeter of the yard with the dogs, and found more and more her thoughts were turning to Tyler. Ty wasn't exactly one hundred percent straight. That was probably why she was starting to crush on him. He was really cute in that sorta rare-redhead kinda way. Mixing DNA from a redhead and a black woman might be somewhat risky, but what the hell? Sometimes in life you have to go for it, and cross your fingers. Besides, she was thinking, the fit of his pants suggested he might put on a spectacular show in the bedroom.

Her hopes about his anatomy were confirmed when she approached the old tree stump that marked a back corner of the yard. This corner of the lot was sheltered from view of the house by an old chicken coop, and she was quick enough to kneel in its shadow before distracting Tyler from his focus.

He wore no shirt, and his jeans were around his ankles. Reclining against the stump, he was lost in animal pleasure. One hand tweaked and pulled at his nipple. The other gripped the very thick shaft of his engorged dick. The taut muscles of his lily-white arms, chest, and stomach flexed and bulged with the effort.

Rachel broke an instant sweat and felt wet everywhere. She wasn't ashamed of herself for watching him pump his swollen meat. She was enthralled. Tired of the "nun's life" for which she had never volunteered. She moved rapidly to his side, causing him to freeze in astonishment. Unable to speak or even move the hand still wrapped around the base of his fat cock.

As she reached him, one of her still finely manicured hands was un-buttoning her blouse, when the other reached to enclose the top of his manhood and the spongy head. She was smiling and had actually jacked it a few times before Ty shook off the shock and forcibly pushed her hand away and tried to cover himself with his own.

"Why?" was all Rachel could manage in her confusion.

"You—you're an awesome girl," he stuttered, self-consciously trying to wipe all the sticky pre-cum from the furry red trail leading down from his belly button, "I mean it. You're a beauty, but I have feelings for someone else."

"You're hot for Darby!" She accused, "I should have known!"

"Not him!" he yelled back, "His sister!"

Rachel hadn't seen that one coming. "You can't be serious. The ice queen?" Rae was incredulous.

"Yes."

"You have a school-boy fantasy about the princess of demons. Is that what you're telling me?" She continued her indignant reaction while he pulled up his pants and secured his belt.

"She's not like that," he answered.

"Oh? How is she, Tyler? This woman that you've known a few days?"

"All I know is, I find her as fascinating as she is beautiful, and she's starting to dig me too. We've been flirting a little, and I hope to take it a lot further."

"She'll have you for lunch, little boy," she had turned to leave, but looked back over her shoulder to add, "And she'll be thinking of her brother while she does it."

Beacon hadn't been searching for Tyler long, when she found him with Rachel in an outer-most corner of the yard. They both stared as she approached, and the princess was convinced that the light-blue sundress Blair had talked her into had been a poor choice after all. She was no more confident about the loose ponytail Paolo had made of her golden hair.

"Greetings," she offered awkwardly when she arrived at the stump.

"Back at ya," Rae barely suppressed her bitterness.

"I was seeking your company, Tyler," Beacon gingerly touched his bicep but quickly withdrew as if burned; "I did not realize you were using my brother's handmaiden."

"What?" Rachel came unglued, and Ty's fast thinking put his entire body in her path as she lunged towards the arrogant princess. "How dare you? You crazy, you devil-lovin', demon seed carryin' bitch?"

"Simmer down," Ty was quiet but forceful, turning Rae away from Beacon and boosting her towards the house. "You know how she is. She's in a foreign world. Cut her some slack," he looked over his shoulder to give the semi-startled princess a wink and a smile, "You go walk it off," he patted Rachel on the tush, "Miss Dragor and I have things to discuss," he waited long enough to be sure she was going to leave them in peace, then returned to the stump and the smiling, fresh-scrubbed face of a little girl who had been living among the wolves.

Rachel didn't go straight to the house. She decided she needed to cry for a minute, and not wanting the others to see her, she entered the cornfield, moving several rows deep. She stopped about 12 feet out, unsure of how far the protection shield extended. She didn't want to find herself on the outside trying to get back in. Sitting in the dirt, she ignored the scratching of the stalks against bare arms. Hugging her knees, she let the tears flow. Suppressing tiny sobs, she decided she didn't need a man to complete her after all. She thought about how the Navaho believe the first human was a woman, and that woman, second to no one, founded a nation. That myth had merit, and from that moment forward, she would be the pilot of her own destiny. She wouldn't need Darby or any other man to forge her path.

That's when she heard it. The deeply male whisper of a voice she knew.

"Who's there?" Rachel was more miffed than afraid.

"Don't be afraid," In a blink Lucien sat before her. His back against the corn, each of his knees outside one of hers. He was resplendent, as always, in a green toga—perfectly matching the stalks behind him.

Rae opened her mouth to scream, but his hand on her knee gave her pause. Knowing she would wonder how he penetrated their shield, Lucien quietly explained that while the force-field was adequate to repel common soldiers, his powers were beyond the laws of physics. After listening, she aborted the scream and said, "What do you want?"

"I want you, golden child. Be my bride and rule the universe at my side."

"First of all, setting the hokey-ness of that statement aside—cause you obviously been watchin' too much TV, I thought you were *in love* with Princess Bitch?"

"I was once. That is passed. The truth is she is an Earthling, no different from you. I prefer a bride who appreciates my attentions," he finished with a small caress of her thigh, which despite her will resonated through her body and touched her lonely heart.

"You have killed my friends and you are currently in the process of enslaving my planet. You think I'm going to sell my soul to the new devil for a little nookie?" She used both hands to remove his from her body.

"As for what you call murder," he responded calmly while she wondered how it felt for him to sit in the dirt when she knew he wore no undies beneath his toga, "It has always been nature's way for the strong—the superior—to survive and conquer. One can not judge the harshness or cruelty of nature as evil. It is simply the order of things—set forth by the Father you all adore." She was angry, but she was listening. And his hands were rubbing her outer arms as he eyed her cleavage. Though she was afraid of him, his blatant desire for her—even if only a ruse—was enticing. It made her feel alive. She felt something she hadn't felt in years at Darby's side, and even as she recognized it, she was amazed by its power. She felt noticed.

"Why me?" She clasped his hands in hers with the intention of removing them, but when her small fingers wrapped around his large ones, she no longer wanted to let go.

"The activities of your cohorts have brought me frequently into your presence of late. How could I fail to be mesmerized by such beauty and loyalty as you possess."

"You could do worse than me," she didn't want to succumb to such obvious flattery, "but you have your pick of any woman or man in the galaxy. You just want to use me to get to the Avatarn."

"You under-estimate yourself, as your friends always do…As for the others, I will destroy them as I must. You only think you have an obligation to intervene. I will never ask you to betray them. I will love you and exalt you in ways that would never occur to them in their selfish lives."

"I need to think about this," Rachel couldn't believe she was saying the words and that she meant them.

"Very well," he dazzled her with a brilliant smile, "I have only a small request, if I am to return for your answer." He leaned in for a brief kiss.

"Here we go…What is it?" She braced herself and relished her tingling lips. He vanished as she heard the words.

"Get rid of the cats."

Josh was checking on the shuttle's shield integrity when Fernie joined him on the small vessel. The old woman settled into the co-pilot's seat and appeared to be checking out the controls.

"Well, to what do I owe the honor?" Josh came across as more sarcastic than he had intended.

"Time we had a talk, dear," Fern hadn't meant to sound so sarcastic either. Though she was no psychiatrist, and wouldn't want to be, she had concluded that Joshua's snappish and volatile behavior suggested some personal insecurity. Those doubts and whatever damage they reflected meant he might be open to a little manipulation on her part. Maybe Atom's soul wasn't the only one of the bunch she could save.

"You need to put away this vulgar lifestyle," she continued, "You can serve God's Hammer without partaking in the behavior He allows them." It was then that his rapidly faltering schizoid brain led him to believe that she wasn't Fern at all. She was his Grandma. Grandma Sue. Never-mind that Grandma had been dead for seven years. Josh knew first hand that the dearly-departed could sometimes communicate with the living.

"What do you mean, Grandma?"

His words caused Fern to flinch with a moment of confusion. She quickly realized how sick the boy really was, and was more determined than ever to save his soul. She decided to play along.

"You must give up this homosexual identity you are so proud of. If you can't live as God intended, you must become celibate. Sinful deeds outweigh sinful thoughts."

"But, Grandma…I am living a celibate life now. Yoshi is gone, and there's no one here that I think of in that way…Besides, how can it be wrong when one of the *Chosen Ones* has a gay lover even now?"

"The Lord has chosen from among the vilest sinners for reasons that are not ours to know. Perhaps he is fighting fire with fire, as they say," she paused for this bit of reasoning to soak into Josh's rattled mind, "Your duty is not to emulate them, but to serve the Lord by helping them carry out their mission."

Josh listened carefully, never one to disrespect his beloved grandmother, but he still appeared to be unsure, so the old woman maintained her twisted tirade.

"Perhaps the Lord Almighty put an end to that Yoshi boy in order to set you back on the correct path. To mend your ways so you can focus on God and helping the Avatarn," she was standing and seemed so righteous in Josh's tired eyes.

"But, Grandma," Joshua was crying, "even if you are right about a life of abstinence allowing me to focus on our mission, I won't believe that God allowed Yoshi to die to punish us for being together."

"You believe what you will, boy. Believing a thing doesn't make it so. I have had a vision, and the Lord showed me how you are to serve," Fern was improvising as she went along, but the young man looked like he might be starting to buy it, so she went with it, "You will be *First Priest* to the wicked but chosen, Hammer of God."

Something clicked in the mind that had once made Josh whole and allowed his melting personality to lock onto the concepts his apparent grandmother was pounding at him. With Yoshi gone, and no easy sex in sight, the title of *First Priest* sounded pretty important. Besides, they probably had been wrong about all the gay stuff. The Lord was giving him a chance to start over. He would be the first of a great priestly order. Leader of the Avatarn monks. Whole-heartedly serving the Avatarn despite the fact that they were obviously evil, being used to battle evil. His devotion would be faultless.

"You are right, Grandma. I will do as you have advised. Forgive me for being lost and blind for so long."

"There is nothing for *ME* to forgive my darling," Fern paused as Josh threw himself into her arms, "Only God can forgive your past perversion, and he will, as long as you do not stumble from this new path."

When Josh flung himself on the floor of the vessel to pray with his forehead pressed firmly against the alien metal, Fern took her chance for a fast and silent exit.

Later, when he told the group of his grandmother's annunciation and his epiphany, he made no mention of Fern ever being there, and her lips were sealed.

Everyone present, including the Avatarn, tried to convince him that there was nothing wrong with being gay—that God chose such things, not mortals, but he wouldn't hear it. He would not disrespect Darby and Paolo, but he would never break his self-imposed priestly vows. They explained that they required no priests or servants—only friends, but he would not be dissuaded. Josh knew his duty, and the others knew Josh had demons all his own.

Chapter 24

Fern had refused the gift of Blair's little red bracelet, because it wasn't *Christian,* but Paolo, Tyler, and even the recently demented Josh, had readily accepted theirs.

After presenting sweet-natured Paolo with his lastly, Blair and the beautiful son swaddling in the carrier draped across her chest, started back towards the sanctuary of their bedroom.

The atmospheric disturbances of the invasion fleet still seemed to be heating the air and she was glad that the unseasonable temperature allowed Atom to spend a portion of his first days outside with her.

Blair looked to the endless azure sky and thought it looked like an ocean. The clouds, cresting waves. The massive three-dimensional clouds drifted and changed and she found herself scrying for signs in shapes as she had with her sisters as a child.

She lingered at the front steps, when cumulous *cotton candy* began to morph into a peek at the future. Quickly the large mass of white vapor took the undeniable form of a dragon, the next moment—a human hand, and finally a single lily blossom floating in the sky. The symbols reverted to formless mist and she was left wondering if she was just projecting her imagination onto the clouds. No. She knew what all little witches intuit before kindergarten. The clouds very freely offer tomorrow's truths and today's secrets. You just have to watch. And know.

She went inside and headed upstairs to contemplate the cryptic portents she had just read in the sky.

As Blair snuggled into the bed with Atom and proceeded to breast-feed him, she thought about how ridiculous she had been to hesitate to feed him this way. Absence of prepared formula had left her little choice, and she was glad in the end. The bizarre modesty of modern puritanical America would probably have deprived her of one of the most natural bonding experiences afforded by nature. Roman was still a bit squeamish, admitting he had been completely agreeable when Brenda had put Janie directly on the bottle. He was coming around though. When she had finally convinced him to taste it, he assured her that while he loved the packaging, he still preferred Pepsi.

Placing her lips on Atom's head, she inhaled the fresh and magnetic scent of him. There was nothing like the smell of a clean baby. If innocence and peace have a smell, that is it.

Blair's joy faded as thoughts turned to her parents. Who knew if they were still alive? She remembered their devastation by the deaths of her sisters. Their sad visits to her in the psych ward when her mind had been beyond their reach. She had wanted to call them after her escape but she feared that any contact would increase the odds of making them a demonic target. She wondered if they would ever see their grandson. She prayed that they would. They deserved it. The birthday parties, Christmas, high school plays and whatnot. They deserved it all.

And what about Roman's parents? She wanted so much to meet them. If they had survived, they were getting on in years and she wanted a chance to know them.

"Time will tell," she cooed to her baby as she burped him, then both surrendered to sleep.

Darby and Paolo were feeding the horses, thankful that the

Tobits had lain in all the necessary stores for the care of the animals.

"What's that face for? You look like an Olmec monolith," Dar teased his lover, curious about the cause of the scowl on his face as they hand-fed the horses treats of apples and carrots.

"What's an Olmec?" Paolo questioned back. Apparently, he hadn't paid as much attention in their Ancient History class as the Avatarn had. Darby did his best to describe the giant, sort of Asian-looking, human head statues located sporadically around the Gulf of Mexico. His explanation earned him a deeper scowl before Paolo answered the first question, "I was just thinking about the cats."

"What about them?" Darby asked.

"Where are they? Any other time they would be shadowing us at our heels or occasionally visible as they patrol the perimeter of the yard. I think I've only seen two all day."

"I'm sure they're around. Hiding from the dogs or resting in the shade."

"I don't know," Paolo refused his rationale, "I think there's something funky going on."

"The shield is in place. No intrusion possible. You're just being paranoid;" Darby rubbed his back. "Besides the horses aren't spooky. They would know if something supernatural was up."

"I hope you're right," he remained unconvinced.

"Jinkies!" Darby interjected when one of the happy horses suddenly popped an erection. Both men were startled and erupted with laughter at the unexpected and impressive display.

Their levity was short lived, as Darby's thoughts turned to more serious matters and his abrupt mood change was manifest on his face.

"What is it?" Paolo was concerned, "You ARE worried about our little band of gypsies."

"*Gypsies* now are we?" Dar's face brightened for a second, "Then who are the *gadje*, the foreigners, the non-Roma? Just the aliens or every other human being on the planet? Now that we've been set apart from the natural order, what criteria define *the other*?"

Paolo ducked under a horse head to join the somber blond Avatarn and take his hand, "No expression of the divine is unnatural. You—*The Chosen*—and we—all of us are exactly what God intended us to be. You know that." The two recent students still enjoyed philosophical debate.

"I know," Darby agreed with a half-hearted smile, "It's just that sometimes I wonder if we—The Avatarn—should be having sex, ya know? Pleasure of the flesh just seems so trivial—great as it is with you—when we're supposed to be saving the world."

Paolo replied in the tone that a father uses to soothe a distraught child, "In times of war and crisis, people have always embraced sexuality…Making love makes you feel alive. It feels real when nothing else does…But Man's courage fades and insights are forgotten when he fears God is watching."

Dar felt the resonance of truth, but he wanted to be sure he followed the smaller man's point, "Okay, *Oracle*. What's that mean?"

"It means—those things that you only think may be wrong in times when you are afraid, are not wrong—and you really know that. Society and organized religion have hard-wired people with that gnawing little twinge of doubt that if God really is jealous and petty and cruel when all the conditions for His love aren't met, then we're going to get in trouble. Be punished. Of course that's not the way the universe works, but when people are afraid, the first thing they abandon is reason. The second is faith."

"Holy fount of wisdom, Batman. He should have made you the Avatarn, Baby." Darby was amazed by his boyfriend's insight.

"Naw, I'm just feeling my way along. Common sense just tells me that nothing oppressive can be a reflection of God's will. Combine that with the concept of eternal unconditional love and everything else just flows. I bet He would even take back the demons if they wanted it. They're His creation too after all. But that's where choice comes in. A creature chooses either to be with God or apart from God. Some people will tell you that choice has to be permanent, but it doesn't. He'll wait forever for you. Sometimes people think they've gone too far to ever go back, but it's never too far. No one's ever too lost. Or too bad. People just can't imagine Him forgiving what they can't forgive in themselves. Hell is self-imposed isolation from The Father. And it's kindled out of shame. Heaven is the Father's incorruptible joy when the prodigal turns one last time towards home and calls out to The Source...My place is at your side, Dar. My destiny is to help you meet yours."

Darby was weeping in wonder at his lover's enlightenment when the first screech pierced the air. A large shadow passed over the farmyard, but it wasn't a shuttle that glided over the house and circled just outside the perimeter of the shield.

The brown praying mantis moved quickly across the dying grass of the front yard. It had crawled halfway up the shuttle door, when it began to grow. The alien-looking creature was six feet tall when it finished morphing back into Lucien.

With a wave of his hand, the hatch descended and he swiftly ducked inside. The shield bubble collapsed with a shimmer, and the airborne intruder plunged inside the previously protected atmosphere.

All those outside were dumbfounded by the sight of a flying dragon from medieval legend breathing fire and screeching like a banshee. And the monster was not alone. On its back rode a modern-day Pan. Half goat/half demon with an over-developed steroidal musculature to boot.

Josh had already started to sprint toward the shuttle. Even before he became aware of the mounted demon attack, he had seen the shield go down and was praying as he ran that he would be able to re-initialize it.

He darted through the open door of the craft, propelled by adrenaline. He was prepared to encounter a demonic foe, but found the interior empty of life. Josh easily re-activated the shield, as the controls had not been damaged. He took no notice of the four-inch praying mantis that watched from atop some leaves just outside the hatch.

Darby and Paolo were still standing near the horse pen when Tyler and Beacon joined them. All eyes were locked on the giant winged reptile soaring above the farm.

"Am I hallucinating? Or is that a fucking dragon?" Tyler spoke first.

"You're observation is accurate," Beacon assured him, "And that is a satyr on its back."

"Say what?" Tyler asked.

"A man with goat legs," Darby offered.

"Not just any man," Paolo interjected as the flying monster made a close pass. "I don't know how, but that is Cinder," to clarify for Tyler and Beacon's benefit he continued, 'My former boyfriend. The one Dar was forced to kill."

Another low pass confirmed for the blond Avatarn that his lover was correct. "I think we're going to need the others," he mumbled. He didn't have to call out to them. Everyone was summoned by Rachel's screams. She had been playing with the golden retriever in the backyard when the green fire-breather flew overhead. She had been stunned at first, but when she recognized the half-goat creature that rode it, the screams of horror had erupted from her lungs. How could that bastard have come back to life? And who had given him the make-over and the new ride when he got to Hell?

Blair was yanked awake by Rachel's ear-piercing terror. Atom also woke, but was quiet and unafraid. Fern ran into the room to be sure the baby was safe.

The witch only hesitated for a second. She knew Fern hated her, and the feeling was pretty mutual, but she also knew the old woman loved Atom. She handed the baby to the temporary stand-in grandmother saying only, "In the cellar 'til we come for you." Fern didn't want to hide while everyone around her was slaughtered, as she had been forced to do before, but Atom's safety was paramount. She had failed her own grandchildren, but she would save this child at all costs. She didn't even answer Blair, just headed for the internal entrance to the small unfinished cellar.

Blair encountered Roman as both ran through the kitchen and then out the front door. They spotted Josh and Rachel racing toward the horse corral and followed suit. Ro's eyes turned skyward to see what held the others' rapt attention. He saw a Pan-like demon wielding a sword and shield from the top of a dragon. He didn't know the satyr's true identity until Darby brought the other Avatarn up to speed.

"I thought he was dead?" Blair was baffled.

"He was. I was there," Paolo's eyes glistened and they remained locked on a mutation of the man he had once cared for.

"You all speak as if resurrecting a dead human were a difficult thing," Beacon tried to mask her fear with royal posturing.

Josh, Blair, Tyler, and Roman exchanged glances. If that was true.....

"Of course, when a corpse is re-animated by Legion, they're really only causing it to become possessed," the princess concluded.

The others rolled their eyes. A moment's hope dashed as quickly. Azazel reined his scaled mount into a dive towards the clustered Avatarn.

"Zoinks!" Paolo was the only one to vocalize before all dove to the ground to avoid an exhalation of flames. Beacon, whom had never been injured in her life, was a bit surprised to find the hair singed off her arms.

"Wow, Paolo. Cinder's lookin' tore up from the floor up," Darby tried to use his customary nonchalance to slice through the blanket of terror that had fallen on the group. Paolo responded with a chastising look and Dar added, "Just sayin'."

"Our only chance is to meet him in his element to keep him from getting anywhere near the baby. Get on the horses," Blair instructed Roman and Darby. Ro swung onto the back of the palomino stallion that seemed to be waiting on the other side of the fence. Darby climbed onto a tall brown and white paint with ice-blue eyes. Finally, Blair, whom had been farther from the pen, used the slats of the fence to reach her perch on a jet-black mare she had named Fand for the Irish Queen of Fairies. Azazel seemed to be loitering in the sky, content to wait for his opponents to come to him. Though the horses were unbridled, their jitters had been soothed when Blair telepathically summoned them to service. They seemed to sense the will of their riders and bravely obeyed.

"What about us?" Tyler was indignant at being excluded from the coming battle.

"All of you find shelter," Roman ordered. "Our son is safe?" He looked to Blair for confirmation. After her nod, Josh grabbed Rachel's hand and the others followed his decisive run towards the shuttle.

Blair raised her voice to be heard above the scouring roars of the monster, and her incantation seemed to echo though there was no obvious source of the reverberation:

"Forelock, hooves and swishing tails,
Carry us where storm clouds sail.
I wish I may, I wish I might,
Grant you now the power of flight."

She had barely finished when each horse in turn whinnied and leapt into the air.

The Tobits' horses galloped into the sky as if they were born to it. Roman took point as was his instinct. Azazel jerked the dragon's head in the direction of the airborne Avatarn, and spurred him forward. Ro was wondering how he was going to defend against the Cinder/demon hybrid let alone dragon's breath, when the silent question was answered for him.

"Oh shit!" was all that left his lips when the winged reptile unleashed a torrent of flames intended for him. Darby hadn't quite caught up with their leader, but a flip of his wrist sent a stream of golden energy from his palm to form a shield in front of Roman's mount. The handsome wheat-colored horse hadn't even had a chance to panic at the shooting fire. The orange licks of heat were dispersed into the air, and Ro flew through unharmed.

Azazel soared past and began to circle back in their direction.

"We need weapons, damn it!" Darby shouted towards Blair.

She responded by reaching inside her blouse to pull out three dandelions she had plucked from the yard shortly after the dragon's appearance. Without a word, she popped off their "heads" and as the blossoms fell away, the stems began to grow. Rapidly expanding, they soon took the form of three lances. She casually tossed one towards each of her partners, and the wind cooperatively carried them to the intended hands.

Once armed, Darby joined Blair in flanking the demon from opposing sides.

Blair's first joust was easily deflected by Azazel's sword, but the multi-pronged attack allowed Darby's lance to pierce a scaled wing. The dragon recoiled from the pain, freeing Dar's weapon and distracting the furry demon (which was predictably naked) from the sword swing he had intended for Blair's neck. Roman was right behind them, and took advantage of the opportunity to make a slashing blow towards the back of Azazel's head. The satyr easily blocked the lance with his shield, and as an after-thought, thrust his sword in Ro's general direction. The metal pierced the Avatarn's thigh, and a spot of crimson quickly expanded across his jeans. Roman cried out in shock and pain, but only for a moment, before a flash of white light emanated from his wound and he was instantly healed. The demon growled in frustration.

"Surrender, fools! You will fail as all his mortal enemies have!" Azazel shouted towards the place in the sky where Blair and Darby had regrouped.

"Not bloody likely, Goatboy," Dar shot back.

Blair chimed in, "Yeah, fuck you, Golem!" She thought the possessed corpse was just about a textbook example of the Hebrew term. Through playing around, Darby dropped his lance, allowing it to fall to the ground far below narrowly missing an angry hen. The blond Avatarn raised both hands above his head, interlocking his fingers. Golden spheres of energy began to orbit his woven fists. The lights plunged into his hands, merging to form a wide beam that shot towards the charging demon and his ride.

The golden energy blast found its target in the middle of Azazel's chest. The muscle-bound monster was completely unfazed. Darby couldn't hide his shock any more than he could protect himself from attack after momentarily expending all of his energy in his offensive effort.

"Prepare to taste my blade, Faggot!" Cinder/Azazel shouted. The dragon glided within range, and Darby was helpless to escape. The demon left his sword planted in the Avatarn's heart, and a swat of the reptile's tail sent Darby plummeting to the ground. He landed on his back, and though he tried to speak, only blood gurgled from his mouth.

No one on board the shuttle in the front yard could see what had happened, but Roman and Blair looked on in horror. Azazel had taken up a position some distance away, and seemed content to enjoy watching his victim die before resuming the battle. It was only when he saw Ro's horse galloping towards the Earth that he caused the dragon to dive, blocking the healer's path to his friend.

Roman held tightly to his rearing steed, unsure of his next move. It was a sob from Blair that jarred him into action. He was suddenly very thankful that he remembered how to throw a curveball. Bringing his hands together in front of his stomach, he rolled an orb of white energy between them. Drawing back with one arm, he fired the ball in an arcing trajectory that curved around the monsters blocking his way and found its mark in the fallen Avatarn's chest. Darby convulsed with the infusion of power and white lightning sizzled around his head and limbs. When the light show faded, so had the sword—out of existence—and the wound was gone. He remained covered in blood (unlike Ro's usual healings), but was fully healed. Dar stood up and saluted his immediate savior and flipped off his would-be killer.

In rage, Azazel prepared the dragon to dive yet again, but Blair had anticipated the move.

Her brave ebony mare brought her within half a dozen meters

of her foe. Azazel had begun to laugh at her pointless display of courage, but stopped to listen when she adopted an air of serenity and simply said, "Bees, please," and opened her mouth widely allowing a swarm of yellow and black to be disgorged. The bees shot straight for their target, the satyr barely having time to recognize his own instinctive fear. They stung his eyes, his tongue, his penis and everything in between. The mutant flailed in agony, attempting to wipe them away, but the damage was done.

The bees disappeared into the cerulean sky, and Roman swooped in to take advantage of the monster's blindness. The dragon turned to snap at Ro's horse, but by that time the swarthy Avatarn had slid onto the reptile's back; unsure of his footing, Roman didn't waste a second. He swung his lance like a baseball bat, connecting with the side of Azazel's head. Hearing a sickening crack when the weapon met his enemy's skull, Ro allowed himself to exhale but didn't have time to celebrate. Losing his balance, he toppled from the scaly green back in the same moment as the demon. Both Blair's horse and Ro's raced towards the falling hero, but only Darby's powers reached him in time. He was caught in a blanket of golden light only three feet from the ground, an extension of Dar's upturned palm. The suffering satyr approached the ground in the same instant, but just before the anticipated splat, he shrunk to the size of a pea, and with a "pop" was gone from existence.

Without the guidance of its rider, the dragon turned towards the clouds, launching itself upwards. The beast was flying at maximum speed, head extended, when it hit the force-field. It was dead on impact. A peach tree and more than a few chickens were smashed when it crashed to the yard below. Only hours later, when everyone from the house had gotten a good look, did Josh use the shuttle lasers to vaporize the prehistoric creature (before the carcass could begin to rot).

After the entire group had gathered on the front porch to hash over the events of the attack, and to speculate pointlessly on what had caused the temporary drop in the shields, Darby and Paolo excused themselves to grab a quick shower together before supper.

"Cinder always had a lot of issues," Paolo was saying as he scrubbed his lover's back, finally rinsing away the blood, "but he deserved so much better than all of this. And if it weren't for me, he would never have been involved."

"You can't blame yourself," Darby countered—smiling at the cliché in spite of the seriousness of the topic. He was glad Paolo couldn't see his face.

"There's no one else to blame," Paolo continued.

"People get their hearts broken all the time," Darby argued, "That doesn't absolve them of responsibility for their actions. He chose evil. At least in his last life. I'm just glad I didn't have to be the one to kill him again."

"I don't think he's dead," Paolo had stopped washing.

Darby turned to face him and pulled the smaller man against his scar-free chest, "I hope you're wrong…Thanks to Cinder, for a second there, I was planning afternoon tea with Yoshi and Honey.

Chapter 25

When the group scattered after a desert of Fern's home-made blackberry pie (just as good from the freezer), Roman kissed the baby and told Blair he needed a few minutes of solitude to pull his head together. He slipped out the front as quietly as the mended old screen door would allow, and, finding *Reverend* Josh monitoring shield status on the shuttle, asked him to lower it long enough to let him slip out into the twilight for a brief sojourn down the dirt road.

The first thing Ro noticed was the welcome quiet. He really hadn't basked in such stillness since before the invasion. The city was insane, and the Tobit House was far too crowded to ever be silent. Even the locusts and other country creatures kept their songs to a subtle hum. Darkness was gently settling over the fields and pastures, and the tightly packed road felt hard below his dusty feet. For a few minutes the Avatarn leader allowed himself to get lost in the sensations of the late autumn evening.

His life had changed so much in the past few weeks, he no longer recognized it. He had gone from being a bitter divorced man mourning the loss of his daughter, feeling like a helpless victim of life, forgotten by God—to a man in love, with a brand-new son. Extraordinary powers, and the default spearhead of God's chosen warriors. Although he was happy to leave behind the paper chase of the corporate world, he would gladly have endured a lifetime of it rather than witness the on-going slaughter of mankind. For so long, his only hope of seeing Janie again had been Heaven. And he hadn't been 100 percent confident about that. Having Joppa enter/return to his life had healed him in ways that even his son did not surpass.

As for finding Blair, he had never hoped to love another woman as much as Brenda, but even though their love was new (at least in this incarnation), she completed him in a way that Roman's soul recognized.

He had never been more afraid than he was now. The world was at stake. Hell—worlds—plural. He had never had so much to lose. And though he would give this battle his all, somehow the outcome didn't really matter—not in a *forever* way. That's how he was able to move forward. To keep moving. Now that he truly *KNEW* that God is real. That His all-consuming love is without limit—without end—everything would be okay. In the meantime, the Creator had assigned him a task, and he intended to carry it out. Besides, he still had to teach Atom to play baseball and ride a bike. As he turned and started back towards the farmhouse, grabbing at pussy-willows and kicking dirt clods as he walked, he thought he might teach Joppa to ride a bike too.

Josh had been watching for the "boss" to return, and dropped the shield long enough for him to slip back into the yard. Ro thanked him with the customary bumping of fists and hurried to find Blair in their room, feeding Atom and struggling to stay awake, exhausted by the day's adventures.

She was torn between horniness for her handsome lover, and the need to discuss important *household* matters about which she wanted his opinion.

He kissed Atom first. The chubby infant had finally been overwhelmed by sleep. It was when he raised his head to kiss the new mother that his thoughts were flooded with shame.

"Why didn't you tell me?" He asked regarding her lips, swollen with more than a few bee stings.

"They're nothing really," she was hurt more by the look in his eyes—because she hadn't immediately asked for his help—"At the time I was more concerned about you helping Darby…And me getting back to this little guy." She kissed the top of the baby's head. "I knew you would get around to it. Last time I use that spell."

"Want me to kiss it and make it better?"

She wondered how long he had been waiting to use that line. "Please do."

He took them both into his arms and gently began to kiss her tender lips. All eyes were closed, so no one saw the small flash of white light between their mouths. Roman knew when she pressured his lips to part that hers were fully healed. He sent up a silent prayer of gratitude for the power to restore perfect health to the woman that in less than one cycle of the moon had become the other half of him. He had been a whole person before, but now that was only true in her presence.

He couldn't help being distracted by her especially full—and still exposed—breasts. Mounds of milky white flesh topped off with large nipples the rusty hue of jasper. One was slowly leaking the life-sustaining fluid and he found that he was learning to understand a fetish he had so recently questioned.

At first he intended only to lick her clean, but soon found himself drinking—feeding—from her body. Dribbles from her body soon led to dribbles from his, and with Atom safely tucked into a basket on the nightstand, they made love, her body fully recovered from the recent birth thanks to Roman's magic touch.

When they were resting in each other's arms, Blair brought up the subject of Fern.

"What about her, Sweetheart?"

"The binding spell I placed on her has run its course. It's no longer in effect," she informed him matter-of-factly.

"Do you think she's still dangerous?" Ro questioned, "I mean, she worships the baby."

"I don't think she would hurt Atom...Or you either for that matter, but I'm not sure that makes her trustworthy."

"Anything is possible, honey, but I really don't think she would do something now to jeopardize her standing as honorary grandma," Roman's finger traced her eyebrows and nose.

"She still doesn't have a lock on that title as far as I'm concerned," Blair countered with surprisingly little bitterness, "She's called me *Satan's whore* a few too many times for me to forgive overnight."

"She does seem to have the most venom for you and Dar," he acknowledged. "I guess it has to be your call."

"I guess she will be all right," she reluctantly admitted, "The old hag seems to be adapting. I guess we'll give her a chance to prove she can be trusted without a magical leash."

"Okay," Ro switched gears. "That's settled. Have you noticed that Beacon's pregnancy is also progressing at a supernatural rate?"

"I sure have," she confirmed. "Thankfully, not quite as fast as mine, but it shouldn't be long. I think she's pretty scared, though she would never admit it...Mustn't show any weakness in front of mere humans, you know...Even now."

"Of course, but we'll all be there to help," Ro really wasn't concerned, "Who knows, she might get a Heavenly midwife too...even Avalon again."

"Don't be so sure her helpers will be angelic," Blair reminded, "Her baby's father is essentially the devil."

"Point taken," Roman wasn't smiling anymore.

It was still fairly early in the evening when Blair and Roman were awakened from their brief nap by very loud music pulsing outside the house. They hurried downstairs and converged with everyone else moving through the parlor to get to the porch and investigate the ruckus.

Paolo had placed a board over the birdbath in the front yard and placed a CD player on it. Mariah's "Through the Rain" was pounding from the speakers, and though the animals were a little scared, the people responded to the rhythm and danced out into the yard. As the diva crooned about surviving life's hardships one day at a time, the Avatarn and their make-shift family leaped and twisted and vogued to the music. It felt good to celebrate life after the recent battle.

Even Fern did a little jig when her unexpected new friend Josh swung her into the center of attention. The group clapped and whistled, all differences forgotten, united by the song.

Beacon and Tyler were grinding their bodies together, her superior station apparently set aside. Darby and Rachel were shaking their booties. Reminded of the good ole days, Rae found herself regretting more than usual that she had killed the cats—every one. She had loved them, but not one kitten remained. She had devised a small noose from some of Fernie's yarn, and it had served its dark purpose well. Rae's stomach rolled at the memory. Slowly but surely she had gotten them all, only one old Tom having put up a fight. When a hug from Roman had accidentally healed the scratches on her chest in a flash of light, she had assured him there had just been a bruise from a run-in with the bathroom door. He had known she was lying, but didn't force the issue. Although she was still horrified by what she had done, she would do it again. For Lucien. The only man who wanted her. The one who would make her a queen.

Blair was sandwiched between Paolo and Roman—a scandalous threesome to stranger's eyes, but in truth, three friends—losing themselves in the uplifting lyrics. Blair's thoughts turned to Atom, as they would in every happy moment for the rest of her life. She saw through the eyes of a squirrel that perched just outside her bedroom window, watching the baby's blissful sleep. As if he sensed his mother's joy, Atom was undisturbed by the pounding notes of the music. Blair mentally released her furry cohort from his duty and he scampered away to check on his own babies. The witch turned her focus back to grooving and was floating on the melody when Tyler said, "Who's that?" and all eyes turned to the lovely girl standing by the road, just outside the protective shield.

"Good question," Blair answered.

No one was still dancing, so Paolo shut off the CD player and an eerie silence settled over the yard. The quiet was a wet quilt, almost suffocating.

Roman took the lead, as was his habit, but all followed to the end of the driveway. Ro only had to nod in Josh's direction to cause the self-appointed priest to separate from the pack and quickly board the shuttle to lower the shield. Blair and Darby took their positions at each of Roman's sides. Battle formation for the Holy Triad.

When the energy barrier fell, the raven haired beauty smiled and immediately stepped forward. The Avatarn held their ground, and Darby requested that she identify herself.

"My name is Lilith," she announced, "But please, call me Lily."

"Why are you here?" Beacon took an imperial tone. In the instant that they waited for her response, Tyler took her measure. The straight black hair reached to her waist. He couldn't decide if her heritage was Asian or Hispanic. Her figure was striking below her off-the-shoulder blouse and long swaying peasant skirt.

"I am an escaped slave," was Lily's reply, "My master, a Legion commander, brought me here to spare my life. I was scheduled for execution for helping others escape, but my master chose to show mercy. I was always a favorite pet. He knew asylum with you was my only option. My home planet is on the other side of the galaxy. I beg you. Be as merciful as my demon lord."

"You are welcome he—"Ty was cut short by Beacon's elbow to his mid-section.

Josh and Rachel each noticed a slight tingle in their left wrists. It was beneath their red kabala bracelets. Neither paid it much mind, it was credited to coincidence.

"Not so fast," Rachel stepped forward, "How do we know you are what you claim?"

"Well, proving I'm not of your world is easily done," the beautiful stranger turned her back to the assemblage and allowed her long prehensile tail to extend through a small hole in her crimson skirt, "Proving I am not Legion is a more complicated task."

"I'll just call the cats," Blair offered.

"We could check the color of her blood," Josh piped up. Everyone was more than a little alarmed when he appeared to be serious.

"That would not provide proof of anything, Reverend Insanity," Beacon snapped.

"Where are those damn cats?" Blair wondered testily—her mood more a reaction to the stranger's exotic beauty than the cats' lack of attendance to her mental summons.

"Forget the animals," Rachel jumped in, "The only way you can be sure of Atom's safety is to bind her anyway."

"True that," the witch turned back to the alien, "Any objections?"

"Assuming you intend to bind me magically, and not with ropes and chains, I offer no resistance," Lilith responded.

"Good! Because resistance is fu--," Joshua cut himself off in mid-sentence when the others all turned to glare at him for repeating Adolphus' joke.

Without ceremony, Blair placed a hand on the new girl's shoulder and said:

"I bind you Lily from doing harm.
I bind you Lily from doing harm.
I bind you Lily from doing harm."

Blair resumed her place at Roman's side and sub-consciously took his hand.

"Well, no fireworks," Darby spoke, "So, for lack of a better plan…Welcome."

Lily rewarded him with a dazzling smile then turned it towards Roman, not really taking further notice of the woman.

"Let's go into the parlor and get better acquainted," Paolo suggested. The group silently agreed and shuffled towards the house.

"And discuss sleeping arrangements," the princess shattered the quiet with her flippancy. She had taken careful notice of the way Tyler and Roman stole every glance possible at the nubile alien wench. Why couldn't slaves just remember their place, she thought before quickly reprimanding herself for backsliding into her old patterns.

"Indeed," was all Fern said, troubled by the notion of returning to sleeping with one eye open.

Having reached the porch steps before the others, Blair turned back to wait for Ro. She was surprised to see that Lily had taken his arm and was casually smashing it against her ample breast. She continued to smile and bat her lashes as the two of them conversed too quietly for the others to hear.

The wind seemed to share Blair's jealously and whipped and tossed her coppery hair as if to display its anger. The witch simply turned and adopted an air of nonchalance, leading the group into the sitting room. She wasn't going to let emotional over-reactions sour her against this flirtatious creature, which had just escaped demon conquerors, and might be a bit over-zealous in expressing gratitude for their sanctuary.

Ro was a little overwhelmed by the alien's attentions, but flattered as well. Aside from her beauty, he found himself distracted by her unusual scent. After careful consideration, he decided she smelled like fresh plums. It was very intriguing. Though he was doing nothing wrong, Ro found himself looking around to see if Blair was watching. He was enjoying the flirty creature, but not enough to be worth pissing off the new love of his life.

"Keep an eye on them, my lord," Lily whispered, looking towards Josh, Rachel, Ty, and Beacon as they climbed the steps, "They are not as selfless as they might once have been. They all have personal motives now. Their behavior screams it."

"Look…You don't know them. This mission has been rough

on them, but they're good people. Don't forget, you are here only as long as they agree," Ro paused, "And don't call me *Lord*."

"As you wish," the alien feigned acquiescence but subtly brushed her thinly-veiled nipple against his hard muscles.

Group discussion in the parlor turned into story hour, with Lily sharing all sorts of fascinating details about life on her home planet of Adamos before its invasion. The residents of the Tobit House began to feel the disarming sense of familiarity that comes from knowing the stories of another's life. By the time everyone went their sleepy ways and Lily was assigned a cot in the mud room just inside the back porch, the holy rebels were at peace with the notion of an alien in their midst.

Atom had to eat again before Blair and Roman could think of slumber. He was fast and content, so the process was actually a pleasure. The happy infant was finished in no time, and with a quick burp, his mother had him securely swaddled in his basket with the easy comfort of routine.

Ro seized the moment to take her hand before she fell into bed, and instead he fell to one knee. Blair held her breath to freeze the moment. Not that she could really stop time, but for her there was only that moment. There was no past or future. She had to force herself back to awareness because Roman was speaking and she wasn't hearing what he said.

"—proudest man alive. I could never be complete now, without you. Will you marry me?" Roman's tear-filled eyes threatened to spill over into his giant smile.

"Yes," was all she could squeak out before falling into his arms. They lost their balance and rolled clumsily on the floor, banging knees and elbows and laughing like lunatics. When finally they were still, Roman's body served as a cushion between his new fiancé and the hard floor, but he didn't mind. He didn't even feel it. All he could feel was joy.

"I'm afraid I don't have a ring," he apologized, lifting her fingers to his lips. He saw that she had removed her band from Thomas, and wondered when she had transferred it to the necklace that sparkled against her chest.

"Those trappings don't matter anymore," she assured him, "I just want to be your wife."

He was getting choked up again, but cleared his throat to bring up the next consideration, "I thought maybe we could get Joppa to perform the ceremony?"

"I love that idea," she hopped up and pulled him to his feet. Happily surprised to see they hadn't waked the baby, both dove onto the bed and sat up against the pillows. Without further discussion, they embraced and laid the sides of their heads together and quietly called to Joppa, requesting that she come to them. Blair reached out with her powers to turn their words into a resonating chant, but without success. After an hour of attempts, they concluded that their mystical guide was either busy, or chose not to respond.

"I guess we could always ask Josh to officiate," Ro reluctantly suggested, "Since he feels that he's the *High Priest* of the Avatarn, might as well be him as anyone else."

"Why not? I think that will be fine," she pretended to be more comfortable with the idea than she was. "He'll be thrilled. Let's go tell him."

Suppressing their giggles, they stole down the hallway to Josh's room.

The self appointed priest was ecstatic at their news, and honored by his inclusion. As soon as they left his room he began praying for guidance and planning the ceremony. Dawn was approaching when he surrendered to sleep and dreamt of tradition and rituals.

Roman and Blair rested the rest of lovers found and rose with the sun to tend to their son. They joined Fern in preparing breakfast, and even she was pleased that Ro was making an honest woman of the mother of her adopted grandson. Everyone was excited by the news, though Rachel fought to conceal her envy. She had dreamed of marriage and family for so long, and had nearly lost hope, but now with Lucien…Just maybe. Even Lily offered congratulations to her hosts.

While Uncle Dar and Paolo gave Atom his bath, Blair led Roman to the front porch swing. He was surprised to realize she was a bit nervous about whatever she had to discuss. Because the weather was temperate, when Josh suggested noon for the ceremony, neither had objected. Ro waited for her to begin in her own time, so as they sipped morning coffee, which Lily had, shockingly, learned to make on a starship, they watched Joshua and Tyler in the yard. The boys had gathered chairs from all corners of the house and arranged them audience-style. Though the day was well illumined by the sun, they created an altar on the handy birdbath and board combo and placed a large candle there. They gathered countless flowers and placed them on the ground to mark a sizeable circle around the altar. Artful arrangements of the garden's vegetables and fruits were created to surround the candle. The life-sustaining harvest to represent fertility, even though the betrothed had already proven themselves in that area. The Avatarn just watched in wonder, until Blair broke the silence.

"About the wedding..."She paused, "I need it to be a handfasting rather than a traditional ceremony. I hope that's okay."

"I'm sure it is," Roman replied sincerely, "But I don't know what that means."

She laughed a little before starting to explain.

"Well, it's the way of my people...Witches, I mean. Most pagans really. Thomas and I had an old fashioned Christian ritual, and that's not what I want this time. I need to be true to my heritage...Don't worry, God the Trinity will still be the guest of honor, the proceedings will just vary from what you probably did with Brenda."

"As long as God is present, we could do it in the bathtub as far as I'm concerned," he kissed her cheek and held her close with his arm around her shoulder, "Formalities mean nothing now. I mean it's not like we'll be filing a license with the state. I just want to declare our marriage in front of our loved ones."

"Same page, my love," was her relieved response. She excused herself and went inside so Rachel could help with her hair. She still had to decide if she would wear a dress or go skyclad.

Roman joined Darby in doing the morning chores.

"Shouldn't you be getting spruced up?" Dar asked as he fed and watered the goats.

"Plenty of time for that later," Roman assured.

"Sorry I can't provide a bachelor party for you, dude, but to tell you the truth—even if I was straight, I wouldn't care to see my sister or my best friend stripping," Darby chuckled, "Might be interesting to see what the girl with the monkey tail can do."

"Don't let Blair hear you say that," Ro scolded, "I think Lily already got under her skin a bit."

"Oops…My bad," Darby grinned, "No joking about prehensile girl around the resident witch."

Ro laughed, "I'm just sayin'…Hate to see you starin' out the wrong side of frog eyes."

"Point taken," Dar finished the chores, "I'll keep my yap shut. Where is Lily anyway?"

"I think Fernie is schooling her on how to behave like a proper human lady—unlike my fiancé."

"Uh oh…I better go rescue her. She's suffered enough," Darby winked and headed toward the house. Roman walked the perimeter for an hour, then headed inside to make himself pretty.

Chapter 26

At the appointed hour of noon, all the residents of the Tobit farm appeared freshly scrubbed and took their seats in the front yard. The farm animals and wild creatures alike gathered around the small group of humans to observe and bear witness. Four attack vessels descended from the atmosphere to hover just above the shield bubble, only to watch what they could not stop.

Roman, dressed in white jeans and sort of a white poet's shirt Fern dug up from somewhere, waited at the altar. Josh stood just behind the make-shift table in a royal blue robe pieced together from the aged remains of high school choir garments. Atom was wiggling happily in Rachel's care. Lily sang a haunting wordless song as Blair and her escort, Darby, started up the aisle carpeted by colorful oak leaves gathered from every corner of the yard.

The bride wore Fern's own wedding gown. She had fought it, because the old woman so clearly hated her, but then the crone had insisted that she do it for Atom. Blair had caved, but not so much for the baby, but for Roman. She wanted everything to be special for him. The old fashioned dress was made mostly of form-fitting white satin. All agreed it was too late for the mysteries of a veil. Instead her long fiery hair hung around her shoulders, not in its usual cascading waves, but in large bouncy curls. She had the look of a gorgeous child who had just run out to play in the meadow in her church clothes. Beacon admired the air of dignity she maintained even in her playful guise. All were struck dumb by her beauty except for the alien songbird, and even she fell silent when Darby placed Blair's hand in Roman's.

Joshua never uttered a word of the speech he had so carefully prepared. The blessed couple had just turned to face him, when they heard gasps from the small crowd behind them.

A creature of horrifying magnificence had pierced the bubble above their heads and floating on massive wings it landed just behind the bride and groom.

"Be unafraid," the being bellowed, "For I come in the name of The Father."

The *animal* as Beacon perceived him, didn't seem terribly out of the ordinary to her, but the others were still awestruck by angels.

The glorious beast continued to speak and his human audience was spellbound. "I am Kong-po. The Son has sent me to officiate at your wedding. He is pleased by this joining, and confirms it in the Akashic records." The being was about seven feet tall and covered in white fur. Even its wings were replete with the snowy fluff. It had the body of a muscular man with arms reaching to the ground and the face of an albino baboon. It wore no clothes, but was draped only in a glowing pink aura.

When the angel moved around to take Josh's place, the wanna-be-priest stepped humbly aside, and the candle burst into flame.

As Kong-po began to speak the ancient rites, all eyes were glued on his long white muzzle and startling fangs, "A handfasting is a sacred bonding of two people wishing to permanently link their souls through divine blessing. Today these two unite for as long as love shall last. We invite God Himself to be present and witness. Please clasp your right hands together and join left hands as well." The ferocious angel paused as they obeyed. "Linking hands in this formation creates a living symbol of infinity, as your love is forever," He then reached a frosty-furred hand above his head, where a length of purple cord materialized in his palm. He proceeded to wrap it around the wrists of the bride and groom saying, "This cord holds fast the hands of lovers bound by a promise they make this day. Roman Perez, do you take this woman to be your beloved wife as long as love shall last?"

"I do," Ro pledged with a quiver in his voice.

"Blair Atwood, do you take this man to be your beloved husband as long as love shall last?"

"I do," she swore, no doubt in her vow.

With a pass of a paw-like hand over their bound wrists, the angel de-materialized the cord. At the same moment, his other long arm reached into the air to retrieve two shiny rings. They appeared to be platinum, but were actually crafted from a unique metal found nowhere on Earth. The bands were engraved with symbols of a Heavenly language which Kong-po read to the riveted assembly. Only the Avatarn somehow understood what he was saying, but everyone understood that he was speaking of the indestructibility of love and its holy nature. He handed one to each of the betrothed and with a nod signaled both to say in unison,

"With this ring, I thee wed," as they slid them into place.

"And now," the angel's voice was like thunder, "with the power invested in me by God, the Omniverse, I pronounce you husband and wife…In the name of the Father, the Son, and the Holy Ghost," he finished by raising his hands into the sky at the instant he invoked the Trinity. In a flash, the four hovering fighter ships exploded in flames. Their destruction was sudden and complete. Not a scrap of debris remained. All present only murmured their delight, as Kong-po continued the ceremony, "What God had joined together, let no being put asunder. Seal this union with a kiss." They happily obeyed, and turned to him for closure… Placing his hands on Blair's forehead and Ro's, the creature from Heaven shouted, "Blessed Be!"

"Blessed Be!" The guests yelled in response.

The baboon-man was coming to the end of the ritual, "And now to all of you who bravely help carry God's hammer, I present Roman and Blair Perez." Fern moved behind the bride and twisted up her hair with the help of two pearlized combs then returned to her seat.

The group clapped and cheered, and a few had started to stand when the angel extended his wings to re-focus their attention, "Guard well the *child of goodness*, for danger is never as far as it seems," Kong-po's pink eyes flickered in the direction of a praying mantis climbing the side of the home-made altar.

"As long as we live, Atom is safe," Darby said from his seat. The angel simply nodded acknowledgment.

"I leave you now," The feral angel was floating a few feet above the special carpet of leaves, "with wisdom the Creator once revealed to a sometimes confused man named Nietzsche—He who fights with monsters might take care lest he thereby become a monster. And if you gaze for long into an abyss, the abyss gazes also into you." Annunciation complete, the winged being soared into the sky.

He pierced the shield like it was gossamer and in a streak of pink light flew into space.

Though still marveling at the visitor, the newlyweds jumped up and down and were still hugging when all the others embraced them; for a moment the world's horrors were forgotten. Paolo and Fern prepared a reception dinner, but there would be no honeymoon. Duty called for the new bride. Atom was hungry.

That night the newlyweds were smiling in their sleep when a cacophony of explosive percussion burst through their bedroom door.

Banging pots and pans clanged in every direction as every member of the household poured into the room. Fern had instigated the *shivaree*, but the others had eagerly agreed to participate. She had taught them a folksy song to serenade the couple in the ancient tradition. Though the younger generation had never heard of this wedding night custom, they all jumped on the excuse to intrude into the marital bed. Roman was mortified, but the new *Mrs.* Perez had been taught about the custom by the elder women of her family. She laughed and welcomed the extended celebration, even as she scooped the crying Atom into her arms to shush his fears. With a few whoops and yodels, the mockery ended as quickly as it had begun, and the impromptu musicians marched out the door and Darby closed it with a wink.

"What the hell was that?" A baffled Ro asked his wife. She explained the old tradition, and assured him it was done out of fondness, and was still smiling about it when both of her confused men had returned to slumber. Blair was pleased, knowing that only Fern would have thought of a shivaree and that her implementation of it suggested that she was finally warming to the new mother.

When Joppa appeared on the front steps of the Tobit House, she was the picture of a modern American girl in her mid-twenties. Her long blonde hair was in a French braid down her back. She wore large hoop earrings and shiny pink lips. Her halter-top was bright blue, and she wore low-rider jeans. She walked into the house like she owned it, and all were ecstatic to see her.

She hugged and kissed each of the resistance rebels, and they were delighted and comforted to have their guide back among them.

"It's so good to see you, Sweetheart," Roman couldn't help thinking of the woman as his daughter, and saw no reason to resist it. "We just finished breakfast. Are you hungry?"

"Hello Blair," the eternal priestess in pop-star gear greeted the witch as she entered the kitchen rocking the baby in her arms.

"Hey, that's right. You haven't met your new brother yet," Roman was so proud; "Joppa, meet your brother, Atom. Sorry you couldn't be here for the birth or the wedding."

Joppa blessed the room with a radiant smile and tears brimmed her eyes. She took a step towards the infant, who as Roman perceived reality, was her brother.

Blair took a step backwards, "That's why she's here. Didn't she tell you? She's come to take him away. HAVEN'T YOU?" She yelled so hard she shook.

"No, Darling," Roman corrected her. "She's just come to see him. Tell her, Honey."

Joppa remained silent as she turned back towards Ro. She allowed a single tear to fall before wiping it away and resuming her normal air of self-confidence.

"She's right, Roman," Their blonde guide assumed a tone of authority, "I am forever sorry, but I must take Atom into hiding for his safety."

"I forbid it," Blair growled through clenched teeth.

"Joppa, you can't be serious," Darby spoke up, "He's brand new."

"I must—" she had barely taken a step in the baby's direction when Fern jumped out from around a corner, butcher knife in hand.

"I'll cut out your heart before you take that child, Bitch," the old woman had never been more serious, "Lord Almighty give me the strength to kill this devil." She lunged, but Joppa easily side-stepped the blade.

"It is the Lord that sends me, Fern Leaves, I act in His name."

"I don't care," Roman stepped forward taking Joppa's arm, "You're not taking him, Jane. That's final."

"Dad," Joppa's face remained stony and became cold, "I must obey the will of our true Father."

After that declaration Ro and Darby took positions at Blair's sides and each of the three raised a hand above their heads. Roman's held a ball of white light, Blair's a ball of blue light, and Dar's a ball of gold energy.

In that moment, Fern used the distraction to slip up and plant her knife in Joppa's side. The guide looked surprised at her bleeding wound, but was not afraid and made no move to remove the abandoned blade. Instead the Barbie-doll priestess raised a hand above her own head. Ro was about to launch his healing power, when a wave of Joppa's fingers made it unnecessary. The knife faded from existence, leaving no sign of the trauma or even the blood. She simultaneously erased the power balls from the hands of the triad.

"Come, New One," Joppa called to the infant watching contentedly from his mother's arms; "It's time to go." Atom dematerialized and re-appeared in the priestess' waiting embrace.

"Please don't," Blair was hysterical; "I have to feed him."

"The Creator will allow my body to provide all that he needs," Joppa assured.

"We can protect him ourselves," Roman yelled.

"You can not," The guide countered. "Just because your lives have taken a theanthropic twist doesn't make you divine."

"Where are you taking him?" Rachel demanded to know.

"To the safest place I can think of," Joppa kissed the top of the baby's head, "I will return him to you Ro-Dad." She raised her chin and in the blink of an eye, they were gone.

When Atom and Joppa materialized in the mountain abbey on planet Eden, she was dressed in a long gown, hair piled intricately on her head. The priestess had returned to her sanctuary millennia later. Her white tigers immediately came to inspect the baby. God hadn't told her where to go, and she prayed her charge would be safe here. Her acolytes entered the petitioner's hall and carefully approached, hoping she would let them observe this most important child.

Blair collapsed in Roman's arms. She didn't faint. She had been through too much to pussy-out like that, but she was in shock. Ro tried to comfort her, but he wasn't in much better shape.

Darby was crying, but the newlyweds weren't. They had cried too many tears. They were trying to convince each other that Atom was safe with Joppa. That she would eventually bring him home. But there were no guarantees. They might never see him again.

Beacon found herself protectively hugging her pronounced abdomen. Tyler patted her lower back, as if to assure that he wouldn't let anyone walk in and take her baby.

Fern had started loudly clearing the table, but stopped to sob into a plate of biscuits.

Darby and Paolo half-carried Blair to a parlor sofa, where she sat silent and bewildered. Roman almost made it to her side, when he fell to the floor on his knees and turned his face heavenwards.

"Why, Father?" He raged, "Not again! I won't go through this again! I will not serve you another day 'til you give back my son! What is this?" He began to laugh uncontrollably, "Do you intend to hold him ransom 'til our mission is accomplished? Perhaps we've taken too long here in our respite from the war, but I won't be fucking black-mailed! PLEASE! Please! Please," his body was racked by soundless sobs. God didn't answer.

It was an hour later when Blair slid into the floor and wrapped her arms around her husband who sat motionless in stoic devastation. With a gentle hand on a trembling chin, she turned his face to hers and said, "Your daughter is SO grounded." He grudgingly mirrored her small smile.

Chapter 27

Beacon had been soaking in her bubble bath for a while when Lily barged in.

"Forgive me, Your Highness. I did not realize the room was in use."

"It's all right, Lily," Beacon was not uncomfortable, she was accustomed to being bathed; "you may enter."

"Do you need assistance, Highness?"

"If you wish," Beacon held out a sponge.

Lily took it, and knelt behind the claw-foot tub. Slowly she began to wash the royal back, "It was shocking to actually see you here, among humans, Princess."

"I must say that it is equally strange for me to see an off-worlder among these people," Beacon sighed at the pampering she missed, "You have made a bold and difficult choice by coming here."

"I had no choice, Mame. If I had stayed in bondage, I surely would have died a horrible death."

"If I had stayed," Beacon swatted at the bubbles, "I would have wished I were dead."

"But now you have a chance at a new life," Lily gently washed the princess' greatly expanded stomach."

"I suppose I do," Beacon smiled and lowered herself into the water, "Lily, I was always taught that all the inhabitants of Adamos were Legion."

"Of course, Mame. But warriors require servants and concubines, do they not?"

"They do…It also occurs to me that your master had the audacity to name you after one of our founders…Legion's founders. *Her* name is Lilith. I find it shocking that one would gift a slave with such an important designation."

"I am told I resemble her," Lily offered allowing her sponge to graze Beacon's breast.

"I never had the honor," the princess didn't bother to look at her; "I suppose that you do."

"Lucien's child comes soon," the alien girl observed.

"Do you think so?" The princess sat up quickly, clearing the bubbles for a better view of her tummy. "And how is it that you know the Pretender to the throne fathered this child? The true prince of Legion."

"It is common gossip aboard the ships, Mame. And yes…It will be very soon, Highness. Very soon." Lily left in a state of fluster. Beacon wasn't sure if she were excited or scared by the slave's prediction. She was a little surprised that the next thought to cross her mind was that the alien had left without being dismissed. With concepts like personal freedom for all, how was this planet going to survive?

Tyler was feeding chickens when Lily found him. The poultry had become something of an exercise in futility. Only Fern was willing to kill and pluck them, and even she wouldn't do it for a group of the size currently residing at the farm. Still, they required care, and everyone loved eggs.

"Why do you keep these winged creatures in confinement?" The alien woman asked as she watched from the door of the pen.

"We don't always," Ty replied. "This pen is necessary to protect them from other predators. We humans can be kind of greedy about sharing our food." He was sure to flex his muscles as he tossed the feed. He wasn't interested in betraying the mutual infatuation he was exploring with Beacon, but the beauty of the creature from outer-space was impossible to ignore. In the city, her mere presence would have caused a ten car pile-up.

"So humans from this planet still eat flesh," she thought aloud, "an interesting trait in common with your demon enemies."

"Is that so damn rare in the galaxy? The eating of flesh?" Tyler was insulted by the comparison.

"Actually it is," she confirmed, "Most of the slave races have abandoned the practice to set themselves apart from their masters. They believe that by observing dietary restrictions their people are distinguished from those that they disdain."

Ty considered telling her that it was a practical and efficient source of protein, but instead just said, "We like the taste of blood."

She smiled seductively in response to his defensive but masculine posturing.

"May I assist you?" She asked.

"Thanks, but I'm almost done."

"Where I come from, only slaves do such menial chores," Lily was careful to hide her disdain.

"Where I come from, if you want something done, you do it yourself," Ty returned without a hint of malice.

"A man named Zoroaster, Zarathustra to those who knew him, once told me that hard work doesn't allow time for Ahriman to turn your head," she recounted as they headed back towards the house.

"Ahriman?"

"Was one of Adolphus' many names," she explained, "Zarathustra thought your people capable of uncommonly ethical behavior."

"My people?" The red-headed man was brought to a stand-still by surprise, "This guy knew humans? He had been to Earth?"

"Did I say—I misspoke...It's been a long morning, what with

that intruder stealing the Avatarn prince and all. You live with a lot of drama in this place." She took his hand, and he allowed it until they reached the house.

"It was brutal," he conceded.

"Just be careful that you don't trade the yoke of desperation for the yoke of gratitude as provided by our most hospitable hosts. You can not truly share in the destiny of the *amesha spentas*, as Zoroaster would have called your holy triad."

"I'll keep that in mind," Tyler gently freed his hand and rounded a corner to join Beacon on the back porch where she sipped a Dr. Pepper. She had become addicted in a matter of days, and was bound to suffer withdrawal when their meager supply ran out. He had expected Lily to follow him around the house, but perhaps it was better that she hadn't.

"No offense, Beacs, but you look like you are about to pop." He radiated too much affection for the princess to get angry.

"If you mean to imply that this baby has nearly completed its gestation, I am inclined to agree."

"Looks like this pregnancy is as magical as Blair's." He sat on the floor beside her, "Maybe the angel, Avalon, will return to deliver your child."

"My baby is half demon," she stroked his pale cheek fondly; "I doubt that *He Who Sits Apart* will send his creature to attend this arrival. Fern can handle the birth; I am more concerned with keeping away uninvited representatives of the royal court. There are those who will want to witness the birth of the true heir to the Legion throne."

Tyler hadn't thought of all that before. It appeared to him that the literal *Prince of Darkness* was going to be born within a few days. Blair and Ro were in no condition for battle, and all Hell might be coming for the baby shower. It might be up to him and the other mortal members of the Chosen team to fight the good fight. They had to keep Lucy-Ann's paws off the kids at all costs.

"Don't worry, Babe," Ty stood and kissed her forehead, "I can't be an army of loyal guardians as Atom has surrounding him, but I will protect your child with my life and at any cost."

"ANY cost?" Her week smile was over-powered by the worry in her eyes.

"Any." Tyler meant every word, but the promise made his stomach hurt, and he had the feeling somewhere someone had started digging his grave.

It wasn't difficult for Rachel to slip out of the house and into the cornfield. Most of the group was semi-catatonic over the loss of Atom. She weaved between the outer stalks and sat in the soft soil near where she guessed the shield barrier to be. Lucien appeared, grabbed her arm and de-materialized with her in tow, before she could object. One blink of her eyes, and they opened in the loft of the barn.

"The cats are gone. You've done well, lovely one," Lucien's words poured over her like warm syrup, providing something her heart was missing. Needed.

"Can't say I'm proud of it," she replied.

"It was necessary…You've always been able to force yourself to do what you must, haven't you? This private place is also necessary…As far as possible from the Avatarn's minions," Lucien dazzled her with his sexy smile. "I want to be alone with you."

"Yeah, so you can continue my re-programming," Rachel wasn't going to make it too easy. If she were going to continue to betray her life-long best friend, she had to be certain that the ancient being that stood smoldering before her really wanted her forever at his side.

He scoffed then laughed quietly, "Why would I go to such lengths to mislead you, my pet? You have no powers with which to aid me, and I am here. I already have access to the blindly servile leaders of your little clan…You are special," he continued after pausing to suppress his temper and impatience. "I need a unique woman to be my queen and raise my son. A human to understand his weaker half. A brave warrior, as you have proven yourself to be. You could not settle now for some common person fit only for the slave herds. You have been a handmaiden to real power. You deserve to live among the immortals, and there are none here that want you—save me. I have come to adore you as I watched from my hiding. You will be my wife.

"Yes…I will," she confirmed with surprising calm. In the moment that she said it, she felt transformed. No longer the faithful sidekick—both appreciated and taken for granted, but a woman, loved by a man. Oh, she knew who he was. What he was. Besides witnessing his vile acts firsthand, she had been warned about him since the first time she was carried into the White Dove Baptist Church, still in diapers. None of that mattered. Who wasn't capable of evil? She was surprised to realize she didn't care what he did to others. She had somehow moved beyond it, and this hotty beside her was going to give her a family and make her the most important thing in his life—in his kingdom. Something clicked inside and she was changed. For a second she thought it felt like someone walking out the door to her heart and closing it. In that second, she was hollow, but that also meant lighter. It was a relief to no longer try to be good and do right. A freedom in giving yourself permission to do or feel anything you want…No more guilt. The Avatarn could have the mea culpa. And then Lu was there, filling her up. Not just figuratively either. She didn't know when their clothes had come off, or when he had turned her, bending her over a wooden railing, all she knew was that he was inside her. He was much too big for her really and too rough as he rode her, but she didn't care. In those times when his hard chest was against her back, she could feel his heart pounding with hers. Only for a moment did she pretend he was Darby as she had with so many others.

Lucien knew her thoughts, but didn't care. For an instant HE pretended SHE was Darby.

When it was over and every position had been explored, she shuddered then rested after the last of a dozen climaxes.

"You know if I hadn't already fallen in love with you, that fuck-a-thon alone would have convinced me," Rachel was blissed beyond reasoning.

"You flatter me, Darling." The demon king was suddenly clothed in his usual toga.

"No," Rae disputed, "I'm just not lying to myself anymore. To others maybe, but not to myself."

"By Jove! I think she's got it," Lucien appeared happy.

"Let's leave Jupiter out of it," she scolded, "We have enough gods up in our cookie mix."

No one knew Fern was digging out behind the buck-eye tree. It was the first chance she had to be alone there since the trespassers had *borrowed* her home. Armed with only a sharp spade, wiry old muscles and unflagging determination, she dug a small hole amid the roots. Soon the blade clanked against a metal box, and she retrieved it without another thought to the shovel tossed on the ground or the empty hole that scarred the ground. She scurried off to the privacy of the nearby garden shed.

She had never had the key to the box, so she had to use wire-cutters to break the lock. It had been her grandmother that sealed the contents in the box and then buried it with young Fernie's help. But that had been at the foot of another apple tree far away. Fern had transplanted it herself when she came to live with her daughter and son-in-law. They had never even known it was there. She had told her granddaughter of course. Shared the ancient stories. The ancient responsibilities. The child had laughed at her, but she had listened. That point was moot now, but there was a new child for Fern to look after. And she would not fail him.

In the dim sunlight that crept in through crevices in the walls, she removed a small journal from its rusted prison. The leather-bound book showed its age, and smelled of decades in the earth. She didn't like touching the mildewed pages, but wouldn't fail in this plan. The spell she needed was easily found, but she took extra time to commit it completely to memory. Returning the fragile book to its metal home, she hid the box below some bags of potting soil. Fern would never understand why folks living on a farm had felt the need to *buy* dirt. People tracked more into the house than a body could ever use. The box would be safe in its new hiding place; besides, she wasn't wasting anymore time on trivial details.

The old woman was briefly overcome with doubt. Had she stared too long into the abyss? Had it turned her into a monster as Kong-po had suggested it could? No. She wasn't happy about what she had to do, but her duty was to God and Atom. She would do what had to be done. Back in the sun-drenched yard, she allowed a couple of the dogs to escort her to the house.

When Darby and the others arrived to investigate the cause of Roman's midnight yelling rampage, they were just in time to see their leader prying something from Fern's wrinkled arms just outside her bedroom door.

Roman forcefully handed a charm of feathers and bones to Rachel as she demanded to know what was going on.

"This crazy old bitch finally went off the deep end," Ro roared. The dark Avatarn had locked a large hand on each of Fern's squishy shoulders and began to shake her.

"What has the crone done?" Beacon interjected, and more than one person noticed that she was sleeping in Tyler's shirt.

"Tell them, you dried-up cu—"Roman was cut short by Fern's forced response.

"All right!" She screamed, surprised to find she was actually afraid of the violence in the eyes of the man that was hurting her. "I put a spell on his wife!"

"What? You're a witch? Paolo spoke before the others.

"Hell, no!" She screeched, "A witch *hunter*—at least my ancestors were."

"What have you done to her, Fern?" Darby demanded to know as he placed a hand on Ro's bicep to stop the man-handling.

"She's just sleeping," the old woman assured the angry group. "She's unharmed."

"When I walked in," Roman had to pause to take a breath, "She was just finishing an incantation, and Blair fell unconscious across the bed. She could have broken her neck."

"I wouldn't let that happen," Fern defended, as if she wouldn't hurt a fly.

"I wasn't able to wake her," Ro had tears in his voice.

"Why in the hell are you doing magic anyway?" Darby asked, "I thought it conflicted with your beliefs."

"Oh, it does, fancy boy," Fern confirmed. "Don't you see? From the dawn of this great nation, my family fought to protect everything good and Christian for the God-fearing citizens who deserved it. By learning the ways of our enemy, we stamped out most witchcraft by using their evil powers against them. Down through the years, a few of the spells they collected were preserved for emergencies just such as this one."

"What did you do to her—SPECIFICALLY?" Joshua yelled out as he pushed forward, backing Fern against a wall.

"Traitor!" She shouted back at him. "I thought we had an understanding."

"Not anymore," he countered, "You think the high priest of the Avatarn will stand by and allow you to harm one of the Holy Triad? What was the spell for?"

"She will simply sleep," Fern answered as if the fallen witch was down for a nap.

"Until when?" Roman was back in her face.

"Until I die." The Widow Leaves had silenced the house.

Chapter 28

"**You will remove the** spell right now!" Roman shouted.

The next sound came from Beacon in reaction to her kicking fetus.

"Look what you've done," Fern pretended to scold. "You've upset the unborn anti-Christ."

"The spell, Fern!" Roman was insane.

"Impossible," she replied, "It can't be reversed or broken."

"Except by your death," Beacon reminded her and everyone else.

"Let's hope that's not necessary," Paolo spoke up.

"But you were so supportive during the wedding," Rachel shook the home-made charm at her, "Why have you done this?"

"The marriage was the appropriate action. No reason to force the child to grow up a bastard, "Fern actually took a tone of aloofness, "Of course it was also not an option to have him raised by a witch. Joppa knew it. I will not have him corrupted if she should ever return him."

"You won't have him at all," Roman grabbed the old lady's arm and yanked her towards his bedroom. "How do I wake her, damn it? Stop fucking around."

"I told you how," she had grown calm; "when I die she will wake."

"Have it your way," he pushed her into the room with his sleeping bride, and removed a gun from the chest of drawers.

"I know you want to, but you won't," Fern wasn't afraid anymore. "You don't have murder in you."

Those who had gathered in the doorway saw that he kept the gun leveled at her heart for several minutes, but in the end she was right.

Ro passed the weapon to Paolo for safe-keeping, knowing that given the chance, Josh might take things into his own hands.

With Darby's help, the recent groom arranged his wife more comfortably on the bed then signaled the others that he needed time alone with her.

Left in privacy, he focused all his powers on healing her, but she wasn't hurt or ill. She was only sleeping. And she was beyond his reach. Just before morning Roman forgave God for taking his wife and son away. He found a fragile peace in the hope that both could be returned to him some day.

He emerged determined to complete their mission as soon as possible. Perhaps then the Big Guy would see fit to restore his family.

When he joined the others in the kitchen, he learned that they had spent the remainder of the night interrogating Fern, but she wasn't budging. Though his forgiveness didn't extend to her, he instructed them to leave her alone. He hadn't realized before what she was capable of, but he knew her well enough to know she wouldn't be bullied.

The others tried to give him his space, and he reverted to his college days' habit of note taking and strategizing on a legal pad. It was past time for him to apply his considerable intellect to solving the global crisis.

He was still scribbling in a forgotten corner of the parlor floor when he overheard Lily speaking to the TV. Roman peeked from behind the sofa to see what perpetual re-run she might be talking to, but was surprised to see only static filled the screen.

The language she spoke was completely foreign to Ro's ears, but he thought of someone who might know the tongue. He exited the room on hands and knees, hoping it wasn't too late.

Only two minutes elapsed before Roman, Tyler, and Paolo walked briskly into the parlor.

"Who you talkin' to?" Ty asked the alien woman.

"What?" The raven-haired beauty was shaken by their sudden intrusion, "I was just singing to myself. You know I love to sing." She tried to look indignant as they briskly surrounded her, but a flicker of fear showed through.

"Don't bother lying," a disembodied voice spoke from the air, "I heard more than enough." With a shimmer, the room's atmosphere rippled and Beacon and Darby moved from invisibility into vivid presence by simply unclasping hands. "You are exposed," the princess continued with a sneer.

"What was she saying?" Roman's eyes never left the spy, and he was thankful he had found the twins in time.

"She was speaking to Lucien," Beacon spat the words as if they were dirt in her mouth, "She was assigned by my father's assassin to protect my unborn child until such time as she could steal him and deliver him to my rapist."

"I'll die first." Tyler stepped in front of his new lover.

"Probably so," Lily had no quarrel with the idea.

"What you are going to do is let us handle this," Darby said from his position at Roman's side. "Ya feel me?" He looked sternly at the brave red-headed boy. Ty locked eyes with the Avatarn, but didn't acknowledge his order to stand down. His woman and the baby he intended to raise were in danger. He would be damned before removing himself from this battle.

Paolo made the first move, swinging a floor lamp like a fighting staff. Lilith easily evaded and launched claw-like fingernails through the air to pierce Paolo's face like so many darts. With the slicing penetration came searing pain. Poison spread across his skin, a growing web of necrosis, until he and Roman bumped fists—Wonder Twins style. Their knuckles collided with a spark of white light and the damaging process was reversed. Lily's nails fell away, and Paolo's health was restored.

Jabbing with his muscular arms, Darby was boxing the air. With each swing, a corresponding burst of energy impacted Lily's body. She grabbed her stomach, until her head snapped back, but none of the punches did debilitating damage.

Lilith leaped in Beacon's direction, but with a jump Tyler met her in the air. One arm brushed him aside and propelled him across the room. A bounce off the wall removed him from the conflict.

Only a few feet still separated the demon from Beacon when Fern came running into the room wielding a large cross sculpted in iron. She tripped over Ty's crumpled body and the cross became airborne as she rolled onto the floor. The ancient symbol of execution sunk into the demon's side just above her hip. Lily refused to vocalize her agony with a scream. Instead she looked at each of them n turn before stealing one last glance at Beacon's swollen belly.

Acknowledging defeat, she chose to survive, as she had from the beginning. She who was among the first, would not be undone by these mortals. Her prehensile tail reached to one of the exposed beams of the ceiling and lifted her, flinging her through a closed window.

The others raced over to continue their attack, as Roman healed Ty and even Fern. Paolo and Darby hopped through the window, but the chase was lost. No sign of Lilith remained, not even her blood.

The entire household joined in the search, but the demon was truly gone.

"I know you'd rather be with Beacon," Rachel told Lucien as they quarreled on the stolen shuttle.

"I will not say again that my only continued interest in the princess is that she carries my child." The demon king was weary of the argument. "After the birth of my progeny, the human bitch will be extinguished."

"I hope that's true," Rae scratched at the itch below her kabala bracelet, "Not necessarily the extinguishing part, but about not wanting her." The itch became too much and she casually ripped the red string from her arm and tossed it aside.

"We don't need her child," Rachel offered. "I would love to have your baby—as many as you want."

"If only that were possible, my darling," Lucien took her gently into his arms and kissed her throat. For only an instant, her mind flashed back to how Heather had died. She wasn't afraid though. They were coming to understand each other pretty well.

"Why not?" She was still jubilant at the notion.

"Alas, you are not magical my eager lamb," He stroked her curly hair. "Magic is required for human DNA to combine with the superior genes of Legion. It is the princess' association with Avatarn blood that makes possible the forbidden child. That is why he must be raised at my side. As my prince…With you as his mother."

"Me…As…And so he shall be," She was suffused with pride and dark but filling purpose. "I will see to it."

Tyler and Beacon were working alone in the garden when Rachel found them. The princess, encouraged by her lover, had been surprised to learn that she could actually enjoy working with her hands. Bending nature to human will and working up a sweat in the process. Even in her new larger size, she liked doing what had been un-thinkable, sitting in the dirt harvesting vegetables with a small scythe and a basket.

As Rae approached the young couple, she imagined herself to be Uksakka, whom in Nordic legend looked after the interests of the new-born child. She just needed to speed along this child's birth.

Tyler smiled a welcome, and even Beacon seemed unbothered by the intrusion.

"Mind if I join you?" Rachel was looking at Ty but it was the princess who answered.

"As you wish," her tone more friendly than her words.

"Never expected to see your hands dirty, Highness," Rae let just a little contempt color her voice.

"Nor did I," she actually smiled and held up a bell pepper. "It seems this baby and this man have opened my eyes to the joys possible in a common life. I would never have believed it."

"A love of your own…A family to raise. I can see the allure. It could become everything," Rachel stared passed them towards the horizon.

"Come to lend a hand?" Tyler asked, offering her a pair of gloves.

"I suppose so," She accepted them along with a pair of gardening shears. She wasn't sure if she could do what had to be done. There would be no turning back after that line was crossed. On her knees, she had joined in the harvesting. It was when Tyler leaned over her to offer the basket for her peppers, that she did it. She let go of the bloody shear handles and met Ty's confused gaze with confusion of her own. Although she was no expert in anatomy, Rachel guessed she had stabbed him in the liver. He joined her on his knees, and for a moment Rae's hand moved towards the puncture and the tool that made it, tempted to try to hold in the blood.

Instead she withdrew when Beacon's screams penetrated the haze in which she was moving.

The hysterical yells brought Darby and Paolo running from the back porch where they had been devising plans to move against Legion.

Rae couldn't turn back, so she reclaimed the bloody shears from her dying friend and simultaneously shot a foot out to connect with Beacon's ankle. The princess had struggled to her feet and lunged towards her lover's slayer, scythe in hand.

Darby was running towards the garden as fast as he could when he witnessed the end of sanity in the world. His sister fell to the ground beside Tyler's blood-soaked body, and his best friend pounced on her. A frenzy of arms and blades ended with both girls painted crimson. An agonized cry escaped his lips, but Rachel gave no indication that she heard. Instead she pried the small scythe from Beacon's lifeless fingers and raised it over her protruding belly.

Dar had reached the garden's edge and roared Rachel's name just as the blade arced towards his twin's unborn child. In the instance before the womb was sliced, it deflated. Suddenly, uninhabited. Empty of life. The royal abdomen was flat and vacant, and an infant boy cried in Darby's arms.

The Avatarn couldn't explain how his nephew had teleported from Beacon's uterus to wallow against his chest; he only knew his beloved Rachel still had the scythe and had turned her obsessive vision on the child he held.

Rae was a wild animal running towards her prey, but Darby felt no fear. He could hear that Paolo had run back to the house to summon Roman for healing, but Dar knew that time had passed.

He didn't raise a hand or purposely engage his powers. It happened automatically. When Rachel reached within ten feet of her target, a golden energy barrier blocked her path nearly knocking her off her feet.

"Why?" was all the Avatarn could say through the tears that showered the squirming baby.

"To have what every human being deserves. A husband. Children. To be someone's partner. To be mutually in love." She had grown quiet and calm. "Surely you, of all people, wouldn't deny me that after all those years."

"In time you would have had all that, Rae," Darby tried to comfort the wriggling child. "But not now. Not this way." She stared at the ground for a moment before looking directly into his red-rimmed eyes.

"You're right," she whispered, "I blew it." The scythe fell from her hand; then she joined it, crumpling to the dirt, racked with sobs.

Watching her heart break, his broke too. Darby dropped his shield and went to her. Cradling the baby in one muscular arm, he used the other to pull his broken friend into his embrace. She let him.

Holding them both, sitting among the onion tops, Darby was almost disappointed to see Paolo and Roman emerging from the back of the house, Josh not far behind. Now he would be forced to deal with Rae's betrayal, and nothing would ever by the same.

He thought some garden creature had bitten him at first. The pain in his hand was sharp but brief. When he looked passed Rachel's shoulder and saw the scythe sticking in his hand, he was too surprised to react. The Avatarn was still stunned when Rachel grabbed the baby and was up and running.

Darby clenched his teeth and yanked the curved blade from his hand. Though bleeding profusely, he jumped to his feet and started after the crazed girl that had his nephew.

The others quickly ascertained the situation, and joined the pursuit; however Rachel's lead was too great an advantage. She rounded the house and temporarily disappeared from view. When the others reached the front yard, she was just entering the shuttlecraft. They all ran as fast as they'd ever run before, but the hatch was sealed and locked when they reached it.

"Don't worry; she doesn't know how to fly it," Josh offered confidently, but the words were barely out of his mouth when the engines came online.

Everyone followed Darby to the front to peer in through the large windows. Rachel was in the co-pilot's seat. Lucien was at the helm. The extended shield bubble was retracted to protect only the small ship. Dar didn't bother to activate his powers. He couldn't stop them.

They moved back as the craft began to hover. It drifted in the air for only a few seconds before shooting into space. Roman and Paolo each took one of Darby's arms to lend needed balance.

Though he was choking on the horror of what had happened, the grieving brother pushed his voice to sound.

"The best friend I ever had just killed a friend, my twin sister, and kidnapped my only surviving blood relative and delivered him to the enemy. To the fucking devil for Christ's sake," Darby wiped his face which was still turned to the sky. "The baby doesn't even have a name."

"Yes…He does," Paolo interjected and every head turned, "Beacon told me just this morning…His name is Bridge."

"Of course," Darby smiled a little, "The prince would have been her bridge between her old life and a new life of goodness and real love. It's perfect…Don't worry, Sis!" He shouted to the air. "Uncle Darby won't rest until he's home."

Roman nodded his own promise. Someday the Avatarn children were coming home.

Chapter 29

"**Believe me, we're better** off," Fern assured Josh. "No good was going to come from the Princess of Hell and the devil's child."

"You forget, Fernie, that the Princess of Hell was also the sister of an Avatarn—The Hammer of God," the self appointed priest reminded.

"They were dangerous, and these fools were too blind to see it."

"Not everything is black and white, Fern Leaves. I would have thought you would have learned that by your age."

"And I should think by now that you would know that loving somebody doesn't make them good and sometimes no amount of love can save somebody from themselves. Besides…I knew that black bitch would be trouble from the moment she walked in here." She offered Josh a refill on his coffee when she got hers. They were alone in the kitchen.

"You know somethin', old girl, you actually had me up until that nasty rotten soul of yours peeked through."

She chuckled, then replied, "Say what you want about me, Reverend, but none of my friends ever felt so alone in a crowd that she sold her pussy to the devil for a hug and a promise."

Joshua returned to the altar he had built in his room. He went down on his knees and lit the candles. Next he placed his fingers in the bowl full of three-leaf clovers he had collected. They were surely out of season; he found they were plentiful on the property inhabited by the Avatarn. Go figure. He then kissed his fingertips and used them to trace a cross on his forehead. His prayers centered on Bridge's safe return, but he found it difficult to concentrate.

They had let Rachel down in a way that he could barely fathom, and as a result, she was lost. Separated from the divine force and His emissaries. If only he and Darby and Yoshi hadn't been gay, they could have given her the kind of love she craved. They had been so selfish. If only his grandmother had appeared to him sooner to show him the way. Conflict crowded his thoughts. On the one hand, he was devoted to serving the Avatarn, God's Chosen. On the other, he had come to understand that homosexuality is wrong. A crucial consideration because of Darby's relationship with Paolo.

As Josh prayed for guidance, a single idea kept sliding back into his mind. Someone needed to remove Paolo's influence from Darby's life.

Fern had just settled into bed for the night with her needlepoint project. She had to do something to fill the hours while they waited for whatever the next big encounter would be. She wasn't sleeping much anymore, so she occupied her time making a blanket for Atom. The other baby was where he belonged as far as she was concerned. Only a few new stitches were added before she was startled by the sudden appearance of a man in the corner of the room. Here we go, she thought.

The apparition wore a long brown robe that so precisely matched his long brown beard, it might have been woven of the whiskers. His countenance was severe, and Fern knew that he would judge harshly her reaction to whatever he was there to say.

"My name is Rasputin." He stepped from the shadows into the lamplight, knowing the tough old woman would not scream. "I am an angel sent by the Almighty." The demon lied and she believed with all of her heart. She had been waiting for the Lord to contact her with instructions. She knew He was bound to use her to keep the *Chosen Ones* from straying. Fern nodded her understanding, so he continued. "As long as the witch lives, she is a contamination threat to the favored child that she bore. She must die tonight."

"But that's not necessary," she was shocked at the suggestion, "I cast a spell to lock her in sleep. She's no longer a threat to anyone. Besides, that Joppa creature has taken Atom into hiding."

"Your efforts have been valiant, but your duty is not yet done. The witch could still wake, and the child WILL return."

"Well…I will obey the Lord's instructions of course. What would He have me do?"

The beast that would be her angel smiled an icy smile. "It's very simple. I've brought you a tool." He produced something vile and putrid from the folds of his robe.

"What the hell is that?" She fought down the bile rising in her throat.

"It's a *hand of glory,*" the monkish being replied.

"There's nothing holy about that thing."

"You're right. There's nothing holy about this or any of the magic performed by you mortals."

"But that looks like a decaying human hand."

"Oh, it is…From a hanged man to be more specific."

"What is it for?"

"You will burn it to accomplish two goals. It will put every human in the house to sleep. Including the witch's watchdog husband. And it will unlock the bitch's bedroom door."

"That seems more like Satan's work than the Lord's."

"Humans must use whatever powers are available to achieve their aims."

"I don't want to kill her," Fern was as surprised as he that she would offer any defiance. "She is Roman's wife now. And Atom's mother. She may be a bad influence, but they would never forgive me."

"Your personal morality and desire for popularity are of no consequence. The Almighty has issued a directive to you. Will you obey it?"

She only nodded yes. He dropped the rotting appendage into her gnarled ones and unceremoniously stepped into her full-length mirror and disappeared.

Fern thought the Lord might have cut her some slack. After all, she had already risked her position in the house by using magic on the witch, AND turning Joshua's life around.

Oh, well, so be it. She made a decision on the spot as she stared down at the ghastly object in her wrinkled hand. Somebody was going to have to pay the dun for the child's well-being. If the price of that were her good conscience, so be it. Besides, the good Lord never asked more than we are capable of.

Fern removed the flue from the kerosene lamp she preferred for her needle work (it wasn't good for her eyes, but allowed her to drift back to long-ago days) and passed the flame under the gruesome flesh. The impact of the stench was immediate. She thought she would throw up, but she fought to maintain control. At first, the skin only blackened, but soon every finger was alight. It took some time for the fire to actually burn down to the wrist, but when it had, the remainder of the ghoulish item simply vaporized and was gone. Fern's eyes burned from the smoke, and she realized that the rest of the house was indeed eerily quiet.

A quick peek into neighboring rooms proved that everyone else was deeply asleep. Rasputin's trick had worked. She had soon made her way to the newlywed's room, and, as expected, the door was unlocked. She carried no weapons, as she had already decided that a pillow over the face would be the least violent way—and the least traceable.

Fern stopped in her tracks just inside the door. Though Roman was beside his wife, he too was a prisoner of sleep. What she hadn't counted on was the large white tiger on sentry at the foot of the bed. Joppa's giant pet raised its head and issued a low warning growl. Neither her mysterious visitor nor her imagination had prepared her for this possibility. She trusted that God might protect her from the feline guard as he had Daniel in the lions' den. Moving boldly forward, Fern squeezed past the big cat and approached Blair's side of the bed. The tiger growled a warning, and she froze.

Somehow Roman stirred at the animal's bluster. Fern wondered if the giant cat had magic of its own to counter the sleep charm, but thought it more likely that Roman's own powers were somehow protecting him from outside influences. The gig was up. He was awake, and she had a pillow in her hands.

"Stop! What the hell are you doing, Fernie?" Roman's fear had him sitting up with a protective arm across his wife before his head completely cleared.

"Just giving her another pillow, dear. No reason for concern."

"Bullshit! First of all, our door was locked. Secondly, Jane's tiger wouldn't have sounded the alarm unless you were up to no good. So back the fuck away from her," Roman was on his knees in the middle of the bed, unconcerned about his nudity, in full protective mode.

Prude that she was, the old lady stole a lingering glance. Even to her, Ro's body and maleness were magnificent to behold. She knew at least one reason the witch loved him.

"You were actually going to murder my wife, weren't you, you crazy old bitch?"

"Why would I bother? She's as good as dead anyway." Fern Leaves didn't appreciate his verbal attack. She was through pussy-footing around with Roman Perez. "As long as I live, she will sleep. She won't have a chance to taint that boy of yours with her sorcery and evil. She claims to be of God, but her kind can't serve two masters."

"You're really certain of that? She will never wake until you die?" Roman sounded defeated, crushed.

"I know it," Fern was both arrogant and bitter, "My people have been dealing with the likes of her since they founded this nation. Not another soul will be corrupted by that misguided girl."

"Very well," Roman was glad no one had come to investigate the commotion. "You've left me without a choice, Fernie." The dark Avatarn reached behind the bed to retrieve the baseball bat he had procured from the kids' room in case of intruder. "Last chance. Break the spell." His quiet words chilled her spine.

"I said it can't be broken. Now put that thing away, fool. You are the last person I would be afraid of. You don't have it in you. It goes against everything you are." Roman climbed to his feet, still on the bed. Fern thought he looked ridiculous in spite of being a perfect specimen.

"You're right. If I hurt you, it will damage me in a way that can never by healed…But I will take that burden on to save my wife."

She wasn't really scared, but she did glance at the door where the tiger had moved to block the exit.

"Roman, don't be such a weak—"Her sentence went unfinished. He had swung the bat with all of his might. An image of Cinder flashed in his mind. This wasn't what he'd been in little league for. A baseball would have been out of the park, but Fern's head simply lay on her shoulder. A broken globe. A bowl of blood and brains. Ro was sick and his mostly digested last meal just missed the bed as he turned and his stomach heaved. He could feel his powers automatically rising to heal her, but he wouldn't release it. Fern's body stood in place for several more seconds before accepting its fate and collapsing to the floor. Roman tossed the stained bat and sat Indian-style on the bed and spoke to the snowy tiger.

"Well, what does that make me, big fella?"

The animal purred a response, then stood and turned in a circle. When its mouth caught its tail, it vanished, leaving Roman to answer his own question as Blair began to wake.

"I guess it makes me a husband."

Everyone in the house had awakened after Fern's death. They

had a pre-dawn pow-wow in the kitchen to catch Blair up on all the crazy events she had missed, and then all volunteered to help clean up the master bedroom. Only Paolo expressed some sympathy for Fern. The others just tried to comfort Roman as they put the old woman to rest with her family in the still-new cemetery.

After Reverend Josh conducted a very short funeral service in the black suit he had reconstructed to have a blue Nehru collar representing the halos of the Avatarn; Roman, who had hardly let go of Blair's hand, wandered off alone to watch the horses and try to figure out if he could keep doing whatever he had to do to save his family and his world. And if he should.

"You need to fix your face." Roman looked around for the source of the voice, hoping it wasn't coming from one of the horses. He was still leaning against the wooden fence rail by the horses' stalls when the voice said, "Over here, Cowboy. I said take that angry, beat-down, sour look off your face."

After a brief search, he found what he was looking for in the horses' giant metal water tank. The gray tub had been filled to the brim, and smiling at him from below the water's surface was his friend Honeydew. Leave it to Honey to appear beneath water when she had met her death in the murky moat of Castle Hades.

"Oh, Honey. Christ, I wish you were still here." He started to raise his voice to summon the others, but the beautiful black girl/boy beneath the water cut him off.

"No no, Sugar. Honey's just here for you this time."

"Couldn't have come at a better time, girl. You won't believe the shit I've been through since you died. Sorry by the way... About the shark and all."

"Bygones, Baby. Bygones," Honey floated near the surface, the brown strands of her wig and the fabric of her sundress undulating in unseen and impossible currents.

"I do know what you done gone through, Captain Courageous. And I'm proud of you."

"Proud?" Roman was shocked, "Honey, I clubbed an old woman to death last night. That's not exactly—"

"You saved your wife so she can help you save the world.

That's what you did last night," the young drag queen assured him.

"We really did try to create a sense of bonhomie with the old hag," Roman was trying to convince himself. "But she betrayed us. I had no choice."

"You're preachin' to the choir, Sweets. I know your heart, Perez." Honey waved at the palomino that approached the tank for a drink. The horse was surprised for only a second before naying hello and choosing to respectfully wait until the water tank was absent of spirits.

"But how am I supposed to live with this, Honey?"

"You won't…You won't. Instead, you will live with your wife and son," Honey wished she could reach through the rippling water to take Ro's hand, but all she could offer was words. "There will always be a scar, darlin'…A wound on your soul that your powers can't heal, 'til one day you'll be touched by the Son—yours or God's—and you will be restored. Repaired….Meanwhile, you gotta stop frettin' about Fern Leaves. She's still in time-out, soakin' up some truth from Papa…Soon as He straightens her out, she will be with us. Her grandkids missed her anyway, so let it go as best you can."

"So what do we do now, Hon?"

"Mothership, Sweets. It's time," Miss Honey was re-touching her lip liner, "Gather your posse and get re'ta-go."

"Big showdown?" Ro was scared but excited.

"The wait is over, Chosen," she said. "You already have God's blessing. Now go to your destiny."

Roman stuck his fingers into the water to connect with her, but instead her image shimmered and was gone. Without thinking, he wiped his tear streaked cheek with his already-wet hand and laughed at himself as Honey's voice whispered one last phrase in his ear, "And kick some demon ass for me."

Ro was still laughing softly when the flaxen horse returned for his drink.

"But how are we going to get to the *Caiphas* without the shuttle?" Paolo asked the group. They had all taken their favorite spots on the front porch for the impromptu meeting Roman called to relay Honey's message, each one wishing they had been selected for her visitation.

"That is our most immediate question," Darby seconded from his place on the steps.

"I'm thinking we'll have to use the Babylon chant to portal there," Blair offered the most viable option from her rocking chair. Roman and Josh nodded their agreement, and it was decided that they would leave right after breakfast. They would need some nourishment for what they were about to face. Most important meal of the day—had never meant so much, so pop-tarts or granola bars weren't going to do. The five remaining residents of the Tobit House prepared a lavish spread, even though none of them was hungry.

All agreed that it was impossible to predict what they would encounter onboard the *Caiphas*. The only weapons they would have were their powers and the mistletoe potion. Josh's skills with technology and computers would be required, but Darby wasn't shy about telling Paolo that he would be staying behind. Of course everyone knew it was just an exercise to protect Dar's conscience. Paolo wouldn't think of staying at the farm. If he died, it would be at his lover's side. He was going along, and not even the *Hammer of God* could stop him.

Chapter 30

They made quite a picture when the group met on the flattened grass where the shuttle had sat under the giant tree. All wore only denim overalls, with the addition of a black bra for Blair. It had been decided that fitted, but comfy bib overalls would provide them a matching uniform that would make for easy identification of their team during battle. Not to mention, the Tobit closets offered limited options. Blair topped the look with a high ponytail.

The Avatarn joined hands, Josh and Paolo (temporarily delayed by a nervous bout of diarrhea) provided the nucleus for the organism created by their linked arms. Outside their circle, dogs' tails froze mid-wag, and the guys saw bird statues hanging in the air. The triad's chants of *Babylon* grew in volume until their shouts echoed off an invisible cone of power. A black vortex opened beneath their feet and for an instant, all were standing on nothingness. Then the fall. Through darkness and empty space, they watched each other plummet. All focused their thoughts on the bridge of the *Caiphas*, and with a crash, they tumbled onto the command floor. The bridge officers leapt to their feet and the holy pilgrims did likewise.

Josh was in technology heaven. Looking around the spaceship's command center, he was blown away by the seemingly simple computer control stations that operated the highly advanced craft. Nearly every surface appeared to be made of a silvery metal. There were countless view screens displaying everything from a complex symbol language to images from around the Earth and beyond. The officers that had been at their posts looked human at a glance, but a lingering eye revealed that they were monsters. His sci-fi geek fascination was cut short by a deafening alarm and he was oddly distracted by the stench as the demons entered attack mode.

Paolo had just recognized the communications officer who stood and laid her headset on her terminal, when she leaped on him. Who would have guessed their old friend Lily had attained such a prominent position.

Darby grabbed her swishing tail in an attempt to pull her off his boyfriend, but to no avail. The others were engaged hand-to-hand by the other bridge officers, when suddenly laser blasts cut through the air. They were being fired upon by security personnel as they arrived in the control center. The overzealous soldiers managed to shoot two of their own before a scorching burn appeared on Roman's thigh. As soon as he had recognized that he was injured, his leg was healed in a flash of white light. He was still thanking God for his power when he saw Josh wrestling with a 3-foot demon with shocking strength. Joshua didn't even see the demon Fern had known as Rasputin approach him from behind. The demon's brown robe had been replaced by a black military uniform, though the long beard remained. Roman saw, but couldn't move fast enough to prevent Rasputin's swinging sword. The long sharp blade separated Josh's head from his neck. Roman dove and managed to catch his friend's head before it hit the floor. Josh's heart was still beating, so the Avatarn leader pressed his head into place. Blair held her breath until the customary white light engulfed the severed neck then faded to reveal a whole and healthy man. Josh was too overwhelmed with gratitude to speak, so he hoped Ro read it in his eyes.

The Avatarn leader's brief smile showed his relief, then he moved immediately to Blair to shield her at all costs. He quickly realized his protection was not called for. Upon looking into his wife's eyes, he saw a thunderstorm brewing behind her irises. Rolling clouds of bruised green. A deluge raged beyond the windows to her soul, and he knew Blair could take care of herself.

Roman had just moved out of her way, when the witch raised her arms and opened her hands to unleash sizzling bolts of lightning that shot from her palms to lift soldiers off the floor and shake them with convulsing electrocution. Each demon in turn fell to the bridge and was reduced to a steaming black pool.

After seeing what she could do, Blair turned her attentions to an alien she knew had directly harmed Avatarn. Rasputin narrowly escaped the bluish lightning streak by diving behind the navigation station, but Blair had been aiming for Lily and she wasn't so lucky. Darby still had her by the tail, when a jagged bolt hit the middle of her back. All present were surprised when as she flopped in pain, her twisting tail came off in Dar's hands. The stunned Blair briefly stopped her electric flow, allowing Lily to live. The ancient demoness took the opportunity to join Rasputin behind the silvery console.

Josh quickly claimed the sword Rasputin had abandoned to the floor, and Paolo followed his lead, grabbing an energy gun from a holster in the sticky goo that had been a demon.

Each approached the navigation station from a different side, cornering the cowering aliens. However, upon seeing who was moving on them, Lily rose to her feet, indicating that Rasputin should do likewise.

"Do not fear, lieutenant," she became arrogant. "These two are not men enough to detain us."

"You're right," Paolo calmly replied. "We're not going to detain you." Without hesitation, he raised the weapon and fired it into her abdomen. Lily only had an instant to react with shock as the purple beam impacted and spread out to consume her flesh until she was gone.

Rasputin had turned at her scream, offering his back to a vengeful Josh. The time was past for notions of etiquette or fairness, so Joshua didn't wait for the bearded demon to turn back to his fate. The self-appointed priest of the Avatarn plunged the weighty sword between the alien's shoulder blades. Josh took a step backwards, both proud and horrified at what he had done, and watched as the sword fell to the floor in a rain of black sludge. Paolo reached to give him a high-five, carefully avoiding stepping in the gore.

Josh wasted no more time in seating himself at the computer station and using what he had learned from their stolen shuttle to begin to analyze the status of the ship.

The Avatarn used their powers and Legion weapons to finish the few remaining soldiers on the bridge.

With the area temporarily secure, Roman peered over Joshua's shoulder and ordered him to report on their situation.

"So how long 'til we're overrun with storm troopers?" Ro asked the team's programming expert.

"Looks like a major security detail is approaching," Josh replied, "but I think I've managed to seal the doors."

"That's good for now, but we have to figure out a way to get to the slaves and captives and get them off the ship."

"Maybe we can help with that," came a woman's voice from a vent in a wall.

All attention and weapons turned toward the duct as bare feet kicked out the screen, and a beautiful but very alien woman emerged.

"Indra!" Blair recognized her immediately and rushed into the four open arms of the slave that had helped her escape when she was imprisoned on board the *Caiphas* with Roman's first wife. "I assumed you had been killed for helping us."

"I would have been, if Adolphus hadn't so looked forward to making me his bride and taking me to his bed. I am alive today because the monster Lucien finds much pleasure in raping the wives of his predecessor." Long black hair, an elaborate jeweled halter (covering four full breasts), and a skirt made up of veils made the new arrival on the bridge appear as an exotic fantasy fresh from the *Tales of Arabian Nights*. Even the gay boys were mesmerized.

Blair was making introductions, and Ro was thanking the

creature who was both a slave and a queen for saving the woman of his life, when Indra turned back to the vent-duct and signaled for someone to join them. Darby subtly raised the Legion weapon he held, not yet convinced to trust.

The handsome boy who emerged from the crawl-space was far from human, as evidenced by the protective horns that grew up from the tops of his shoulders. Darby was reminded of many of the myths that Rachel had taught him over the years. This strange but alluring boy might have been a *huldu*, the male version of the Scandinavian huldra, a seductive being that lured men or women as the case may be into the depths of a forest for their delight or destruction depending on the creature's whim. Indra introduced her cohort as Geb and explained that he was from the planet Gam-in, a world where no one lived into adulthood. This was why she had made him her foster child. It remained unspoken that no one else present could think of the sexy and nearly naked youth as a child. Josh correctly guessed that even by Earth standards the boy met the age of consent. The fact that he took notice was very troubling to his new *heterosexual* mind. He dismissed the entire notion by turning back to the display screen and focusing on the vital information it provided.

Indra went on to explain how she had guessed from the sounding alarms that the ship had been infiltrated. She had sent Geb, as she often did, to eavesdrop on the bridge to see what had happened. When he returned to the royal harem through the well-explored duct system, and informed his foster mother of the battle in the command center, she had joined him to lend whatever support they could provide.

"You really are a sight for sore eyes." Blair pried her emerald green ones from Geb and looked into Indra's. "We have to find a way to get all the captives off this ship, and we don't know where to begin."

"I think the only viable solution will be the life pods," Indra suggested. "Each escape craft can hold ten persons. There should be enough for everyone."

"Let's do it," Blair gestured towards the vent. "I'll go with them to provide a little fire-power. You guys figure out how to find Baby Bridge and bring down the rest of the fleet."

"Is that all?" Paolo was sarcastic but smiling. Roman wasn't happy as he kissed his wife and watched her disappear into the crawl space with Indra and Geb, but he had quickly learned that when it came to marital arguments, his bride was made more in the mold of modern TV witches, not the nose-wigglers of his childhood.

The security force had begun to pound on the invincible metal doors with some kind of make-shift battering ram, but they couldn't make a dent.

"Can you use internal sensors to locate the baby?" Darby had returned to Josh's side.

"It's our best chance," Josh answered, "but it's hard to sort out these bio signs. With so many aliens aboard, the readings are all wonky."

"Do your best." Ro joined them as he tried calling Blair's cell phone with his. When she didn't respond, he assumed—hoped—that the ship's hull must be blocking the satellite signal.

"So what are we going to do when the soldiers decide to start teleporting in?" Dar hoped their leader had a plan not yet shared.

"You should have thought of that before embarking on this doomed mission, heretic," Lucien's voice rang out from the other side of the control center. He had materialized strangely perched on the shoulders of Azazel, the demon hybrid that had once been Paolo's human lover, who had been reduced to serving as mounted steed.

"What in the hell?" Roman didn't know what to make of the bizarre visual across the room.

"Exactly," Lucien replied with a sneer. His lofty perch didn't really provide much of a battle advantage; he just enjoyed subjugating the human slave. And the expressions on the Avatarn's faces were priceless. The demon king had traded his usual toga for cowboy clothes, and Azazel wore a black leather harness over his chest and abdomen to match black leather pants. There was actually a bridle in his mouth with black leather reins, but he didn't seem to mind. The re-animated hybrid didn't flinch when his rider dug metal spurs into his sides starting him forward.

Darby was relieved that their adversaries seemed unarmed, but knew they might fare worse in hand-to-hand. He was thankful they still had the weapons they had just fought to procure.

"Love the overalls," Lucien scoffed. "Who would have thought the long prophesied Avatarn would turn out to be hillbillies?"

Under different circumstances, Josh would have had a wry remark regarding renegade Village People, but fear suppressed his ready humor. No sooner had he raised Rasputin's sword above his head in a double-handed grip, than Lucien waved his fingers teleporting it to Azazel's waiting hand.

Without a word of planning, Darby and Paolo both fired their laser guns at the demon king. Azazel's arms moved with mechanical speed to block the energy blasts with the massive sword, the deflected energy ripping holes in the surrounding computers.

Azazel continued to charge forward, ducking his head to allow Lucien to land on his booted feet. In a single leap, he crashed into Darby, the Avatarn not even having a chance to instinctively raise his protective shield. The handsome monster was raining blows on Dar's face too quickly for him to resist, let alone remove the syringes of potion from his pocket.

Roman moved to help, but Azazel's blade sliced the air before him, cutting short his progress. Ro hesitated as he considered his next course of action and stared into the face of the smiling corpse that had been a man named Cinder.

Neither of them saw Paolo jump from the top of a console to land on Azazel's back and wrap one of Indra's veils around his throat. As luck would have it, if there was such a thing, the exotic slave had left behind the swath of fabric when it caught on the ventilation grate. Paolo couldn't believe he was trying to strangle Cinder, but under the circumstances he had no choice. Besides, the man he had cared about wasn't occupying this body alone, if at all.

The sword clattered on the floor, as Azazel attempted to free himself, giving Roman the chance to kick Lucien in the back. The demon spun to face his attacker and Darby fell to his knees, his shield rising to insulate him from further harm.

"Now what, Roman Perez?" Lucien challenged him, "Your little bitch wife isn't here to protect you. You don't have an offensive power. What ya gonna do?" The demon rammed his fist into Ro's stomach, doubling him over. He didn't see the syringe in Roman's hand until the Avatarn tried to stick it in his thigh. The needle bent and bounced off without breaking the demon's skin. "Surely you knew Rachel would tell me about your little potion. I took the liberty of casting a spell to make my skin impenetrable to cutting or stabbing. Anymore great ideas?"

"Hey, a…royal asshole." Paolo called to Lucien confidently as Azazel seemed to be weakening from the oxygen deprivation, "You need to scrub down your horse here. He stinks." It was then that a burst of rage enabled Azazel to toss his burden from his back and tear away the cloth cutting off his air. Paolo lay stunned by the wall he slammed into meters away. Josh only had time to raise his fist before Azazel punched him in the temple and watched him crumple into unconsciousness.

"I tire of this fiasco…Finish him." Lucien gestured towards the bent Avatarn between him and his soldier. With only a grunt of acknowledgment, Azazel reached between Roman's legs from behind and grabbed his testicles in a crushing grip. Ro cried out in agony, then jerkily raised himself to his full height. This allowed Azazel/Cinder to hook his arm around Ro's neck, slowly suffocating him as he placed his other large hand on the Avatarn's chin, preparing to snap his spine.

When a golden beam of energy emanating from Darby's forehead reached Azazel's head and lit him up like a Christmas tree, causing excruciating pain, Darby mumbled, "Fuck you, Cinder," just as Lucien tried to punch the Avatarn still on the floor. Dar's force-field blocked the blow like break-proof glass and the demon kissed his tender knuckles and seethed.

Though Darby's golden energy was torturing his friend's captor, the beam was not strong enough to disable the monster, and any second the creature would steal Ro's life. Darby maintained the beam and cried out to their only possible savior, "Jesus, please. Give me strength as your servant to protect your disciple, Roman, and free Cinder from enslavement to the devil. I ask this in your holy name, Yeshua. Help us." In that instant Darby felt a surge of power that tripled the force of his beam. Azazel exploded into a billion pieces, every cell blasted apart. The hybrid was blown into oblivion, freeing Cinder's soul, and releasing Roman to heal himself.

Lucien reached to finish Roman on his own, but not before Paolo fired the laser gun he had scrambled to recover during the battle.

"Ouch!" The demon couldn't stifle himself when the scorching weapon burned his shoulder. "Don't get too comfy on my ship." He was gone in a blink.

Blair, Indra and Geb emerged from the ducts in the starship's traveling harem. Pillows, silks, and tapestries covered every surface of the large quarters. The women were relieved at Indra's safe return and greeted them enthusiastically.

Geb quickly outlined the plan to escape in the pods as Indra and Blair moved to the only door and summoned the guards stationed just outside.

When the door slid open, Indra commanded their attention by opening her jeweled halter revealing the four most beautiful breasts Blair had ever seen. The two demon soldiers stood mesmerized for nearly a minute before deciding to risk life and limb by entering the forbidden sanctum of the harem. It was then that the auburn-haired witch stepped from the shadows and chanted her couplet:

"No time for the devil's cop,
So I command your heart to stop."

The guards looked stricken and clutched at their chests and

collapsed on the rug. Indra and Blair commandeered their weapons and handed Geb a sword. They made short work of getting every wife and concubine into an escape pod, and with the aid of surprise, slaughtered every demon who crossed their path. Much of the crew was on Earth duty so resistance was relatively weak. Soon nearly every slave had been launched towards safety except those few butchered by the aliens as the revolt took place.

If not for the hairs on her arms coming to attention, Blair might not have made special notice of the mother and baby waiting in line to board one of the escape pods. A second glance confirmed that it was Rachel.

"Stop her!" Blair called to the alien slaves as she tried to push through the throng. When no one readily responded, Rachel cradled Bridge to her and dove towards the hatch. A flick of Blair's hand caused the door to slide into place and seal. Rachel turned to run, but the bustling crowd prevented her from fleeing.

"Back off, Bitch!" Rae screamed as she opened a trash shoot and held the baby over it. She knew she could never do it, but she hoped that Blair might think her recent acts of desperation could extend that far. Her only real hope at holding off the witch now frozen in her tracks was that Lucien would intervene. Rachel found herself doing yet another thing she never thought she would do. She prayed to the devil.

Chapter 31

After being awakened by Roman, Josh resumed his post at the operations station, and Ro turned to healing Darby's swollen face.

"Guys, there is a ship identifying itself as *The Uruk* closing on our position. It seems the alarms and escape pod launches have drawn the attention of the fleet," Joshua reported.

"Do you have weapon control?" Paolo leaned over his shoulder.

"Let's find out before they start teleporting back-up on board," Roman said.

"I think I can block them from teleporting here with the ship's shields," Josh sounded far less than certain. "Here goes." The long time friend turned priest of the Avatarn delicately tapped a series of symbols on the display panel and a volley of purple energy balls were fired at the approaching starship. All but one made contact with the giant saucer and a series of explosions erupted in massive damage. A string of curses flooded the communications transmissions as *The Uruk*'s crew tried unsuccessfully to teleport to the *Caiphas*, but only for a moment. The fiery damage escalated until a thunderous bang broke the ship into huge pieces that rained down on the city.

"Can we do that to the rest of the armada?" Darby suppressed his awe and asked with hope.

"We could, except now that they know we control the *Caiphas*, their shields will be raised. I don't think their weapons can penetrate them." Josh's sense of victory was short-lived.

"Set a course for the next saucer and leave the weapons upgrade to me," Dar assured him with a wink.

"Aye, Aye." Joshua smiled and put the ship in hyper-speed. The next ship they encountered was over Denver. The make-shift pilot locked weapons and fired without waiting for instruction. As he predicted, the shields easily dispersed the purple energy.

"Thank God we have shields too," Roman offered to counter everyone's disappointment.

"Don't be so quick to give up, fearless leader," Darby placed his hand on the display near the weapons control. "Now!" He ordered.

Josh fired the weapons and a golden glow encased Dar's hand and illumined the computer controls. The energy balls flying towards the enemy vessel suddenly changed from purple to gold. The golden light balls easily moved through the defensive shields and the ship was blown to oblivion far more quickly than the *Uruk*. A minimal amount of scrap fragments fell to the city below, and the *Caiphas'* new bridge crew cheered the discovery of an expedient way to destroy the invasion fleet.

As the Avatarn and their disciples flew the flagship from city to city annihilating the alien armada, Roman couldn't help wondering why Lucien hadn't reappeared to stop them. He chose not to risk jinxing their endeavor by vocalizing his concern, concern that would have turned to terror if he had known the lord of demons was busy with his wife.

Rachel's prayer was answered. Lucien appeared in a flash at her side scattering the remaining slaves like squirrels avoiding an angry dog. Rae smiled and handed the baby to her lover.

"I see you've decided to join my harem after all, Miss Atwood," Lucien smirked and pretended not to notice Rachel's jealous rage.

"It's Mrs. Perez now, Fuckwad. And as you can see, I just rescued your harem," Blair couldn't help gloating. "Looks like Rae is all you've got left."

"I'm all he needs, you cunt!" Rachel could hardly contain herself.

"No need to fight, ladies. There's more than enough of Uncle Lu to go around. And that's just what I told your husband, sweetheart, before I crushed his skull."

"You're lying," Blair replied confidently. "I would have felt it if he died."

"Check for your self if you don't believe me, dear."

"I'll return to him as soon as I take care of you, honeycakes," she finished sarcastically.

"Hold this," Lucien instructed, handing the baby back to Rachel. "Wait over there out of the way. I'm gonna do to this witch what I just did to her friends."

Blair didn't know if she could kill him, but she knew she could incapacitate him for a while.

"I bind you, Lucien
Body and powers
I bind you, Lu— "

Her chant was cut short when he teleported to her and materialized with his hand over her mouth. She might have been done for, had Geb not chosen that moment to attack. Lucien easily stopped the swing of the sword by grabbing the boy's wrist, but in that moment the youth lunged forward ramming the horn protruding from atop his shoulder through the cowboy shirt into the demon's unguarded ribs, Lucien howled in pain and released the Avatarn.

He swatted Geb away like a troubling fly, and Blair resumed her spell:

"I bind you, Lucien
Body and powers
I bind you, Lucien
Body and powers
By the guardians of the watch towers
Powerless to harm the bold
Hand and foot in bondage hold."

Metal bands that looked like iron appeared around Lucien's arms, wrists, legs, and ankles. As he struggled to maintain his balance and remain standing, he called upon the fires of Hell to consume the witch who presumed too much. To his amazement, his magic wasn't working.

"You little whore," Lucien was genuinely astonished. "He has granted you far more power than I imagined. Brava."

"Thanks, Lucy. Now if you don't mind, I'm just gonna park you someplace while we get on with our mission." With her last words and a flick of her wrist, Blair levitated the demon king to the trash shoot Rachel had opened earlier. The evil alien started to say something but knew it was pointless, so merely glared at her as another wave sent him plunging down the shaft to the refuse collected below. The king took comfort in thinking of all the ways he would make the twat pay.

During the distraction, Indra had inched ever closer to Rachel and little Bridge. When the beautiful alien grabbed for the baby, the former friend to the Avatarn blocked one arm with one of hers and held the baby tight with the other, but she couldn't fend off Indra's other three arms and soon the child was safely in the slave queen's care. Rachel would have attacked her, had Geb not swung his sword to intervene. In a move of surprising agility, she avoided his blade and twisted to thrust a dagger of her own towards his belly.

Blair couldn't hesitate to decide. Lightning shot from her palms lifting Rachel into the air and tossing her body against a bulkhead. Blair closed her hands to stop the flow and ran to the side of the girl who had been like a sister to her.

Rachel was barely conscious, but she reached out to take her killer's hand.

"I'm so sorry, Rachel. I had no choice."

"Lu was going to be my Gilgamesh, and me his Enkido," Rae mumbled with a fading smile. "Tell Darby I still loved him. Always loved him."

"He knows that, Rae."

"And tell God," the dying girl lost consciousness for only a moment and was back, "Tell God I'm sorry. I was consumed by desperation. Remind Him how alone He felt when He was on the cross. That's how alone I felt. Forsaken. When you're that alone, you give yourself to whoever answers your call. Whoever wipes your tears…You remind Him of that, and maybe He'll let me come home." She finished with a whisper.

"I will." Blair promised, but vacant eyes told her Rachel was already gone. The Avatarn shed a tear of her own and got to her feet. Indra handed her the baby for comfort, and when the last of the slaves was safely away and every soldier they encountered was dead, the threesome and the infant headed for the bridge.

When the *Caiphas* was the last remaining saucer-ship, Josh steered the craft back towards Kansas City. With everything under control, Roman decided to try to use his psychic link to Blair to find his wife. Sensors told them something had lured away the soldiers outside their doors long ago. They had probably been summoned to stop the escaping slaves, a supposition Ro was none too comfortable with considering his wife's role in their revolt.

Armed with laser guns and a sword, he set out on his own. He instructed Darby to stay with Josh and Paolo. They couldn't risk losing command of the ship.

In only a few minutes the *Caiphas* was back in position above Kansas City. Darby and Paolo were holding each other and looking down on the smoldering city, damaged by falling sections of the first ship they had battled, when Joshua's hands became a flurry of activity on the computer panel.

"What are you doing?" Paolo was startled and confused. "I thought we had gotten every ship."

"We did…On Earth," Josh was frantic. "But this is Planet Gehenna. That's Castle Hades below us. We've got to vaporize it," He yelled as the first wave of energy bombs impacted the unsuspecting city.

"Dude, you've lost it!" Darby screamed at his schizophrenic friend. "This is Earth. You're firing on a human city. Hold your fire man!"

"I can't; you're delusional, Dar. But don't worry; I will eradicate all traces of life on this demon world."

"I've been watching him. I think I can operate the ship," Paolo attempted to shove Josh away from the controls.

"I can't let you stop us, spy," Josh grabbed a laser gun and leveled it at Paolo.

Darby saw Joshua's finger tightening on the trigger, and his instincts took over. Shimmering golden light shot out from his heart and lifted a sword from the floor. There was no time for the Avatarn to stop what he knew must be. His golden aura flung the sword with flawless precision into Josh's stomach.

The shock on Joshua's face broke Darby's heart once again. He ran to catch his friend as his knees buckled and Dar was awash in his dear friend's blood.

"Roman!" Darby screamed, but Ro didn't hear. There would be no healing. Paolo pulled out the blade and another crimson gush flowed. Josh was going fast.

"I'm sorry, Joshy," Dar was sobbing, "Forgive me."

"What?" The fallen wanna-be-priest was still confused. All three heads turned to find the source of a glow across the room. It was Yoshi. Yoshi's ghost. A faint white glow emanated from his translucent body. The somber spirit walked calmly to the place where his wounded lover lay.

Without realizing, Darby and Paolo moved back to give him space. Yoshi's shade seemed to wink out and reappear kneeling at Josh's side. The ghost, which seemed without substance, somehow lifted the dying man into his arms, kissing his forehead. Caressing his face.

"I've been sent here in your moment of transition, my love, to restore your mind. I bring you healing more important than the body. My sweet beloved," Yoshi was smiling and his peace flooded Josh's rattled brain, lighting the dark corners. Returning clarity and understanding.

Joshua was smiling back and only said, "Thank you, Baby."

Just for an instant, the old Joshua was back, and somehow Darby actually felt happy as his old buddy closed his eyes and released his invisible soul from the flesh.

Yoshi's ghost gently placed the lifeless form on the floor and turned silently laughing his joy towards Dar and Paolo as he faded back into the ether.

The grief-stricken couple were still sitting on the floor beside Josh's body when Roman and Blair, with friends and baby in tow, returned to the bridge.

"What happened?" Ro cried out and rushed to heal their fallen comrade.

"It's too late," Darby's voice was husky with mind-numbing sorrow; "I had to kill him."

Blair responded to his sobs in kind, "I had to kill Rachel," she coughed the words, choking back a scream.

"Oh, God!" Darby didn't think he could hurt anymore, but this seemed more than his sanity could bear.

"Breathe," Paolo reminded him. Dar didn't have to ask why she had done it. The fact that Bridge was in her arms explained enough. Talking a hundred miles an hour, Paolo went on to tell what happened with Josh, including Yoshi escorting him home, the last bringing a moment of peace to the other Avatarn.

Still, nearly overcome with loss, it was decided they would return to the Tobit farm to regroup and plan their next move. It was only a matter of time until Lucien would free himself. All were confident that their powers had grown enough that they could teleport themselves through the shields if they left them up to keep out the demons.

With Indra and Geb's help, they located the trash receptacle where Lucien had landed, but no trace of him remained. Blair searched the ship with her mind and concluded that he was no longer on board. It seemed they would have to deal with him another day.

They loaded the bodies of Rachel and Josh onto a small shuttle, and after seeing Indra and Geb off in the last of the pods, the holy pilgrims boarded the shuttle and headed for the farmhouse.

Darby even managed a brief nap with his nephew sleeping on his chest.

The Avatarn were surprised how good it felt to return to the familiarity of the farmhouse. Though she was delighted to have him home, seeing and caring for Bridge multiplied the agony of missing Atom, and Blair prayed that Joppa was taking good care of her son. They buried their friends before even going inside. Only a short prayer served as a memorial. They didn't have the strength for anything more.

Paolo turned on the news expecting reports of the demons teleporting off world, returning home in defeat. He wasn't the only one surprised to learn that most of the aliens had stayed to retaliate for the destruction of their ships. They were mercilessly attacking humans around the world. No longer interested in taking slaves, they simply killed in vengeance wherever they could.

The Chosen Ones were ecstatic to see, however, that men and women around the globe were rising up against their oppressors in unstoppable numbers. Over the next twenty-four hours, humans took back the Earth. Many died, but those who lived would live freely. With a vast array of freed aliens on their side, mankind's victory was accomplished.

The Avatarn's small party managed to get a decent night of sleep. Bridge slept with Blair, as she was forced to breast feed him. Though it seemed odd at first, the baby and the new mother seemed comforted by the process. Bridge had never had the chance to feed directly from the source (though Lucien could have easily granted Rachel that wish); however, she showed him how and he got the hang of it.

Darby tossed and turned more than the others. Two more of his long-time best friends were dead. One by his own hand. He wondered why God had to exact such a terrible price for the blessings He gave. Several times Paolo lay awake watching his lover struggle with haunting dreams of the day's events.

Eventually, they all rose to find Roman again in front of the TV. Die-hard reporters from around the world were showing video clips of the demon invaders being killed by Earthlings and freed aliens. It wasn't over, but people were starting to pick up the pieces.

Looking around the parlor, Paolo thought about how they would look to someone who didn't know who they really were. Just a normal country family. A Rockwell painting from simple times. It consoled him somehow. To think that they could all be normal again. His whole life he had dreamed of the great Avatarn. Now he just hoped they could find their way back to ordinary. He knew better though. Ordinary would never mean what it had before.

Darby announced he was going upstairs to soak in a long bath. He hoped it would soothe his unquiet mind. Paolo stood to go with him, but a small gesture from Dar indicated he should stay. Very slowly the Avatarn ascended and started the steamy water in the claw-foot tub.

Darby felt his tensions begin to ease as he slid into the almost-too-hot bath. He allowed himself to slip deeper into the liquid therapy. The magical fluid gently renewing achy muscles.

He was half asleep when a shimmering image in the water returned him to sharp awareness. Beacon was there. Below the surface. His sister was also naked and her long blonde hair floated and billowed around her. He moved his fingers through the water to touch her face, but her visage only rippled in the current. There was nothing solid to feel.

"Looking between his legs, the princess said, "I see why Paolo is so devoted to you."

Darby chuckled softly as tears streamed his face, "Come on now. I don't think my twin crossed the great divide just to flirt. I'm so glad to see you, Sis. Everyone is dying. We've lost so many."

"I know, Brother. I know."

"Between Josh going crazy and Rae giving herself to the devil, I don't even know if they made it to Heaven...The things they've done...That all of us have done," his pause was brief before he asked, "Are they there with you? With God?"

"Yes, of course," she shushed his sobs and reached as if to touch his leg, though she could not. "Let me explain a few things to you, darling...I had not yet allowed Jesus into my heart when I was killed...I died without knowing him. Darby tried to speak but no sounds would come out.

"It's okay, though," she hurried to erase the fear from his eyes, "You see it's all about mercy, Brother. His mercy is without end. When I died, I found myself walking on the clouds of Gehenna. It was the only after-life I had ever imagined. My father had always promised that I would live eternally with him in Castle Hades, but somehow I knew that would never really be. I thought too that I would miss my baby, and Tyler, and you—but I didn't. Not at all. All of you were part of a different life. All exactly where you should be, and somehow it was okay.

"I thought you said you are with God?" Darby tried not to wiggle his feet and disturb the water.

"I am getting to that, impatient one," she scolded without losing her serenity. "As I strolled among the prismatic clouds, I came upon one other being. A magnificent man. So very handsome and charismatic, though not classically so. He looked like many of your Jewish people. He told me His name was Yeshua. That he is the one I was raised to call *He Who Sits Apart*. He said if I was sorry for my sins that I was forgiven. He said if I wanted to be with Him forever to take His hand. And I did...Endless mercy. Endless love."

"I'm so glad, Sis," Darby was relieved beyond measure. He finally felt better about all of his losses.

"There is another reason I'm here, Darby. I must ask a great favor."

"Anything, Sis."

"I want you and Paolo to raise my son, Bridge, as your own. You will be his parents."

"Are you sure? Two dads? Gay parents?"

"It's what I want. It's what God wants."

"Nothing would make me happier. We'll do it."

"Be at peace, Brother. And know that He is well pleased with you…We are close, Darby. Heaven is only a breath away."

It was then that the Avatarn's face broke the surface of the water. His head was thrust up to gasp for air, shaken like a dog to remove the clumping hair from his eyes. He had been talking to her from under water and hadn't even realized. Wiping rivulets from his face, he looked for her. For some sign that his dead sister had been there. There was none, but for her sweet floral scent. She was gone, but her message had done something not even Roman's powers could do. It had lifted his grief, leaving only selfish loneliness where an impossible burden had been.

Darby hopped out of the tub and grabbed some fluffy towels to mop up the splashy mess he had made.

Chapter 32

Time went by and the people of Earth tried their best to return to their old lives. The invasion and occupation had been short-lived so the elements of human civilization had not been destroyed or forgotten. But there were differences.

Many people had been killed. Women and men had been raped by all manner of demons and creatures.

The freed slaves from a hundred worlds were equal in number to the surviving humans. Some were taken in by human friends; relationships were forged in the new holocaust. Others were forming camps and villages wherever possible.

It had been two weeks since the Avatarn returned to the Tobit House. Bridge had been a wonderful distraction for the group as they planned a journey to Gehenna to rescue the remaining slaves. Each day the half-demon child grew and aged the approximate equivalent of one year. The accelerated growth finally slowed to a normal rate when Bridge appeared to be about eighteen, settling adult fears that his aging might not stop. He was unusually handsome and strong with long blond hair and blue eyes. He adored his parents, Darby and Paolo, and was very dear to his Aunt Blair and Uncle Roman. So far he had demonstrated no special powers, but nothing would have surprised them anymore. Someone was with him at all times, as all were aware that Lucien, his biological father, might try to claim him at anytime.

Word of the Avatarn spread fast from those they rescued to the rest of the Earth's population. The location of their base, however, was kept secret. There were still demons scattered around the planet, and given the chance, they would converge on the holy triad. Would crucify them in parody of the most famous execution of all time. The new residents of this world held their tongues, speaking of God's Hammer only in prayers for the continued success of their mission.

Though Bridge had developed into a young man, he still had the inquisitive nature of a child. His family struggled daily to keep up with his need to explore. On the seventeenth day of his life, he was feeding the horses with Paolo when he grew bold enough to implement a plan. "I'm going to run inside to pee, Papa," Bridge said as casually as possible.

"Okay," Paolo didn't look up from the mare he was brushing.

As soon as he rounded the corner of the house, the mischievous boy broke into a sprint. He ran to the end of the driveway, two of the dogs as his escorts.

When he had gone a hundred feet down the road, the corn, already past prime harvest, obscured his view of the house and vice versa. He slowed to a lazy walk, not wanting to miss any of the change in scenery. There was no point in rushing. It would only be a few minutes until his pop missed him, then there would be a shuttlecraft hovering over his head. That is if Aunt Blair didn't just summon the wind to carry him back home.

Though he had seen a few dusty farm vehicles shooting down their road, he was surprised to see a faded blue pickup come around the bend. Dust flew as the vehicle approached, and Bridge had to balance on the edge of the ditch to avoid being hit. The friendly-looking driver came to a stop when his window was next to the fair-haired boy.

"Hey there," the darkly handsome stranger greeted the curious expression.

"Hey," Bridge warily replied. Of course he was forbidden to talk to anyone from the outside.

"I have something for you," the possible neighbor/demon reached to retrieve something from the seat next to him.

Bridge immediately struck a defensive fighting pose as his parents had taught him. The brown-haired driver chuckled lightly, "Whoa there, Big Boy. This little guy isn't gonna hurt you."

The driver handed a human baby through the window.

"What are you doing?" Bridge was flabbergasted. "Why are you giving—? Who are you?"

"My name is Tom Atwood...I'm a friend of your family."

Bridge recognized the name, but couldn't remember the significance. Tom's arms had withdrawn, leaving the boy no choice but to take the child.

"Could this—? Is this Atom?" Bridge was astounded.

"It is," Thomas seemed to shine a little. "Just take him to your Aunt Blair. Tell her I kept my old promise...That someday I would give her a son."

Bridge had been cooing to the happy babe, but looked up to ask more questions. It was then that the visitor slammed the truck into gear and sped away.

"Wait!" The half-human young prince yelled, but the stranger wasn't coming back. Bridge tried to use his own long hair to shelter the baby's face from the dust cloud, but hurried towards home as fast as he could go.

"What have you got there? And where have you been?" Darby was folding laundry on the front porch when Bridge approached.

"It's amazing, Dad!" The boy was bouncing with anticipation. "Where's Aunt Blair?"

"Is that what I think it is?" Darby started down the steps.

"Yes, it is," Blair almost whispered as she opened the screen door. "Atom!" She screamed, leaping from the porch and rushing past Dar to scoop her son into her arms.

She was dancing and screaming, as were Darby and Bridge, but Atom wasn't afraid. The baby actually laughed when he heard his father's voice ringing out across the barnyard. Roman and Paolo came running from their respective chores. Seeing the infant and hearing the joy left no doubt that Roman's son was home. His other child had been true to her word.

"Thank you, God!" The Avatarn leader shouted again and again as he swept his wife and son into his embrace.

As Paolo joined hands with Darby and their son, he thought about their extended Avatarn family. Though no one watching could doubt the boundless love they all shared, before the invasion their sudden and non-traditional family would not have been accepted. Perhaps not even tolerated. But he kept smiling, and his next thought was—what God has joined together, let no man put asunder…Paolo was pretty sure that rule applied to everybody.

Lucien sat on the window ledge watching the comings and goings of the Tobit House. No one noticed the twig-like praying mantis observing their every move.

The fags were all wrapped up in the television news. Entranced by stories of humans and aliens trying to mesh to form a strange new society. Though many were gleeful now, there would be much conflict and distrust. Lucien would see to that.

He couldn't be so careless again. Over-confidence had been his downfall in the battle on the mothership. How quickly it had all slipped away. If Adolphus were still alive, he would have exacted a terrible price from his second-in-command, but he had successfully taken care of that problem. The ancient fleet of spaceships was a great loss. So was the army he could not replace. However, Gehenna was home to plenty more soldiers. He would have his revenge. He would have the respect and fear given his predecessor if he had to strangle it from every being he encountered.

The witch appeared in the parlor briefly to take lunch orders. Lu was surprised at how abruptly the powerful young woman could fall into the age-old role of subservience to men. She disappointed him.

The demon king's tiny eyes scanned the room for Blair's pussy-whipped husband. Not that he really cared where he was. He was the weakest link in this charm*(ed)* bracelet anyway.

A new guy entered carrying a baby. At first, Lucien assumed the infant was his son, but luckily as he was about to morph back into his human form, he saw that this baby had black hair. It wasn't his.

It was Darby who revealed a turn of events the demon hadn't expected. He addressed the golden-tressed young man toting the child. The faggot called the man *Bridge*. The beautiful boy with long hair and sky-lit eyes was the new prince of darkness. His son.

Lucien was surprised to find that he longed to take the boy under his wing. Literally. The Legion lord had not displayed his massive wings for a long time, but his instincts were to wrap them around his unholy child. To protect him from the influence of the Father's plodding sheep.

But this was not the time. Beacon's royal child was being raised by these mortals. Lucien's blood boiled when Bridge called Darby *"Dad."* How could his mother allow the child to call his uncle *"Dad*?" He knew that the princess was attracted to her twin, but he had thought the Avatarn would draw a line at incest. Where was Beacon anyway? She probably thought all was right in the world since the chosen fools had recovered her child. The kidnapping had presumably devastated her, though Rachel had refused to even speak of the birth or the princess who was her rival. Moot point now that the black bitch was dead. He had hoped to steal a glimpse of the girl he was still determined to make his bride. No matter. He would attend to her later. She would have to be punished before their nuptials. Or maybe on the honeymoon.

Everyone in the house was startled by the crashing thunder created by Lu's frustrated anger. Assuming a storm must be coming, Paolo moved to each window in turn, closing them to the elements. He casually swatted the unusually large brown mantis off the ledge, sliding the pane into place. As Lucien hit the ground outside he decided Paolo would have an extra portion of suffering for that.

The demon in insect form would return to Gehenna. He knew the Avatarn's mission would not be complete as long as the Legion homeworld was secure. They would not leave all those slaves in thrall to evil.

Since no one was watching, he stretched and morphed back into his brooding and very male human form. He didn't bother to manifest clothes. There was no one to see him, but he wore a silver crown of laurels. After his recent, partial defeat, he needed it to remind him of his rank in the universe. He was a king and these people were candle-flames in the wind. His ego took solace in that.

Fortunately, he didn't need a ship to go home. He raised up his arms and in a lightning flash he was gone.

Bridge didn't mind helping watch Atom. Blair was never far away, but her attention was required by the other Avatarn as they planned the destruction of the planet Gehenna.

The sweet-natured boy didn't miss his mother. He was curious about her, but while he couldn't remember her, he recalled every moment of his life with Darby and Paolo as parents. His fathers had explained to him as delicately as possible that his mother, the Princess Beacon had been forced by Lucien, the demon king. The monster still believed his mother was alive and continued in his obsession. Some would think a child didn't need to know these aspects of his history, but on the Tobit farm, ignorance was dangerous. The alien was a threat to his family, and Bridge would protect the baby and the rest anyway that he could.

As he changed a diaper and half-listened to the adults planning the raid, he tried not to think about the devil's blood flowing through his veins. He chose not to accept that identity. Though he was scared, he would follow his dads' example. He was *good*. He *wanted to be* good.

Paolo had relieved his son of baby-sitting duty and was rocking Atom to sleep on the front porch when he noticed. The baby's breathing seemed labored. Scarier still, his skin seemed a little blue.

When he burst into the kitchen with Atom in his arms, Blair broke into an instant sweat simultaneously leaping to pull the baby to her chest.

"What's wrong?" She almost screamed at Paolo.

"Don't know," he stammered, "I was rocking him, and even in the fading light on the porch, I could see his color isn't right. And he seems weak."

Roman was at his wife's side in the time it took her to raise her eyes. She didn't have to tell him to heal their son. He placed a hand on Atom's head. The other on his belly. Instead of flowing from his appendages, the healing white light exploded from him like a supernova. So intense, all present were blinded for a moment. As the glow of the room faded, Darby stepped around the table expecting to see the infant restored. He was horrified to see that Atom's pallor and breathing were getting worse.

"It's not working," Dar was baffled by the failure of Roman's powers. Blair was starting to cry, but Ro was too stunned to react.

"We have to take him to a hospital," Blair locked into *mommy-mode* and automatically started making the decisions necessary to save her child. "We'll take the shuttle," she instructed as she flew into action and was out the front door. The others were right behind her.

"But we don't even know if there's anyone at the hospitals," Paolo couldn't help stating the obvious.

"What are hos—?" Bridge was frightened by the uncommon fear motivating the adults, but his dad anticipated his question.

"I'll explain on the way," Darby assured him.

Blair took the craft's helm herself, handing Atom to his father, knowing Roman would continue to try to use his gift to heal whatever was killing their darling baby.

They were already in the air when she realized they should have checked a phone book for hospital addresses. She set a course for downtown and stayed low enough to scan by eye for any building resembling a hospital.

In anguish, Roman vocalized what Blair was thinking. "How can God allow Lucien's child to live, while mine is dying?" He spoke to no one but the air. It was for God's ear. But Bridge was slapped in the face by his *uncle's* lamentation. The boy opened his mouth to ask how Ro could say such a thing, but his dad took his hand and silently shook his head *no*, shushing him with his lips. Darby would explain their leader's panic later. Bridge would have to endure the feeling of betrayal until then.

Roman was breathing into the baby's tiny mouth by the time Paolo spotted the sign for House of David Hospital. Blair wasn't shy about landing on the roof. The guys would have to deal with any security they encountered.

It became a non-issue when a laser gun blast melted a lock allowing them access to the building. There were no guards to bar their progress.

Blair wanted to carry Atom herself, but she trusted Roman, and he ran as fast as she.

There was only one nurse at the first desk they approached, but she sounded an alarm which summoned a black male doctor in only seconds. He took the baby from Ro and rushed into a room with a treatment bed, asking questions all the way. Oxygen was administered. Vitals taken. Blood drawn. Though she wasn't about to give up, Blair hadn't felt so helpless since Thomas had died in her arms. Only she and Roman had been allowed into the room.

Outside the nurse assisting the doctor had been replaced by another. Nurse Salome was less cooperative. She insisted no one enter the room without the doctor's permission. After only a few endless minutes, the first nurse scurried out with the samples she would personally run to the lab.

"We need to get in there," Darby started towards the door thinking how the hospital, like every hospital, smelled like death. Reeked of it.

"Sorry. Family only," Salome blocked his entrance.

"After all that's happened," Darby was trying not to raise his voice. "Don't you have bigger concerns than who goes in the room? Do you know who we are?"

"What I know, Sir, is that rules exist for a reason and apply to everyone. The staff needs space to do their job. Family only."

"Well, I'm the mother's brother and I'm going in!" Darby had resorted to shouting (and lying). "My boyfriend's coming with me!"

"Okay, if you're the uncle, you can go in. However, this man will have to wait out here. The hospital does not recognize homosexual relationships."

"Fuck that!" Darby was prepared to use force, but Paolo's hand on his bicep stayed his anger.

"It's all right," Paolo piped up. "We don't need to create a distractive scene. You go in. I'll wait out here. Just keep me posted."

"Very well. You wait here with OUR son," Dar was still steaming, "I'll be back in a flash with an update."

Salome stepped aside to let him pass, unfazed by the Avatarn's hateful glare.

Bridge stood aghast at the blatant refusal to recognize his family. He knew his dad had lied about his relationship to Blair, but that fib was a minor thing compared to the cruelty the woman had directed at his papa. His parents had not refrained from teaching him that their family was different from most, but he hadn't truly believed that anyone would try to keep people from their loved ones. He understood then that demons weren't the only monsters on Earth.

"Keep an eye on her," Darby added as he went through the door. "Since the fall of Legion, there'll be demons trying to pass as human again. They could be anywhere."

"How dare you?" The nurse snapped.

"No…How dare you?" Bridge's indignation seeped out between clenched teeth.

Chapter 33

Blair was doing her best to comfort Atom, but he was lost in his struggle to survive another minute.

The addition of Darby to the room was no consolation, though Roman had wondered fleetingly what kept him.

"I wish we had those test results." The doctor had no idea what was causing the cyanosis, but he was already administering the oxygen which was the only immediate treatment for the deprivation signified by the bluish skin.

"Roman! Do something!" Blair pleaded.

Ro knew he couldn't heal his son, but something occurred to him for the first time. Without a word, he held his hand—open, flat, and palm down—above Atom's small head and passed it over the length of his body. Darby recognized instantly that Roman was scanning for a diagnosis.

The doctor looked at the desperate father with surprise and then pity.

"He has a genetic blood disorder," Ro stated as a matter-of-fact. "His red blood cells don't produce normal hemoglobin, and his case is especially severe."

"Thalassemia," The doctor said. His expression of doubt replaced by the logic of the diagnosis. "More specifically, Cooley's Anemia."

"What's that mean?" Blair suppressed the urge to scream her question.

"If your husband is right, Mame, it means your son is one-out-of-a-thousand people in the U.S. that have this disease. The malformed hemoglobin can't properly carry oxygen through the blood."

"Well, what's the prognosis? How do you treat it?" Blair finally began to scream.

"Prognosis is chronic life-long anemia and frequent transfusions," the doctor replied, "Although in a case this bad, removal of the oxygen tube might result in suffocation."

"You said transfusion?" Roman was frantic. "Hook us up. We'll give him all the blood we have."

"Transfusion would solve the immediate crisis," the doctor replied, "but you have to be compatible. As soon as that nurse calls with his blood type— "

"He's type O." Roman sounded certain.

"Are you sure?" Blair knew a mistake would mean death.

"Positive," Ro confirmed.

"But I'm AB," Blair stated as if her own blood might as well be sewage water.

"I'm O," Roman voiced the obvious.

"Me too," Darby offered, but the nearly hysterical father was already pulling off his shirt.

Blair returned to cooing to her baby and watched bug-eyed as the doctor prepped her husband for blood donation. She couldn't know that the reason the normally very skeptical doctor was accepting the diagnosis of a layman was that he could see Roman's blue halo shimmering around his sweat-soaked head. Though her mouth was singing to her child, her mind was begging God.

Lucien was glad one of his soldiers had resumed her charade

as a staff psychiatrist at House of David Hospital. Her friend Salome had called her to complain about the bitchy fags accompanying the Perez family. The nurse hoped to convince her friend to make up some excuse to slap one of them into a straight jacket. That would keep them laughing through their next smoke break.

However, the demon doctor had better use for the information, and quickly relayed it to her king.

Although Lucien would have liked to pop in and grab his son, he knew that would only solidify Bridge's hatred of him. For the moment he would have to be satisfied with taking the progeny of the Avatarn.

In a flash, Lucien appeared at the side of the treatment table opposite of Blair. Before she, or anyone else, could react, he grabbed for the baby. When his hands made contact with Atom's skin, the demon king convulsed with electrocution. Startled, enraged, and in more than a little pain, Lucien recoiled from the child. As Blair and Darby raised their hands to attack, the alien settled for his last choice. No one anticipated Lu snatching Roman. The demon's hand lashed out grabbing Roman's wrist, and in a blink both were gone.

The remaining Avatarn and the doctor were too shocked to respond.

"We'll get him back," Darby promised.

"I know," Blair said, but she didn't sound convinced.

It took five full seconds for Roman to fully understand that he was no longer in the hospital room.

He was lying on a marble floor staring up into a night sky and an eternity of stars.

Lucien sat nearby on the mangled remains of huge platinum doors that now lay on the weedy ground.

"Where are we?" Roman demanded.

"We are in the ruins of a once great palace on Planet Eden. On the far side of your galaxy. My people destroyed this world eons ago."

"Take me back!" Ro fearlessly ordered. "My son needs me!"

"Your son? YOUR SON!" Lucien was incredulous. "Why would I wish to help your son, when you holy fools deny me mine?"

"I command you in the name of God!" Roman shouted.

"You command me?" Lucien scoffed. "The Father grants free will to *all* of His creations. And I no longer acknowledge His laws or His name."

Roman stood up, looking around the broken palace.

"I banish you here," the Legion lord continued. "If your witch-wife ever finds a way to rescue you, you'll be too old to please her and too insane to recognize her face. Be glad that you have soft hands. They'll be your only lover from this day forward." Then he was gone.

"Don't leave me!" Roman screamed into the foreign night, but no one heard.

"Next." The doctor said turning to Darby. The Avatarn was already slipping out of his shirt.

As soon as the doctor had started the process of collecting the donor blood, he summoned additional staff members to assist in the transfusion. There was no time for the appropriate processing of the blood, but Blair and Darby assured him it was not necessary. He believed them, as their heads too were encircled by radiant blue light.

The procedure was completed without further interruption, and Atom seemed to receive immediate relief. Blair felt the return of oxygen-rich blood to her brain as well, and realized she had been holding her breath.

The doctor, who finally introduced himself as Dr. Evans, was kind enough to clear the room and offer them a few moments of privacy. Darby was sure the kindly physician would bend the rules and send in Paolo and Bridge to be with their family. He only had time to recognize how typically cold the room was and how unusually quiet the entire hospital, when his boyfriend and son burst into the room, desperate to confirm their well-being.

Though Atom rapidly returned to his usual serene demeanor and slept the peaceful sleep of the recovering, it took some convincing for Bridge to get Blair to let him hold her son.

Dr. Evans returned within the hour to check on the favorite of his many patients. He informed them that he had reserved a room for little Atom and that he would need to stay a few days for observation and to develop a long-range treatment plan.

Blair thanked him and said God would bless him for his good works. Then she said they were leaving.

"You can't possibly," Dr. Evans argued.

"I'm afraid we must," Blair looked less than sure. "I promise we will return for the treatment protocol, but first we have to find his father. And I could never leave him alone here."

"He would be under my protection," Evans said.

"I appreciate that," Blair countered, "but we have no choice. Trust that God is guiding us."

Dr. Evans still saw the blazing halos around the mother and her gay friend. He would have to have faith that the baby was in the care of God's servants.

"So be it." He eventually said aloud and gestured towards the door. "But Heaven help us if you're wrong."

"Heaven does help us—all the time," Paolo thanked him with a smile as they each filed out into the waiting area and past the objecting Nurse Salome.

In only minutes they had returned to the roof and their shuttle. Paolo took the helm and they hovered above the roof for only seconds before shooting towards their country home.

Though theirs was a peaceful order, Joppa was teaching her acolytes battle techniques when she felt his presence. The spiritual leader had just demonstrated the Vishnuvian defense posture as best she could with only two arms, when she felt the first tingling behind her eyes.

She sensed her beloved Roman. More near than reality allowed. It felt like he was on her world, somehow within the reach of her mind. But he couldn't be on Eden. The priestess reached out with her thoughts. She searched the abbey. Then the entire mountain.

He wasn't there, but he was on Eden. Somewhere. Joppa continued to train the young sisters to fight, showing one kick or stance after another, even as she sent her shade to look for her human charge.

Roman had just left the ancient remains of a giant throne room and was wondering along the grassy edge of a forest older than Earth, but younger than the crumbled palace, when he saw movement at the corner of his peripheral vision. He had feared that Lucien left him on a lifeless world to finish his existence alone. He had seen strange reptilian birds. Some animals resembling squirrels darted among the trees, and even a fox-like creature was following him at some distance, but no sign of people. Until now. On a low branch.

His eyes were playing tricks. Wishful thinking. It was Janie. But she couldn't be there.

"But I am here, Roman," Janie said aloud. "As much as I am anywhere."

"It's good to see you, Sweetheart." He still didn't believe his rattled mind. "Just keeping me company?"

"No, Dad. Joppa's looking for you. This is her world."

"Darling, I thought you were Joppa?" He was puzzled.

"I am. Confusing, ain't it?" She smiled her precious smile.

'"Isn't it," Roman corrected his dead daughter automatically.

"Anyway. Now that I've found you, Joppa will come to take you home." She scrambled down from the limb and dropped into

Roman's arms directly below. She hugged him tightly around the neck, and whispered against his stubbled cheek. "I think my brother needs you." Then she vanished.

Roman stood with his arms still outstretched, embracing the empty air. He swallowed another wad of grief and wandered back towards the ruins. He had despaired of even seeing home again, but as always, God was providing a way where there had been none. Ro silently thanked Jesus for synchronicity and just prayed that he would be returned in time for Atom.

Atom was sleeping contentedly when the shuttle landed in the front lawn of the Tobit House. On the flight home, they had discussed options for finding Roman, but no bright ideas had developed. The only avenue seemed to be some as yet unimagined spell Blair would have to dream up. The witch hoped she could just astral project herself to her husband's unknown location. The problem was, as Paolo pointed out, if might be a trap. Not to mention, Blair couldn't bring herself to leave the baby so soon. They were still brain-storming when they disembarked and walked to the house. It was nearly dawn, and all were exhausted. Though tired, everyone was still too wired to go immediately to bed, so all settled temporarily in the parlor.

"How can I ever thank you for the gift of your blood?" Blair hugged Darby close to her and the baby. "You saved my son's life."

"You've done as much for my son." Dar replied quickly kissing her mouth.

"Well, I already loved you as much as I thought I could," she replied, "but now you are truly my brother."

"The feeling is mutual, honey." He assured her and pulled away. They had done enough crying for the night.

Bridge was blissfully curled up against Paolo sleeping the deep sleep of the innocent, and Blair realized she wouldn't sleep again 'til her husband was found. She thanked God again that the children were safe.

Ideas had run out, and everyone was sort of zombied-out staring at CNN while Blair kept watch with a mother's tenacity for any sign that her baby's health might be in jeopardy. No symptoms presented. For now, he was okay.

Golden fingers of light reached across a hot-pink horizon to illuminate the rural sky. Sunbeams reflected off the silvery mothership contributing extra dazzle to the chilly morning. Darby's attention had drifted to the front door to watch the morning bloom when he saw them mount the stairs. Roman and Joppa were holding hands. He thought they were a vision in matching jeans and T-shirts, back-lit by the sun's nearly blinding glow. But they were real. They were coming inside.

Blair lifted off the floor to literally fly across the room into his arms. Greetings and hugs were shared all around, and Roman explained, as best he could, where he had been and how their guide had found him and used her powers to bring him home in the time it took him to say her name.

Blair did not hesitate to pull Joppa into her embrace. She easily forgave Atom's kidnapping after learning that the girl rescued her husband from permanent exile.

Roman immediately inquired of Atom's condition and his wife informed him that he was fine for the time being. The Avatarn leader ran to his son, and narrowly resisted the urge to wake his slumbering child.

Paolo explained how Darby had saved the day, and Ro expressed the most genuine thanks any of them had ever heard.

Bridge awoke just in time to see from the safety of his papa's shoulder that a beautiful blonde stranger had left the house and started down the driveway before disappearing into the ether.

"Was that the Joppa that you all speak of?" He asked softly.

"It was." Paolo said, smoothing his son's long hair.

"And who and what is she again?"

"How long have you got?" Paolo kissed his forehead and began to tell the tales of Janie and their encounters with the guide persona. When everyone was caught up on their separate misadventures and miracles, Darby suggested everyone should try to get some sleep. Blair said a quick spell to shield the house against intruders, and all retired to their bedrooms.

Bridge's room was across the hall from his parents, and the occupants of both were possessed by slumber as soon as their heads hit the pillows.

In Ro and Blair's room, the couple stood at the crib, fighting the urge to take Atom into their bed. They knew he would sleep more soundly where he was, but it was hard not to be touching him. The newlyweds eventually took to their own cozy bed.

They snuggled and kissed with the gentle intimacy that most couples take decades to find. Though both were still full of adrenaline, they soon found sleep. The daylight wasn't an impediment to any of them.

Blair awoke in a panic around noon. She had to make sure the baby was still in his crib. Her next act was to unleash a wrenching scream. The household was instantly returned to consciousness and rushed to the master bedroom. Blair and Roman were staring silently when the others entered. The entire crib was encased in a thick fibrous cocoon.

Blair suddenly dove at the mass, trying with all her might to rip it apart.

"Wait," Darby yelled, causing her to hesitate. "You can see the chrysalis glowing and moving inside. Maybe you should leave it alone."

"My son is in a fucking cocoon," Blair was losing control, "and you're suggesting I just leave it?"

"Let me look at this," Roman said, stepping around his wife and gently passing his hands over the seemingly impenetrable shell. "He's okay."

"What the hell do you mean '*He's okay*'?" Blair was baffled.

"I mean I scanned him for sickness and health crises and he seems fine. Even his genetic disorder barely registered. I think for the moment he's all right."

Blair had to sit down on the foot of the bed. How could this be happening to her baby? How much did God expect them to endure?

"What's wrong with him?" She cried to the ceiling.

"Nothing's wrong." Roman joined her and placed an arm around her shoulders. "This was supposed to happen."

"Huh?" Darby and Paolo said in unison.

"No, I'm serious," Ro appeared less upset. "In nature, when a creature makes a cocoon, it's because it's undergoing some kind of intended metamorphosis. It's changing."

"So now our son is a *creature*?" Blair was channeling her fear into anger, and couldn't believe her husband's nonchalance.

"You know what I mean," he responded. "I think the transfusion of Darby's blood set in motion some kind of planned change. Something that was meant to be."

"Hey, dude, don't put this on me," Darby was slightly indignant.

"I see what you're getting at," Paolo spoke up. "Maybe the presence of DNA from all three Avatarn, when brought together in one body, triggered a transformation. It's not science, but we live in the world of magic now."

"I had so hoped he would just be a normal human being," Blair was much calmer. "Guess, I can write off that dream."

"What's important is that Atom comes out of this okay." Darby offered. "We just have to wait out this change process."

Bridge finally broke his awed silence, "The question is, Dad. What's he changing into?"

Chapter 34

By the time twilight came, the cocoon had become more opaque and they had all stopped straining to see inside.

The men had distracted themselves with plans to destroy Gehenna, but Blair never left her bedroom. Bridge brought her food and tea, but no one could convince her to take a break from the observation post she had established at the head of her bed.

Roman checked periodically with a scan of his hand over the bizarre living bubble. Though he could no longer read specific details of his son's health, he still felt that he was well.

Though darkness had not yet settled on the house, Blair was mostly asleep when the cocoon began to pulse with a much brighter light than before. When she had reached full wakefulness, she saw that the bubble was stretching and distorting in every direction. Something was trying to get out. Something big.

A loud yelp from the witch brought the others on the run. All could see the being inside was struggling to break out.

"We have to help him," Blair raised her hands thinking to somehow use her powers.

"No," Roman stopped her. "We don't know the plan. He needs to do this on his own."

The point became moot, because the fabric of the shell finally tore and everyone held their breath waiting for a hideous claw or tentacle to emerge from the deflating cocoon. Instead the strong arms of a man stretched the hole to shoulder width and a perfectly sculpted human male stepped out.

"Sweet Jesus," Blair exhaled.

"No, Mother, It's only me." The fully-grown Atom blessed her with a magnificent smile before climbing naked out of his crib.

"Thank God you're all right," Blair only hesitated for an instant before reaching up to hug her son—now a head taller than she.

Atom stretched out a muscular arm to pull his father into their embrace. Roman returned his kisses with a mix of shock and relief.

Paolo was saying how no one could deny his lineage, with Roman's black hair and Blair's green eyes; he was the spitting image of his parents.

Though he remained quiet, Darby was thinking the same as the other Avatarn. Their son, Atom, was the powerful *Sovereign* from their vision on the crosses. This was confirmed by the violet halo they saw around his head. That also meant Joppa would become his wife.

They didn't know how much to tell Atom about his future, so they avoided telling him anything specific from their vision.

Over the next few days, as the Avatarn continued to plan the destruction of the demon homeworld, Atom and Bridge played together like boys in the farmyard. Though they possessed the bodies of men—Atom actually appearing older than Bridge—they reveled in the distractions and curiosities of the animals and the country landscape.

Though all the parents would have preferred to leave their sons on the farm, they didn't dare leave them unprotected. The boys would be making the journey to Gehenna as well.

Darby started training the next generation to fight, hoping

they would at least be able to defend themselves if necessary. Both boys proved to be naturals, demonstrating combat skills already beyond their experienced parents.

It was not unusual for them to return from the barn or field so dirty that Blair forced them to strip outside, where she sprayed them down with a garden hose, her magic making the water temperature a little less harsh. The boys displayed no embarrassment over nudity, and their parents saw no reason to teach them shame. There would be time enough to learn the restrictions of society later.

Roman worried that weeks were passing, and they still hadn't made the journey to Gehenna. No one wanted to take the children into danger so soon after their homecoming. It was impossible to know if they were ready, but with only one ship in orbit, the climate was beginning to normalize. Soon it would be winter in Kansas City. All agreed it would be better to conduct the mission before true cold settled in to complicate the arrival of even more alien refugees. Though doubts lingered, he called a meeting and announced they would leave for the demon planet the following morning. No one wanted to go except the boys. The trip was unavoidable, so the parents remained silent while the boys high-fived.

It was difficult for Darby to refuse when Bridge wanted to bring one of the dogs on the shuttle, but he had to put his foot down. Although there was plenty of space for pets on the *Caiphas*, the young prince couldn't be distracted in the coming battle. The boy had to content himself with feeding the scraps from the breakfast table to the mongrel pup before joining the others on the quick trip up to the mothership.

Blair's magic set a course for Gehenna and moved the spacecraft out of Earth orbit. In the days that followed, Atom and Bridge displayed an intuitive knack for handling the ships systems. They left the driving to witchcraft, but used the time to familiarize themselves with alien technology, drawn to any device or gadget as the young usually are.

The Avatarn spent the wait watching from viewports as stellar systems streaked by. The trip had begun to feel endless when the ship finally entered orbit around a vibrant blue planet half the size of Earth. Holographic displays came online, appearing above several command stations. Three-dimensional images floated in the air representing data about Gehenna.

The ships shields, augmented by Darby's powers, were never lowered. They would prevent infiltration by any average demon.

Sensor scans indicated that few Legion warriors had teleported back to their homeworld after their defeat, and the Avatarn's shuttle met no resistance as they left the giant saucer and glided to the ground just outside Castle Hades.

Otherwise jaded peasants and alien slaves were curious to see humans leaving a shuttle without a Legion escort. Some of the captive species could sense Bridge's demon biology, but he wasn't like their masters. This one seemed to answer to the bold humans he accompanied.

The holy pilgrims slowly walked to the road that led to the draw-bridge, casually joining the march of the downtrodden.

Blair was the first to speak after their disembarkation. "I had forgotten how beautiful this place is," She flung her arm to indicate the fields, forest, and sky. "Or maybe it's just easier to appreciate when you are less afraid."

"Perhaps you feel conflicted, Mother, because your eyes are surrounded by the splendor of creation," Atom offered. "But your heart insists that there can be no beauty where people live in slavery."

"You know you're sounding more like your wi—our friend, Joppa, everyday," Blair was mostly impressed but slightly annoyed with her son.

"I think I really must have a reunion with my former kidnapper slash sister slash whatever," Atom replied.

Darby and Paolo met each others' gaze with raised eyebrows, and the group moved onto the bridge. They stayed near the center as they crossed. The adults needed no reminder of the leaping shark that had taken their beloved friend, Honey. Roman herded the curious boys away from the half-rotted edges.

All eyes were on the massive entrance ahead, when Paolo accidentally bumped into the large man covered in brownish fur—Natives of North America and Canada would have recognized him as a sasquatch. The beastly slave reacted by grabbing Paolo's shoulders and growling, "Grrravar dopponee trikoden!"

Paolo just swallowed hard, prepared to meet his maker.

Darby was raising his hands to intervene, when the ebony-haired Atom stepped towards the alien holding his uncle, shouting an intercession in the creature's own language. "Diyama mekas arevy shubber!"

The *Bigfoot* froze and locked eyes with the bold human. The first one to ever speak the Yeti language. Releasing the Earthling that trembled in his grasp, he nodded briefly to the unusually brave human and continued his rambling lope over the moat.

"How did you—?" Paolo began. "What did you say to it?"

"Well," Atom began, still in surprise himself. "He said '*How dare you, Earth-born piece of shit*', so I said '*Forgive our clumsy misstep, friend*'. I guess he bought it."

"But how the hell did you know that language?" Roman asked his son.

"I don't know," Atom admitted, "but it was as clear to me as English."

"*Hell*—is how I understood every word," Bridge sheepishly informed them, ashamed of his demon ancestry.

Darby placed a comforting arm around his son's shoulders, saying, "This newfound skill you have in common with your cousin will no doubt help us in countless ways in the days ahead. Be proud of your gifts. Regardless of the bloodline, God is still the source of all magic and powers. After all, He created all those that would eventually make up the darkside."

Bridge rolled his eyes at his dad's corny speech, but grinned at what he knew to be true and consoling. Show over, the flow of peasants and slaves resumed toward the mouth of the castle.

When they finally reached the entrance, Blair mentally prepared a spell to deal with the sentries standing guard at both sides of the doors. However, her efforts were not required. Atom and Roman were in the lead and upon their approach, the demon sentries found themselves unable to look upon the magnificent face of the Avatarn's son. Both soldiers turned away allowing the holy party to pass unmolested.

Atom did nothing to acknowledge his extraordinary effect on the Legion soldiers, seeming to take the on-going revelation of his powers in stride.

Blair and Roman joined hands, proud of their baby, but in fear and awe of the extent of his powers and the nature of his destiny…*What will he become?*

The travelers from Earth moved into the cavernous great hall. Bridge and Atom were overwhelmed, never having been inside such a structure.

As always, peasants scurried about, cleaning, preparing food for the few remaining demons, and processing new slaves. Though they had been forewarned, Atom and Bridge were alarmed to see whips and electric prods used to train and control the recent captures. More than a few of them were from Earth.

Even in daytime the great fortress was gloomy, prompting Paolo and Darby to move to one of the giant pillars that reached to the lofty ceiling in order to procure a couple of lit torches.

"Which way first?" Blair asked. "Dungeon or nursery? Anybody have a coin?"

"Got use to money having no value," Roman said. "Guess that's one evil we'll have to get used to again."

"Dungeon first," Darby threw in. "We may need extra hands to help with the nursery."

Only two demon warriors attempted to intercept them as Blair led the way to the stairs that spiraled down behind the huge central stairway.

The witch pointed at one of the soldiers and wiggled her finger in a spiraling motion. Much to the demon's horror, only he could see the invisible snake that wrapped around his body, constricting to crush out his life. He collapsed to the stone floor changing to a black puddle. His cohort started towards Blair to deliver revenge in the form of a short sword.

Not far from his mother, Atom lunged to grab her attacker's forearm. The instant he touched him, the demon registered shock before his green skin liquefied in Atom's hand.

"He only has to touch them," Roman was astonished.

"No wonder he grows up to be—"Paolo was silenced by a look from Darby.

"But I'm not harmed when he touches me?" Bridge was baffled.

"I think you can thank Beacon's genes for that," Ro vocalized the only explanation.

Atom couldn't help being a little pleased with himself at the discovery of this...perhaps his greatest gift. Though Blair was as amazed as the others by her son's awesome powers, she harbored a conflicted sorrow that her baby was blessed with the *touch of death*.

The intrepid little group pushed onward, beginning to descend the seemingly eternal staircase that plummeted into Gehenna's depths. The dark bowels of the castle were cold and damp and the boys took care not to make contact with the slimy walls.

"Hey, guys, I don't mean to get all philosophical on your asses," Paolo began, "but has it occurred to anyone else that with Adolphus gone, if ya'll finish Lucien off, there will no longer be one true devil. Adolphus said they had secretly ruled Earth for at least a millennium. Does that mean our actions may bring on the second coming of Christ?"

"He will arrive when the timing is right," Darby spoke up. "But I think it may be a while. If His return were at hand, it wouldn't have been necessary to call us to duty. There would be no need for Avatarn to battle demons if Jesus were coming soon. Seems like He's chosen us to hold it down 'til He gets there."

"I agree with Uncle Dar," Atom said. "Yeshua, our Savior, will not be compelled by the actions of the fallen. He will return at the appointed time…And when He does, we will serve Him. Again in the bliss of His full presence."

Blair leaned close to her husband, her words sotto voce, "I swear Joppa's gotta be whisperin' this stuff in his ear."

Roman softly chuckled, then began changing his mindset to fighting mode as they heard the boys—who had enthusiastically raced ahead—reach the echoing chambers of the dungeon level.

Atom and Bridge were surprised to find so many corridors spoking from the central landing. Fortunately, their parents remembered the way.

With a wave of his hand, Darby erected a golden force-field at the foot of the stairs, preventing any guards from following.

They quickly reached the dungeon, and found no demons standing watch. With no one to impede the search, they separated to search cell by cell.

"They're all empty," Paolo reported what the others were discovering for themselves. "Why?"

"I have a theory," Roman said. "My guess is that trouble-makers are usually just killed. Judging from the undisturbed dust layers, I'd say most of these rooms haven't been used in centuries."

"Well, we had to check," Darby said.

The group started back towards the stair-room, greatly relieved that there would be fewer captives to evacuate. Just as they were about to re-enter the *hub-room,* Blair decided to obtain her own light source for the climb back to ground level. She grabbed the last torch of the corridor, but instead of the wooden club coming out of its sconce; it proved to be a lever. The downward pull triggered a mechanism to activate a secret door in the stone wall. A portion of the wall slid aside revealing another short hallway. And total darkness beyond.

Chapter 35

"How did you know?" Bridge asked his aunt.

"I didn't," Blair answered. "Just luck." She took her son's hand and started to investigate the hidden space. All present knew she didn't believe in luck.

There was only one door in the short hallway. It was constructed of heavy wooden planks, and it was slightly ajar.

Blair and Atom approached with trepidation. The others immediately behind them.

When Bridge saw Atom's jaw drop, he pushed passed his aunt to see what had stopped them where they stood.

Two people sat at a small rickety table. A young man with carved muscles wore nothing but shackles, his skin so pale it nearly matched his white hair and beard. Across from him, a delicate maiden perched lightly on a wooden stool. The girl's long black hair was mostly covered by a powder-blue veil that flattered eyes the color of the richest soil. Her olive-skinned body was enticingly wrapped in complimentary silks. Her fingers and ears were unadorned. Until they became aware of their audience, they were conversing in Aramaic.

"Hello." Blair was the first to recover her voice.

"You speak English?" The pretty girl asked in surprise. "If you are fresh arrivals from Earth, you should be in the holding corrals. You'll be harshly punished if you are found here."

Bridge was deeply touched by the prisoner's concern for strangers, but touched deeper still because her gaze met his, not with fear, but with genuine caring—deepest empathy.

"We are from Earth," Roman confirmed. "The question is, how do you know English...Unless...Are you demons, or from Earth yourselves?"

"We are of Earth," she replied, but I know your language because I am personal valet to Lucien. He prefers that I know the tongues of all his slaves."

"You're not American then?" Darby asked.

"I am not familiar with that province. The Roman Empire is vast. I am Hebrew," she answered. "I am Veronica."

"And I am Melchior of Catalonia," her friend stated.

"How long have you two been here?" Atom asked.

"Nearly two-thousand years," Veronica replied with numb sorrow.

"Two thou—"Blair was stunned. "How can that be?"

"It was a terrible time in Jerusalem," The lovely girl stood to tell her story."

"I was taken before this dear one," Melchior chimed in, and as the twosome began their story, the would-be-rescuers filed into the small cell to better hear the tale. Only Paolo remained outside the room. After his previous captivity in the dungeon of Castle Hades, he couldn't stand the crushing confines of the dingy space. "Not an hour had passed," the bearded man continued, "since the other magi and I had left the presence of the divine child."

"You mean *Jesus*?" Atom asked.

"Of course I mean *Yeshua,*" Melchior was a bit indignant. "There has been only one." The handsome prisoner made no effort to cover his nakedness. He had forgotten its significance long ago.

"You met the Christ child in person?" Blair was in awe.

"Indeed." The mage smiled.

"Are you saying you're one of THE three wise-men that followed the star to find the infant messiah?" Paolo asked from the door.

Melchior chuckled and said, "There were many more of us than three, but yes. Our caravan of astrologers, magicians, and learned men had studied the portents and signs to find the most blessed babe. We missed his birth, but found him in time and were welcomed by the holy family. We had just returned to the desert when the spaceship appeared above us. We were terrified. We thought it was God. In an instant, demons materialized at both my sides. My next memory was waking in the ship's cargo hold. I don't know what happened to the others. I never saw them again."

"My story is similar," Veronica addressed the group, but spoke mostly to Bridge. "I only tell you this ancient truth because I see the halos radiating about some of your heads. The light of God marks you as His own. It is a sign I've seen before." The snowy-haired mage nodded his encouragement to the girl he loved as a daughter, and she rushed to reveal her secret. "I was in the city when He carried His cross to Golgotha. He was near me when He fell in the street. Collapsed under His burden. Blood poured from the wounds in His head 'til He could hardly see. I ran to Him, though the crowd and my parents attempted to hold me back. I knelt in the dust and wiped his face with my veil." She hiccupped a sob, but never paused in the telling. "It was then that He smiled at me. Smiled. Through the sweat and grime. I was crying, but I smiled back. Before I could speak, soldiers kicked me aside and forced the Rabbi back to His feet. The crowd was too great and my chores too many for me to follow and witness his brave death, but as I crawled away, I clutched the ruined veil to my chest. I turned into an alley to escape the crowd and spread the veil, thinking to wipe my own dirty face. I was astounded by the miracle in my hands. A perfect image of the Master's face was preserved in the cloth. I knew then that the rumor so few had dared to whisper was true. This carpenter from Nazareth was the flesh and blood Son of God. And within the hour He would be crucified...The last thing I heard was my father calling my name when Adolphus himself appeared at my side.

"Of course, I didn't know him then. He was dressed as a centurion of Rome. He grabbed my throat, and I dropped the veil to clasp his hand in both of mine. I also remember nothing until awakening in the ship's cargo hold. I later learned that Adolphus had returned immediately to the hill outside the city to bask in the pleasure of seeing God killed by His own creations. Of course, I was thrilled beyond measure when I later heard Lucien and the king raging about the resurrection. All hope was restored to the universe. Even me...I had no way of knowing then, that Adolphus would feel the need to find special torture for Melchior and myself because of our contact with the Savior. He collected scientists from galaxy to galaxy and force them to alter our DNA. The bio-chemical treatments combined with the powers originally granted him by Heaven extended our lives indefinitely. Provided we receive no fatal injuries, we are immortal."

When Veronica stopped to catch her breath, Melchior took a turn. "My torture is to spend eternity chained in this cell. Forever alone, if not for the stolen moments when Veronica visits."

"As I indicated," the slave girl interrupted, "my living hell is to serve as Lucien's hand-maid. Though he values me, he never misses an opportunity to disgrace me. I have been violated and abused beyond your capacity to understand. My only anchor to sanity is the time I slip away to spend secretly here with my adoptive father. I believe our relationship survives because Lucien has forgotten that Melchior still lives."

"But now," it was the mage's turn to inject, "who are you, besides perhaps our heroes?"

"We are the Avatarn," Darby said placing his hands on Ro and Blair's shoulders.

Veronica gasped before he could continue, and gushed, "The holy triad, chosen by God Himself to battle Legion. Everyone on Gehenna has heard this heretical prophecy...And this one?" She gestured towards Atom.

"Our son," Blair answered slipping an arm around his waist as Roman tousled his hair.

"And you are?" Veronica stood only inches in front of Bridge.

"I am their son," he indicated Darby and Paolo. The maiden raised a questioning eyebrow. "I'm adopted," he explained. "My mother, Beacon, is dead. Lucien is my biological father."

He expected her to be afraid or disgusted, but she wasn't.

She only said, "I should have recognized you, Prince. You have your mother's pretty face." She knew she was staring and smiling at him longer than she should, but couldn't help herself. Her weary heart recognized the man that would be her husband.

"The shackles?" She turned back towards the Avatarn.

"Let me," Blair said as she moved to the wise man's place at the little table and took the iron cuffs in her hands. "The damp atmosphere down here must increase oxidation at an alarming rate." As she completed the sentence, the metal bands turned to rust in her hands, crumbling and falling away. Melchior looked at her with such disbelief and gratitude, that Blair knew the tears in his eyes were matched by her own.

Veronica too was overcome by the sight of her beloved friend's release. Bridge's hands on her sides steadied her on her feet.

"As amazing as all of this is," Roman took charge, "we have to get up there and evacuate the nursery."

"Any suggestions?" Blair turned to Veronica.

"This is where centuries of sneaking around this castle pays off," the maiden said as she removed her veil and passed it to Melchior signaling him to tie it around his waist. "Though the fortress looks primitive, there is technology hidden everywhere. There is a secret elevator. We can take it directly to the nursery level."

The newly enlarged group returned to the hub-room, where Darby turned opaque the force-field blocking the stairs. Some guards were staking out the foot of the stairs, waiting patiently for the strangers to attempt escape—He didn't want them knowing they had located the elevator.

Veronica guided the group to a huge column in the center of the chamber. Placing her palm flat against the granite, she moved her hand in a counter-clockwise or *widdershins* circular motion. The stone surface before her faded out of existence, de-cloaking a large oval doorway.

None were anticipating that the elevator would be occupied. Lucien met their shocked expressions with his always smug smile.

"Well, lookey who's wondering around my dungeon," the king bellowed. "I can't say that I am surprised to find the Avatarn trespassing in my home, but you, Veronica? I am disappointed that even after millennia in my service, you would betray me with these nascent do-gooders."

"Haven't you heard, father?" Bridge stepped forward, "The war is over. You lost."

Lucien's smile was gone. Such insolence from his own son. He wished the princess were there, so he might beat her as a lesson to the boy. Alas. He would catch up with her later.

"Prince Bridge," the demon's grin returned. "You will modify your attitude or I will be forced to kill this cocksucker that you call *Daddy*."

"If you could do that," the boy raised his chin, "You already would have."

Atom moved in between the friend he called cousin and the lord of demons. He was surprised when their eyes locked, and the king didn't look away.

Lucien laughed, "Did you really think I would be unable to look upon your splendid visage *Child of the Chosen*? I am much more powerful than the minions you encountered outside."

Atom lunged then to grab the king's arm, eager to see him melt to sludge. But Lucien remained. Instead of dissolving, the alien's skin began to burn Atom's hands like soaking in acid. "Fuck!" The Avatarn's son yelled, pulling away. Blair started to scold him, but thought better of it.

Roman quickly tossed his son a ball of healing white light. Atom caught it in both hands and they were instantly restored to perfect condition. For a moment the handsome boy turned to his mother in confusion. He had never really been hurt.

Lucien laughed as Blair kissed Atom's hands, but her son's confidence returned on the spot.

Suddenly from nowhere, the king produced a sword, plunging it into Roman's stomach. But as it was withdrawn, the Avatarn simultaneously healed. The demon arched an eyebrow, realizing that his foes were becoming ever-more difficult to destroy.

No one except Atom knew that Bridge was carrying a weapon until he lunged towards Lucien, slamming the tazer-like device against the alien's bare shoulder. The weapon was of Legion technology. The boys had discovered it in an armory onboard the ship. It worked as designed, shocking the demon with a massive pulse of electricity. Lucien only laughed at his son. The weapon didn't even cause him discomfort.

The king was only briefly amused, but rather than retaliate against his own son, he turned to the nearby Paolo and with a casual swat of his hand knocked him across the chamber. Bouncing off the stone wall, too dazed to stand, the human experienced déjà vu.

Darby's anger exploded in a golden wave from the fist he jabbed into Lucien's chiseled jaw. The alien adversary was stunned by the barrage of punches Dar continued to pound into his face and stomach. Golden energy emanated from each impact. Bridge, slowly freed from the surprise of his failure, moved immediately to protect Veronica.

The king lost his composure and balance, stumbling out of the elevator pillar and nearly falling. Only his outrage provided the determination to right his stance.

"Enough!" Lucien blared. He didn't like being embarrassed by lower species.

"I agree," Blair shouted. The witch had stepped in front of her son, knowing that his fantastic powers were unable to affect this devil. Still without a way to administer the mistletoe potion, she improvised a spell to keep Lucien out of their way long enough to accomplish the mission:

"Stone surrounds on every side,
In this place where secrets hide.
You too now are made of stone,
And cannot move a single bone."

Before she had finished the incantation, the demon had started to vanish, but the strength of her power forced his molecules to re-solidify. Surprise was frozen on Lucien's face when he continued to transform. After his skin turned grey, his fine features continued to blur and roughen as he became a roughly carved statue of rock.

"Damn! You're a one man strike-force," Darby said to Blair. She blushed slightly at his praise.

"Yeah, way to go, Aunt Blair," Bridge was impressed. Atom simply smiled his pride in his mother. Veronica and Melchior were impressed by the strength of her power, but not particularly dazzled by magic. It wasn't that uncommon on Gehenna.

"No time to admire your work, Darling," Roman said. "Everyone in. We have to get up to the nursery before Lucy figures out a way to free himself."

They all obeyed, packed into the relatively small elevator. As soon as everyone squeezed into the hollow column, Veronica said *Nursery Level* and a door appeared in the opening. After a very slight sensation of movement, the oval door dissolved again and they all filed out, finding themselves just around a corner from the massive nursery.

Chapter 36

The holy group lingered out of sight, allowing Veronica to go first and speak to the Head Governess. She had informed the Avatarn that the devout old woman was truly good, and she wanted to remove her from harm's way before the revolt began.

Roman realized as he watched the hushed encounter, that the decrepit old woman in a nun's habit was actually THE Mother Teresa. The people from Earth were astounded to see her there, especially since they all knew she was deceased.

Veronica returned to them shortly, careful not to draw the attention of the few guards.

"Mother refuses to leave the cribs of some of the infants who are ailing," she reported.

"What is she doing here anyway?" Darby asked. "Surely if anyone deserves to be in Heaven—"

"She could be," Veronica explained. "She asked God to post her here, that she might safeguard the children. She will assist us any way that she can."

"So what's the plan?" Paolo asked.

"The other nannies aren't demons," Veronica said, "though obviously most are aliens. Most, if not all of them will help."

"So that just leaves the guards then," Atom said.

"Let's go," Roman ordered. With Blair and Darby at his sides and the others following, they rounded the corner and passed through the pillars that connected the corridor and the open nursery. Frightened children, some of which looked like monsters, scampered to hide behind their nannies' skirts. The startled caregivers all grabbed up babies in each arm. For some of them that meant carrying four infants.

When the first Legion guard lurched forward, Mother Teresa moved into his path, pretending to be confused. The soldier barked at her to get out of his way, and when she failed to move quickly enough, he shoved her. He gestured to the other three guards to converge with him where the intruders had paused in the play area.

The soldiers found it difficult to approach the trespassers, since Atom had moved into the lead position. They couldn't look directly at him and were forced to watch the strangers through their peripheral vision.

Finally within range, two of the demons lunged towards the Avatarn. Atom grabbed one by the shoulders and seized the other's wrist. They only had time to cry out in agony before liquefying and forming black puddles on the floor. Happy to see he still had his powers, Atom looked to the other demons, but they were well beyond his reach.

Melchior and Veronica took advantage of the brief engagement to circumnavigate the guards and get to the nannies and children. The two immortals and Mother started herding the toddlers and nurse-maids towards the corridor.

When one of the Legion guards turned to see what the kids were up to, Darby raised his hand and with a flip of his fingers launched a gold energy pulse that struck between the demon's shoulder blades and flung him into a wall. The crack of the impact confirmed his finish, before he too became a puddle.

The last guard raised a spiked metal glove and moved in on Blair. The witch didn't have time to say a spell, so she instinctively froze in place. Her irises and pupils disappeared, leaving eyes of solid glowing white. The demons eyes locked with hers and he became dizzy. Stumbling, he lost his balance and toppled to the floor.

Roman took advantage of the warrior's incapacitation. Grabbing an antique rattle from a nearby crib, he plunged the handle into the alien guard's back. The creature met his end on all fours, first becoming slimy, then flowing to the floor.

For the moment, the coast was clear. With Blair and Veronica at his sides, Roman led the procession towards the central stairs. As they made their way through dark halls, the powers of Blair's mind lit torches on both sides to prepare their path. They encountered only a few patrolling guards, and each time Atom came forward causing the demon to avert his eyes. That's when the son of Avatarn would place a hand on them, turning his enemy to a soup of evil.

The little group of rebels descended the grand stairs as quickly as the children allowed. It wouldn't have been such a big deal when Darby stumbled into Blair causing both to fall down a few stairs before either could engage their powers, but in the same instant a toddler lost his footing and two infants wiggled from their nurses' grasps. Some of the nannies couldn't help screaming. There was no one close enough to catch them, until in the blink of an eye, each babe landed in protective arms. From the ether, Yoshi and Josh appeared to catch the two infants in mid-air, cradling them to their chests. The toddler hadn't been agile enough to use his fluffy tail to correct his balance. Mercifully, he fell right into the waiting arms of Honeydew who was kneeling a few steps below him. With a hug and a kiss, she returned the squirming child to his feet.

Joshua and Yoshi handed the crying babies to the grateful nurse-maids who rushed to claim them, before offering brief waves to their astonished friends. The Avatarn were just whispering their names when the three ghosts vanished. Paolo quietly explained the significance of the apparitions to Veronica, Melchior, Atom, and Bridge as they reached the floor of the great hall.

As peasants and slaves watched dumbfounded, the group hurried toward the main entrance. A misguided minotaur rang a gong, which triggered a loud computer-controlled alarm claxon. A woven metal door began to drop to block their exit. Darby paused long enough to whip his arm up around his head like an invisible sling-shot, swinging it to unleash a golden ball of energy that flew into the dropping gate. The iron structure exploded as if made of paper.

The Avatarn and their party of half a dozen nannies and four times as many children still faced obstacles in the form of demon soldiers.

Darby raised his arms, simultaneously raising a golden forcefield that formed a bubble around the fleeing group. Neither weapons nor fists of the rival warriors could penetrate the protective shield. Once the holy sojourners were safely across the drawbridge, Blair took action. She grabbed a twig from the dirt path and turned back towards their pursuers. She snapped it into several pieces and watched happily as the bridge spanning the moat cracked and splintered rapidly plunging into the water, taking the Legion guards with it.

Slaves and peasants in the castle entrance and on the land side shouted "Huzzah!" and cheered wildly. They had never witnessed such open defiance. The witch turned back to her family, their pace slowed with the abolition of eminent danger.

Only Melchior saw that the minotaur had crossed the bridge before them to lay in ambush. As the group neared the shuttle, the half-bull human hybrid sneaked from behind a boulder. The beastly slave charged the unsuspecting escapees, propelling the ancient wise man into motion. Melchior doubled back to intercept the larger alien. By the time the Avatarn heard the snorting of the creature, the mage was wrestling with him.

The chosen triad started to intervene, but Veronica stopped them. "He's felt helpless all these centuries," she said. "He needs to do this, regardless of the outcome." She choked on the last words. She loved the man in the white hair and beard as a parent. The others marveled that the old pilgrim, naked again, appeared to be in his prime. Melchior fought bravely, but the battle was lost before it began. In a swift change of tactic, the minotaur lowered his head, plunging his horns into the mage's chest. Melchior screamed when the incredibly strong slave raised its bovine head with the man still impaled. Blood poured, the beast roared, and a wise one embraced destiny with a smile.

A nanny who anyone on Earth would have called a werewolf handed Roman a dagger and he ran towards the brawl. He reached the loyal slave just as he was tossing Melchior to the ground. Ro sank the knife into the beast's back, and withdrew to watch him struggle to reach the blade. When too much blood had been lost, too much damage done, the creature tumbled, a final thud in the dust and gravel.

The lead Avatarn rushed to the wise man's side. Roman's hands were already glowing when he crouched by the torn mage.

"No!" Melchior commanded in the loudest voice he could still muster. "The time is past due for me to face my creator. The girl is safe now with you. I don't have to stay any longer. Complete your mission. Destroy this beautiful hell. We've each had a role, but I must go…Please."

"Okay…If you're sure." Roman let the light go out in his hands. Veronica reached them then and threw herself on top of her dying friend.

"I'm sorry you didn't have a chance to know freedom again, Mel." The girl blubbered.

"Me too, dearest," he said, "but you shall know it for me. Go and live a wondrous life with the prince I can tell that you fancy. Be happy, cherub. Promise me."

"I promise," she was still crying, but no longer sobbed. Bridge blushed a little as he and the others were accidentally privy to the intimate conversation.

Melchior was gone then, leaving his body in the arms of a woman who had loved him for two thousand years. Though there were no more soldiers in sight, Darby reminded them that they were too close to the end to linger any longer. Bridge took Veronica's arm and coaxed her from the ground. She didn't resist. She knew her substitute father was gone. With the prince's arm around her waist, she was led behind the group to the waiting shuttle.

After opening the hatch, Paolo led the refugees inside.

"What are we going to do about the thousands of other slaves?" Darby asked. "We'll never get them all to the ship with this shuttle."

"I'll take care of that," Joppa said casually walking around the shuttle, flanked by her white tigers. She was dressed in one of her long blue gowns, but breaking with her traditional priestess guise, her long blonde hair flowed around her shoulders instead of towering above her head.

Blair suspected their lovely guide was already beginning the process of seducing her son. That knowledge made her a little jealous, but she knew their eventual marriage was meant to be. Still it was hard. She already had to share a part of Roman with her.

As if on cue, Ro went to the being that was sometimes his daughter and pulled her into a hug.

"How can you help us, Sweetheart?" He asked.

"Though I may not survive the effort," Joppa replied. "I will attempt to teleport all of the slaves of Gehenna to the cargo holds of the *Caiphas*."

"Drama queen," Darby teased her.

"I won't let you risk yourself," Ro started to lecture.

"I'll be fine, Roman," she re-assured him. "Dar is right. I over-exaggerated. Besides, there is no other way. It would take weeks, if not months, to move them by shuttle."

"She's right, father," Atom said staring at the priestess in a way that made her heart feel warm and made Blair's feel cold.

"Of course I am," Joppa returned Atom's fascination. "Go now," she continued. "You still have to find a way to destroy this evil place. I'll see you again on Earth. Do not worry about harming me. I will already be gone when the demon homeworld meets its end." She kissed Roman's chin and shoved him towards the hatch.

Everyone boarded, unsure of the priestess' intentions. They hesitated to leave, but with a wave of Joppa's arm, the engines activated and lifted off. The shuttle soared into the atmosphere to land on the mothership. Blair didn't even have to use her magic.

On the planet's surface, Joppa was more scared than she dared admit about whether she had the power to move so many people. She said a silent prayer to The Trinity and closed her eyes, raising her hands and pointing them in the direction she knew the ship to be. Wind whipped around her causing her hair to dance. The sky filled with rolling clouds and lightning. When it seemed certain she would be devoured by the storm, she was gone. All that remained on Gehenna was a few scattered demons and a clear sunny day.

As the Avatarn and crew disembarked in the shuttle bay, Mother Teresa hurriedly made the sign of the cross on the head of each child, regardless of the species. Darby, Ro, and Blair were about to head for the operations bridge, leaving their guests to make themselves at home, when the old nun moved to a clearing in the bay and raised a shriveled hand as if to address the group. Instead, when she had everyone's attention, she simply waved goodbye. With steps that seemed too fast for her age, she walked to the large bay entrance, where only a force-field held in the atmosphere created by life-support systems. She did not hesitate, but impossibly stepped through the energy field into space. Defying all laws of physics, she kept walking into the darkness of space. The others had all run to the bay doors, and watched as she seemed to climb invisible stairs into the black void until a white light opened before her and she stepped through. The saintly lady had finally gone home. Some of the children cried and some clapped.

The rescue team just went to the elevator, eager to complete the mission. Upon reaching the bridge, Paolo scanned the holds and all were relieved to learn the slaves were all on board. Joppa had found a way. Roman and Atom shared a glance, still worried for Joppa's well-being.

Blair found herself wondering, as the others probably did, why the priestess couldn't have *beamed* everyone aboard before they had even gone down to the planet, but then it occurred to her that it was all just part of God's plan. If they hadn't gone down and fought with Lucien, he probably would have prevented Joppa from teleporting anyone, let alone everyone to the ship.

All took seats at what had become their usual work stations, except Veronica who stood behind Prince Bridge, her hand on his shoulder. The blond boy hoped that his dads didn't notice, but of course they did. There would be no end to the teasing.

Darby locked all weapons on the planet. As he commenced firing, he did something he had never done before. He called on every ounce of his God-given powers to amplify the weapons beyond anything he had ever attempted. The entire ship hummed as the laser-like beams changed from lavender to gold and struck the planet with the force of a colliding moon. The planet Gehenna shook and contorted very briefly before breaking apart. An entire world shattered. Molten rock and debris all that remained to tear through space at great speed.

The Avatarn family cheered, jumped, and danced. Below decks aliens of many species had been watching from viewports in the holds and their response was identical to that on the bridge.

"Sensors are still indicating flashes of life signs out there," Blair cut into the revelry from the work station she had returned to. "What's that about?"

"They're teleporting back…the demons," Veronica suggested. "They sensed something was wrong on Gehenna, and they are teleporting back."

"Bonus!" Darby yelled. "Let those fuckers finish themselves off."

"But imagine," Paolo was only a little more sympathetic, "finding yourself materialized in deep space."

"They made their choices, Uncle Paolo," Atom felt no mercy. "They could have changed their minds anytime. Each day they chose to serve evil. You can only make that choice so many times before knowing regret."

Days went by as the mothership sped back to Earth. The Chosen Ones became friends with many of the former slaves. The children were all united with parents or relatives, thrilled beyond measure to have their babies back.

Blair had pointed out that her witchcraft might be required to restore the world's neglected harvests with the addition of so many alien refugees to feed, but these concerns were abandoned when they approached Earth orbit. Sensors showed that at least three billion human life signs were missing. Half the population had been massacred. There would be plenty of food for those that remained. It just needed to be distributed more evenly than it had been before the invasion.

The *Caiphas* moved back into orbit over Kansas City, and earthbound people returned to panic, fearing a renewed incursion. Soon, however, members of the more telepathic species on board the ship were able to relay to more sensitive humans that the Avatarn had come home.

It had been decided in transit that the former slaves would remain aboard ship until the newly arrived winter was dispatched in the spring. At that time additional shuttles would be collected to ferry all the refugees down to settle in the countryside surrounding Tobit House. The *Caiphas* would be dismantled to build houses and the other necessary facilities. The aliens might need the fortified dwellings as fragile humanity learned to live with their new neighbors.

Governments throughout the globe had collapsed, and vigilante leaders were calling for the Avatarn to suggest someone to govern the new world society. The Holy Triad wasn't comfortable with that responsibility, but when people saw the miracles performed when Atom moved among them, the burden of decision was taken back from the Chosen Ones.

When Atom and Bridge ventured into the city, people saw that the *cousins* communicated telepathically, and that the Son of Avatarn could speak every language. On the rare occasion that they encountered a demon straggler, Atom dismissed them with a touch. Because he had been given the divine power to kill their adversaries with a laying on of hands, many thought Atom Perez was the second coming of Christ. He assured them that he was not, but continued to have to stamp out cults that arose over night to worship him and his family. Neither he nor the Avatarn would tolerate it.

Just as quickly a movement started to elect Atom *Sovereign of the Earth*. It was suggested that the Avatarn could serve as his council, and for the time being, martial law would be best. When an international vote was almost unanimous among all those participating, Atom agreed to serve, with the conditions that terms in the office need not be limited, but elections would be held every five years. The members of his extended family would act as his cabinet. The aliens' votes would have the same value as each human. At first he requested a less royal title, but the people insisted that the new era needed a ruler that was beyond question, as long as the best interest of the people was maintained.

A small inaugural ceremony was broadcast around the world, via satellite and internet from the Liberty Memorial in the city. Though Atom would have preferred to skip all the pomp, Joppa had explained to him in a dream that the recovering populace needed visual confirmation that the Earth indeed had a new leader. A ruler seemingly appointed by God Himself to help heal universal wounds. Heeding her advice, Atom was just glad to talk to her again.

The feeling was mutual. Joppa knew what he did not. This relationship, this love, was to be her reward. A reward for unwavering service from the beginning.

Chapter 37

Darby and Paolo were riding horses on a dirt path past the small village that had sprouted up in the fields around the Tobit Farm. Those who had come to learn the ways of the Avatarn called their village Emmaus. Atom intercepted them in an open black Jeep. He was alone although the Avatarn had encouraged him to make use of the secret service volunteers who had offered their protection, not from lingering demons, but from humans, people seeking an audience with the Sovereign to settle some dispute or grant some request. So far Atom had only allowed the bodyguards to provide a secure perimeter around the Tobit Farm to protect his family and the alien refugees.

"Hey, Uncle Dar," Atom hopped out of the Jeep. Paolo was no longer surprised when their nephew approached and the horses bowed in reverence to the Son of Avatarn.

"What's up, Atom?" Darby wondered what was too urgent to wait until they returned to the house.

"I wanted a chance to talk to you guys alone. In the last several weeks I've heard you two talking about the dream of getting married, so I'm here to tell you I'm going to hook you up. I'll officiate at your ceremony."

"That's a sweet offer," Paolo said, "but we don't want to do it until it will be legal."

"I am Sovereign of Earth," Atom countered. "Whatever I say is legal."

"Touché," Paolo actually applauded.

"We've been talking about this for a while," Darby said. "What made you conclude that this was the time? Paolo and I agreed that we should wait until after we get Lucien, then start the process of over-coming the political challenge regarding our civil rights."

"Okay, I confess," Atom replied, "though I love the idea, it originally wasn't mine."

"This smells like your mom's handi-work," Dar suggested.

"It does. You're right," Atom laughed, "But not this time. This morning, while I was in the bathtub, of all times. I had a visitation. An angel named Apsara appeared to me."

"Blonde ponytail to the floor? Gold Amazon armor?" Paolo asked.

"How'd you know?" Atom wondered.

"He knew because she was my mother," Darby answered. For a rare change, Atom was speechless.

"Well," Dar continued, "What did mamacita have to say?"

"She said that God sent her to deliver a decree. The covenant of marriage is for all people. And whosoever shall declare their love and swear vows before Him are wed by His grace. He has been witness to the bond between the Avatarn and he who found him. Their union is to be sealed by His blessing."

"Well," Paolo said. "your mom did predict this relationship when I was eight. What do you say, Mr. Zaid?"

"I say if God sanctions our marriage," Darby gazed adoringly at his lover, "woe to those who stand against us…I said '*woe*'."

"I liked that," Paolo grinned.

"I was tryin' to sound all Biblical," Dar was indulging his sense of humor because the profound weight of the moment threatened to either crush him or lift him to a level of personal validation that he had never realized.

"How soon can we do this, Sovereign?" Paolo asked.

"Please, Uncle, just call me Atom. We can do it this afternoon. The others are already preparing the house."

"Let's getter done," Darby thought about how happy he was, and that Rachel would have said he was *over the moon*.

As instructed by his mother, Atom blindfolded his uncles on the front porch before leading them inside and up to their room. Unbeknownst to the grooms-to-be, Blair had gone shopping in her mind and managed through witchcraft to create the two white tuxedoes laid out on their bed.

They spent the next hour primping, and descended to find the parlor transformed into a chapel of red and white splendor.

The witch playing wedding coordinator had turned everything in the parlor white. Floors, furniture, drapes, every knick-knack. A thick layer of crimson rose petals made a path from the stairs to an altar also of white. On the altar was a large bowl containing blessed water and floating red roses. A snowy sash lay folded before the bowl. On a platform above the water was an alabaster tray. It contained a matching chalice of red wine and a loaf of bread. The fragrance of the room was intoxicating, as vases and baskets of blood roses covered every surface. Previously, Darby would have thought red roses cliché, but the sheer abundance and rich decadence of this display overloaded his senses with primal, consuming, unstoppable love.

The family was equally beautiful. Bridge was in a black tux and white shirt and tie. Roman wore a black suit, shirt, and tie. Blair was in a long black gown, fiery hair piled on her head. Veronica dressed to match her. Atom wore a short red tunic and cape. His mom wouldn't have that kind of gear even for his Majesty. Darby knew the new Sovereign's timeless girlfriend, Joppa, must have provided the royal wardrobe. Atom also held a shepherd's staff, drained of color by the ages; it too was white as bone. The Avatarn didn't know that this symbolic prop, also supplied by the priestess, had belonged to one of the very shepherds that worshipped Yeshua in the manger. Song was provided by albino birds of many species that had gathered at the open windows. And thanks to magic, the gentle breeze that wafted through was warm and comforting.

A few of the secret service men watched from the doorways in fascination. Not coincidentally, they were also in black.

Recent alien friends tried to watch from the front porch, as the family alone filled the parlor. Though no one saw them except Atom, Bridge, and Blair, ghosts fluttered all around the ceiling. Beacon was there. Dar's adoptive parents, Paolo's parents, and all their dearest friends. Blair thought Heaven must be half empty that day.

When Atom took his position behind the altar, Paolo and Darby joined hands and stood facing him before it.

"Who presents these men at the throne of Earth to be joined in wedlock?" Atom's deep voice filled the room.

"I do," their son said proudly, taking his place behind them.

Their vows were traditional Christian ones, leaving out the part about obeying and changing *'til death do us part'* to *'beyond death, into eternity.'*

The Sovereign then instructed them to cleanse each others hands in the bowl, washing away their pasts, to make themselves new for the marriage. Atom then took the loaf, breaking it in half to reveal the many rose petals baked in. He offered it to the grooms and each broke off a bite. The Son of Avatarn said, "Eat this, which is the body of God. Consume His flesh and know that He is in you."

After the men chewed and swallowed, Atom raised the chalice and said, "Drink this, which is the blood of God. Imbibe this liquid, which is the elixir of life and know He sustains you."

The rings were composed of circles of large rubies, set in something that looked like silver, though it was not. No one knew that Apsara had somehow provided them. Atom had simply found them at the base of the wine chalice.

He held them up for inspection by the gathered, one in each

hand, saying, "Exchange these rings in a sacred promise before all who love you, and Jesus, our honored guest."

Each of the guys took a band and placed it on the other's finger. Both men fought to remain dry-eyed. Too many tears had been shed.

"And now," Atom proclaimed with authority, "By the power invested in me by the people of Earth and the Holy Trinity, I pronounce you husbands all. What God has joined together, let no creature put asunder. Blessed Be!"

"Blessed Be!" The family echoed.

"Kiss your spouse," the Sovereign commanded his uncles. As the grooms lips touched and they fell into the kiss, the gold glow of Darby's power swathed them in sparkles and lifted them slowly off the floor. They spun gradually into the air, spirits dancing around them.

When the lovers' feet again touched the floorboards, the illusion began to fade. Only the newlyweds and the Sovereign's clothes were real. The other garments all reverted to T-shirts and jeans. Every rose faded away, and the pristine white parlor changed a few items at a time back to their original color. Even the altar disappeared, but the rings remained. The family rushed forward with hugs, kisses, and handshakes. Congratulations and applause came from the bodyguards and alien guests.

Darby and Paolo clung to each other like mad fools, each so overcome by joy, they thought their hearts might burst.

When they had met months ago, Dar didn't see a serious future for them. He thought the Italian hotty from his class would just be one more notch. Instead, this devoted man had become his husband. This hodge-podge family had ended up meaning everything.

Though it was still light out, Mr. and Mr. Zaid excused themselves and went up to their marital bed. Their son and nephew just whistled inappropriately from the bottom of the stairs.

The newlyweds were very hesitant when Bridge told them he wanted to drive Veronica into the city for a date. He wanted to show the ancient saint what human society had grown into while she was gone. Ironically, he wasn't very familiar with it himself. After the blond boy assured them he had been practicing teleportation and that he was mastering his demonic/angelic powers, he explained that he would just teleport him and the maiden to safety if necessary. Paolo insisted they be followed by secret service just in case, and his son reluctantly agreed.

They took a black SUV that was part of the royal fleet of cars provided for the Sovereign's use. Efficient use of carbon fuels was no longer an issue, since the population had been halved. Green energy was off the political table until social order was better stabilized. Bridge insisted no one actually ride with them, so the security car followed at a discreet distance. Veronica loved the skyline and architecture of the city, just as her fledgling boyfriend had predicted, though neither fully understood that only half of it was still standing.

The two of them would have been content to drive around all day, but when Bridge's stomach started to growl, they decided to get lunch. He was proud that Uncle Roman had taught him how to use money.

After calling the secret service behind them for a recommendation, the couple followed the security car under some golden arches and went inside for their first fast-food burgers.

"Atom?" Veronica was shocked to see him in a booth stuffing fries into his face.

"Shhhhh," the Sovereign attempted to quiet her. "Trying not to be recognized here." He pulled his ball cap lower over his face.

"Hello, Veronica," Joppa beamed at the girl.

"I'm sorry, have we met?" The maiden was confused.

"Oh, of course," Joppa laughed at her own thoughtlessness. "You only knew me in the form of a child. I was the candle-lighter in Adolphus' court."

"Then by what magic are you an adult now?" Veronica asked.

"It's complicated," Atom joined in. "Bridge will explain it to you."

Why don't you explain what you two are doing here? Bridge projected towards his cousin's mind. Atom heard him loud and clear, though the prince never spoke.

Joppa thought that you guys might be in danger. The Sovereign's thoughts told his young friend.

"Rude," the priestess in blue jeans and a sweater said aloud to the boys to inform them she knew they were reading each other's minds. "Join us." She said flashing an image of the peasant child version of herself to Veronica to prove her identity. Only the maiden saw the child's face, and her surprise turned instantly to recognition.

"We need to order our food first," Bridge said aloud. "Besides, I have my own powers you know." He wasn't too mature to pout.

"I know that, cousin," Atom couldn't help being a little patronizing. "Joppa and I were going out for supper anyway, and we thought we might as well keep you company."

"Well, I don't need a damn babysitter, Perez," Bridge's cheeks were turning red. "You're barely older than me."

"I'm older than either of you," Veronica threw in.

"And I'm older than this planet. Let's eat." Joppa closed the contest, and Bridge and Veronica went to the counter to order their meals.

The teenage girl working the register was star-struck the moment she recognized them. The cult of celebrity had survived the invasion without a dent. "Hey! Aren't you a member of the holy family? You're Darby's son, right?" The girl was waiving over her co-workers. "So what's it like being half demon?" She was starting to flirt, despite Veronica's presence.

Before Bridge could even respond, he heard, "No more demons!" and "Die Asshole!" Two rednecks had jumped up from their booth and without hesitation, whipped machine guns from under their long coats. They were already raining bullets towards the front counter, by the time the secret servicemen stood up. Two of the counter girls were riddled with shots, and the bodyguards paid for their lack of preparedness with their lives. At first Bridge was amazed to find himself unharmed, despite being splattered with blood, but he soon realized Veronica's choice to shield him with her body had cost her dearly. Her life leaked from a dozen holes.

The Sovereign and Joppa ran to the spot where the dying maiden was crumpling in Bridge's arms. "Quickly! Teleport us home!" Atom ordered the prince. They each grabbed one of Bridge's biceps and with a shimmer of the air, the foursome disappeared.

When the boys and their ladies materialized on the front porch instead of driving home, Paolo knew something was wrong. When he saw all the blood on his son, he started to shout in wordless fear.

Blair had been washing dishes and was the first to reach them after Paolo. By that time Joppa had explained the situation. Roman had been feeding horses, but was sprinting across the yard as fast as his legs could carry him. His witchly wife called to the wind, and it lifted the startled runner and deposited him on the porch steps. Atom wondered where Darby was, but he had gone jogging to distract himself from worrying about his son's first date out in the world. Later, his guilt would be merciless for not being home when the children needed help. Roman's hands were already emitting white light when he stumbled onto the porch and passed them over the gasping, sputtering girl.

"Veronica, listen to me!" Ro shouted trying to focus her attention. When she tried to clear her vision and lock eyes with the Avatarn he continued. "You have to make a decision…I can heal you, if you still want to live. After two thousand years, I won't force you to go on. You have to make a choice."

The girl answered immediately, but her voice was so weak it couldn't be heard. Joppa leaned in and placed a hand on the maiden's cheek. When she repeated her reply her voice came through the priestess' mouth and was amplified. "For millennia on Gehenna, I prayed that I would die. That I might lay down my burden, and go to my God. But now…I have found the other half of me." She struggled to turn towards Bridge. "And I must remain with him. I would know love in this life, before I go to the Savior."

"Right answer, Hon." Roman placed his hands on her abdomen and the healing glow spread over her body. When the light faded, not even the copious blood remained. *Veronica of the Veil* was restored.

Bridge tackled his uncle with a giant hug, then returned to bathe his girl's face in kisses.

"Easy, Tiger," Paolo gently scolded. "This is still your first date."

Chapter 38

"**Well speak of the** devil," Darby said when Lucien appeared. "I knew that statue spell was too good to last." The Avatarn were in the yard discussing ideas for destroying the demon king, helping Bridge round up the little goats. Dar had just warned his son that Atom was going to kill him for using his ancient shepherd's staff to herd the buggers when Roman said Lucien's name for the third time. That always got a demon's attention.

The king stepped rapidly to his son's side and when Bridge moved the historical staff between them, Lucien took it in hand. "Owww!" The demon yelled, "Get that fucking thing away from me, you little traitor!"

"Get thee behind me, Father," Bridge replied. "Before my dad kicks your ass."

Lucien laughed deeply, "That faggot wet nurse of yours has never been a threat to me."

Darby started to object, fully prepared to exercise his powers, when the front of his shirt became wet with mother's milk. He was indeed lactating, and the milky substance poured from his sore nipples. The Avatarn grew red with embarrassment and humiliation.

Though she was tempted to laugh, Blair knew Darby might

never forgive her. With a subtle wave of her hand, the flow was stopped. Dar nodded his thanks and turned back towards the intruder.

"What do you want, you son of a bitch?" Darby launched a gold energy ball at the demon, but the king easily swatted it away with the palm of his hand.

"This is your last chance to come back to me, son," Lucien placed a hand on Bridge's shoulder. "I won't offer absolution again."

"Father, just go back to Hell," The prince smiled his defiance. "Oh wait, that's right. You can't. We blew it up." Bridge made his point with a wad of spit that landed on the demon's cheek.

"I'm sorry you can't appreciate the way I feel about you, my son. I will mourn your death," Lucien actually seemed sad, but no one missed the threat.

The Avatarn and Bridge all raised their hands in battle stances, but it wasn't necessary.

Lucien raised his chin, reaffirming his pride in the wake of his son's rejection and was gone. Where he stood, only wisping smoke remained.

It wasn't until late night that Lucien returned to the Tobit Farm, the humble residence of Earth's new throne.

Silently, he searched room by room. Though all slept in the Avatarn household, the demon wore a hooded black robe, and planned to take the form of one of the family dogs should anyone stir. Eventually, he found what he was looking for in his son's room. If you could call it a room. The faggots raising him had stuck his bed in some kind of converted closet. Lucien wondered what kind of symbolism that held for the Sodomites parenting his boy. Though Bridge was oddly absent, it appeared that his mother was sleeping in his bed. The Legion king wondered what delicious perversions led the princess to still share the boy's room. No matter. It was Beacon he sought anyway. He had decided the ancient law of Talion, an eye for an eye, was appropriate retribution for the Avatarn who had corrupted his child. Darby took Bridge, so he would take the fag's twin sister. Lucien marveled at how after all their encounters, the holy fools still didn't know who they were fucking with. Not really.

Beacon woke with a start, sensing a predator in her slumber. She opened her mouth to scream, but the lord of the fallen was upon her. Before a sound escaped, he pounced. Lucien felt himself to be a lion, wrapping four sinewy legs around his prey, and perhaps for a moment he was, but he reined in the beast. He would not harm the princess yet. His meaty, bump-covered tongue had filled her mouth to silence her warning. By the time the lion possession receded, Beacon and Lucien were gone. Her family none the wiser.

"Hey, schnuckems," Blair kissed the top of her husband's head, being silly and snatching away the newspaper he was reading at the kitchen table. She was still impressed that the papers were already operational again, and more so that Roman had convinced the secret service that Atom should have it on the table by the time he rose each morning. "Please call everyone for breakfast, including Sovereign Lazy-butt and his sidekick." Ro knew she meant Bridge, because Joppa had not started staying overnight. "Oh yeah," the witch continued, "Drag Veronica down here too. I think watching TV and appearing in the media has caused her to worry that B's head might be turned. I won't have her skipping meals in fear that some scrawny celebrity is going to come along."

"I'll see that she comes down," Roman couldn't help chuckling as his wife doled out motherly concern for a girl two thousand years her senior. Veronica had insisted on making a bed for herself of fabric and bunting on the sewing-room floor. No one would have objected to her bunking with the prince, but her personal morals were still intact, despite what seemed an eternity of demonic violation.

Bounding up the stairs, Roman decided to wake the kids first. Atom had graciously made a bedroom of what had once been a walk-in closet. The Avatarn silently entered his son's room and jumped on the bed. "Rise and shine, Majesty!" He yelled in the boy's ear. Atom was not amused. Grabbing his father's robe, and lifting him into the air with one hand, he would have flung him across the room, had his sleepy vision not cleared just in time.

"Damn it, Dad! You scared the crap out of me," Atom was mad, but already starting to laugh. "I could have hurt you."

"You're not grown enough to take the old man yet, Brat," Roman teased. Both knew that he could. "Mom wants you down stairs in five for French toast. Up! Now!"

The lead Avatarn moved to the next room as his son pulled the covers over his head. Bridge's room had once been a spacious linen closet. With the shelving removed, it provided the boy with a bit of privacy. Soon though, he would out grow it. Roman knocked once and entered without waiting for a response.

Bridge's rumpled bed was empty. Already up and about Ro thought. He was turning to leave when he saw the scroll. It was mostly obscured by an errant pillow. Though he didn't want to snoop, the parchment scroll was definitely not native to the farm.

He snagged it and was moving back towards the stairs as he unrolled the regal document and started to read. By the time he started descending three steps at a time, he was simply yelling for Veronica, Darby, and Paolo to join them in the kitchen.

When all had groggily gathered, Darby asked "Where's Toll-Bridge?" It was one of the nicknames, along with Bridge-Work and Bridget, that he had taken to calling his son. The prince hated the jokey names but didn't really get the references.

"That's what this meeting is about. I found this in his bed," Roman held up the scroll and read aloud:

"Be it known.
The Princess Beacon is my precious guest and hostage.

To prevent her untimely death,
The Avatarn and their mutant son will meet me at the Arch of War above this city.
When darkness falls,
so does this misbegotten rebellion against my authority.
God's Hammer shall be broken.
I await you.
King Lucien"

"Oh, Jesus, He has Bridge," Darby's knees buckled.

"He doesn't know the princess is dead?" Veronica was nearly as hysterical as Bridge's dads.

"He must have done a glamour with his demony-angel powers, whatever," Blair said, "to convince Lu he was his mother. But why?"

"B didn't even know what Beacon looked like," Ro said.

"Sure he did," Atom interrupted; "her ghost was at the wedding." News to Roman. He had been unaware of the spectral guests.

"Either he thinks Lucien won't hurt her," Paolo offered through tears, "or he's got something trickier up his sleeve, hoping for some payback."

"Well, then, I guess we know what we're doing tonight," Joppa offered from where she appeared on the kitchen counter.

"We can't just leave him in the devil's clutches 'til then," Darby was angry.

"It may help that the king has coveted the princess for a long time," Veronica said. "He would rather keep her than kill her."

"Besides," said Blair, "it will take us until sunset to figure out where the hell he's talking about."

"How about some direction from our guide," Darby turned his frustration on Joppa, "Well?"

"Google it." Her placid response made Dar boil.

Chapter 39

Blair called upon Gaia, the spirit of the Earth, to slow her spin and delay the coming of night, but she could only slow a little and maintain sufficient gravity.

The Tobit Farm was provided every technological convenience by the temporary world government, so it was no problem for Paolo to open a laptop and hop on the Web.

A word search for "Arch, War, and Kansas City" pulled up a number of hits, but the desperate parent rapidly reviewed the information until finding what he intuitively knew to be the answer.

"Got it!" Paolo announced to the small remaining group, halting their strategizing.

"Share," Blair invited.

"Rosedale Memorial Arch," he announced. "It's a war memorial on top of a hill. What's more, it's a 34 foot limestone archway modeled on the Arc De Triomphe in Paris. I think I even know why he chose it." Paolo was proud of his research and analysis. "This monument is designed to reflect a famous structure in Paris, France. Paris is known as the City of Light. Lucien is Latin for light."

"Sounds logical to me," Roman said. "These ancient power

types are big into symbolism. I do believe Paolo Zaid, honorary Avatarn-by-marriage has just located his kidnapped son."

"You rock, Baby," Darby kissed Paolo gently on the lips, then held him. A brace to shore each other up in a terror storm.

After a brief argument, it was agreed that Roman and Atom would take a map and the shuttle to find the arch and do a dry run to assure they would be there at the appointed time. Darby, Paolo, and Veronica tried to comfort each other and plan for battle, but each of them was more horrified than the next. Blair and Joppa carefully packed the only weapon they had outside their powers. The mistletoe potion. They had yet to discover a way to administer it since needles could no longer penetrate Lucien's skin, but it was all they had. They were short one syringe, but they figured having lost only one in multiple confrontations was pretty good.

Roman and the young sovereign reported finding the memorial with ease. After lunch, they passed the day practicing combat and listening to Veronica relay everything she could recall of the demon's traits and habits; then they went upstairs to dress.

All would wear white from head to toe. They might as well look the part. Veronica wore a long dress and shawl, as she had never worn pants and didn't plan to. Joppa wore a shiny white ski outfit, consisting of leggings and a fur vest. Blair opted for a turtle-neck, pants and knee-high boots, and the guys' styles were just as varied.

They decided not to notify the media. It would just place additional lives in danger.

When sunset arrived, the seven-person crew boarded the shuttle. Floating above the scarred city, the Avatarn looked down with sorrow and gladness. So much had been lost, but freedom had been regained. None felt ready when the craft descended on a small hill-top park. They emerged in the brisk darkness and traversed the three steps of the mini-amphitheatre leading down to the grand arch. The lighting from below the monument cast it in a yellowish glow, a temple altar gate from another time.

None of them would have noticed Lucien and *Beacon* standing atop the monument, had *she* not called out a warning. The king and his reluctant consort each wore togas the blood red of devil lore. The demon enjoyed playing his part.

"Well, if it isn't the new Sovereign Elect and his holy-roller entourage and hangers-on. The whole coven's here." Lucien's voice boomed through the moonlit night. He was well pleased with the spot he had selected for this final showdown.

"You, Paolo, are perhaps the bravest of this lot…Or the most foolish," Lucien pointed a finger at Paolo who was surprised to be addressed. "You alone here are powerless AND mortal. Do you think because you are of the House of Peter, you are protected?"

"What the hell are you talking about, Asshole?" Darby interceded, nervous about the demon's focus on his lover.

"Isn't that why you chose him, Avatarn?" The king was astonished. "To embrace his apostolic lineage?"

"Are you claiming that Paolo is descended from THE Peter? Jesus' disciple?" Roman had not become too jaded or de-sensitized to feel awe.

"Of course," Lucien could not believe their ignorance.

All eyes turned to Joppa, who simply nodded confirmation.

"I guess the Universe contrived to bring us together by providing a purpose, Lulu," Darby called out with a combination of pride and contempt and held Paolo's hand as the demon held *Beacon's*.

"Adonai works in mysteries," Joppa put in.

"Yeah, whatever," Lucien wanted to get on with it. "This is how it's going to go." He raised his hand to the back of *Beacon's* neck. "Each Avatarn will in turn proclaim that *God is dead*." Veronica actually gasped at the beautiful monster's demand.

Blair's reaction was to laugh, "Aaa…yeah, that's gonna happen, Jackass."

The king's response was to lift the *princess* by the neck and dangle *her* over the edge. "She would probably survive the fall," Lucien stated calmly, "But her neck will be broken well before impact with the ground."

Beacon screamed, and Darby urgently climbed the iron fencing that shielded the base of the arch from graffiti artists. He was prepared to catch the son passing as his sister in a net of golden energy. Roman came over the fence studded with dragon heads shortly after him. He could heal his nephew if he was still alive when Darby caught him. Blair raised two fingers of each hand and waved them towards the gate, saying *'disparaissez'* which is French for 'disappear' and it did. The holy family crowded closer to the monument, but none offered to comply with the Legion lord's order.

"If not one of you says it in the time it takes me to close my hand, the princess shell be no more," Lucien meant what he said.

"Say it!" Paolo cried.

Then the demon shook his captive and *she* screamed in pain. Darby could take no more "God is dead!" He yelled and the night held its breath. He sobbed then and everyone felt his utter anguish like a blow to the stomach.

"No...No...No," *Beacon* whined from *her* lofty view. Darby felt a traitor and alone in the world. He regretted his paternal impulse, until *Beacon's* torture caused *her* to cry out again, and he knew that he would do it over and over.

"Please!" He roared at Roman and Blair. Neither wanted to voice such a horrible lie, but they too loved Bridge. And Darby's heartbreak was breaking theirs. In unison, they softly complied.

"God is dead." Echoed two more Avatarn. Anticipation over, the sickened night returned to city sound and motion. Thunder rolled and wind gusted around the little grotto. Lucien returned *Beacon* to *her* position at his side.

The holy triad felt empty. Blair and Darby both raised their arms, thinking to use their powers in the brief window of opportunity to bring the child to safety.

Nothing happened. All realized in the same instant what the devil had done. By convincing them to deny God, he had robbed them of their magic. God's human hammer brought low by the power of words.

"Oh, no," Blair was crying yet again and sank to her knees.

"What have we done?" Roman asked the stars. *Forgive Me,*

Darby's lips silently mouthed to the illusion of a girl high above him.

"Where Adolphus failed, I have triumphed," Lucien pumped his fist in the air. "A prophecy older than Earth is undone by me. And now, before I destroy you, know that you were defeated by blind allegiance to a Creator that rarely cares enough to intervene in the happenings of this planet or any other. Witness as I claim my well deserved prize." Pulling *Beacon* to him, he ignored *her* struggle and stole a violent kiss. Though *she* fought to resist, eventually passion seemed to overwhelm and *she* yielded to his lustful aggression.

Her helpless family yelled below for them to stop, but the *princess* indulged his deviant pleasure at forcing *her* loved ones to watch, and when his big tongue ended its rampage in *her* mouth, *hers* slid into his.

Lucien hadn't actually planned to hurt her, but the opportunity to punish her for daring to reject him was too tempting to let pass. With one vicious chomp, he bit off her small pink tongue and swallowed it.

Chapter 40

Both of their chins dripped with blood, and the horror on the faces of Beacon's family matched the initial expression on her own. However, her grimace rapidly became a smile to rival the one on the demon's face.

"What have you done, bitch?" Lucien masked his sudden fear with bullish posturing.

As the *princess* morphed into the figure of the demon's half-breed son, the laughing boy's lips began to move, but the voice came from Atom, "It's not bitch. It's Bridge, Father. My mother died when I was ripped from her womb."

The shock that infused the Legion devil was so complete he lost his footing and would have fallen had he not levitated long enough to step back onto the ledge. Next the handsome king clutched his cramping stomach. He began to realize what his son had done.

"That's right, you evil fuck," Bridge was again speaking through Atom. "I drank the potion made by Aunt Blair with the help of a nature spirit."

Lucien was trying in vain to retch up the poison tongue, but without success. He realized it was too late; even if he had an alexiteric to counter the effects, it was already too late.

"It will kill you too in time foolish, Halfling," the king coughed and spat at the prince.

"Perhaps," Atom sounded Bridge's words again. "A worthy price for your long-sought demise, Father."

"Call out to God, Lucien," Blair shouted. "He would still forgive you. Even for you, it's not too late."

"If I did that," he responded, "my very long and glorious life," he choked, "would have been for nothing."

"Sadly, it was," Roman said.

"I played my part," the demon said, "as expected."

Veronica was shaking, and Darby and Paolo were trying to devise a way to climb the monument. They wouldn't let their son be martyred for this cause.

Lucien fell on his back, beginning to convulse. Bridge stood proudly over him, and with one kick sent the lord of demons plummeting to the grass below.

The Avatarn and family set upon him with their fists as soon as he hit the ground. To their macabre delight, he came apart in their ripping hands. Arms. Legs. Even his head rolled into Darby's chest. The pieces quickly dissolved into sticky black gel and then nothingness. God lived. The devil was dead.

With a flicker, Bridge appeared with the others at the base of the monument to warriors. His mouth still bleeding, he was becoming unsteady and beginning to weaken.

"Do something!" Veronica yelled, her arms going around her love to try to support him as he collapsed to the ground in stages. Roman had to try, so he joined the rest of the family, kneeling in the grass around the frightened boy. Ro placed one hand on his nephew's cheek and the other on his stomach, but no amount of desperation could spark the white light that flowed with his healing powers.

The three Avatarn looked up at each other in synchronized epiphany. Raising their faces towards a sparkling black Heaven, their voices rang out in harmony as if prepared in advance:

"God, forgive us our shameful denial.

Our belief never faltered, only our tongues.
We worship only you, whose existence is the Omniverse.
We ask not for the restoration of our holy powers,
Only that in your eternal mercy,
You allow life to remain with this servant who sacrificed all to stop the adversary.
Grant us this prayer, that his light not yet pass from the world.
We ask in the name of Yeshua."

And then only sobbing as Bridge closed his eyes and became still.

Honeydew Johnson's voice boomed from the night sky all around them. No vision accompanied the annunciation, but all knew it was her:

"You are God's Chosen Hammer.
In ya'll He is well pleased, best believe.
Issa say get on with His business.
Only look inside to find Zion and know you wasn't never alone.
Turn to He that dwells within you, and know It is God."

As the echoes faded from the hill-top grotto, the familiar white light emanated from Roman's hands still blessing the dying boy. The healing power surrounded the former prince, and though it took longer than they were accustomed to, Bridge regained consciousness. Darby and Paolo rained kisses on their son and sang praises to God for sparing their child.

"Are you all right?" Veronica urgently asked her beloved undistracted by the fact that the Avatarn's blue halos were all radiating more vibrantly than ever.

Bridge opened his mouth to answer, but only a garbled moaning sound came out. His dad opened the boy's mouth with his fingers, and saw to his horror that his tongue was still gone.

Joppa wasn't surprised, but held HER tongue, as she knew the others had to recognize the extent of Bridge's sacrifice on their own. His disciples earned their enlightenment.

"Try again!" Paolo demanded of Ro. "It's not finished." Each of the Avatarn tried in turn, and though their powers were all restored and active, Bridge remained unchanged.

Eventually, it was the boy himself who stopped them. "I'm okay," he declared through Atom's mouth. "It's a small price for our victory…Besides that dork over there that calls himself the freakin' Sovereign and has the purple special effects around his head—," Bridge paused as Atom gave him a dirty look for the words coming from his own lips, "He and I have always read each others thoughts, easy as *Dick and Jane*. Long as he's got my back, I'll be cool."

"And I always will, my geeky cousin," Atom concluded in his own voice.

Though the Sovereign's attention was focused on his injured friend, Bridge saw in the back of his mind that Atom and Joppa had planned to announce their engagement if the day ever came when Lucien was destroyed, but knew they would be content to keep their joy to themselves until a more appropriate time. He hadn't asked Veronica yet, but was sure some day she would be his wife.

With the boy on his feet, joking and being comforted by Atom, Paolo, and the other women, the Avatarn wandered off to lean against the shuttlecraft.

"Does this mean it's over?" Blair asked her partners.

"I think we completed this job for which we were chosen," Roman replied. "But it doesn't mean we're done."

"Bingo," Darby said. "The kids are gonna have their hands full running this show. Even with Joppa's guidance, your son's gonna need all of us."

"And he'll have us," Blair agreed.

"You know guys," Roman said, "not long ago this shared destiny brought havoc into our lives and each of us thought we had seen happiness for the last time, but here we are. This family we found provides hope not only for us, but for the planet."

"Blah, blah, blah," Darby teased. "Let's just go home. We can solve the rest of the world's problems tomorrow."

"This is supposed to be the heart-melting climax of this story," Roman laughed, "Fuck you."

"Sorry, I'm married," Darby winked.

"And it didn't even cause the universe to implode," Blair mused, patting his cheek.

"Near miss though," Ro mumbled, earning him a play punch from Darby… "I'm just sayin'." The Avatarn leader added pulling his friends to him.

The threesome fell into a group hug, and God blessed them again and again until each of them knew it was good **TO BE CHOSEN.**

Character Introductions

(in order of appearance)

Roman Perez (pronounced pear-ez)—is a 35-year-old divorced real estate investor.

Jane Perez—is Roman's 8-year-old daughter. She is dead.

Toto Perez—is Jane's dog. He is also dead.

Brenda Perez—is Roman's ex-wife.

Joppa (pronounced jaw-puh)—is the high priestess of a mountain abbey on planet Eden. She is also magical guide to the Avatarn. She is immortal and wears many faces. One of them is Jane.

Blair Atwood—is the beautiful 30-year-old wife of a preacher. And she is a witch. By faith she is Christian; her minor magic is a family gift.

Thomas Atwood—is a Baptist minister and Blair's husband. A kind man, he is not threatened by his wife's family secret.

Sarah—is Blair's blonde sister. She is also a born witch.

Molly—is Blair's brunette sister; a hereditary witch too.

Joseph Jenkins—is a bitter judgmental old man.

Susan Myerhoff—is the church pianist.

Lucian Jones (pronounced loo-see-un)—is new in town. He's a highway patrolman (and a fallen angel).

Harold—is the church maintenance man.

Tiffany Chambers—is Thomas's secretary. And she is in love with him.

Darby Zaid—is a 21-year-old college student and part-time fitness trainer. He is also gay.

Professor Taylor—is one of Darby's teachers.

Paolo (pronounced pal-oh)—is a handsome Italian boy in Darby's history class.

Apsara—is an angelic vision from Paolo's childhood. And the birth mother of an Avatarn.

Cinder Gorchowski—is Paolo's possessive boyfriend.

Rachel—is a lovely bi-racial girl, and Darby's best friend.

Miss Luna—is an elderly black psychic.

Yoshi—is a dear friend of Darby's, and achieves double minority status by being both Asian and gay.

Grand Emperor Skylar VII—is the ruler of four galaxies in a time long ago.

Empress Draden—is Skylar's wife.

Issa (pronounced ee-suh)—is a king who founded Skylar's family line. It is also the Muslim name for Jesus.

Kali—is a unicorn and Issa's loyal steed.

Agape (pronounced uh-gaw-pay)—is Issa's daughter. It is also a word for divine unconditional love.

Juna—is Issa's lover and Agape's mother.

Adolphus Dragor (pronounced uh-doll-fus)—is the lord of Legion. King of demons.

Beacon Elisondre Dragor—is Adolphus' adopted daughter.

Jerry Dobson—is a psychotic killer.

Carter Sodderby—is Brenda's boyfriend.

Sampson—is a child-like mental patient.

Jack—is an obsessive compulsive self-abuser in the psych ward.

Jacob—is the leader of a white supremacist group.

Wendy—is Jacob's woman.

Charlie—is a biker and follower of Jacob.

Gibril (pronounced juh-breel)—is a crew member on board the *Caiphas*.

Ramses (pronounced ram-zees)—is the leader of an inner city gang.

Chantel (pronounced shan-tell)—is a little girl and the victim of a drive-by shooting.

Dre (pronounced dray)—is Chantel's brother and a member of Ramses' gang.

Honeydew Johnson—is a teenage black drag queen (a man who impersonates a woman by wearing female attire, etc.)

Jo—is a bartender, and another face of Joppa.

Tyler—is a red-haired homeless boy, forced to prostitute himself to survive.

Mateo (pronounced muh-tay-oh)—is a homeless Hispanic teenager. Like his best friend, Tyler, he also is a hustler.

HeaTheriel (pronounced huh-thear-ee-ul)—is a punk rock homeless girl. She hangs with Tyler and Mateo. And she has a secret.

Chaos—is a waiter and friend of Heather's.

Simone Woods—is an attorney, and Rachel's aunt.

Indra—is an alien concubine of Adolphus. She is from the planet Vishnu.

Hashup—is a dwarf slave, and personal servant to Indra.

Major Teardra—is a female demon warrior.

Zanzibar—is a black slave from another planet.

Fernie Leaves—is grandmother of the slaughtered Tobit family.

Azazel (pronounced uh-zay-zul)—is a hybrid composed of a human corpse (Cinder's) possessed by a demon.

Dashwood—is the royal scribe of Adolphus' court.

Grandma Sue—is Josh's deceased grandmother.

Lilith—is an escaped alien slave, and much more.

Bridge Zaid—is the half-breed son of Princess Beacon and Lucien.

Atom Perez—is the son of Blair and Roman.

Veronica—is Lucien's personal attendant, and a witness to the torture of Jesus.

Melchior (pronounced mail-key-or)—is one of the three wise-men of the Bible's nativity story.

Glossary

Abbey — A convent. The premises or community of a religious order.

Acolyte — a follower

Adamos — A fictional planet, named for the first man (Adam) in Judeo-Christian mythology.

Adolphus — Fictional leader of demons. Name based on Adolph Hitler, often considered an anti-Christ.

Adonai — Hebrew for "My Lord."

Agape — Greek word meaning "Christian Love." The reference is spiritual. There is no romantic or sexual connotation.

Ahriman — (or Angra Mainyu) – Devil-like being in Zoroastrianism.

Akashic Records — Tibetan word. Ethereal hidden library of records of the past, present, and future.

Alexandria — Ancient Egyptian city, home of the greatest library of the ancient world and Cleopatra.

All Hallows Eve — Original name of Halloween. The night preceding All Saints Day. Also, originally the pagan celebration of Samhain.

Amazon — Legendary female warriors of Greece.

Amesha spentas — The seven archangels of Ahura Mazda in Zoroastrianism.

Anathema — Detested.

Angels — Literally "messengers." Immortal beings in service to God.

Annunciation — An announcement.

Apostles — The twelve disciples of Jesus. The leaders or advocates of a new cause.

Apsara — Hindu spirit of nature—water or forest. Inspiration for lovers. Can change shape at will.

Aramaic — A Semitic language. The language of Jesus.

Armageddon — Final battle between the forces of Good and Evil.

Aryan — A non-Jewish Caucasian, especially a Nordic type.

Asmodai — a demon from the Book of Tobit and some Talmudic legends; in this story, another name for Lucien

Astral projection — When one's soul leaves the physical location of its body to visit another location.

Atlantis — Ancient island nation of an advanced civilization. Lost to history, believed to be under the sea.

Atom — The smallest part of an element that retains its identity.

Aura — An emanation of light, usually around a living thing.

Avalon — Island burial place of King Arthur.

Avatarn — A variation on the term Avatar.

Avatar — In Hindu philosophy, an incarnation. The embodiment of a quality or concept. A temporary manifestation of a continuing entity. An aspect of God in physical form.

Azazel — A leader of fallen angels. A goat demon.

Babylon — The ancient city name translates as "gate of God." Capital of Babylonia in western Asia. Many thousands of years old, perhaps founded by Sumerians.

Banshee — Gaelic folklore. Female spirit whose wailing warns of a death in the family.

Blessed Be — A general blessing used by some pagans and witches. Often used to express farewell. Used at the end of a prayer or statement to express approval.

Bonfire — A large outdoor fire. From Celtic "bone fire." Midsummer festival in which animal bones were burned to ward off evil spirits.

Caiphas — High priest of the Jews in Biblical times. Leader of the Sanhedrin. Instrumental in the arrest of Jesus.

Caligula — An emperor of Rome. Infamous sexual deviant.

Catacombs — Underground passages used for burial or entombing.

Catalonia — Part of Spain. Was colonized by Greeks and was part of Roman Empire.

Centurion — A Roman officer commanding 100 men.

Cerne (Cernunnos) — In Celtic polytheism, a horned nature god. Associated with produce and fertility. A pagan god of the forest.

Chakra — In Buddhism, points of energy concentration in the body.

Charm — To effect with magic.

Christ — Greek word referring to the Hebrew word "Messiah" which means "the anointed one," anointed meaning "blessed and/or chosen."

Christian — Relating to or derived from Jesus. In reference to a person, someone who strives to be like Jesus and follow his example.

Christos — Another Greek version of the word "anointed."

Chrysalis — A protected stage of development, such as a butterfly inside a cocoon.

Clairvoyant — Able to discern that which is beyond ordinary human senses.

Cleopatra — Famed queen of Egypt. She was actually of Greek descent.

Concubine — A woman possessed by a man, not a wife. Usually kept for sexual purposes.

Courtesans — A prostitute associated with the royal court.

Courtiers — An attendant at a royal court.

Coven — A group of witches, sometimes, but not always, numbering 13.

Cowans — Among freemasons, a pretender. To witches, someone who has not been initiated.

Crucifixion — The act of putting to death on a cross. A common form of execution in ancient Rome.

Dashwood — Character named for Sir Francis Dashwood of England. He was rumored to have been a devil worshipper.

Demesne — In the Middle Ages, all the land attached to a manor

Demon — An evil being, a fallen angel. An angel who chooses to leave God's presence rather than serve him.

Devil — The major spirit of evil, the foe of God.

Disciple — A believer who spreads the teachings of a master.

Drag Queen — A male who dresses to impersonate a female, often to perform or entertain.

Dragon — Found in mythology around the world. A giant reptile, usually winged and fire-breathing.

Dragor — A surname based on the word "dragon."

Druid — A member of the priesthood of the Celtic religion of ancient Britain and Gaul.

Dun — A bill

Dwarf — A small person

Eden — Paradise; in Judeo-Christian mythology, the first home of Adam and Eve.

Emmaus (pronounced ee-may-us) — After his resurrection, Jesus appeared to two travelers on the road. He spent time with them and went with them to their home in Emmaus.

Enchant — To cast a spell over, to delight

Enkido — In Sumerian mythology, a wild-man raised by animals. Fights Gilgamesh, but is later tamed and becomes Gilgamesh's best friend, perhaps more.

Epiphany — A revelation, often spiritual.

Ether — Substance without mass, once thought to fill space. Of the Heavens.

Ethereal — otherworldly, unearthly, delicate

Fairy — A magical being, often small and mischievous.

Fand — In Irish mythology, the Queen of the Fairies

Gadje (non-Roma) — Anyone not a gypsy.

Gaia — Greek goddess of the Earth. The Earth as a living entity.

Gamine — Fictional planet. Originally, a girl who roams the streets, an urchin.

Geas — a vow or obligation on a hero, from Irish mythology and folklore

Geb — In Egyptian mythology, the personification of the Earth. Father of Isis.

Gehenna — Greek word referring to the garbage dump of Jerusalem. Bodies of crucified criminals were tossed into its continuous fire. Possible origin of the concept of Hell.

Genghis Khan — Military leader of Asia who united tribes to create the Mongol empire.

Ghost — Usually the spirit or apparition of a deceased person.

Gibril — A fallen angel serving on board the *Caiphas*, later choosing to return to God. Also a variant of the name Gabriel, an important archangel.

Gilgamesh — A Sumerian king of Urek. A great adventurer.

Glamour — A magical alteration of appearance.

Golem — In Jewish folklore, an artificially created human being supernaturally endowed with life.

Golgotha — Calvary in English. A hill outside of Jerusalem called the place of the skull on which Jesus was crucified.

Goshen — Area in Egypt given to Joseph's family of shepherds. Shepherds were detested by Egyptians.

Green Man — Refers to a nature spirit, often represented by a foliate mask (a face surrounded by or made up of leaves) He symbolizes the god or incarnation of the forest or woods, all of nature.

Gwrddni — Welsh for the green man

Gypsies — The Roma, nomadic people, originally from India. Some believe they came to be called gypsies by people mistaking them for Egyptians.

Hades — In Greek mythology, the abode of the dead, Hell.

Halo — A circle of light around the head, an aura of goodness.

Handfasting — A wedding-like Wiccan commitment ceremony.

Hand of Glory — The dried and pickled hand of a hanged man. Some Europeans believed it had the power to render people motionless and unlock doors.

Harem — Rooms for the women of a household or the women themselves. Often with sexual connotation, as they are kept for the master of the house.

Hashup — Name of dwarf character, possibly Egyptian in origin.

HeaTheriel — Imaginary angel who appears as a girl. Her name is a combination of Heather and ethereal. Also, the "el" sound often found at the end of angel names usually means "of God."

Hebrew — A member of the Semitic people claiming descent from Abraham, Isaac, and Jacob. God's chosen people in the Old Testament. Those who would become known as Jews.

Hecate — often thought of as the goddess of witchcraft in Greek mythology; sometimes associated with the dark side of the moon.

Heretic — A dissenter from orthodox beliefs; someone who breaks from set religious beliefs.

Hindu — One of a people native to India, a believer in Hinduism.

Hitler, Adolph — Leader of Germany's Nazi party. Responsible for genocide of Jews, known as the holocaust. Some speculate that he was the anti-Christ.

Hocus Pocus — Nonsense words or phrase used by sorcerers, trickery.

House of David — Refers to the third king of ancient Israel (the Hebrew people). God said David's line would endure forever. Judaism teaches that the Jewish messiah will be a direct descendant of King David. He was described as an ancestor of Jesus.

Huldu (huldra) — In Scandinavian folklore, a seductive forest creature.

Huzzah — Medieval shouted expression of joy.

Immaculate Conception — Commonly confused with the virgin birth of Jesus. It is the Roman Catholic doctrine that Mary, Mother of Jesus, was preserved by God from the stain of original sin at the time of her own conception. Became dogma in 1854.

Immortal — Exempt from death, lasting forever.

Incantation — The chanting or reciting of a magic spell.

Indian Summer — A period of mild weather in late autumn. Also known as "Old Wives' Summer" in the United Kingdom. Possibly originating from the autumn Native American harvest season, or the fact the Indians sometimes raided European colonies throughout summer up until autumn.

Indra — A male Hindu deity. God of weather and war. In this story, the name of a female concubine.

Issa — Isa is the Islamic name for Jesus.

Jacob — Hebrew. Pretended to be his hairy older brother to obtain his father's blessing and fortune.

Jane — Hebrew. Means "The Lord is gracious."

Jehovah — An English transcription of God's Hebrew name

Jerusalem — Ancient middle-eastern city of key importance to Christianity, Judaism, and Islam, the three great religions that all originated with Abraham.

Jesus — English version of the Greek name of the Son of God.

Jihad — A holy war, Muslim origin.

John Barleycorn — the green man

Joppa — Is a Biblical name for the Israel city of Yafa, otherwise known as Jaffa. Now a part of Tel Aviv-Yafo. A port city on the Mediterranean Sea. Historic gateway into Israel. In Joppa, Peter had a vision that Jesus was not just the messiah for the Jews, but for everyone (Gentiles too).

Joshua — Similar name to Jesus. Hebrew for "The Lord is salvation."

Jove (form of Jupiter) — Leader of the Roman gods. Zeus to the Greeks.

Judas — The apostle Judas Iscariot thought to betray Jesus with a kiss to identify him to the Romans. However, another interpretation is that he was serving God. Jesus said Judas would do what was required that scripture might be fulfilled.

Juna — Variant of Juno. Latin for "Queen of Heaven." Roman version of Hera, wife of Zeus (Jupiter).

Kabala — Mystical teachings of rabbinical origin. Based on esoteric interpretation of Hebrew Scriptures.

Kabbalists — One who studies or follows Kabala.

Kali — Sanskrit Hindu's divine mother. Destroyer of evil spirits.

Kong-po — Tibetan mythology's first human ruler. Descended from the sky.

Kyrie Eleison — Latin phrase meaning "Lord, have mercy."

Law of Talion — Revenge equal to the crime. An eye for an eye.

Legion — In the New Testament, a multitude of demons acting as one.

Lilith — An Arab ghost or night demon. In some stories, she was Adam's first wife. When she insisted on being on top during sex to prove she was equal, he cast her out and she became a man-hating demon.

Lucien — Name based on Lucifer, whose name in Latin means "light-bearer." Lucifer was a favored angel until being cast out of Heaven for pride, greed, vanity, and refusing to serve God as an inferior. Also known as Satan. His rebellion and fall are not actually mentioned in the Old Testament. In Greek mythology, he is the *morning star.* Milton explores his Christian connections in *Paradise Lost*.

Luna — Latin for "moon."

Magi — Plural of mage. Often a reference to the "three wisemen."

Magic — The art of controlling the supernatural.

Mage or Magus — A magician or sorcerer.

Maricón — Spanish word for "sissy" or "effeminate." A derogatory term used like "faggot."

Martyr — One who makes great sacrifices or suffers to advance a belief or chooses to die rather than renounce a religious principle.

Mateo — Spanish version of Matthew. Means "Devoted to God."

Mea culpa — Latin meaning "my fault."

Merci — French for "thank you."

Mer-people — A being that appears half human and half fish.

Messiah — A liberator or deliverer, especially of the Jews.

Minotaur — From Greek mythology, has the head of a bull and the body of a man

Mistletoe — A parasitic plant that grows on trees and has evergreen leaves and white berries. In Norse mythology, it was the only thing with the power to kill favored god, Balder.

Ma chère — French feminine for "my beloved" or "my dear"

Mortal — subject to death, human

Mother Teresa — (of Calcutta) a Catholic nun famed for her work among the poor.

Muggles — From "Harry Potter" by J.K. Rowling. A human with no magical abilities.

Nativity — The place, conditions, and circumstances of being born; especially of Jesus.

Navaho — Native American tribe living mostly in Southeastern states.

Nazarene — Of or from the city of Nazareth

Nazareth — A small town of ancient Israel, legendary home of Jesus.

Nazi — A member of the fascist party that held power in Germany under Hitler.

Nestorian Christians — Believed that Jesus had two persons, the man Jesus and the divine Son of God, instead of one unified person. Believed He was a human made divine by God.

Nietzsche — An influential German philosopher (1844-1900).

Nimbi — halos

Olmec monoliths — Giant carvings of human heads, found throughout the lands bordering the Gulf of Mexico, created by an early Mesoamerican civilization.

Omniverse — Made up of all existing universes, the multiverse. A euphemism for God.

Oracle — One who gives wise advice, a shrine consecrated to a prophetic deity.

Pagan — One who is not a Christian, Muslim, or Jew. A heathen. Originally referred to any country person.

Pan — From Greek mythology, the god of woods, fields, and flocks. Human head and body; with legs, horns, and ears of a goat. A satyr.

Paolo — Italian name meaning "small." A form of "Paul."

Paramour — old French for "lover."

Peter — Greek for "the rock." He is the apostle Jesus assigned the task of starting His church.

Pilate — The Roman prefect of Judea who ordered the crucifixion of Jesus.

Pilgrim — One who goes on an extended journey with a purpose.

Pixie — An elfin or mischievous creature.

Pogrom — From Russian meaning "violent riot."

Portents — An omen or sign of a future event.

Pow-wow — A North American Indian prayer ceremony, a meeting or conference.

Princess Diana — Now deceased. The former wife of Prince Charles of the United Kingdom. Beloved around the world as "the people's princess."

Prophecy — a prediction

Prophet — One whose revelations are divinely inspired. One who foretells the future.

Proselytize — to convert someone to a religion or political stance

Psychic — One who is sensitive to the supernatural, knowing more than the input of one's senses.

Puma — a cougar or mountain lion

Puto — Spanish for "male prostitute."

Querent — A questioner, a seeker. Person for whom a tarot reading is done.

Rabbi — A scholar qualified to interpret Jewish law. A teacher.

Rachel — Hebrew for "female sheep"; wife of the Old Testament patriarch Jacob.

Rainbow flag — symbol of gay pride and community

Ramses (probably the II) — Egyptian pharaoh during the exodus of Hebrew slaves led by Moses.

Rasputin — Religious advisor to Nicholas II of Russia. Assassinated by noblemen who feared that the monk's debauchery would weaken the monarchy.

Reincarnation — Rebirth of the soul in another body. At one time there were positive references to it in the Bible, and some believe that comments made by Jesus refer to its existence.

Resurrection — The act of returning from death to life.

Robin Goodfellow — the green man

Roite bindele — The red string bracelet worn by kabbalists for protection from the evil eye and evil in general.

Roman — Character named for a "citizen of Rome." In this story, it symbolizes the fact that though Romans were partially responsible for Christ's death, even that can be forgiven. God doesn't hold grudges.

Saint Joan (of Arc) — Translation of French: Jeanne D'Arc. A young girl led by voices to command a French army against the English. Though she succeeded, she was later burned as a witch.

Salem, MA — Though named for the holy city (Jerusalem) this colonial village became the site of corrupt witch trials in 1692.

Salome — Hebrew for "peace." Most famous namesake danced for her step-father, King Herod, and in return asked for John the Baptist's head on a platter.

Samaritan — Refers to a New Testament story, in which a man in need is helped by a citizen of Samaria, who was good and kind despite the reputation of his people.

Sarah — Hebrew for "princess." Wife of the patriarch Abraham.

Sasquatch — Native American term for a large hairy human-like creature living in the wild. Also known as Bigfoot.

Satan — Literally "the adversary." Refers to the opponent of God.

Satyr — In Greek mythology, a humanoid male having the ears, horns, and legs of a goat. Horny forest creature.

Scrying — A form of divination using a reflective surface, such as black glass, a crystal ball, or a bowl of water, to aid psychic abilities to know the past, present, or future. Also done with clouds, smoke, and flames.

Shade — a ghost or spirit

Shaitan — An Islamic name for the devil, or a rebellious jinni who leads men astray.

Shamrock — A three-leaf clover. Thought to be good luck. Represents the Trinity to Christians.

Shem — Noah's son. Ancestor of Abraham.

Shining — A gift of supernatural ability. An extra-sensory power.

Shivaree — A noisy mock serenade (made by banging pots and kettles) to a newlywed couple in the middle of their wedding night. An American regional form of a French word.

Siren — In Greek mythology, sea entities that lured sailors into danger with their irresistible song.

Skinhead — A neo-Nazi racist

Skyclad — Wiccan term for naked

De Sortilege — French for witchcraft, divination in which an outcome is predicted using a seemingly random means, such as throwing bones or dice.

Sovereign — The head of state in a monarchy, a king.

Sotto voce — quiet voice, whisper

Spell — A magical working, often a word formula

Spirit — soul, ghost

Stigmata — Marks or sympathetic wounds resembling the crucifixion wounds of Jesus.

Strega — Italian for "witch."

Supernatural — Beyond the natural world, attributed to a divine agent, of or pertaining to an order of existence outside the norm.

Swastika — An ancient symbol, taken by the Hitler-era Nazis as their own.

Synchronicity — Term coined by Swiss Psychologist Carl Jung, referring to when two or more things happen coincidentally in a manner that is meaningful to the person or persons involved. There may appear to be an underlying pattern or plan.

Terrans — People of Terra (Earth in Latin)

Thalassemia (esp. Cooley's Anemia) — An inherited form of anemia occurring chiefly among people of Mediterranean descent, caused by faulty synthesis of part of the hemoglobin molecule.

Theanthropic — Having qualities of both human and the divine.

Thomas — Aramaic meaning "twin." He was the doubting disciple who had to feel Jesus' crucifixion wounds to believe his leader had risen from the dead.

Threnody — a poem or song of lamentation offered for the dead

Tobit — Refers to the Book of Tobit which is part of the Catholic canon. Tobit was known for attempting to provide proper burials for slain Jews, a righteous Jew himself.

Toto — The name of Dorothy's dog in "The Wizard of Oz."

Triad — a group of three persons or things

Trinity — A group of three persons in unison. The union of the Father, Son, and Holy Ghost in a single Godhead.

Uksakka — Nordic legend – In Finnish mythology, deity helpful to pregnant women.

Unicorn — A fabled horse-like creature with a long spiral horn in the center of its forehead.

Urek — An ancient city of Sumer. The name of Iraq is derived from Urek.

Vassal — From Feudal Europe, a serf, a servant or slave, sometimes called on by a lord for military services.

Veronica (of the Veil) — Her story is told in this novel. Though a popular legend among Catholics, she is not actually mentioned in the Bible.

Viridios — Celtic for the green man of Roman Britain

Vishnu — A Hindu deity worshipped as the preserver of worlds.

Watch towers — In Wicca, homes to the guardians of the North, South, East, and West. Invoked for protection.

Werewolf — A person capable of taking on the appearance of a wolf.

Wiccan — A practitioner of Wicca, a pagan religion of Earth, nature, and magic.

Widdershins — counter-clockwise

Wirdjos — proto-Celtic name for the green man

Witch — An individual who engages in witchcraft. Someone who has supernatural powers or practices sorcery. Sometimes the followers of a pagan nature religion. Sometimes Wiccan.

Yahweh — Old Testament. A vocalization of the Tetragrammaton, the name of God.

Yeshua — True name of Jesus. His name in Aramaic, the language He spoke. This is what His mother, family, friends, and disciples would have called Him.

Yeti — In Tibetan, "a little man-like animal" living in the Himalayas. In the West, incorrectly referred to as the "abominable snowman."

Zaid — An Arabic name meaning "abundance" or "growth." Darby's last name is derived from the name of a slave adopted by Muhammad as his son.

Zephyr — Name of the West Wind (Greek god of the wind)

Zion — Originally a mountain near Jerusalem. Just as Jews in Babylonian captivity longed for home, so Christianized black slaves prayed for a place of safety. Zion became a metaphor to wandering peoples seeking a homeland of freedom and peace.

Zoroaster — Called Zarathustra in his time. A spiritual leader of ancient Iran (Persia). Believed to be the origin of many Judeo-Christian beliefs, including Heaven, Hell, resurrection of the body, the messiah, final judgment, and Armageddon.